THE STORIES OF

john
edgar
wideman

ALSO BY JOHN EDGAR WIDEMAN

A Glance Away
Hurry Home
The Lynchers
Damballah
Hiding Place
Sent for You Yesterday
Brothers and Keepers
Reuben
Fever
Philadelphia Fire

THE STORIES OF

john edgar wideman

BY JOHN EDGAR WIDEMAN

PANTHEON BOOKS · NEW YORK

Library of Congress Cataloging-in-Publication Data

Wideman, John Edgar.
    [Short stories]
    The stories of John Edgar Wideman/John Edgar Wideman.
      p. cm.
    ISBN 0-679-40719-7
    I. Title.
  PS3573.I26A6   1992
  813'.54—dc20   91–50839

Book design by Debbie Glasserman
Manufactured in the United States of America
First Edition

to Danny and Maimuna
the circles widen—
the waters reach back and reach forward and
reach out

contents

I. ALL STORIES ARE TRUE *(1992)*
    All Stories Are True   3
    Casa Grande   18
    Backseat   22
    Loon Man   50
    Everybody Knew Bubba Riff   64
    Signs   74
    What He Saw   96
    A Voice Foretold   112
    Newborn Thrown in Trash and Dies   120
    Welcome   129

II. FEVER *(1989)*
    Doc's Story   145
    The Statue of Liberty   154
    Valaida   165
    Hostages   176
    Surfiction   189
    Rock River   198

When It's Time to Go   205
Concert   213
Presents   218
The Tambourine Lady   225
Little Brother   229
Fever   239
Notes   266

III.   DAMBALLAH *(1981)*
Damballah   275
Daddy Garbage   285
Lizabeth: The Caterpillar Story   301
Hazel   318
The Chinaman   331
The Watermelon Story   343
The Songs of Reba Love Jackson   352
Across the Wide Missouri   370
Rashad   379
Tommy   389
Solitary   407
The Beginning of Homewood   420

PART I

all
stories
are true

1 9 9 2

all stories are true

My mother is standing on her porch. May 10, 1991. Early morning and the street is quiet now, as peaceful as it gets here, as peaceful as it always stays in other neighborhoods, invisible, not a half mile away behind the tree-topped ridge that separates Tokay, Susquehanna, Dunfermline, Seagirt from their neighbors to the west. The litany of streets always sweet on my tongue. I think I murmur their names, a silence unless you are inside my skull, sing them as a kind of background music that doesn't break the quiet of morning. If I'm not reciting them to myself, I hear the names anyway coming from somewhere else, a place that also knows what lies within the sound of these streets said to oneself again and again. Footsteps, voices, a skein of life dragged bead by bead through a soft needle's eye. And knows the names of streets can open like the gates of a great city, everyone who's ever inhabited the city, walked its streets, suddenly, like a shimmer, like the first notes of a Monk solo, breathing, moving, a world quickens as the gates swing apart. And knows my mother is not alone on her porch this May morning. Knows she hears beneath the stillness enveloping her the sound of street names, what is animated when they are recalled. The presence of other souls as palpable as light playing in the

3

edges of her robe. Her mother and father and children. Her brother and sisters. Grands and great-grands. The man I have become and those whom I've lost becoming him. The song of street names a medium in which we all float, suspended, as if each of us is someone's precious, precious child who must never be allowed to slip from the arms cradling, rocking. And knows my mother is listening to time, time voiced in no manmade measurements of days or minutes or years, time playing as it always must, background or foreground or taking up all the space we have, a tape of the street names chanted that releases every Homewood footstep she's ever heard or dreamed.

I'm afraid for her. Experience one of those moments of missing her intensely, her gone, final good-byes said, though she is here, just ten feet away, through the front door screen, framed by two of the rusty wrought iron columns supporting the roof. A moment where fear of losing her overwhelms me to such an extent that I am bereft, helpless, unconsoled even by her presence, one price I pay for other moments when she's thousands of miles away and I've needed her and she is there, *there* beside me. After nine months of chemo her hair has grown in again, softer, curlier. Many shades of bushy gray and a crown of lighter hair, nearly white, nearly spun to invisibility by morning. I'm aware as I seldom am of her dimensions, how tall, how wide, how much this woman on the porch with her newborn's hair weighs. I need what is tangible, no matter how small she turns out to be, to offset words like frail and vulnerable I can't help saying to myself, words popping up though I try not to think them. I hate words with the power to take her away. *Frail. Old.* The effort of denying them makes her disappear anyway. My eyes cross Tokay, counting cobblestones as they go, remarking the incredible steepness of the street slanting out of my field of vision, the broken curbs and littered gutters, settling on the gigantic tree islanded in the delta where Seagirt and Tokay converge and Bricelyn begins. If the downtown wedge of skyscrapers where three rivers meet is the city's Golden Triangle, this could be its Green Triangle. A massive tree centuries old holds out against the odds here across from my mother's house, one of the biggest trees in Pittsburgh, anchored in a green tangle of weeds and bushes, trunk thick as a Buick, black as night after rain soaks its striated hide. Huge spread of its branches canopies the foot of the hill where the streets come together. Certain times of day in summer it shades my mother's front porch. If it ever tore loose from its moorings, it would crush her house like a sledgehammer. As big as it is, its roots must run under her cellar. The sound of it drinking, lapping nourishment deep underground is part of the quiet when her house is empty. How the tree survived a city growing around it is a mystery. For years no more than a twig, a sapling, a switch someone could have snapped off to beat a balky animal, swat a child's behind. I see a dark fist exploding through the asphalt, thrusting to the sky, the fingers opening, multiplying, fanning outward to form a vast umbrella of foliage. The arm behind it petrifies, other thick limbs burst from knots of hardened flesh, each one duplicating the fan of leaves, the delicate network of branches, thinning, twisting as they climb higher and farther from the source. Full-blown in a matter of seconds, ready to stand here across from my mother's house forever, till its time to be undone in the twinkling of an eye, just the way it arrived.

I didn't say any of this to my mother as I pushed through the screen door with my cup of coffee to join her on the porch. Then it was just one quiet thing after the other, a matter of seconds, the sight of her standing still, her back to me, me thinking thoughts that flashed at warp speed but would take forever to unpack, the door creaking, her turning slowly towards the noise, *You up, Baby,* a quick welcoming smile before she turns back to whatever it was, wherever she was gazing when I saw her first, small, bathed in the soft, remorseless light of morning, when I heard the sound of Homewood street names playing, transforming a commonplace scene into something else, restoring the invisible omnipresence of time, the enabling medium, what brought you to this moment and will carry you away, how things begin and end, always, you about to step out onto your mother's porch, catching her staring off at something, somewhere, home again, morning again, steamy coffee mug in one hand, sure of what you will do next, your fingers press the doorframe, pushing, absolutely unsure, fearing what will happen next, wondering what's in her eyes, behind them this morning in May, and which ghosts crowd the porch, regretting her privacy you are invading with yours. Who will the two of you together summon if you steal her attention, if you are ready and willing to offer yours, if you can break away from the tune playing over and over in your head and maybe in hers of the street names, sorrow and loss in every syllable when you say them to yourself the way you must to locate yourself here, back home in Pittsburgh this morning, Tioga Susquehanna Seagirt Cassina, praying your mother won't move, won't be gone before you reach her.

You hug each other. Not hard, not soft. Briefly. Long enough to remember everything.

I love my flowers.

A guy was selling them in the gas station. At Braddock and Penn. You know. The two big stations across from one another. A white guy in Mickey Mouse bermudas. He said these hadn't been out in the sun. Too much direct sun's not good for them, he said. These were shoved under a folding table he had set up. Pansies or some other kind, I forget. They just looked pretty to me and I thought you'd like something pretty and growing.

Impatiens. They're beautiful.

And you already have a hook by the door to hang them.

I used to keep a few little plants out here. Then one night just before Easter the flowers grew feet. Woke up one morning and everybody's flowers were gone. I only had a couple nice little plants. Nothing special. But they were gone just like everybody else's up and down both blocks. Flowers grew feet that night and walked away.

You mean somebody ripped off people's flowers.

Should have heard Eva. See the house with the green and white aluminum awning. That's Eva's. You know who I mean, don't you. Small brown-skinned woman always dressed nice. Used to ride the bus to town with me to work. Eva had big-time flowers on her porch. Gone that morning like everybody else's and Eva's fit to be tied. She said she was marching down to the corner and beat the black off him with her own two hands if she caught him with one of her flowers. Said she'd know her flowers if she saw them, pot or no pot or new pot she'd know her own flowers and strangle him with her bare hands if she caught him with her flowers.

Somebody selling flowers on the corner.

Right there on Bennett. Day after the night the flowers walked.

No. You got to be kidding.

Huh uh. Some guy down there big as life selling flowers. Had his stand right on Bennett and Bricelyn. No pots. Dog probably sold people's pots somewhere else. He wasn't completely crazy. A flower sale day after everybody's flowers disappeared off their porches.

He's lucky he didn't get shot.

Eva said she was going down there and look for her flowers. Tear him up if she found any. But how could you know for sure. I kinds looked for mine when I passed by that way, but he had everything tied up in plastic bags of dirt so how you supposed to tell. Flowers are flowers. Eva swore she'd know hers, but I didn't notice any commotion down there. Did his business all day. Gone next morning. Walked away like the flowers walked. Never saw the guy before. Don't care if I ever see him again.

A brazen brother.

That's how they do us. Steal anything and everything. Stained-glass windows out the church. I worry about one of them getting into the house.

Sorry-assed junkies.

Dope turns them crazy. Knock you down as soon as look at you. Kids you've watched grow up around here. I don't believe they intend to hurt anybody, but when that sickness is down on them, my, my, my, they'll do anything. I shudder when I think of your brother crazy that way. Him hurting someone or someone hurting him. Those so-called friends of his he'd bring home. Yes ma'am and no ma'am me and all the time I know their dope eyes counting up what they could come back and steal. Tommy knew it, too. God have mercy on me for saying this about my own son, but I believe now that's why he brought some of them around. To steal from me.

Coffee's not hot. Not cold. I try the porch railing with my hand. It feels solid enough. I remember helping Wade from next door mix concrete for the porch. The good feel of doing hard work with my brothers, the three of us, Dave, Ote and me, Wade's crew sweating into the wet cement, the moment during one cold Iron City break we all felt the presence of the brother missing who should be with us building this porch for our mother. I sit on the rail anchored in our concrete. Ask about Wade.

Poor man had a tough year. Dog died, wife died, he hit that paperboy. Old Wade was way down. Said he wouldn't have made it if it hadn't been for the boy's parents. They didn't blame him. People who witnessed the accident said Wade never had a chance. Going normal speed. The boy rode his bike straight into Wade's car. And thank goodness Wade was on his way to work. So he hadn't been drinking. Wade said if the parents had blamed him for the boy's death, he wouldn't have pulled through.

Dog died. Wife died. That's a rather strange order to put things in, Mother Dear.

You know what I mean. Didn't mean one thing worse than the other or first things first. You know I didn't mean anything like that.

I'm just teasing.

Teasing your fuddle-brained old mother. I know. I know most the time nobody understands what I'm talking about. Half the time don't know my own self. Pay me no mind. I didn't intend any disrespect. Wade loved Nadine dearly and misses her terribly. Loved that raggedy, stump-tailed dog, too. It was just one terrible thing after another falling on the poor man. I don't know how he survived. Thought for awhile he was going to drink himself to death. But he'd clean up every morning and drive off to work. Wade's a strong man. A good man, too, in his way.

Sounds like he was Job last year.

I prayed for him. All alone in his house. I know how that feels, rattling around in a house all by yourself.

The porch is holding up fine, isn't it. A little crack by the glider and one where the steps come up but this porch will be here awhile.

Youall did quite a job.

Wade the only one who knew what he was doing. Me and Dave and Ote supplied the muscle.

It was one hot day. I was worried about youall. None of you used to working out in the broiling sun that way.

Little sweat mixed in the cement makes it stronger, last longer. Why you think the Pyramids been standing all these centuries. Good African blood gluing the stones.

What do you think about this idea going around that Egyptians were black.

Better late than never, Mom. I guess. Most of them a mixture of black Africans and brown Asiatics. Look at what part of the world we're talking about. Look at them today. Not exactly a matter of color, though. More about culture. People migrating and invading and mixing since the dawn of time. Everybody's a mongrel. The wonder is it's taken this long for the obvious to be said out loud. Wonder is it's 1991 and the obvious still resisted in some quarters.

I try to change the faces of the people in the Bible. I can't do it. They still look like the faces I saw in Sunday school, in the little picture books we had to study from. No black faces, except for that one dark wise man with Jesus in the manger. When I close my eyes, I still can't put black faces on the Bible people.

Well, we must of had the same books when I was in Sunday school. Maybe that's one of the reasons you had to drag me. Child abuse every Sunday morning.

Bit more child abuse might not have been a bad idea. I felt terrible knowing I was raising a bunch of little heathens.

Anyway, what I started to say is we used those same jive comic books, but the Bible people never were white to me. They never had a color, really. The funny-looking robes and beards and turbans stuck in my mind. But as far as color, well it's Reverend Felder I think of when I think of Bible days and Bible stories. Him up on the pulpit of A.M.E. Zion shouting and strutting and banging his big fist. Old Frank Felder black as coal and that's the color of everything he preached. Like his voice tar-brushed the Bible. If the faces in the books weren't black it didn't matter cause black was in charge, telling the story.

I did think of Job more than once when I prayed for Wade. And I guess Job surely did have Wade's face and Wade's face, God bless him, surely isn't white. Poor man bent down under all his burdens. I needed the story of Job to understand how Wade could handle it. Strength to bear up to the worst, no matter what, has to come from somewhere. I needed God and Job. Needed them both to understand how Wade survived what he did.

You know, Mom, people look at you and what you've had to deal with and you're just as much a miracle to them as you say Wade is to you.

God doesn't give you more than you can handle.

Not everybody has that kind of god.

I worry about your brother. Where will he turn now. He's still a Muslim, isn't he. He still goes by his Muslim name.

Told me not long ago he's not as active in the group as he once was. But he does pray. Not as regular as he once did, he says, but he keeps the faith.

I hope he has something. Because this last blow. The pardons board turning him down again without a hearing. He believed they'd almost have to let him go. Didn't see how they could say no.

They say whatever they want to say.

Other times he held something back. In his heart he hoped they'd give him a chance, believed he'd earned a chance, but like you say. He knows they don't have to answer to anybody. Do what they want to do. Every time but this he'd held something back to fight the no.

He's in danger now. Like when he was first locked up and wild and determined to tear the prison apart with his bare hands. Worse now because he's on his own. No crew of young wild ones like him fighting back. All he has is us. And we're out here. All he has really is the chance anybody has. To keep pushing on and try to make something of a life, whatever.

Don't think I can go with you today. I'm too shaky today to face that evil prison. Tell him I'll come next week with Denise and Chance.

Don't want to leave you if you're feeling badly.

I'll be all right here. You go talk to your brother. It's just one of those days. I'll take my pills and sit myself down awhile. I'll get it together, Babe.

Is something specific hurting.

Just one of those not so good days. I'm shaky. I have bad days every now and then. Hug him for me. Tell him I love him. I'll be fine here.

I rise with her. The porch one of those quiet, extrawide, featureless elevators in the hospital where she goes Tuesdays for treatments. Below us the map of streets, veins, arteries. We wait on this floor, at this height. The porch rocks like a Ferris wheel car stopped at the apex of the ride. Perhaps the huge motor's broken. Cable snapped. Gears stripped. We wait and listen for music to drift up from the streets.

. . .

MY BROTHER'S ARMS are prison arms. The kind you see in the street that clue you where a young brother's been spending his time. Bulging biceps, the rippled look of ropy sinews and cords of muscle snaking around the bones. Skinned. Excess flesh boiled away in this cauldron. Must be noisy as a construction site where the weightlifters hang out in the prison yard. Metal clanking. Grunts and groans. Iron pumped till shoulders and chests swell to the bursting point. Men fashioning arms thick enough to wrestle fate, hold off the pressure of walls and bars always bearing down. Large. Big. Nothing else to do all day. Size one measure of time served. Serious time. Bodies honed to stop-time perfection, beyond vulnerability and pain. I see them in their sun-scoured playground sprawled like dazed children.

Hot today in the visiting area, fiery heat like the day we paddled round in Wade's cement. Row row row your concrete boat. It ain't heavy, it's your brother.

Hey, bro, I'd be the last one to deny I'm fucked up. We both know good and well I've had problems all my life doing what I been supposed to do. Here I sit in this godforsaken hole if anybody needs proof I couldn't handle. Something's wrong wit me, man, but the people who runs this joint, something's real wrong wit them, too.

Pressure in my face muscles from the permanent squint I'm wearing to keep sun out of my eyes. A mask of age. Forehead furrowed, cheeks tensed and hollow, eyes narrow, tiny creases incised at their corners, vision dimmed by the hazy porch of lashes and brow pouting to shade the eyes. Sun cooks my right side. I look past my brother to avoid the direct glare, beyond him to the bricks of the visiting room wall, the glass doors opening to this roofless enclosure where we sit. I listen closely but he's a blur in the center of the space across the round table where my eyes would naturally focus if I wasn't hiding from the sun. I don't need to see him. He will be wearing the same face I am. Pinched and sweaty. Older than it should be. Glazed eyes seeking something other than me to fix on, so what I say is a voice-over, as his is to me, listening while I tour the stones stacked forty feet high that surround us, the glass doors black as water, reflecting scraps of the yard.

Motherfuckers don't say shit for three months. Know I'm on pins and needles every minute of every day since I filed my commutation papers, but don't nobody say one god-blessed single solitary word good or bad for three months. I'm going crazy wit the waiting. And too scared to ask anybody what's happening cause you know how that works. Ask a question and they say *no* just to spite you, just to get you out their face. Limbo, man, for three months. Then last week I'm by the desk in the visiting room waiting for Denise and Chance and the guard at the desk hands me the phone, call for you. Lieutenant's on the line and he says to me Board turned you down. Tells me I can cancel my visit and speak to him now or check by his office later. That's it. Boom. Turned down.

Like getting hit in the chest wit a hammer. Couldn't breathe, man. Couldn't catch my breath for three days. Still can't breathe right. Felt like somebody had taken a hammer and whammed me in the heart.

No warning. No explanation. I'm standing in the visiting room trying to catch my breath and Denise and the baby be in here in a minute. Dying, man, and ready to die. My life was over soon's the lieutenant said Board turned you down.

Weird thing is the night before I had a dream. Woke me up. Couldn't go back to sleep. Dreamed I was in one the offices around here and my papers was on the desk. My papers. What I'd been waiting for all these months and finally there they sat. On top the desk and nobody else around. All I had to do was peep at the last sheet, right. There it'd be in black and white. Yes or no. Couldn't believe it be this easy. So much waiting and praying and begging and cursing boneheads out cause they wouldn't give me a clue. Wouldn't tell me nothing, nothing, and now alls I had to do was turn to the last page and I'd know.

Awful thing was I already knew the answer. Couldn't peep at the bottom sheet cause I already knew. Knew in my heart so I kept standing, staring, too scared to read what I knew I'd find.

Right when the dream ended I did look. Couldn't hold out. Looked and saw *denied* stamped on the last page. Whole dream came back to me soon as I put down that phone in the visiting room. Been *denied* all along. And all along I guess I knowed.

Nothing for three months then I'm waiting for a visit from my old lady and son and I get a phone call. Turned you down. Bam. Take that.

Like a hammer in my chest. Tell me that ain't evil, man. Saying no is bad enough. They don't have to treat people like dirt saying it.

My own fault I'm in here. I know I done some bad things. I'm in here, man, doing my time. Uh huh. Hard time. Lots of time for doing wrong. But they treat us like dog shit in here and that's wrong too. Guys get killed in here. Go crazy. But nobody cares. Long as they keep us locked up they can do us anyway they want. Figure we in here, so they don't owe us nothing. But wrong is wrong, ain't it. Just cause we down, is it right to keep on kicking us. Guys get meaner and crazier in here. Every day you see the ones can't take it slipping further and further off. Distance in their eyes, bro. Ain't nobody home in them eyes. They shuffle around here like ghosts. Stop speaking to people. Stop keeping theyselves clean. Gone, man. If you been around here any length of time you seen it happen to a lot of guys. You understand how easy it is to tune out and drop off the edge into your own little world. Another planet. You see why guys go off. Why they so cold and mean if they ever hit the street again.

Now our eyes are meeting. The sun's part of the meeting. A sting, a rawness you try to blink away but only make worse as sweat drips and irritates. Only one other table occupied when you sat down at yours. Now no free ones. The visiting room wall forms one end of the outdoor enclosure. Its other three walls rise forty feet at least, smooth blocks of stone topped by razor wire, a walkway, a guard tower in the far corner. At the base of the sheer stone walls fresh plantings, shrubbery dense and spiky bordering the concrete pavement. A few trees, also recently planted, have been spaced along the inside of the walls, each in a square collar of earth the size of a missing section of paving. You register these details for later. You think it will be crucial at some point to remember this yard exactly. You are uncertain why. Then, still listening to what he's saying, you realize how little of your brother's life you can share. This yard, detail by detail, is part of what you do share. You would be compromised if you come away with only a vague recollection. To fight this place, to force it to disappear, you must not miss anything. The map of it in your head makes its horror real, but also is what you must depend upon to plan an escape.

I think I'm finally beginning to understand why they so evil to us. They're scared of the black man. Really scared. More scared than I ever knew. More scared than they know themselves. When I first come in the joint I knew something about the fear. Knew we had something on them. Wild as we was we didn't give them no chance to run game on us. We had learned the hard way coming up running the streets what they thought of us. Crazy killers. Animals. Dope fiends. Niggers you got to lock up or kill before they kill you. That was the deal. So we played the hand dealed us. We was stone outlaws. Fuck wit us you better be prepared to take us down cause if you don't we coming down on you. I was young and hot-blooded and that cowboy and indian gangster shit okay wit me. Bring it on. Let's git down and dirty. Rock and roll. We saw fear in their eyes. We fucked with them to keep it there. But they didn't kill me and, all praises to Allah, I didn't kill a guard. I changed. Wasn't really me in the first place. I was just playing the outlaw role I thought I needed to play to survive the joint. I changed but they stayed scared of me. And they hate me for keeping them scared. My buddy Rick. You remember Ricky from up the hill on Tokay. Took him dying to make me really understand what I'm telling you now. You know he got sick in here. Come in when I did, one of our wild bunch. Take no shit from nobody, none of us. But Rick changed, too. Wised up. Then he got sick, real sick, like I said. They wouldn't treat him. Wouldn't try to find out what was wrong. Why should they. If you scared of somebody, why you gon try and help them, fix them up, make them well so they can jump in your chest again. Huh uh. Ricky just rotted. Chased him away from the clinic. Or handed him a aspirin. You know the story. He shrunk down to nothing. Ninety-three goddamn pounds. Finally they had to stick him in the clinic. Let him rot in the clinic till his mother got to somebody and they transferred Ricky out of here and chained him to a bed in a locked ward in a real hospital and diagnosed stomach cancer. By that time Ricky too far gone to help. Drugged him up so he just nodded away. Didn't know people when they came to see him his mother said. Said he was so weak they unchained him. A cop in the room when she visited, but Ricky just laying there. A pitiful sight, plugged up to machines, not even recognizing his own mama. She was in a chair beside his bed on a Sunday she said it must have been Sunday cause she'd been there a couple hours that afternoon and she works six days a week so it must of been Sunday and Rick been sleeping like he always did the whole time so she was just sitting half sleep herself when Ricky's hand reached over and patted hers where she'd laid it on the blanket. She couldn't believe it she said. Tears started rolling down her cheeks she told me because what his touching her meant she thought was that he was ready to die. Too far gone to get better so she just knew Rick using his last strength to say good-bye.

The cop in the room had a different idea. See, he was still scared of Ricky so Ricky moving that hand meant Ricky was dangerous again. Cop jumped up and started refastening the chains.

None of it makes any goddamn sense. Who they keep. Who they let go. Never give you any reasons. They don't have to give reasons for what they do. They just do it. Denied. They stamp your papers *denied* and that's all the reason they got to give. Denied.

One the dudes they didn't deny, a white boy, he busted out of here not too long ago. Busted out and stayed out till he got tired of running and turned hisself in. Escaped the joint, man, and now they granted him a hearing with the full parole board. What kind of sense do it make.

Maybe you ought to arrange a little vacation for yourself before you apply next time.

Don't think I ain't thought about it. Been keeping my eye on that tree over there. Shimmy up, leap over to the wall. Gone.

Not much of a tree yet.

Yeah, well, it's still pretty scraggly. But I been watching it.

Long time before those branches grow as high as the wall. And you'd still have a pretty good leap.

Guys in here would try. Plenty of them. Scoot up that tree in a minute. Do a super monkey jump.

Branches awful skinny at the top. Even for a monkey.

Right. Right. Skinny enough so you get up there it'll bend to the wall. Ride it like a surfboard.

You got it all figured out, bro.

Told you I've been keeping my eye on that little tree.

This is where you and Denise were when the leaf got out.

At the table closest to the wall. In the shade. Uh huh. We was sitting there but by the time that leaf blew up near the top of the wall both of us on our feet cheering. Other people had got into it, too. Saw what we was watching and that leaf had a whole lot of fans when it sailed over the wall. Would have thought people cheering for the Steelers or somebody's lottery number hit. Wasn't nothing but a leaf me and Denise noticed that had started blowing higher and higher. Each time the wind would grab it, it would circle up higher. Over in that corner like it was riding a draft or a whirlwind or some damn something keeping it up. You know how something dumb catch your attention and you can't let it go. Leaf kept spinning round and round and rising each time it spinned. Like on a yo-yo. After watching it a while you know that leaf has flying out of here on its mind. Every little whip and twist and bounce starts to matter. Before you know it you're blowing with your breath to help it over the wall and you know something inside you will be hurt if that silly leaf can't finish what it started. Whole visiting yard whooping and hollering when it finally blew over the wall.

Denise cried. And damn. It was everything I could do to keep the tears out of my eyes. Everybody in here needed that leaf to go free.

Kind of magic, man, if you was here in the yard and seen it. Know I sound dumb trying to tell you how it was. But that's how it was. Specially for Denise and me cause earlier in the visit she told me she was carrying my baby. We'd already picked names: Jazz Melody for a girl, Chance Mandela if it was a boy. Couldn't help taking the leaf as a sign.

Chance because the odds were stacked against him ever being conceived, let alone born.

Million to one, bro. And Mandela cause Mandela's my man. You know. In the joint like me but still taking care of business.

Chance Mandela. When Mom called and told me he was born the day after Mandela walked out of prison, I couldn't believe it.

Little day late rascal. But my little guy was close. Real close. Bust out right behind Nelson.

The leaf, the day, the name. Pretty amazing, little brother. Has to be a sign. Gives you something special to fight for. A son, a family. You've come too far to let this denial turn you around.

I think a lot about it. Everything I mean. When I'm alone at night in my cell. Ain't never really alone no more since they double-bunking everybody, but you know what I mean. When I think about giving up, truth is, nothing but me can pull me back from the edge. I got to do it for me. No matter how much I love Chance and Denise and Mom and youall, nothing, not all the love in the world can fill the hole that opens up when I get down, really down. Only way to save myself is to do it for me. I got to be the reason. I got to be worth saving. Can't live a life for nobody else. Nobody can live one for me. You understand what I'm saying.

I'm trying.

The leaf. I told you how it finally blowed free overtop the wall. Couldn't see it no more. Denise grabbed my hand. She was crying and we was bouncing up and down. People shouting. Some even clapped. But you know something. I'm gonna tell you something I don't tell nobody when I tell about the leaf. The dumb thing blew back in here again.

casa grande

About a month ago I discovered a long-lost story written by my son:

A Trip to Jupiter

One morning I woke up floating in space because the gravity pull decreased. I was sailing nice and smoothly right towards Jupiter. I sailed for 0:100 hours and then landed. The atmosphere was very cool and I heard a sound: "Mee, Meep. Earthling intruder."

"Where are you earthling name caller." I asked.

"Right before your eyes. I am green with black spots but no thing can see me. I cannot see you. Where are you?"

"Who, me? Oh. Well I guess I might be near the end of the universe because it is very cool here. I also think I might be on Saturn because of the rings."

"Well, earthling you are dumb because you are on the biggest planet in the Universe, Jupiter. The rings you see are our moons. They make a circle around our planet. Earthling, are you well educated?"

"I am. I am. Mr. Unknown."

"Well you don't sound that way. Our schools are green and our

18

only force is a cannon that shoots out Juperballs. Juperballs are balls from the sky and they kill whatever they touch. We have great leaders named: Nansi, Rasher, Lack, Spirital and Malcomba. Spirital is our only man from another planet, Earth. You live in Earth too, right?"

"I do. But how do you know?"

"We Jupers have 3 different powers. Each Juper has different powers. Mine happen to be: disappearing power, able to speak English, and E.S.P. My E.S.P. allows me to look into your body and know everything about you. For instance: You're 10 years old, you go to Washington school, and you're from a family of 5. Well I have to now go back to tending the Juperlies. Goodbye." And he went away. When I got back I told everyone what I had learned and where I had been and the writers named me student of the year. But when I told my parents they didn't believe one bit of it. They just laughed. "Ha, ha, ha," they said.

My son wrote his story, as he says, when he was ten years old. Eleven years later, just after he'd turned twenty-one and I had celebrated his birthday with him in the Arizona prison where he's serving a life sentence, I was attempting to write in my journal about the way it feels when the terrible reality of his situation comes down on me, when I exchange for a fraction of a second my life for his. Longer than that I can't bear. Even that fraction of a second, brief and illusory as it is, has the effect of a pebble dropped at dawn in a still, clear lake. Everything changes and keeps on changing, but not with the simple elegance of ripple within ripple expanding rhythmically outward. What I feel when I cannot help myself and our shadows collide, are superimposed for a millisecond, is the instability of the earth's core, the tremor of aging that's already started in my left thumb, convulsing my entire body, the planes and frames of being rattling and shattering, a voice too familiar to name crying out in pain and I can't do a damn thing about any of it. I couldn't write either so I straightened up my study instead. That's when I found "Trip to Jupiter" in a manila folder in a box of our kids' things and read it again for the first time in eleven years, thinking as I read, My god, here's something I've totally forgotten, totally lost.

That's what I thought anyway until later that same day, browsing my journal, I came across an entry from the previous year, written after another visit with my son:

He sits on a planet ten million light years away, waiting for time to change the place he is to another. Darkness shrouds him. He would be invisible from ten feet if there were someone else on the planet looking at the space where he sits. He peoples the darkness with many such *someones,* teaches them the language of this planet to which he is exiled, instructs them how not to be blind to his presence. They help him pass this time till it becomes another. To himself he is far too visible, a presence screaming light, insistent, tedious as neon. Dim warmth beneath his skin defines him, fills the void he must occupy until time drifts as far as it must drift to open again for him.

He dreams a forest of green creatures, some tall as trees, many man-size, others a foot or two high. They repeat themselves, could be the same prickly, stumped-armed form over and over until you dream differently, stare at the cacti clustered around you, scattered on rolling hills, in stark ranks on the desert floor.

They say the Hohokam dwelt here. Those who are gone, who are used up is what the word *hohokam,* borrowed from the Pima Indian language, means. Hohokam cremated their dead in shallow pits. Only ash and bits and pieces of ornament and bone remain. Named Hohokam by archeologists because the ones who dwelt here are gone, gone, gone and cannot speak their own names, sing their songs, claim this land they peopled nine centuries ago when the Gila River was young and filled with fish and waterfowl nested on its green banks and game roamed the marshes, when this dry land supported fruits and vegetables and flowers no one has seen growing here in a thousand years. Because they left so little behind, not even skulls for anthropologists to measure, the Hohokam culture remains mysterious. No one knows where they originated nor why they disappeared completely after flourishing here for hundreds of years, building towns, canals, their Casa Grande I decide to visit since I've come this far anyway, this close, and my heart is bursting so I'll come up for air here, near Coolidge, Arizona, off Route 289, just fifteen miles from the prison at Florence, blend in with the old white people hoping to find in these ruins something they didn't bring with them, hoping to leave something burdensome behind in the dust they do not need or will not miss when the vacation's over and its home again, home again.

On his distant planet he invents the word *hohokam.* It slips into his unconscious as a way of understanding where he once was. The sound of it almost like laughter, a joke on himself he can tell over and over without becoming bitter. Where he stays it doesn't snow but something is always falling from the sky, gritty, grainy, like shredded husks of insects—wings, legs, antennae, dried blood sucked from long-dead hosts, the desert floor lifted and reversed so it is a ceiling, then shaken ever so gently, sifted through the finest sieve down on his head *hohokam hohokam.* It could be a word of welcome, a whispered promise, That which is, soon goes away.

I can't help thinking the cacti are deformed. Truncated men missing limbs, heads, fingers, feet. Clearly each cactus is incomplete. Not what it should, could be. Or once was. Asymmetry reigns. Ladders with rungs missing. Functionless protuberances. Each cripple a warped facsimile of the perfect form yet to be achieved by a builder who keeps trying in spite of countless disasters jammed upright, headfirst into the desert sand.

Among these legions of failures some believe they are better than others. They laugh at the lost ones, the outcast, the *hohokam.* Their laughter rises and becomes dry rain on the planet where he sits in darkness, where time runs backwards, *Zamani* to *Sasa,* Great-time to Little-time, and oceans disappear down a drain no bigger than the pinhead upon which he dances his angels, counts them as they exhaust themselves and one by one plummet back to earth.

backseat

We made love in the belly of the whale. More times than I could count I'd laid her across the funky backseat of Uncle Mac's 1946 Lincoln Continental rusting in the backyard of 712 Copeland Street and opened her fat thighs, jiggly as they wanted to be, but like a compass too, hinged, calibrated so you can keep track of how far they're spreading, a school kind of feeling, a lesson in this thing you're doing to her and you will be tested later, spread her legs and hiked her bottom to one end of the seat so I could crawl in after her and draw the rear door shut behind me. No telling who might look out the kitchen window. What would they think bare frog legs poked out the gaping door of Uncle Mac's pride and joy gathering rust and dust now like Mac himself in the basement playing with his electric trains.

Her name was Tommy. The Lincoln Continental gun metal red in its prime. Short for Thomasina. A silver spoked spare wheel attached to the back bumper lengthened the dream car, already long as a limousine, a foot and a half. I'd heard someone say, Ain't she pretty today. Four portholes on each gleaming flank of the hood for extra, nautical elegance. Huh uh. Not in that dirty old thing. Red leather interior. Buck Rogers instrument panel. I'd stolen the blanket over

22

where Italians live from a clothesline after dark, when everybody in my neighborhood knew better than to leave their wash hanging. See how nice it is now. Uncle Mac sported a white yachtsman's cap with a fictitious ship's name in gold stitched on a blue badge above a shiny visor seamed and edged with gold braid. Sail on. Sail on, Mac, with your bad self. She couldn't have been all that ugly. Didn't my mother call her pretty dressed up one Easter in her best. I'm not making this shit up, man. Really don't care what you think, really. Look who's talking, anyway. Many times as I've seen you slinking out the side door of the Bellmawr show with some boogy-bear. Trying to hide and pretend she ain't with you. A fine ride in its day. King of the highway. It was the first year Lincoln put out the Continental, I think. Uncle Mac said when you're old enough to get a license, you can have it. Fix it up. Drive it away. I'm through with it. Just lean on back, girl. Cock your leg up out the way. Hook your heel on the front seatback. Won't give you no baby that way. You be wide open I just be fucking your pussy.

I do. I do. I do do do wop love you.

Don't get bashful with me. No need in you trying to blush. You know you wasn't bashful and shy then. Trying to get me out in Mister Mackinley Overton's nasty old car.

It was like the compasses in plastic trays at school. Most of them busted. Either so tight you can barely prize them open or just flap cause the hinge pin bracket's gone. Start out tight and stiff you push the legs apart till she loosens up, little quivers start in her thighs, her butt muscles pump then she starts doing the Booty-green and its soft and soppy where your hands up under her and the legs moving on their own now, beating on you in the dark, clamping, dancing.

I hadn't seen her in fifteen years, hadn't touched her in thirty-five, but today she decided to remind me and my main man Scott of the good old days.

He used to beg me go out there with him. Didn't always look like I look now, did I. Been big as a house after my kids start coming. Daytime, nighttime, didn't make him no nevermind. You know you did. You know. You know. You know you was a dog. Standing here all tongue-tied like you don't remember.

Scott laughs. Well, did you or didn't you, homeboy.

Man. You know after all these years. Be damned if I can remember, man. Pittsburgh all those years ago. Growing up, trying to get slick.

I wink at him. Shield my mouth and lip-synch *Yes. Yes.* So he can read me and she might. And then she says, Good too, wasn't it, and laughs and we all crack up. *Yes. Yes.*

I HEAR THE latest news from Pittsburgh in a phone call from my mother. Grandma holds on. Not eating. Little sip of water or coffee. She seems not to be in pain. Oxygen tube in her nose. She talks, then drifts off. To rest. To sleep. Very weak, very thin. The doctor said, I'm doing nothing to keep her here, nothing that will take her away. Grandma is ninety-eight. Her children were Edgar, Catherine, Eugene. Eugene killed on the island of Guam in the Pacific, a few days after the war with Japan declared over. Sniper or booby trap. Her husbands were Mackinley Overton, the Reverend J. R. Morehead, Otis Fallen, and the first, my grandfather, Harry Wideman, sire of her three children, including Edgar, my father.

I cannot close the great distance between us except by letting myself get too close. Too close means imagining myself beside her bed in the hospital room in Pittsburgh and holding her hand and dealing with the meltdown a touch, flesh to flesh, would begin.

Skin and bones. She's down to skin and bone. Wasting away. We thought she'd live forever. She'd be sick, real sick but she always came back. Flesh has deserted her now. Shrunken down to a whisper under the hospital sheets. She is a large-framed, big-boned woman. Have the bones lost their density, their heft, the power to support her upright, propel her through the world. Flesh is baggage. What good would it do her now. Yet my mother's description makes my grandmother too little, too frail for the journey ahead of her. I don't like to think of her weak and exposed. To survive the passage, she needs padding, meat on her bones. She's not afraid of anything. She carries herself with great independence, dignity. Her style is to be polite, soft-spoken, and sometimes, around white people, invisible, but her manners are superfluous to the iron core of her will. A cover story. A means of getting by, making ends meet. She couldn't be a scared person and remain as tough as she is. Her height, her bearing protect her. I don't like to think of her lying in a bed, reduced in scale. There will be long darkness and cold and shocks of many kinds to meet. I want her robust, those wide hips and broad shoulders bumpered with flesh. She would handle whatever she had to meet, but it worries and hurts me that she's starting out the journey so small.

Pittsburgh is a city of hills piggybacked on other hills. A jumble of streets that climb, jut, slant, crisscross, loop, jook, dead-end as if once there was a plan, an immense symmetrical mound arching towards heaven and houses in neat rows terracing the hump as it thrust upward, but one day the whole thing karate-chopped. Everything split, crumbled, slid. Furrows yawned, gullies opened, houses, trees, streets were stranded on precipitous inclines, the original, stately, turtle-back shape unrecognizable. The whole mess on edge, barely clinging to forty-five degree hillsides, resigned to the next convulsion that will pitch what's left into the rivers that gird it.

If you're raised in Pittsburgh you grow up aware of edges, ups and downs, the give and take back economic rhythms of the mills, boom and bust cycles, the crazy quilt patchwork of borders and turf defined by bridges, trolley car tracks, skin color, language, hills and valleys. People of every imaginable ethnic origin, religion, race, balkanized by the fractured terrain into clans, neighborhoods and ghettoes isolated as islands in the sea.

My grandmother took me for a ride on the Incline, a funicular railway connecting the lower west end of the city to the heights of Mount Washington. At night in the Incline car, gliding, rattling up the mountainside, Pittsburgh spreading out beneath us, I was mesmerized by the tapestry of lights that winked and twinkled brighter than stars, more real than stars because I could hear them humming and sang back to them, a little Jimminy Cricket my grandmother told me years later, me up on my knees against the seat back, face pressed to the window of the cable car that would have been from another perspective part of the spectacle I was enjoying, an elevator buzzed up to the top floor of Mount Washington, a spark escaping from the profusion of illuminated bridges, highways, chains of auto lights, the wedge of skyscrapers jammed where three rivers—Ohio, Monongahela, Allegheny—converge, turning night to almost day.

My grandmother smiling at the other passengers in the cagelike car, wondering if any of them mind the noise the little boy is making. That's John, my first grandson. I call him Doot. Little Scooddely-Doot chirping like a cricket at the city lights. She wouldn't have spoken aloud to anyone except me and that would be a whisper, close to my ear, twisting in her seat, leaning to peer over my shoulder and see what I was singing at out there. Lookit all the pretty lights pretty lights pretty lights she said I said over and over. Lights lights lights, making up a one-word song and chanting it at the black window. Glowing in the darkness the city before the fall. The city they'd been planning when all the broken hills were still one perfect ark. Lights restored that vision, and I couldn't open my eyes wide enough to take it all in. So I opened my mouth, heart, the works. I remember my grand-mother's hand opening, squeezing mine, my weight shifting back off my bare knees that had been pressed into the weave of the seat cushions. Then as I turned again to the window our eyes met. I pointed to the faces suspended out there, ancient versions of hers, mine, hovering in some other place we were passing on our way to the crest of the mountain.

Distance always compounded of distance and closeness, one impos-sible without the other, you know you are in one city because you are not in another. Distance expresses itself that way. She is in Pittsburgh and you aren't there. Distance announces itself as the necessity of a journey. Of choices. Either go or stay. Plane or car. Time, money trade-offs. Reckonings. Calculations. Everything intervenes. Distance a fence and closeness the green on the other side, always greener, closer because it's on the other side.

Either go today while she's still alive or wait till someone phones to say she's gone. Then go. Go then to gather with the family, one last communal ritual signifying closeness in spite of unbreachable distance. Wait too long and the choice will be snatched out of my hands, or that will seem to be the case, but it's really not, because I know better, know now that I'm deciding as I wait and write.

She's my last surviving grandparent. Two died, Harry Wideman and Freeda French when I was grown, their deaths announced to me long distance over the phone by my mother. John French, Freeda's hus-band, the first grandparent lost. He was sitting on the toilet, knees rammed against the bathtub rim, a large man in a bathroom too small for him, much too small for a family of six, my grandmother Freeda, my mother Betty and her siblings Martha, Geral and Otis, a tiny bathroom at the top of steep hallway stairs (I'd hear my aunts fly in from work or shopping, hit the front door and make a beeline straight up the steps and slam the bathroom door behind them before the front door stopped shaking), John French was sitting in that bathroom when his heart stopped and he slumped into the space between toilet and tub, unable to fall further, his knees wedged, one arm slung across the sink, no room for him to slide down further into that tight space he cursed every time he slipped off his suspenders and dropped his trousers, but far enough down, big man that he was, none of the women in the house could get him unstuck. Geral ran hollering for Mr. Clark next door. Mrs. Clark drove off for my mother while her husband Fred with the women's help propped and dragged my grandfather from the bathroom to the bedroom and laid John French across his son's bed.

I was ten then, going on eleven and it was wintertime. We were hustled into the Clarks' car and driven through icy, snowbanked streets to the house on Finance Street where John and Freeda French had raised their children, where my mother had been forced to raise the five of us when there was no money or no love between her and my father. Going home in a way, my second home on Finance Street in Homewood, but a sudden trip, with no warning, no explanation, a storm-burst of screams and tears and tight-lipped composure, my mother's pale face paler, her eyes red, nothing to say to any of us as we were bundled and bundled ourselves quickly into whatever heavy clothing she grabbed first from the hall closet. No careful layering and buttoning and zippers pulled tight to chin, galoshes fastened toe to shin, scarves wrapped so we were mummified against the cold, the coughs and sneezing and fevers she scared us into believing, because she believed, might steal us away. No. We were dressed helter-skelter in a hurry in anybody's mixmatch stuff. And that was so different, so unlike my mother I knew something terrible had happened. It was that rush into the winter streets, a deep stillness in my mother I knew I should not violate, the questions I couldn't ask, the foolishness and fear hitting me I knew better than to act out in the ride to Finance Street, the firmness and distance of adult voices that said youall sit down here and be quiet, Daddyjohn is upstairs very sick and the hurrying overhead back and forth across the ceiling, the sound of Mr. Clark from next door plodding down the hall stairs, his sigh and low, weary muttering I'm sorry Miss French sorry sorry and the front door eased shut behind him and one of my aunts flying back up the steps as soon as Mr. Clark was gone, that's how the death of John French, first of my grandparents to go, was announced.

TUNNELS, BRIDGES, TUBES, inclines, trolley tracks, giddy banks of steps are the connectors, arteries joining busted pieces of a city. Each has distinctive physical attributes but is also immaterial, a metaphor that contains a message about distance and how we negotiate it, how we build things to embody our deepest desires and fears, arrangements of steel, concrete, stone, timber that fashion us as we use them, speak a language we must learn in order to reach where we're going. Inside the earth, suspended above it, gliding over it as if we've conjured the secret of gravity, control the fickleness of a spinning planet, lift our feet while the earth rotates like a roulette wheel and then set them down again in a different place.

My father's dead brother Eugene, lost in one war, says this about the latest: They're crowing now about winning. You watch. In a while it'll turn to Jim Crowing. Then what will those black boys think who risked their lives and lost their lives to keep a grin on the face of the man who rode Willie Horton bareback to the White House. Twelve, fourteen cops on TV beating that boy with sticks long as their legs. Our young men not even home good from the war yet. What you think they be thinking when they see a black man beat to his knees by a whole posse of cracker cops. Somebody ought to tell them boys, ought to have told me, it happens every time. After every war. Oh yeah. They tell us march off and fight in some jungle or desert. Be heroes and save our behinds. We'll be here rooting for you. But when you come back across the pond, if you make it back, don't forget where you are. You ain't no hero here. You know what you are here. And just in case you don't remember, here's a little reminder. A forget-me-knot upside your nappy head. Bop bop a loo bop. Bop bam boom. Rolling around on the pavement beat half to death just in time to welcome our boys home.

I ONCE ASKED my grandmother Martha to talk to me about her earliest memories. Storytellers on my mother's side of the family had supplied me with bucket-loads of family history, but I knew next to nothing about my father's mother, little about Harry Wideman, his father. Later I would travel to Greenwood, South Carolina, and begin researching my father's father's origins. My father's mother's roots were closer at hand but remained uninvestigated, a few notes at the back of a journal I recorded from one sustained conversation with her about her past, if twenty minutes or so can be considered "sustained." She said her people came from Wrightsville, Pennsylvania, near York. Baers and Lawsons on her father's side, Johnsons and Wrights on her mother's. Though she was called Martha Lawson, Rutledge her real name she said. Her father a white man named Rutledge. She didn't use the word "illegitimate," but when I asked her if she meant that Rutledge was her natural father but never married to her mother, she nodded and replied, Uh huh, a loud, definite *uh huh* her eyes fixed directly into mine. Not a half clearing your throat Uh huh, but an answer she wished to imprint, to leave no doubt about, an answer foreshortened, abridged, suggesting much she could have said, perhaps should have said, might say on some other occasion, but for now, for her own good reasons Uh huh assumed the weight of all the other untold stories about a girl born out of wedlock in 1892 in a remote, rural southeastern Pennsylvania community, fathered by a white man upon a black woman. A matter-of-fact Uh huh. As matter-of-fact as newspapers at that time reporting on Teddy Roosevelt's charge up San Juan Hill, the massacre of Native Americans at Wounded Knee, Kitchener's expedition in Egypt, the King of Belgium pacifying the Congo, West Africa partitioned, European gunboats in Peking, Indochina annexed by France.

Nothing to regret or be ashamed of. The world was a certain way then and few challenged the rightness of that way. The white man tall in the saddle calling all the shots. His world. His child Martha Irene he could claim, deny, ignore, orphan, kill. The absolute sovereignty he had usurped over all God's children, the irresistibility of his will, superiority of his culture, the inseparability of his destiny and dictates from Divine will, these grandiose fictions had penetrated even into the backwaters of Wrightsville, Pa., and abided there so a girl child the instant she emerged from her mother's womb was swaddled in the clothes the emperor had decreed for her, a gown of invisibility, of dependency, the status of illegitimacy she must wear all the days of her life, that she would acknowledge nearly a century later, its tattered remnants still clinging Uh huh, uh huh to her grandson. But the thing she acknowledged, and as far as I know never told anyone else, she also denied by not putting the whole sad story into words. *They,* her father, his fathers and sons, all their white cousins scattered across the globe stealing, burning, raping, beating people into submission, *they* and their big sticks had fashioned a world in which she could never be much of anything. She understood that. The power of that world. The harm it would do to her and hers. How they had cheated, abused and disposed of her. But she could also dismiss them and their dirty dog ways. All that was not worth repeating, the whole ugly world they'd created wasn't worth a word, hardly worth a grunt. She was being generous when she uttered Uh huh. That's what the things they'd done amounted to. Not even that. She was granting them the credit of an Uh huh only because her grandson had asked. Needed for some reason to know, to hear her say out loud what they both already knew or *ought* to know as a birthright. Uh huh. She was passing on/sharing with me her gift of language, the power to name, claim and disclaim. One scornful, curt, clear-eyed, distasteful to her lips part grunt, part incantation in which I heard how *they* for all their fantasies of authority and control and endless scheming and libraries of words, they could never tell the simple truth of her life. Try as they might, they could not usurp her story. In her own good time, in words or deeds or fiery silence, the truth of her witness would be heard. Oh yes. Their side was on the record, it *was* the record according to their books, laws, customs, schools and laboratories. Illegitimacy, all their lies and shit, whatever. It was there alright, but it was also nothing. She summed it up and turned it to Uh huh. She'd suffered her life, earned it and it had little or nothing to do with what *they* said about her over there where they held sway. She had stripped them clean, down to the bone, to their bare asses with no place to run and hide and nothing to cover the shame of their nakedness uh huh.

So you didn't live with your father.

Huh uh.

Did you know him to see him.

Oh yes. Little bitty place like Wrightsville everybody knew everybody else.

You were raised a Lawson.

Yes, sir. Proud of it. And my mother was a Johnson. Baers and Wrights mixed in there, too. Lots of Johnsons and Baers up around York then.

Do you remember anything else. Other family . . .

But the tape stops. The rest of the conversation's lost to me, I'm beginning to fabricate what might have been said. Devise a history I don't know. We can guess it, can't we. Crucial features, at least. How much discipline and silence were required of people growing up black, marginalized and poor anyplace in America at the apex of the white man's century. But the tape stops because the witness fades from the stand. My grandmother's memories were sparse. She was over ninety when we talked that time. Too late to go back. For her *back* shuttles unpredictably in and out of now. Why chop time again into those little ungenerous cells that confine us most of our lives. Those dark, blind moments when the short view overwhelms, when we're so busy rushing forward we forget about back and up and down and sideways too and the only way out seems up ahead, tomorrow, maybe, in a hurry to be gone.

Been a long time, Doot. Long long time. Your grandmother's an old lady.

Grandma didn't have much she needed to say. Yet I could read things happening in her eyes, in the corners of her mouth where age lines, incised like tribal markings, twitched. Off a screen inside her brow a third unseen eye was reading the story of her life. Pages, chapters consumed faster than a blink. Years, decades displayed on the screen, handfuls of years chewed and swallowed and savored or spit out between breaths. Her long history was being enacted again, her face betrayed the action in minute adjustments. Her chipmunk cheeks, the only place she ever got fat, trembling, flexing, bitten from inside, expressive as the skin of a lake. She was back reliving whatever her memory called up, but living at the speed of light, a fast fast shuffle of scenes people places they say occurs between your next to last and last breath of air on earth.

The show, the spectacle was hers and hers alone to view. No way in. No way out. She wasn't consciously withholding, she simply couldn't do otherwise. Distance between us was not of her making. No more than she had intended to distance herself from Martha Irene Lawson, a skinny yellow girl child playing in a field in Wrightsville, Pa. She was comfortable with distance, its necessity, its tease, the hard passage against all odds and expectations had not left her stranded here, now, an old woman. Instead it freed her to return. To pick and choose. She could verify her life. It continued to happen inside her head, flickering across her invisible eye. And that's all that mattered, perhaps. The force in her yoking her days together. From the beginning to the not quite end yet. Not quite. Yet. The not quite of the end no more distant, illusory or real than the beginning, as it dances and sways and plays itself out for her again. Energy released some day some instrument may harvest, energy made available for broadcast and replay by technology as commonplace then as what we employ today to hear the dead sing and watch ghosts flutter across a screen.

Long time ago, Doot.

Blankness a moment. My grandmother's eyes unfocused. Or rather focused inward instead of outward. Rolling back the stone. The long-gone days a throng of children exiting into sunlight from a dark cave. Black Orpheus music. La la la la. Lala la la. They are nothing more than a flash of color, a splash of chatter, squabble, singing, laughter. Kid noise and then you begin to make up lives for them. To remember.

We were playing one time in the backyard and my brother, Otis, he said . . . By the time you open your mouth and turn around the children are gone. You're lying. You're alone. Distance increases driving the vision away, like when you attempt to tell a dream, destroying it with every word. I'm left to construct what I need from her thoughtful silence.

If I hopped a plane to Pittsburgh today, would there be more. More than we've shared already, the infinite history of our lives intersecting.

But I need to be beside her bed. In person holding her actual hand. A last touch. On this side. Of what.

I REFUSED to taste let alone eat scrambled eggs till the time my grandmother cooked them for me. Though she was a good cook, even a professional at times—living-in and cooking for white families, chef at an Isaly's restaurant on Penn Avenue in East Liberty where my best buddy Scott Payne and I would check in for lunchtime leftovers on our way home from Peabody High School—the first time I ate Grandma's or anybody else's scrambled eggs had less to do with how well she cooked than with where she cooked them the first time she set down a plate of scrambled eggs, bacon and toast in front of me. Because of where I was, I couldn't say no. Couldn't say much of anything except *yes ma'am* and *yessir,* speaking when spoken to by my grandmother or one of the white faces at the breakfast table in the Ricks' kitchen. My grandmother like a member of the Rick family they said. Bring your grandson to meet us they said. So one morning I tagged along in the back of a Lincoln Continental driven by Mr. Overton, the Ricks' chauffeur. Mr. Mackinley Overton who became Uncle Mac when Grandma left Harry Wideman and moved into Mackinley Overton's place above the Ricks' garage. The scrambled eggs happened right after that move when I was five or six years old. My grandmother chattered all the time about how cute and smart I was and since the Ricks were still holding out hope that one of their children would soon be presenting them with a grandchild they thought maybe a preview would be fun, a vicarious taste through my proud grandmother of what they longed for in their own family. Thus I was invited to breakfast and found myself one early early morning driven through the quietest streets in Pittsburgh. Broad streets, tree-sheltered, immaculate. Houses twice the size of apartment buildings in Homewood, the community where my other grandmother Freeda French lived.

The Continental's plush backseat swallowed me. My eyes barely reached window level, windows that magically rose and fell with the touch of a button. I remember leather smell and a reddish glow, a color something like the way our bedroom feels now on sunny mornings when dawn filters through the plum blinds. But then, the color, the softness, the smell, Mr. Overton's board-straight back and big, black, chauffeur-capped head, my grandmother's dreamy self-absorption, my worry she was drifting further and further from me, becoming someone else as we passed from the familiar skimpy streets of my neighborhood into a region where houses were too large for anyone to be living inside, then the stillness, the rosy hue immobilized me. I was losing my bearings. Scared to reach out, speak out, reorient myself. I didn't want the ride to end, but I also didn't want to be driven one inch further from home. For some reason in that leather pit I couldn't help picturing myself as a king on a throne. A tiny, shrunken, frozen king, a Little King like the one in the comics, dwarfed, overwhelmed, so meek and mute no one cares, especially him, that he's king. There I sat, a different color, no bigger than a pea in that immense, upholstered pod, the city tamed and harmless as I'd ever seen it. A warning in the calm, however: You better not stop, better not touch. I prayed we'd turn around. Knew we'd gone too far. Beginning to lose track of who I was, of everything, the dark, wrinkle-necked man in the front seat, the lady gazing out a window humming to herself. Where were we headed. Why. My tongue swelled dry and heavy. I'd lost the power to speak. Only thing making sense the sound of the Lincoln's huge tires buffing those pretty streets clean.

I am a black boy five or six in the kitchen of a white family for whom my grandmother is hired help. Sitting at a table with the white folks while my grandmother in her apron, hair netted into a lump atop her head, serves us a scrambled-egg breakfast. She was beaming as she bustled around, making sure everyone receives enough of what they want on their flower-rimmed plates. Everyone (except me) in their glory. The Ricks because they were treating my grandmother royally by indulging her grandson with a seat at the intimate family table, a little black boy welcomed decades before Sidney Poitier and *Guess Who's Coming to Dinner*. My grandmother because her fabled grandson had achieved one more legendary plateau, sitting big as life at the emperor's table, her rich white employers stamping their seal of approval on the precious Doot she'd advertised to them as cute and smart as a whip, here he was and here she was bathed in reflected glory. Things were changing, maybe they would never be the same again.

All that mellow glory and feeling good just about killed me. I sat through breakfast intent on doing the right thing, determined not to disappoint anybody, not to spill food or get my mouth greasy or talk like a little ignorant pickaninny. Only the Shadow knows what was running through my five-year-old mind. But the effort glazed my eyes and twisted my tongue. No matter how hard I tried to be something else, I knew I was sitting like a bump on a log, brown and nappy-headed, afraid to say a word other than *yessir, yes ma'am,* eyes down, locked on my plate so nobody could steal them. Was I the only one who knew about the lion crouched in the middle of the table, ready to spring and destroy this nice kitchen, all these fine people, me first, tearing off my head, swiping open my belly with one huge paw. It stinks, it slobbers, its claws drip boogers of red meat. Couldn't anybody else hear the gurgle of its stomach, the low, menacing big-cat purr as its yellow eyes stared at me, waiting for me to commit the mistake that would trigger its charge. A beast as palpable to me as the strips of bacon, triangles of toast, and mound of soft eggs on my plate.

I replied yes ma'am when eggs were offered because everybody else did. With a salty mouthful of crumbled bacon and buttery crunchy toast, I could barely taste the buttery eggs. A lion to deal with demoted eggs into a minor consideration anyway. What would happen next. Would I explode from the effort of keeping the beast at bay or would it attack, for its own hidden reasons, whether I committed a mistake or not. Maybe a tie, a dead heat. Two big bangs sounding like one. Me self-destructing as the lion rips my guts out. Quitting as I'm fired.

So busy lion taming I was actually surprised when I noticed the eggs were gone. Clean plate. One more sign of good breeding, of what a nice little gentleman I was. Except everybody else left lots of stuff on their plates. Garbage for my grandmother to scrape into a can, in the kitchen where she periodically disappeared. Because we weren't eating in the Ricks' kitchen after all. It was a breakfast room. Skylights. Green plants. The more I think about the morning at the Ricks' house, the more I remember, the freer I feel to invent what's needed to fill in my memory. A special room for eating breakfast. As unexpected, as bizarre a concept to me as the live lion centerpiece.

I'm sure the Ricks were kind and unfailingly polite, probably bent over backwards to make a child feel at home in an alien atmosphere. I'm sure my grandmother did her best, too. But the experience was dreadful. I summon it up and not many details remain. No specific Rick faces. No Rick names. Just a collective, overwhelming white presence, the smells and noises of the white people responsible. Fear of scrambled eggs overcome, a thousand other fears rushing to fill the vacuum. A funny, deadly lion that somehow accompanied me home, miniaturized but not one iota less threatening or dangerous, bounding up onto a shadowy ledge in the cave of my heart where it feigns sleep but never closes one yellow cat's-eye.

HEY MAN. See the way that lady coming up the street is walking. Check her out. She old now but you can tell by the way she swish that old booty she done a whole lot a fucking in her day. We were on somebody's stoop. Charlie, who we called Patches or Patchhead because a severe case of tetters had left lighter-colored blotches in his scalp, Charlie, a newcomer who'd only been living on Copeland a couple weeks was mouthing off about a woman on her way up the block from Ellsworth Avenue where buses and trolleys ran. She sported a dark, white-bordered straw hat, a matching purse squeezed under her bare arm. Summertime. Her bright print dress was fitted at the waist but hung loosely in pleats from her hips, ending halfway between knees and ankles. From the hem of the dress her bony straight legs slanted inward. You'd guess she was bowlegged from the side-to-side pitch of her walk, the steep angling downward from broad hipbones to ankles just inches apart.

Charlie and I didn't get along too well. This was going to make it worse. Because the woman he was sounding on, forcing me to observe in a fashion I never had before (even though once upon a time I had pushed open the bathroom door and she was standing naked in the tub, soaping herself and both of us were so surprised I took another half step into the steamy room, seeing and not seeing her, and she scrubbed a few more licks before she said, Oh, it's you, Doot, and I dropped my eyes and backed out, pulling the door to without saying sorry or anything else and now couldn't help fusing and refusing to fuse that close-up of my grandmother's wet anatomy with whatever foul-mouthed point Patches was announcing about the peculiar gait of the woman coming up Copeland), the woman was in fact my grandmother, a fact I wasn't exactly conscious of and Patches didn't know but everybody else on the stoop definitely was aware of so when I finally woke up and smacked Patches hard upside his patchy head, and he leaped for me and we were into a long-overdue rumble, everybody knew Patches was in the wrong and deserved whatever he got. And hoped he got plenty cause it was a shame to put somebody's nice old grandmother in the dirty dozens.

Man, I'da killed Patches he put the mouth on my grandmother that way. But it was not exactly clear if putting somebody's grandmother in the dirty dozens was as bad as putting somebody's mama there. Could be worse. Maybe. But it wasn't clear. We fought, anyway, more scuffle than fight, enough room and other guys between us we mostly hollered back and forth and Patches learned he'd insulted my grandmother and said sorry he didn't mean it man, but he wasn't scared of me and he'd fight me any day, any time but it wasn't over nothing he meant to say cause he hadn't meant no harm, I don't play that shit, man. The air quieter if not entirely clear by the time my grandmother passed the stoop and said, Hi fellas and What a nice bunch of boys and Doot, you come on home in a little minute so you can visit with your grandmother.

I should have kicked his ass good. I never liked him. I think I gave Patches the Patchhead nickname he hated. What I didn't like about him was the permanent sneer on his face. The curl in his lip, the look-right-through-you eyes that said I know you think you can whip me but you better not try. It wasn't even about who was badder, who could whip whose behind, it was about attitude. An ass whipping, no matter who won, wouldn't adjust Patchhead's attitude. I should have tried anyway. He gave me an opening and I should have finished it there and then.

A COLD MARCH RAIN rains down. Some person somewhere may be counting by Marches. Nine Marches left till the end of the century.

Then will come the first March in the year 2000. You could count by months or count raindrops striking. How many raindrops will fall before the century ends. A fast count, total mounting higher and higher till rain stops. Then numbers piling up again, flashing faster and faster during the next March downpour, faster even than the numbers registering the national debt accumulating second by second on an electronic billboard in Times Square, but do you reach the new century any quicker counting raindrops or counting months. Is fast sometimes slower. Slower fast. What difference does it make. Approximately 3.2 billion seconds equal a hundred years. If I'd been counting the seconds in my life, I'd be up to about 1.6 billion. My grandmother close to a whole 3.2 billion century's worth. Count down or count up. From either direction you arrive at the same place. No place. The circle closes. An old gospel song asks God: Will the circle be unbroken. Answers itself, closes the circle of faith: *By and by, Lord, by and by. / There's a better home awaiting / In the sky, Lord, in the sky.*

My grandmother Martha Irene was a regular at church. Two of her husbands preached. For nearly twenty years she lived in various parish houses with the Reverend Mr. Morehead who built churches for the greater glory of God in the name of A.M.E. Zion. Since the Reverend's death—bless his roan wig, his brace of pastel Cadillacs, the sesquepedalian vocabulary he trotted out in conversations with his college-teacher, writer step-grandson—in the years since she's been in Pittsburgh, finding Otis Fallen at the Vintage Senior Citizens' Center, marrying him then outliving him too, my grandmother has attended Homewood A.M.E. Zion. I don't know if she ever severed officially her ties with Reverend Morehead's last church in Ohio, but she's clearly part of the Homewood congregation, a mother of the church, respected, deferred to, a consensus marvel. Though she lies about her age, even if she only carries the ninety-six years she claims in public, she has no right to be as strong, spry, quick-witted as she is. She dresses as if there's still some man, or men, paying special attention to how she looks on her own two good feet, stepping down the aisle of Homewood A.M.E. Zion to her accustomed bench in the right center section, two rows from the pulpit. Church members are aware when she's not in her spot. No one in the congregation would dream of occupying it, even when she doesn't. The thought that one Sunday

her place will be empty and she might never return may cross someone's mind, but just as quickly is dispelled. She'll make it back. She
always does. And if her progress through the front door and down the
crimson-carpeted aisle is half of a half step slower, it's also more
stately, more dignified. A bad case of flu or a fall or whatever keeps
her away, must surely take its toll, she is, after all, constructed of the
same flesh and blood as everybody else so we can expect her to slow
down a tiny bit. That's part of the marvel. Not so much a matter of
Mrs. Martha Fallen getting away with anything. Rather, the grace to
bear affliction, to come out the far end of trouble and be recognizable,
undefeated, ready for whatever comes next. Uh huh. She'll return next
week. In a feathered hat and candy-striped dress, shoes matching
purse, fresh and unpredictable. What's Mrs. Fallen wearing today. Did
you check out that beautiful silk blouse communion Sunday. Girl, I
ain't hit fifty yet and I wish I looked as good in my clothes as Mrs.
Fallen. She seems to wear outfits only once. A trick of rotation.
Changing accessories, establishing a unique, personal style so you're
aware of her, always beautifully dressed, not necessarily the particular
suit or dress. She possesses ten or twenty years' worth of choices in
her wardrobe because her clothes don't date, classic materials and cuts
you don't just pull off a rack. That's also part of the marvel. Not only
does she manage to appear in church on her own two feet most every
Sunday, but she looks good doing it. A fashion show. Easter parade
each Sunday morning.

   In spite of preacher husbands and her role as matriarch in Homewood Church, I do not associate my grandmother with religion. Not
in her speech, actions nor the depths of her as I perceive them from
a cloudy distance, two generations removed. To me she is the worldli-
est woman in the family. A hardheaded practicality governs her. She
seems utterly unsentimental. My father's definitely her son. Aloof,
detached, self-sufficient. A habit of masking emotion that's so thor-
oughgoing, so convincing, you wonder sometimes if emotions really
are percolating behind the mask or if the elegant, stylized mask itself
has become an emotion, the ultimate, unchanging protective shield of
cool indifference. Does what is not expressed count. If so, for what.
For whom. Since I'm my father's son, these are not neutral questions.
In an unbroken stream I feel the cold rush descend on me, the icy

reserve, the cutting off of feeling if feeling threatens to disrupt the illusion of self-control. Is this power to separate myself from my feelings, from my people, a gift, a curse, some unstable mix of both. Should I ask others to trust me, depend on me. Where does the withheld emotion, the denial accumulate. Will it come crushing down one day, the irresistible weight of remorse, or will it be emptiness, a gaunt, turkey-necked bird perched on a fence digesting my insides in its pot belly.

Grandma's different because unlike the other women in the family she's never, in my hearing, spoken passionately of God or spirit, heaven or hell. Never spoken the language of salvation, love and redemption the others speak. Neither praised transcendent glories above nor testified about here below, the trials and tribulations, toils and snares that try the spirit, break the heart, snatch flesh and breath away. I've never heard her speak of losing a child, or voice the terror that one might be lost. She's never admitted aloud her helplessness, her dependence. My mother, her mother Freeda French, my aunts, I've seen each one scared. Or hurt or soul weary. Bent down. Dismayed. They would not have survived without their god, his promise of love and divine intervention that doesn't itself resolve trouble but prepares the miracle of faith, the possibility of belief and belief for them becomes a kind of overcoming and resignation that keeps hope alive. I've watched them, heard them when they were knocked down past the point of prayer or singing, yet their religion sustained them, instructed them: *All you got to do is fold your arms and moan a little while.*

The few statements I recall my grandmother making about religion are businesslike, factual, high-church formulaic and cool. She was a preacher's wife responsible for organizational matters, not the mourner's bench. She writes a beautiful hand, letters perfectly formed according to the manual of classic penmanship little black girls copied from diligently at the turn of the century when writing itself, like cleanliness, brought colored people a bit closer to heaven, at least the writing which faithfully mirrored models in the white man's books. Ecstasy of a perfect copy. Starched dresses, ironed hair, skin scrubbed and oiled against ash, shiny shoes, fingernails crisp, snowy ankle-socks, desks in ranks as symmetrical and straight as rows of crosses in

Flanders Fields. Church for my grandmother a neat garden, an efficiently arranged chest of drawers. Money in the bank, money kept
Swiss clean, hidden, private, in the vault where it belonged.

They say losing her last child Eugene broke her heart. She waited
for the mailman every day Eugene was overseas in the war. No one
was allowed to touch the mail before she did. Her trips to the mailbox
each morning kept him alive, kept his letters, though few and far
between and in a childish script nothing, nothing like the good old-
fashioned way she'd learned to write, her hand the envy of every
church secretary who ever read her quarterly reports, her ritual kept
Eugene's letters arriving from distant places and kept away a dreaded
telegram from the War Department informing her of her son's death.
A vigil unbroken the final two years of World War II. First Edgar
gone, then Catherine to the WACS, finally Eugene, last born but the
biggest already, finally old enough to enlist if he lied on an extra year.
She knew Edgar was a guard in a prisoner-of-war camp, safe, away
from the fighting, and Catherine typing at a desk in Washington, D.C.,
but Eugene was in the Pacific, the bloody, island-hopping road to
Tokyo, so it was him mostly she worried about, they say, up some
mornings at the crack of dawn and back and forth like a crazy woman,
a dozen trips before the time she knew good and well the mailman
would arrive.

Perhaps that has something to do with her composure now. The ice
in her, the iron, the almost peculiar reserve and quaint sense of
decorum. After services, in the fellowship hour when people gather in
the church basement for chicken wings and gossip, she'd whisper
when she'd ask about my brother, her grandson in prison, as if his
whereabouts were a secret, a family shame to be guarded even though
everyone in Homewood knew Rob's story, the stories of all the young
men cut down, shipped away. But nothing causes her to flinch. I never
saw her cry. Or worse, fall into the states my mother and her sisters
got in, swaying, quiet, arms folded, dry-eyed when crying would have
been a luxury, a release of raging feelings visibly tearing them apart.
I'm sorry to hear that, Grandma would say. Or John French was a fine
man. Freeda will miss him. Phrases she'd cobble to wall herself behind,
a wall constructed of the bricks she'd counted on the path to the
mailbox two years' worth of mornings between 1943 and 1945; senti-

ments precise as the clipped hedges lining the brick walkway. Perhaps she'd exhausted every ounce of emotional energy and disciplined herself to live on what was left. Shadows and substance. A memory of anxiety, of pain, of giving away everything and receiving nothing in the return mail until weeks after the war was over, weeks after the trek down the brick path from front door to sidewalk was less about hoping for a letter from Eugene or fearing a War Department telegram, than it was a mother's too-good-to-be-true expectation that maybe, just maybe Eugene would be standing there, huge and smiling in his uniform. Weeks of waiting for a surprise she didn't dare speak aloud.

Instead of him home again what the mailman brought her in return for daring to hope, for dying by inches on every trip she took down the brick path, was the notice, finally, weeks, months after the war had ended, that her son Eugene was gone.

THERE HAVE BEEN times when I didn't know my grandmother's name. I had to stop and try to figure it out. What is she calling herself now. I'd be too embarrassed to ask, if anybody was around at one of those moments to ask. Mom. How does Grandma spell her name. Oh yeah. Right. I couldn't remember whether Fallen's spelled with one *l* or two. And he's Otis, right. Like Ote. Like your brother Big Otis and my brother. Otis. Only my brother Otis Eugene goes by Gene now. And my sister. I never can get her name straight either. She converted to her second husband's religion, the American Moorish Church. Exchanged both names I knew her by. And added a few extra. My father subtracted names, gave his as Edgar Lawson when he was picked up by the cops in raids on those joints where he drank and gambled after hours. He told them the truth. Those were in fact his names. He just left off the Wideman part. My brother Robby became a Muslim. In the joint lots of inmates have never heard of a Robert Wideman. He's Farouk. Another name I couldn't spell till I checked it out. When I published my first novel, I wanted my father's name to be part of the record so I was John Edgar Wideman on the cover. Now the three names of my entitles sound pretentious to me, stiff and old-fashioned. I'd prefer to be just plain John Wideman, but can't shake the Edgar.

It's my trademark, my brand name in the book trade. Is my grand-mother's name Martha Irene Rutledge-Lawson-Wideman-Overton-Morehead-Fallen. Does she drag that dragon-tail baggage wherever she goes.

Hannibal Wideman, my grandfather from Greenwood, South Carolina, changed his name to Harry when he migrated north. Who had named him originally, whose sense of history included the memory of the Carthaginian general, African conqueror of Rome. Ironic that such a name would become an encumbrance as Harry crossed his Alps, south to north, an elephant of a name he shrunk, discarded, refused, seeking anonymity, ordinariness. Didn't pay for a black workingman to stick out, to draw attention to himself in Pittsburgh in 1901. A fancy name would brand him, clearly as his accent, as a down-home country boy fresh to the city. What happened to the history inscribed in *Hannibal,* its power to connect Harry Wideman to the past and assist in forging, determining a future.

My grandmother's last husband, Otis Fallen (my mother always claimed poor Otis so old and befuddled he never actually realized he was married again) pronounced his last name so it rhymed with "Allen." On paper it reads like the adjective meaning to have dropped, tumbled, etc., "fallen." Fallen, Martha.

She anointed me with many names. Each one appropriate for a particular time, place, occasion. *Spank. Doot. Spanky. John-Edgar. John. Doodlebug. Mr. Wideman.* She employed them with an exactitude that matched the perfectly formed letters of her handwriting. Part of the game was slipping up on purpose. Calling me *Spanky,* my name inside the family, in front of people who weren't family. Spanky . . . I mean *John,* her eyes twinkling, her face suddenly sixty, seventy, eighty years younger, a teasing little girl smile and she's Martha Lawson again, back in Wrightsville, PA.

What did you call me at the end. Your grandson half a century old now himself. Did you believe in that mannish *John* name yet or would there always be a tongue-in-cheek grin tucked away somewhere within that sound when it issued from your lips. Towards the end I couldn't gauge how much Grandma actually heard. We all learned to speak louder, to face her so she could read our lips as well as pick up sound. In a crowd she'd settle into herself and seem to drift away from the conversations rattling around her. Sometimes I thought it wasn't so much her difficulty in hearing as it was the preogative she granted herself to hear what she wanted to hear, ignore the rest. She'd earned the right. Listening so long to the snow of words that never seems to diminish. People always needing someone to listen, to say something. Words, words, words, never an end in sight. She'd sit, slightly slumped, hands in lap. Was she asleep. Was her chin sinking onto her chest. No. Right on time, on target, she'd perk up and snap into the flow of words. If my name happened to be in what she was contributing, it would be the correct name, the one that fit precisely unless she winked slyly at me and brought her hand up to shush her mouth. Doot . . . I mean *John*. Hamming up the corrective gesture for everyone to see, walnuts in her cheeks or balls of dough, a smooth hilly pouch under each eye when she smiles and covers her offending lips with her hands. My long shanked hand, my brother Rob's lean fingers, my sister Tish's color, my father's thick veins, a sucked-in hollowness below the puffy cheeks that belongs exclusively to her, her age when her false teeth are out and the flesh collapses inwards on emptiness. If you thought of me when you were in the hospital, what name did you think. When you asked after your missing eldest grandson, what was the name in your question. Do you know a name that stands for all the others. One present when they are absent, one that existed before they were invented. Do you ever speak aloud the name of that place where all the names converge, become no name, nothing. Where I am known by you and only you, nameless, a place empty as a grave you decorated with names. Identities like seeds planted there. But you must remember the ground untilled, untouched, unbroken, unsown. When you played your name games with me, is that the place I felt solid under my feet. You possessed the power to land me there, take me back, free me. When I wasn't beside you at the end to grip your hand, what did you call the emptiness you patted and consoled.

THIS HAS BEEN one of those Marches of interminable rain, grayness, clamminess, gusting winds. If winter is earth sleeping and spring a wakening, the transition has been fitful, violent, unsettling dreams prematurely ripping the land into consciousness. Alert, aching because sleep is ending without fulfilling its restorative function, without bestowing its bounty of rest and peace. A few days of Arctic blue sky. Too pure, too distant for the pale green shoots that are beginning to push up, no matter what. A vast chilling blue. Trees skeletal. A few dead leaves cling, tatter of meat on the bone. A scouring wind. Anything vertical shivers and ripples and you realize the invisible wind is a medium thick and dense as water, the earth a pebble plummeting through it. Seasons are not heavy, solid blocks of time abutting one another. They lean, sway. Seasons are the records of billions upon billions of infinitesimally minute particles, each one cycling through its changes, its weather of metamorphosis, transition, adjustment. They determine the larger patterns we observe. Little pictures seeming to mirror the big one, but correspondences are a measure of our lack of understanding of either. Middling creatures. Caught in the middle. What we know always the limiting factor in what else, how much, we can know. March is winter spring summer fall, the stripping bare of certainty, all seasons present no matter how convenient it would be for us to have it another middling way, for our categories to maintain their separate identities, our centers to hold.

Yesterday, Thursday, March 26, 1991, around eight-thirty in the evening my grandmother died. Now my bargain rate, advance purchase ticket to Pittsburgh will be used for her funeral, not a visit to the hospital. So it goes. I was on the phone with my father, letting him know my plan to arrive in Pittsburgh Friday. He was down, way down. Though he'd never admit it directly, I could tell, because his voice was low, uninflected. Childhood buddy of his had recently died. His girlfriend's mother had died. Uncle Dave, Grandma's last surviving brother had died in California the week before. And of course his mother lay dying, no longer alert, no longer speaking or recognizing people or focusing her eyes. Occasionally she started awake, made noises, blinked her eyes. She'd drifted into a comatose state after the doctor had begun morphine injections. To ease her pain. But everyone had told me she hadn't complained of pain. Her doctors must have anticipated the discomfort of dehydration, the slow starvation that was inevitable since they applied no measures to force-feed her or irrigate her failing system. Why not. I wanted to know who made these decisions. Someone to hold responsible, to blame.

Of course I should have been there. Or tried to call her. But I refuse the luxury of guilt now. For whatever reason, I didn't do what I should have done. Buying a plane ticket to Pittsburgh a half-ass measure. As much wishful thinking as a serious attempt to get home before she died. The odd thing is I began to believe she'd stay alive till I got there. Just a few more days, Grandma. Then it will be convenient for me to come. Hold on till Friday. Then it will be OK for you to die. But hold on. Welcome me home. I was relying on the possibility that my schedule and Death's would mesh, be in step. Began to believe that's how things would happen. Till I got the call from my mother. She said Catherine had called her and Catherine was on her way to the hospital with her friend Lil and my father if she could reach him. Catherine hadn't been able to reach my father because he'd been on the phone with me when Catherine called him, hearing about my plan to arrive on the weekend. My plan to see my grandmother before it was too late.

FOR ABOUT A YEAR while we were waiting for an apartment to open up at 702 Copeland, we lived on the third floor of my grandmother's house at 712 Copeland in Shadyside, an almost entirely white Pittsburgh neighborhood with good schools my father worked two and a half jobs to keep us in. That's when I saw her in the tub. We almost died in that house, my mother, myself, my four siblings, gassed by a leaky stove. Robby, the baby then, saved us when his crying woke my grandmother and she came to our rescue. I made love for the first time in that house, on the couch in the downstairs apartment. My first lover the daughter of the man who boarded on the first floor of my grandmother's house.

Wanda was visiting from Harlem, where she lived on Convent Avenue. She was a gift out of the blue, as truly heaven-sent as Harlem-sent. Harlem just added spice, danger. Small, perfect, clearer about what she was doing than I would ever be. She said she liked me because I wore my jeans low on my hips, the way the Spanish boys did back home in New York. Liking me, forget the reason, whatever, reason, was blessing enough. And to like me enough to pull down her own tight, low-slung jeans and then step out of her panties and lie down beside me, kissing and hugging on the couch in a corner of Mr. Lennox's sitting room. Wow. Her daddy was a waiter, like my father, and wouldn't be home before midnight. Uncle Mac I'd lost track of. Grandma was upstairs, probably in bed, with no reason to return down the steps so Uncle Mac was the only one who might enter the front door and catch us in the tiny anteroom off the main hall, Mr. Lennox's parlor with his radio where he listened to the Pirates' baseball games. We'd been warned that the rest of the apartment was out of bounds. Don't youall go back in there. If you need to sit up and make google-eyes at each other, sit in the parlor. And don't stay up late. No locks or doors between us and whatever traffic passing in and out the front entrance. Maybe Mr. Mac was upstairs, maybe he was working late at the Ricks' or at the storefront church on Tioga Street where he was assistant sometime pastor. He could bust through the door any moment and see most of the couch from the hall. But Wanda liked me and was prepared to show me how much so I was prepared to risk shame or death.

What I wasn't really ready for was the way things speeded up and tangled up, her body with mine, mine with hers, legs, hair, fingers, touching and moaning, little increments of mixed-up back- and-forth sallies, then a landslide, stuff I'd only imagined or read in stolen paperbacks, or tried on myself locked in the bathroom or daydreamed under the covers when I thought my younger brother Otis had finally stopped flopping and farting for the night and was snoring himself to oblivion on his side of the bed. Her smells and wetness, squeezing, opening. Starting slowly inch by inch, amazed at what I was seeing, at how simple it was once you got started, and trying to prolong, imprint and hurry at the same time everything new and incredible and scaring the shit out of me while I enjoyed it to death. No. Huh uh. I wasn't ready for all that instant joy and pumping away with my bare behind mooning Uncle Mac if he happened to bust through the front door. It was like swing low sweet chariot, my buns lifted, her sweet gold buns—gold, gold is exactly how I remember her, gold, golden, her skin soft gold light of candle glow and honey—lifting me and sweeping me away and then I was someplace else, watching a cool minute, till I was caught up again in a whirling daze and didn't return to earth, didn't care if I ever returned, didn't think of returning till whipped to a frazzle, everything I owned squeezed out the needle's eye in one of those big bangs that jump-started the universe. I rolled my thighs off hers to recapture my bearings, get a good look at where I'd been, what had been causing all the excitement, and saw the half-dollar-size puddle of cum between us. She scooted back to prop her head against the couch's armrest. There it was. A dollop of custard. Did we do that. A little baby lying there between us wouldn't have surprised me more. And I half expected that creamy stuff to osmose itself into a mouth and start yelling. Where had it come from. Who did it belong to. How many days had we been lying naked from the hips down, cooling out, exposed to the world on this couch in my grandmother's house. And even if we'd managed to get away with something, wasn't all the evidence anybody'd need to find us out, convict and punish us, right here, indelible, plain as day. Wherever else I'd been, I was home again that quick. A boy who'd been given permission to visit Mr. Lennox's daughter. But don't stay late. And behave yourself. And don't youall dare go back in his apartment. I'd messed up. Ruined the couch and sure as night follows day somebody was going to pay.

Wanda mopped up with her underpants, balled them and stuffed them in the back pocket of her jeans, a place I couldn't imagine with room for anything more than the tight, apple mounds of her cheeks.

Rest will dry right up, she smiled.

And it did. Nothing to worry about. Just a spot. Something to remember me by. Are you going to remember me when I'm gone. You gon keep being nice to me. I like you cause you're nice. Not like them nasty boys at home want you for just one thing. Will you write.

I didn't but she did. One or two letters, then a third one a year or so later: Dear John . . .

My mother didn't say a word when I returned home that evening from my grandmother's couch. Next day I was up and out early. Where you going in such a hurry already this morning, boy. Don't bother answering. Your grandmother's house mighty popular all the sudden. Don't you go waking people up. You know Mr. Lennox works late.

Grandma's front door unlocked. Wanda and her father probably still asleep. Uncle Mac and Grandma gone by now. I crept in. Checked the couch for a spot. You could see it only if you were looking for it. Maybe still the slightest bit damp. I brushed the purplish nap. Blew on it. And since my nose was so close, inhaled what I could of her sweetness. A good thing, too, because that whiff was as close as I ever got to her again. Or loving again for two long years till I was fifteen and talked Tommy into the backseat of Uncle Mac's rusty Lincoln Continental in the alley yard behind my grandmother's house.

loon man

Foster's in the garden on his knees. His hands bleed. Foster's not very bright. Not very bright. That's me, Foster, in the bitch's garden on my knees digging. I am not very bright to be doing this. No. Certain deep roots are better left alone. You grip them and pull, the bristles strip skin from your hands. On my knees, hands bleeding. Foster, Foster, Foster. You're not very bright, Foster. Why didn't you wear the gardening gloves, Foster. The gloves. The gloves. The gloves. Look at your hands you silly man boy person whatever it was she called me I do not recall it does not matter anyway in this piece I'm saying to stop the bleeding. Gloves. Gloves. Gloves. In the garden on your knees you must wear the gardening gloves. They are like a piece of someone else's body. A discarded body part. Road-killed hands scraped up and laid here where I see them but do not remember to put them on. Not very bright. No. I go down on my knees and grub with my bare hands the hairy roots scream and dig deeper, curl around rocks, braid themselves into entanglements with other roots, assume the dead weight heaviness of earth itself and I'm tugging at the same ground I kneel on crazy crazy as earth rips and cracks and heaves under me trying to raise myself by these ropy bootstrap roots. Not very bright. Not very Foster. Hard skin of a pair of hands run over years ago by a bus, mashed and scorched and tanned till they're tough as leather. How could I slip my hands in those hands whose hands they belong to someone somewhere else my hands pull and bleed do not belong either except if I go on digging sooner or later they'll fall off or she'll stand over me scowling, thick ankles, the frilly-edged apron Foster you're not very bright. Where are the gloves. How many times have I said wear the gloves, Foster. Use the gardening gloves in the garden. Now look at your hands. My hands. My hands. You're bleeding like a stuck pig. And dirt in the cuts. If they begin to rot, I'm going to cut them off. Off, Foster. Cut them off and toss them in the compost pile if you don't remember the gloves.

So I know better but I forget again and go on working till she comes for me sooner or later when I have no hands when I've watered this ground with them. I forget because the brain is one long root twisted back and forth on itself, hugging itself, hidden in itself in its own shadows of loop and bend, a booger that grows while you pick it, Loonman said and said with a special curved needle the sly priests extracted all of it intact, not a nick not a crimp or bruise the whole endless string of spaghetti through one nostril of the corpse. Leaving no marks. Leaving sullen, wet emptiness which soon in the dry desert heat of Egypt becomes a skull. A harmless toy. He said left nostril always only the left and told me magic reasons why but Foster is Foster's not very bright. She always buys a brainless handyman like me when the one before goes bad. She says these are the handyman's gloves. You must wear them in the garden. You must wear them on your hands when you are the handyman. Wear what the others have worn. Handymen. Your soft bare fingers burrowing into stiffness, into tunnels like the roots claw for themselves deeper and deeper till there is no way to wrench them free. You know that if you pull one breath harder you will lose control, flip over and tumble down deeper and deeper twisting and bleeding into the darkness where those devil-tailed roots thrive. You can't let go. You can't poke your fingers into those handy handy things the others before you are still inside, parts of them trapped, lost inside let me out let me out let me go. The ones who came before me squealing if I stuff my fingers in the gloves. When I pull my fingers out the cork pops, a howl, a pitiful whine each finger a bald genie popping free to suffer all over again her wishes.

I see one handyman almost daily, the one before me who I sometimes mistake for myself. Loonman says that's crazy, really crazy not even keeping straight who you are not. Who you are is hard. But Foster, any bird or beetle knows who it is not. Not very bright. Not very bright. I see him almost every day, my predecessor with his peculiar style of walking. His duty must be patrolling this road. His body if you follow it from behind leans at an unnatural angle, so steep you believe any moment he'll topple over. Loonman said that guy's job should be delivering pizza. The miles he logs on these country roads, the T-shirt he could wear: Leaning Tower Pizza. But I didn't laugh. I don't think humor at some poor soul's expense is polite or funny. Especially when a person's sick in body or mind and can't help themselves. The wall-eyed, pigeon-toed fellow who tilts and doesn't even know it. His feet on the dirt shoulder of the road, the top of him cockeyed, leaning so far into the road's airspace that a trailer truck, if one ever passed, would bang him, spin him like a top, nobody's fault, round and round he'd go spinning in place like a duck you ding in a carnival booth three shots for a quarter.

Where have my predecessors' hands been. What nastinesses committed. Nose picking, crotch scratching, God knows what else. Where else. Who else. Handyman chores around here extract sweat, scum. Finger holes like sewers. Too much intimacy to bear. Too bright, Foster, too bright to bear. If you itch, how could you scratch with those thick gloves on your fingers. She buys new men, no new clothes. She introduces me to the gloves, reminds me of their purpose, threatens me, lops off my hands. I forget anyway. He kneels in the garden. His bare hands beg for mercy. Foster. Me.

Foster lives in a house along the road, at the top of a steep rise, some miles from town. Not much of a town, not much of a road. The sorrowful crooked not very bright ones shuttle up and down the feeble road with so little traffic they are in no danger. They are the traffic. If you cross the road to fetch her mail and don't stop and look both ways, stop and look both ways stop look listen you are more likely to be bumped by one of them, the retards on their endless errands up and back the road, more likely to be struck by one of them, glaze-eyed, muttering to himself, leaning like a cockeyed tower, than be struck by anything with wheels, with drivers or cargo worth a shit.

There are many features of this house on the crest of a gradual incline of a winding, hilly, empty road going absolutely nowhere. Features you must memorize in order to find the house if you leave it and need to return again and again. If it's where you live, it's called your home and you will indeed discover many occasions when it's to your benefit to return. The house gives you a way of going places and coming back from places even though it is not yours and never will be, even though the bitch doesn't allow you to claim one square private inch for your own. You can leave and return. Sleep here nights. You are not a yo-yo spinning nonstop between the cold hand that tosses you out, the string round your neck that jerks you back.

You shut your eyes and this house you've learned appears like a face in a dream. Countless features you have memorized magically arrange themselves into someone who would be different, who would not exist if just one of those countless features was missing or changed. Yes, that is the house where you live. The eyes, mouth, nose, the sallow cheeks, thinning hair. Count the ears. Are there enough. Too many. Does what you see in your mind materialize when you open your eyes after trudging to the top of the hill and asking yourself, Should I go in. Is this the list of items I've submitted to my memory. Am I home again.

Foster is not very bright, but this house is easy for him to find. Many stone steps. A miniature fountain and waterfall. Tarry railroad ties to cordon clumps of this and that growing here and there. Trees, shrubs. Ornaments. A little grinning groom, Foster's color, in a vest and jockey cap, hand stretched out for someone's horse. The house is a crown studded with many jewels that do not shine but are busy busy everywhere, a clutter begging for attention, for a handyman to polish and neaten, dig and snip and clip. Crown the bitch queen wears, atop the helmet of her hair.

Thus it's easy to find. No matter how long you've been gone. Top of hill. Three heads stacked one on the other. The first a face so mean you quickly look away, look up and find the other two—helmet, crown.

We live here as a family. Mama Bear, Papa Bear, baby bears. We are lucky to be in a real home. There are worse places. Far, far worse. Be grateful this kind lady has consented to take you in. She is the Mama Bear. Papa Bear and the other little bears are dead. The handyman tends their graves. The handyman is Foster who sometimes is a baby bear because all the baby bears are dead. She comes to tuck Foster in. Mama Bear on tiptoe, tippy-paw so she doesn't wake the others. But she never does because the others sleep the sleep of the dead. They are dead. Nevertheless she is considerate of their rest, sneaks in on tippy-toes her big burly body shrunken tiny as a mouse. Sometimes I don't hear her just the whisper of the bedsheet she raises to get at me, a breeze on my sweaty thighs then nibble nibble mouse moth gnawing nipping as I pretend to sleep as I watch the room fill up with the yellow of her smell, the things she cooks and chews her breath never forgets. I dream four little feet and downy fur its darting its hurry-up hurry-up and scared rabbit heart thump thump thump, form these things into a dream so I feel them happening far away in another country and do not move a muscle deep in fake sleep so the game won't end. She's never fooled. She bides her time, darting, nibbling till my own heart's pounding gives me away. Very much awake. Very. Then its her rough hands grasping and pulling. It could be a tooth she's yanking out but I'm afraid to scream, to make any sound at all. It's too late. She has the root of me. Jerks, squeezes. I shudder. Except for one long gasping sigh, a whistle nearly, I keep my noises to myself. She lumbers out thick again as a she-bear.

I say to Loonman, We're a family.

Well, that makes me the bouncing baby boy, the new kid on the block, right mate. Winking and licking his lips and rubbing his hands together. He is a mistake, no doubt about it, furloughed too soon among normal people, the kind you must watch like a hawk until he gives himself away and you can march him straight back to the locked ward where he belongs.

He didn't let me finish what I wanted to say. We are a family. Very lucky to be here. Fortunate there are people like this generous lady who will accept us into their homes, treat us like family members. That's it. That's why you must be grateful and show respect at all times. Obey. Do exactly as you're told. A privilege to be welcomed into someone's home. You must demonstrate that you are ready, responsible. Stay neat, clean, don't eat too much. You must never fuss or fight or wander off. Your host must know your whereabouts at all times. Worse places. Far worse.

You are lucky to be part of a family, I wanted to tell him. The living and their dead. You must learn to be a ghost and one day if you master the secrets, the patience and skills of a ghost, after you've learned to hold your breath, stifle your noises, wipe every trace of yourself so there is no animal trail of you on pieces of furniture, walls, counters, no hairs, no rings in the sink, no footprints in the soil, none of your blood on the roots, no fingerprints because you've remembered the handyman gloves every time, when you hear speak nor see any evil and can dangle for hours on end motionless, invisible from the monkey tail of your unraveled brain, then perhaps she'll touch your forehead with her sword and you'll be free.

I call him Loonman but Loonman's not his name. Foster, call me Foster. I told him mine he told me his the day of his arrival. I don't remember what he told me. Foster's not too bright. Doesn't matter anyway. Don't need names around here. Just come when you are called. No mistaking who she wants, when she wants, what she wants. Those metal eyes, that linger like a hook. She's posed on the side steps to the kitchen, on the top one, nearest the door, her hand on the knob. He stood smiling above me on the middle step, the one I had fixed five times before she was satisfied, him with his duffle crushed under one arm, wearing a Boston Red Sox cap, grinning down on me as if he knew all my secrets or knew I possessed none. Either way I was laughable, silly. As pitiful as that crooked man on the crooked road. The county person slammed a car door out front. They're always in a hurry. Running from the danger of catching whatever it is they're afraid to catch from us. County door slammed, county motor gunned. County tires spit gravel. He's still grinning; she's twisted the door knob but hasn't pushed through into the kitchen. She had said, Don't stand there like a dummy. Introduce yourself. Barked those words at me, not him. As if already he was further along than I was. Fresh from the county car, too dumb to care it was leaving, but already further along. As if my days and nights of being a ghost counted for nothing and already, if I didn't know already how things stood, the two of them had arranged themselves on the back steps to announce she's always boss and he's one step above you already. You're not on the bottom, you are the bottom. After she orders me to speak, he grins till I tell my name. Foster. Hello, Foster. That your first or last name, pal. Another question, another order from him before he offers the courtesy of his name. Bitch hovers above us. Staring, approving. As if this newcomer has every right and I have none.

He squawks his name. She cuts in. He'll need to hear it plenty before he learns it. Maybe never will. And she's absolutely correct, on the money. Whatever name he smirked is gone, gone gone as soon as he said it. It doesn't matter. One name or two. Or none. First, last or middle. Here you come when you are summoned. She knows how to get your attention. Curved needle of a finger stabbing. Squabble squabble out of his duckbilled cap, many insulting names, many nasty words run together squawking from the mouth of his cap the instant her back is turned so no one hears but me. Remember those shiny scrubbed doll baby dressed little girls sticking their tongues out at you when their mothers aren't looking. Or raising their dresses, flashing their dirty bloomers. Loon gabble like a squishy fart in my face as he hitched his bag in his arm, grabbed for the screen door swinging shut behind her.

Now two of us sleep here in this house where she does. The rest of the family, Silas and Walter, appear early each morning in the county car. They are farmers. She turns them loose every day and they farm. I know nothing about their work. I don't care what they do all day. They farm. They never talk at lunch or supper when we are one big happy family gathered around the picnic table in her kitchen. A very tall man could lie on that wooden table and not hang over either end. You can't reach everything from your seat, but even when they need something passed, Walter and Silas who are brothers alike as peas won't open their mouths and ask. Sometimes I watch them move a salt shaker, a bowl of mashed potatoes, a water pitcher with their minds. You know they want something and without speaking or pointing they get what they want to slide within reach. I know they have this power. But some days I practice the power to resist. I hoard what they want at my end of the table, ketchup, sugar, pepper beside my plate and fight the rays they send to fetch them. They suffer. The rays are strong and urgent. They plead, beg, try to trick me into releasing what they require. Like a meter reader I measure red escalating in their faces. They know they are losing the game but refuse to speak. Farmers. I let them squirm.

They must gossip when they're alone together all day in her fields. Exhaust their supply of words, their energy for conversation. Perhaps. Or perhaps they are mutes. Dummies. What I know is their sullen silence oppresses me. Though they are members of our little family I'm glad each evening when the county car fetches them. Sundays they never come. That used to be the best day of the week. A long silence their silence didn't disturb.

Now Loonman never shuts up. He is Loonman not because he spit that glob of loon gabble at me his first day but because he tells me the Loon Man stories.

Loons nest in hidden places on the long lake you can reach by crossing the road in front of this house and following one of the trails down through the pine woods. Not very far away, a half mile at most. Except the trails are not easy, meandering through thick undergrowth, trees, muddy bogs you might get turned around or discouraged or lost completely if it's dark. On full moon nights the loons howl like crazed dogs. The Loon Man understood their language. Barked back at them. Echoed their screams, hollers, giggles, their anguished wails, the single rounded notes of longing the birds bounce at night from one bank to the other off the sounding board of black water. Loons, he claimed, commanded him to haunt the cottages along the lake. Peek in lighted windows at night, pick through garbage, spy on the cabins till he was like a member of the family, privy to their habits, their secret lives. He should learn, the loons ordered him, which families had children they didn't love. These children the Loon Man should steal. Set them free in the water so the loons could teach them to swim and dive and catch fish and float and speak the loon language of wandering spirits. Loons were dying out. Too many cottages, too many motorboats. The shells of loon eggs were thinning. Could not withstand the clamor, the crowding of summer people and their machines. Fewer and fewer chicks hatched. Soon soon the birds hooted we old ones will die out, no young will replace us and the new moon's sad face will not be comforted by our cries, no one will sing for the unquiet souls we were sent here to soothe.

When the third child disappeared that summer, two weeks after divers had pulled the first missing child from the lake, people in the cottages understood a monster was stalking them. The Loon Man drowned some say in August of that terrible summer, attempting to escape. Officers from the posse that pursued him claimed he called the state police station and confessed, told them where and when to meet him, promised to read a statement from the loons that would outline a plan for peaceful coexistence between birds and men. At midnight the cops parked their cruisers along the road at fire lane fifteen, the spot and time the Loon Man picked. Flashlights strobed the darkness. Cops crashed heavy-footed down a steep slope through tangles of brush and spiky trees. When a view of the lake opened before them, ghostly daylight hung over the water. The Loon Man had waded out so only his head and shoulders were visible, silhouetted against the shimmering water. They say you couldn't tell his screams from the birds'. As the cops rushed forward he dived, his body arching like a trout's as it broke the surface, splashing scales of light, before it's swallowed by blackness. Seemed like hours passed before he emerged, silver-edged, hooting and cawing over his shoulder, stroking towards the hundred-foot-deep center of the lake where other dark shapes bobbing in the water cheered him home.

The Loon Man's body was never recovered. And so the story goes, you can still hear him howling on full moon nights. Oldtimers around here are real careful to lock their doors, shut their blinds at night.

Fairy tale crapola from the new man. Loon Man gibberish so I call him Loonman.

They say the Loon Man was an escapee from the county home. Locked ward on the seventh floor. Dressed himself up in a doctor's smock, stole keys and just walked away. Say he lived two years in the woods before he attacked the cottages. At home in the woods as a beast. Prowling. Foraging. Killing what he ate. Missing about two years by the summer of the murders. No trace of him till then. They know the killer's name because the Loon Man telephoned and confessed. Didn't call himself the Loon Man. Huh uh. That name came

later, when stories about him began to go the rounds. Legends of the
Loon Man. A local hero kind of. Bogeyman to scare the kiddies to
sleep.

I think his real name was . . . Foster. Like yours. First name or last
name. Maybe both names. And his middle name, too. Foster Foster
Foster. You're not too bright, Foster. Calm down, Foster. I'm just
teasing.

They say if he hadn't killed himself that night he was a goner
anyway. Cops had vowed to do the honors. No room on the planet
for a crazed baby killer. Especially here in Hicksville where everybody
knows everybody else and all the townsfolk dependent on that summer money from tourists who rent cabins on the lake. Folks under-
standably upset. Rumor is the posse primed for a little do-it-yourself
mayhem. You know. A bit of all-American rough justice when they
caught the guilty party. Who could blame them. And who would ever
tell what really happened out there in the dark. Cops part of it, so
who's going to snitch. Who gives a shit anyway about what happens
to a cornered animal that's been slaughtering your lambs.

One of our comrades, Foster, a colleague, an alumnus of our alma
mater. He put our institution on the map. People demanded that the
county home be closed. They fired the superintendent. Security got
tougher. Couldn't find a place to go off and tickle your balls in peace.
More gates, locks, rules and guards. Weren't you there then. Don't you
remember Foster Foster. Eight, nine years ago. No talk of furloughs
then. No halfway houses. Huh uh. Lock'em up. Throw away the key.
Out of sight out of mind. Out of mind out of sight. You remember
the good ole snake pit days, don't you.

Funny thing is some people claim the Loon Man sneaked back into
the booby hatch. Different name or same name. Who worries about
a loony's name. Who keeps track. They say he swam to the other side
of the lake. Yeah, it's a long way. Normal person couldn't make it. But
he's the Loon Man, right. Swam to the opposite shore and sneaked
right back where he belonged in the first place.

Now that's a good one, isn't it. A happy ending for our side. For
once we grab the upper hand and keep it. I can see him stretched out
on his cot, puffing a Lucky Strike, smiling and blowing smoke rings
at the ceiling. That dungeon they built to snuff him, saving his skin.

How you like them apples, Foster. Ain't that a nice ending to the story. But there's more. What if he did it again. Over and over again. The Loon Man regular as rain, as spring summer fall winter. Like some goddamn swarm of locusts every seven years returning to take a bite. Then back to the loony bin to rest up. Pretty scary, huh. Lock your door, Foster. Stay away from the lake after dark. And don't believe a word those loons say. Next time the Loon Man may be hunting crazies. Chowing down on sweet retard meat, dummies like us, Foster.

He's not prejudiced. Might even be curious how darkies taste. Not many of you around these parts. Nobody knows when he'll strike again, but you can bet your ass the Loon Man's coming back.

Foster is frightened. I know better. I have nothing to fear. The Loon Man's dead at the bottom of the lake. Fish have picked his evil bones clean and soon even his bones will rot and disappear, sucked down into the lake's muddy heart, roots dragging him down, down, roots twisting round his arms and legs and breath the night he tried to flee. Now he's fish food or just plain Loonman bullshit. A story he makes up as he goes along. But Foster is not too bright. He is a child. So I must stay awake with him, squeeze his baby-soft hand, calm his fears. Poor Foster believes anything. I talked him to sleep once tonight, earlier, then he popped up all in a sweat believing an army of heavy-booted men hunted him with spears of light. Light stabbed the darkness. Buzzing and zapping, slicing bushes, trees, everything in its path lasered dead, a ruined smoking forest disintegrating around him, his pursuers only yards behind leveling all cover, all safety with hissing beams of light.

Foster is an asshole. A burden. He believes anything and Loonman is merciless. His cheap Jack Nicholson imitations of leer and menace. His comic book tales of the crypt. Foster, I say. Go to sleep, man. Go to sleep, man, boy, child, person, whichever.

I am afraid the next time the bitch comes for me I won't hear the familiar noises, only feel the swift chill on my skin when she sweeps off the sheet and I'm suddenly vulnerable, ripe for taking. I'll think she's the Loon Man stealing my life and leap from my bed, battle till one of us is gone.

I'm afraid she's on her way tonight and Foster doesn't understand yet the cruel trick Loonman is playing on him. Not funny. I don't think it's humorous at all. Especially since Foster's not too bright. Not a joke. Not funny you grinning bastard. To lie awake all night trembling when silly birds babble at the moon. Tonight Foster must sleep, sleep. He needs peace. Rest. He's dying from lack of sleep. I leave him stretched rigid as a plank, staring at moon fire consuming the edges of a blind. He fears for his life. Fears for hers. If she comes for him and he is confused, if she doesn't come but he lies awake through the wolf hours of night waiting, someone will die.

So I slink from the bed, leave the closet allotted for my sleep, creep through the kitchen, out the side door, down the steps, tiptoe on damp grass, just beyond the loud gravel of the driveway, circling until I reach her window. It's not covered. Loonman hasn't poisoned her with lies.

Bright August moon. Like noon I think as my eyes, in spite of deep night, accustom themselves effortlessly to seeing everything they care to see. Don't need eyes. I've memorized the features of this house, this home. I could be struck blind as sin and still find my way anywhere, find anything I need. Her low window is half open, screened to keep out bugs. They've stopped biting me. Or rather I let them bite and they never take too much. After a month here scratching my skin raw I made a truce. Said take what you need but don't overdo it. I'll stop swatting and spraying and scratching. Just don't be greedy. So there is a gentle nip, nip on my bare skin like summer rain I don't mind from the kitchen to her bright window. Closer, I see everything inside. Furniture, bed, discarded clothing, magazines on an end table, her stack of fluffy, fringed pillows. She must be in the bathroom now. How many times have I scrubbed mopped and polished that white, cold place were she shits and washes, shits and washes, washes and shits. Each time I wipe the toilet seat I think of her heavy ass bearing down, stamping its imprint into the wood. If I watch, if I slip inside her, anticipate every step of her nighttime routine, I can keep her here, in this room where she sleeps, lock her inside for the night. My force outdueling hers, defeating those rays which might drive her to Foster's room. She is stronger than Walter and Silas. Silas and Walter. But I am strongest. I begin thinking all the reasons she must stay here, all the actions I've observed many nights that she must perform to draw this room tighter and tighter about her body, tight so the blazing light is drowned, so the walls collapse and pull tight as gloves over her flesh and she's finished for the night, still as a potato in the bottom of a sack. Pea in a pod. Foster in the armless jacket they lace like a shoe.

Warm water splashes her mannish shoulders, runs down her broad bare back Foster has never seen, its warts, pimples and mottled colors of dead leaves Foster must sweep and sweep. Leaves everywhere. Wind his enemy till he burns them. Flames lick, smoke belches. Careful. Careful, Foster, don't set the damned woods on fire, don't burn down the damned house. She will wrap a towel around the wet helmet of hair, crown on crown, and that's all she'll be wearing when she steps in from the bathroom. Naked as I am outside the window. It's putter time then. Grooming and oiling and plucking the huge whiteness of her body. She'll stop to play with herself sometimes. A surprised look on her face, as if she's dug a piece of candy from her crotch. I have memorized the tasks she performs preparing for bed. I have memorized her body parts. Would know if anything's missing. Without counting I know the number of hairs rooted between her legs, the number of cratered rings circling her thick nipples. Foster has never seen any of this. Cow tits, backside slung like two fifty-pound bags of flour. He knows her only in the dark. Only the touch of fingers and lips, lips and fingers, her fist squeezing like a vise. Foster knows nothing. Except fear. He's afraid of the Loon Man. Afraid of her polar bear flesh.

One hoot from the bathroom. Sudden. Startled. Pleasure or pain or both. It's different. A sound I haven't heard from her before. I make myself ready for anything.

Loonman pops into the lighted square. *Twist again like we did last summer.* He is grinning. He is ugly, hideous beyond belief. White and doughy, black hairs like feathers spit curled on his wet body. He pulls a towel side to side across his back, knees bent, obscenely sashaying his bony hips. *Twist twist twist again, like we did last year* stringy pecker donging back and forth, flapping like a lynched worm. Then she's behind him, twice as wide, helmets on her head, nakedness filling the doorframe. She's cracking up. Ha ha ha ha ha as if Loonman's the cutest, funniest act she's ever seen.

I duck as quickly as I can below the window ledge, but I know he caught me. He winked at me as if to say I know you have a weapon in your hand you've been pretending till this very moment you don't know anything about.

Thought I heard a noise outside, Sweetie.

I know he's winking at me again, though I'm huddled out of sight, his mine hers down in this dark pool beneath the window.

Raccoon probably. Or maybe that stupid Foster's out there spying on me again. Nothing, Babydoll.

Loonman squawks out the window. Squawk. Squawk. Answers echo from the lake. *Yes. Yes. Yes.* I slash through the light to join them.

everybody knew bubba riff

Voices are a river you step in once and again never the same Bubba here you are dead boy dead dead dead nigger with spooky Boris Karloff powder caked on your face boy skin lightener skin brightener and who did it to you I'm talking to you boy don't roll your eyes at me don't suckee teeth and cutee eye look how that boy's grown come here baby gimme some sugar baby look at the feet on him they say you know the size of the dog by the puppy's feet his long feet this one be a giant some day I swear some man's long feet and his Mama's curly eyes Mama's baby Daddy's maybe I wonder if Bubba's feet bare if his big ass and gorilla thighs and donkey dick are naked down inside the coffin under the snow white satin naked as the day he was born a big bouncy boy on his mama's knee touch him touch him he won't bite he's yours now too man boy your daddy brought you into this world but I can take you out the man wags a finger in the boy's face the boy sees the yellowed long john top three undone buttons at the chewed neck and bagged about the man's middle he's scared them funky pants slide down the man's hips man be standing there fussing at him in his long johns his behind hanging out the holes his knees bagged out like the baggy middle what he wants to do is put his thumbs in the

64

suspenders and hike them back on the trifling runty little man's narrow shoulders here you are that's better ain't it little fellow you was about to lose your britches now go play sit back on down where you was sitting drinking your wine before you got all up in my face about nothing cause you ain't my real daddy and you can wave your finger and holler all you want but if you ever lay a hand on me again I'ma break you in half old man don't care how much my mama need the shit you bring around here no more whipping on me you touch me or put a hand on her ever again it's rumble time mano a mano motherfucker me and you on the green and if you can't stand the heat get out the kitchen this ain't no Papa Bear Mama Bear and li'l Sugar Baby Bear jam no more I'm grown now ain't taking your whiskeyhead shit no more hit my mama hit me Ima bust you up my sweet Bubba how I loved that boy seem like he came out smiling like he arrived here knowing something that made him the grinningest baby you ever seen he was easy easy girl my first and the only easy one I ever had I didn't know better I thought pain and blood and walking the floor all night the way it spozed to be you know stuff you spozed to learn growing up to be a woman so you mize well go ahead and get on with what you got to do no way round it like falling off roller skates when you little learning to skate and scuffed up knees bloody elbow you climb back up off the ground ain't nothing the matter with you girl you sneak back up on your feet and look around hope nobody saw you down on the pavement wipe the tears out your eyes make sure your clothes ain't ripped and go ahead about your business you know you learning a lesson you know how it is dues you got to pay Mama Mama look at you boy look what a mess you made out the side of your face it always hurt you worse than it hurts them you bound to fall once twice three times falling falling and tear up your ass as many falls as you need to learn your lesson then you starts understanding you know better you know ain't no lesson and ain't no learning you just keep on falling your babies keep falling you pick yourself up pick up that boy put him down he's big enough to be carrying you around woman look at where he bit me little devil he's too young to start him on a bottle the falling ain't teaching nobody nothing you keep on falling because falling down's what you born to do all the days of your life amen till one time thank you Father amen you can't stand back

up no more little devil knows when he's biting me he look up all
cutie-pie wide-eyed and I'm seeing stars think the bloods trickling
down my chest boy oh boy next time Ima smack you balder headed
than you already is you know good and well you ain't spozed to be
biting your Mama like that got the nerve to have teeth little bitty nubs
pushing up I rub his gums help his teeth come in rub a ice cube on
his gums when he frets please don't lose your little smile now ain't
no time to take back my titty let him nibble if he needs to nibble he
needs me now I rock him and rub his tummy he grin up at me I lifts
him and wiggle him he shakes like a bowl of jelly my little old man him
diaper droopy and creases in him thighs him knees wobble shake him
bake him paddy cake him sing him froggy went a courtin and he did
ride this room uh huh these walls uh huh she lifts the dumpling baby
uh huh uh huh tastes its rubbery flesh she is dressed in black beside
the coffin her face veiled her gloved hands somewhere out of sight the
music winds on she must not stand too long the others behind her
prop her ease her along the line fed from rows of benches into the
center aisle Amazing Grace you would think they'd get their fill of
young black men's bodies but no no end to it she must not hover too
long over the crib because the others are lined up for their turn passing
passing down the rows of benches onto the carpeted aisle then down
towards the flower-decked altar flowers flowers everywhere who pays
for so many flowers pays for the dope nobody around here has
nothing not one red cent so he stands there in them yellow past
patching long johns trembling like a rattle snake he would break the
boy apart if he could but Bubba too big for that bullshit now I can't
do nothing with him find me a stick break a board upside his big hard
nappy head maybe he start to listening to someone no no no that's not
the way Bubba's a good boy just needs a man to talk to him tell him
wildness not the only way to be a man please help me I try try I talk
till I'm blue in the face snapped a broom handle over his back he
laughed and ran out the kitchen big old boy like that he should be
carrying you around put him down woman you got a muscle in your
arm big as mine it ain't nothing it's a pimple look big cause my arm's
skinny put that boy down on his own two feet feets big as mine
already his shoes cost as much as mine already put that boy down boy
you got teeth in them feet boy chewing out the toes of your shoes they

ain't a week old look like dogshit already I ain't made of money smack some sense he's just a boy don't mean no harm let him be Bubba Bubba too late for crying he's gone gone gone the others push out their hard wooden seats the rows empty one by one Amazing Grace how sweet the sound his cold cold eye on the sparrow the mourners shuffle they squeeze past ancient knees the ones too tired too old who keep their places on the benches too weary to move they sit alone left behind while the others are a river flowing to the altar and the waters part and rise again two streams returning up the side aisles to the rear of Homewood African Methodist Episcopal Zion Church where the ushers stand in white and once upon a time one of them my first love dimple-cheeked almost old as my mama she smiled at me and melted every hard leg dusty butt knucklehead I don't want to be here in church in the first place anger fear and awkwardness of being a boy force-marched Sunday morning every Sunday morning to this woman-haunted place their cries and prayers and wet-eyed singing and hats and moans and veils and bosoms Jesus help me legs Jesus in love and the loneliness beneath those closets of noisy clothes they packed their bodies in Jesus help me the organ when church finally had one when we chased out the white people and moved into their big church on Homewood Avenue first thing you hear the organ when you come in think it some old sister humming in the amen corner as you tiptoe you always tiptoed you always stumbled or shuffled or slid like on ice because your feet would tattle on you how much you didn't want to be in church how much you wanted to fly back out the door and you'd be long gone if it wasn't for your mama dragging you in dragging you away from Bubba and them and what they into Sunday morning you set down one foot after the other careful as rain pitta patta look at the dogs on that boy Bubba you gonna be a big man pardner when you grows into them dogs must cost a pretty penny just keeping you in shoes I'd rather clothe him than feed him on his stoop we ate two dozen hot dogs and drank a gallon of grape Kool-Aid Bubba'd wait till his mama watching then cram a whole hot dog bun wiener and mustard in his mouth shove the end till it disappeared like a train in a tunnel you do that again boy Ima smack you bald-headed but she smiled when he tricked her into catching him in the act same smile on my first love's face greeting me as I crossed the threshold of A.M.E.

Zion but her skin shades lighter and not as old and blemishless and warm to the touch of my eyes and her smile sliced me melted me undressed us both her smile crackling like her swift white uniform so white I could see her brownskin sealskin underneath and her smooth cheeks and dark lips part swelling the rustle of wings of power of furled wings behind her back as she handed me a Sunday program and I tripped onto the purple carpet falling head over heels in love with everything I'd set my jaw against Sunday mornings being gathered being plucked from where I was happily minding my own business dreaming of Bubba and them free as birds somewhere they shouldn't be I'm back again in line pushing forward in stiff new shoes the soles still slick I'm slipping I glide feel static electricity charging my body the green worm of flame that will spit if my fingers touch the metal-edged fountain in the church lobby who's in such a hurry this morning why do I feel the push the rush can't stop for a drink of water somebody's breath on my neck she peers down at Bubba is he sleeping is he dead babies die sometimes just lay there dead a cat suckee breath steal breath a fat white cat in her dream in his crib a green-eyed Chessy cat grin too late too late cat got his tongue all his sweet breath sweet smile got it and gone gone don't you hear me talking to you boy Sunday morning the bells stroll up and down Homewood Avenue black hands ring them our bells now telling time for all Homewood the biggest church on the block on the corner ours now the pretty stained-glass windows till some junky steals them an organ high-domed ceiling we must wash white as snow again tall scaffolds and ladders for the men to climb Bubba won't be there it's Wednesday your mother promised you'd help the men Wednesday evening old deacons and ushers and trustees ancient monkeys in the web of pipe and board rising to the arched ceiling jack be monkey quick angels they are lighter and faster than you've ever seen them in these work clothes they never wear to church I climb one foot after the other into heaven through the door she guards in white welcoming me each finger in white and I love every one her touch veiled but warmer washed white as snow in white glove softness the white that sighs and stretches and must abide her brown body within its shape her fullness her secret scents and white teeth perched within the blackness of her lips her heavy lashes bowing as if she's been waiting shy and puzzled

too as the smile sinks back into her entering and warming the ebb
returning as sure as the outward flow if you were a spider high up in
the tit of swelling vault you would see the pattern how rows empty
one by one and the mourners file towards the coffin and the line
breaks on the rock of the flower-draped altar returning them in two
streams to the source the rear aisle and street door narrow and straight
where she nods and smiles at you and touches your cheek once once
more gentle scratch than touch more of a tracing her pointy nail inside
the glove some bright winged humming insect testing the field of your
cheek faint brush of its breathy legs a path with no destination just
there an instant then gone back to wildness as if your face is a flower
as if your whole life has been nothing till now nothing before nothing
after just this quick brush this kiss you wish now as you remember
it you wish the world would go away again as it did when she lifted
her white winged hand touched her lips teeth breath on your cheek
Bubba how long how long behind me beyond me over yonder on the
bank one of the old ones too stiff and ridden to shuffle down the aisle
shouts like that rock did crying out no hiding place don't leave me this
morning weak and desperate as Old Charley Rackett's voice in that
down home story I told you Bubba about my people you said you
never had no people your Mama found you in the trash you said you
liked that Charley Rackett story tell it again man that tough old nigger
got some Bubba in him weak and feeble and old but they knew he'd
push hisself out his chair and crawl after them to the fields how old
was he then my great-great-Bubba grandfather maybe a hundred
maybe more they called him the African because when he first landed
in this wilderness he spoke a bubba dubba language no one understood not one word of English and even after he *could* speak most days
he *wouldn't* speak Charley Rackett whipped till he'd answer to that
Charley Charley Charley shit a language of blows and animal noises
as if he was the beast not them in those old time slavery days then it
was Freedom and my people working our own briar patch of land in
South Carolina and Charley he's too old go to the fields every morning we sit him in his chair by the door so's he can look out and little
Bubba one the gran kids his job to mind the old man from can to
cain't from sunup to sundown in that chair by the door then one
morning old rusty black Charley Rackett said him say don't leave me

behind this morning I gwine wit youall this godblasted morning and
up he stood and bram down he tumble out his chair and Oh my God
Oh my Blessed Savior they's running around hollering and pull bag
of bones Charley off the floor and stuff him back in the chair but he
flies right out again quick as a grasshopper and bram hits the floor
again his nose bleeding lip cut ain't nobody seen him rise out that
chair for years he's hollering and nobody don't know what to do help
me Jesus Charley Rackett's mind made up he'll drag behind them on
his bloody elbows bloody knees so they gathers him up and ties him
on the mule and that's what happens every day till he dies one night
after supper in his bed Charley Bubba Rackett riding on the mule with
them to the fields he worked a hundred hundred years slavery days
and the slaving days after and they couldn't keep him down I was
Bubba the boy left behind with him I follow Charley Rackett's stare
through the open doorway across the scraped-clean place our cabin
sits on like a turned-over bucket study rolling hills and broccoli tops
of trees that rise from a crease where the creek runs to a river and river
to delta fanning draining to the dark sea where her teeth flash like
waves at night my job to fetch him coolish water shoo flies and plow
his dinner from the skillet I left too long on the stove fasten scraps
of button at the neck of his long johns tend his knobby hands the
color of turned earth wipe the corner of his mouth always the silvery
web the slobber the grunts groans wheezes of words he can't twist his
mouth around he grinds them on the stumps of his teeth chews and
spits them at me I sit much of the time as far away as I'm able in the
space we occupy him in his pew me scattered in a corner on the floor
sucking a tit of cane worrying a hard kernel of something anything
caught in my teeth playing funny little tunes in my brain bird cries
train thunder lightning crickets the women washing snap beans crack
crack drumming in a tin bowl he coughs the walls shake I wipe sweat
from his brow wet from his chin it's broad daylight flies buzz I tuck
him in pull up his suspenders he calls my name a word a sound
nobody else in the whole world knows Bubba and next morning he
tries to stand hits the floor and steals from me the long peace of day
after day alone with him listening learning my name because next
morning they take him and I trail the mule's mulish stink mulish
swish of its shitty tail its pitta pat clomp to the fields that morning

lost to me unremembered until Bubba lying up there like you sleeping like you ain't got a care in the world boy and you say tell it one more time the old timey story I like and your mama looking down at you her little brown bouncing baby broken boy Bubba I hear one of those stones behind me send up your name in a prayer like Charley Rackett hollered Take me goddammit take me this godblasted morning saying Bubba to myself the sound before the sense of it Bubba Bubba Bubba everybody knew Bubba how old was he was he was he was the sound of it before the sense Big Bubba that's the way we talk we say it make the sound the sense of what we're talking about when I return home I walk up Susquehanna Street the people if people had been outside on their porches would have been close enough to touch their voices loud in my ear if I'd have stopped and squatted on one of these stoops we would rap about Bubba you know Big Bubba yeah oh yeah that was some sorry shit man you know how they did him some evil cold blood shit sure enough man you know I must be getting old because it don't bother me that much anymore I mean you know for a minute or two I want to wring a million motherfuckers' necks but then I let it go got to let it go got to chill out I seen too much be crazy if I don't chill out brothers cut down every day shit it don't mean a thing everybody got to go one day you know like a shooting gallery or some motherfucking evil ass lottery we all got a number just a matter of sooner or later today or tomorrow all the brother's got a chain round they necks and a number on the chain and somebody pulling numbers daily bang bang down you go it's just a matter of time bloods be extinct you know like them endangered species and shit don't laugh it's true we ought to fire up a campaign shit they got one for elephants and whales and ring-tailed sap-sucking woody woodpeckers why not posters and TV ads and buttons and T-shirts *S.O.N. Save Our Niggers* go on man you crazy man I pass by on the sidewalk listening but nobody on their stoops maybe everybody knew I was coming up Susquehanna Street with my sad self and ran inside shut their windows shut their doors hiding till I pass with my mournful lost-my-best-friend self I wish for voices hear empty porches hear my own feet on the pavement hear a car pass at the intersection of Braddock half a block away the oldest Homewood streets Albion Tioga Finance these streets where Bubba's known where they say his names *Junior*

June Juney Junebug JB J Bub Bub Bubby Bubba all the silent names hidden behind curtains and blinds the darkness of old walls and tight corners and lids and hoods and secrets you can't tell without giving their power up Bubba Big Bubba I thought when I returned home one time it would be different I didn't know exactly how but maybe better somehow things supposed to change I'm older and heavier and slower now can't disappear down an alley streak like a panther part of black night when I need to rendezvous with my kind who once ruled here talking trash knocking heads the fly arch rulers and kings of pussy and bullshit and smoke Bubba June-Boy Sonny Bo sitting high up on the wall of our pretty where nothing no one could touch us one time it will surely be different these empty porches and empty footsteps and lights of empty cars whizzing by on Braddock but the only difference now Bubba Big Bubba gone they say the junkies tired of him dealers tired of him cops tired of him stealing and muscling people carried a baseball bat and you know Bubba never could play no baseball what he look like carrying around a bat he wouldn't listen that hard head still hard as brick man couldn't nobody never tell Bubba nothing he'd bogart and stomp people take their shit and walk off like dudes don't be remembering like you can do shit to people today and just walk on away and like it's over like all you got to do is get yours today and turn your back and walk away like ain't nothing happened like tomorrow ain't another day yeah he was stone crazy Bubba leave me alone now I'm not for no play today Bubba say fuck you punk and your mama too and snatch people's shit like he's Superman or Br'er Bear with that tree slung over his shoulder that was Big Bubba man big as he was ain't never growed up your boy your old time boon coon and cruising cut-buddy main man yeah we go back don't we bro way back to the olden days you me Bubba the Golden Knights and badass Laredos those banging gangs we runned wit runned from we was bad in our day but it's a new day out here cats ain't seeking glory punching some bad dude's lights out no way see everybody carries these days mess wit my shit I blow you away in a minute see Bubba living in the past Bubba a throwback man like them old time big hat eldorado Iceberg Slim pimps beat they women with coathangers and shit it's all business today dude making it on the street today got to have computers and beepers no time for cowboys and indins and gorillaing people's dope that two-bit King Kong gangster jive ain't what's happening out here today it's business business build yourself an organization man power to the people good product good distribution good vibes spread a little change round keep the boy off your back everybody gets what they want plenty to go round if your shits tight it's these free-lance Rambo motherfuckers fucking things up just a matter of time before somebody waste Bubba don't care how big he is how many bad brothers he busted up with his bare hands his big bat Bubba go down just like anybody else you bust a cap in his chest no man the word on the set is nobody knows who did it but nobody in business don't care neither cause he was way out of line overdue for getting done man cause everybody knows the way it goes moving west mister moving on out bro up and out to star time don't fuck with the product product won't fuck wit you you got to remember today's today and yesterday shit yesterday's long gone we was kids back then you and me and Bubba playing kid games then time runs out it's spozed to run out things spozed to change and we sure ain't babies no more Big Bubba a dinosaur man wasn't even in the right century man living by the wrong clock man he was Bubba all right your man Bubba Bubba Bubba everybody knew Bubba.

■ signs

She thinks of fighting back. How there is no end to ways of fighting back. Consider the lowly termite. How one predator, the aardwolf depends on a particular termite species for 90 percent of its protein. Fox quick on thin, giddy coyote legs is what she thinks watching on a nature special this bizarre, lean-muzzled aardwolf claw open a termite mound and lap up with its long, curly tongue hundreds of scampering black bugs. The narrator explains how soldier termites rush to defend their mound, protect their bloated queen. They fire a gassy tasting liquid from their snouts. Waves of soldiers are consumed but their acid flavor drives the aardwolf to abandon his feast, move on to a fresh nest of victims. Could this be called fighting back. Offering up your flesh and blood until the beast chokes on your bitterness.

Someone sings her name. Kendra. Kendra. Come here, baby, gimme some sugar. Aunt Bell scoots forward in the armchair. Slippers on her tiny, stockinged feet, feet that don't reach the floor, feet not as long as Kendra's short hand but swollen so they balloon over the edges of the house shoes like Aunt Ethel's big behind splayed on a kitchen chair. Aunt Bell's fat little arms wiggle, reeling in Kendra. C'mere, baby. C'mon to your Aunt Bell. Bloated feelers stuttering in the air.

Her old heart must be thumping a mile a minute with the effort of stretching those dumpling arms out to me, hands churning, dewlaps of soft, sweet meat jiggle off the bone. Aunt Bell smiling ready to pull her grandniece down into the chair and drown her in perfume and butterball pillow bosom or reach up and lock her arms behind Kendra's neck as if she wants to be lifted. Aunt Baby Bell all four-by-four, two hundred some pounds of her hiked out of that chair old and mushy as she is and clasped to Kendra's breast in some miracle of reversal, legerdemain, levitation and get your pretty self on over here and give your Aunt Bell a hug, girl.

Leave her lone, Bell. Let the child through the door. Bell's sister Ethel is saying not you first, not you always first Bell as you always think you got to be Bell as you struck me down so many times in this life just to keep one step ahead one year ahead because that's all its ever been between us Bell that one year thirteen pitiful months between our births and you running ahead always and backhanding me if I get too close so I never forget it. Ethel talking over and through everybody gathered in the room at her sister Bell who is trapped in her overstuffed chair by high blood pressure and sugar and god knows what else ails her a ringing in her ear Bell claims never stops the ring Ethel swears is just one more trick to get attention to be the first thing everybody has to talk about everybody must bow down to and shuffle in line behind. Ethel's voice jumps over peoples' heads, is a hand shoving Bell back into the womb of the ancient, bow-bottomed chair while Ethel's eyes frame the prettiest picture for her grandniece to glow in. My girl. My darling girl. Kendra enters through the front door into this photograph never real except when Aunt Ethel smiles on her and stares and stares to chase everything that doesn't belong in the frame and then there's only Kendra, undeniable as a poster child mounted in some heart-stopping, heartrending pose, the only person who matters, victim, star in this bitter world with no mercy, no justice except what's been lost, except this fallen version of what once was the apple of god's eye, this world in which everything good's gone, until, except what Aunt Ethel makes of her grandniece Kendra and hangs for the world to view. And even if no one else sees the picture, Kendra sighs and enjoys it, quietly, shyly, the grace bestowed by that mean old wild-haired woman who almost never smiles except to greet her grown grandniece, to dress her girl in all the resplendent finery Eve could have been wearing if she'd graduated number one in her high school class and graduated college first one in her family and took a postgrad degree no one back home had ever even heard of and left that nasty snake alone.

So proud of you, honey. But can't you find no job closer to home, baby. I know . . . I know. You the best judge now of what's good for you. I just wish . . . you know. Atlanta. Seems so far away.

It's not really. A good day's drive is all.

Don't you never be in that big a hurry, darling. Drive all those miles in one day. Too far. Too fast. We can hold on an extra day.

Amen.

Take your time on those bloody highways. You know how much we want you home, precious, but take your time.

G'wan, Bell. She ain't no child no more. This a grown woman you're addressing. Been halfway round the world and back. More good sense in her pretty little toe than you got in your whole roly-poly self.

She always be my baby. C'mere gimme some sugar.

When she thinks of home, returning, leaving, her dead mother's house is full of people, loud talk, eating and drinking and it's like standing in the ocean, so much surrounds you, swells you, wind and sea and salt air, the rushing of waves you would be frightened if it weren't for something beneath it all, a pulse, a familiar rhythm, like those breaks in a hellfire sermon, the simple call and response breathing room when you are you and the preacher a man you've known most of your life and you can speak to him, him to you, *Uh huh, Amen, Preach, Tell it, tell it, Sister,* breaking the spell of the sermon turning you inside out roasted on the spit of your sins, anchoring you somewhere other than the threatening words swirling round you. She counts on the ancient quarrel between the sisters to break through and save her, remind her where she is, who she must be. Her Aunt Bell and Aunt Ethel wrestling, two-stepping, predictable, everlasting in the house of her dead mother.

PROFESSOR CRAWLEY. Over the weekend I read the part you said to read again. Still doesn't make sense to me. You said to come in if we still didn't understand.

He wavers out of focus. Robert Beausolay. His last word *under-stand* replaces him. Sound for sight. *Understand. Understand.* As in an echo chamber or stuck record that doesn't simply repeat, but mocks itself, booms, hisses, howls, these sounds blurring the face of Robert Beausolay who once sat in the split-cushioned chair beside the metal bookcase in her office while she sat behind her desk, hands folded atop it, legs crossed beneath, her face painted on a balloon tethered by a string to the desktop, a happy face, bobbing, nodding in the wind of the word *understand, understand.* She's afraid to reach for the string. Out the window in the green air of the campus bells are ringing. If she tries to steady the string, it might snap. Her smiling head would shoot up to the ceiling, spatter eggy white and dripping yolk. Her vision clears suddenly. The student materializes, fidgeting, a blond, blue-eyed angel in front of her in this seedy cubicle of office she's ashamed of, dust on the windowsills, dust under the desk, tarry streaks in the cracked flooring, flaking paint on the walls. Another word *seedy* threatens to drown everything. On the radio deejays scratch their records on purpose, music blurs, speeds faster than light, than recognition. Who is this white boy and why is he testing her.

ROBERT, THE INFORMALITY is like touching a hot stove. In an instant, even before pain seizes, she's learned her lesson. Snatches back her hand.

It's about pride. Pride that goeth before a fall, Mr. Beausolay. We've encountered it before, haven't we, at the beginning of the semester. What the Greeks called hubris. Overreaching. A violation of the golden mean. You recall our discussions, don't you. Well, Mr. Beausolay. Milton's examining another version of the same offense. Since he's a Christian poet, for him pride is a sin. A sin that drives men and angels to want more than they have. An insatiable lust for more, always more, that tempts Milton's glorious angel to forfeit his place in heaven.

Remember the Iran-Contra mess. You remember that, don't you. That's one kind of situation Milton was warning us about. Pride and greed, contempt for the rules. The evil done by Reagan and his crew because they considered themselves above the rules.

I'm sorry, Professor Crawley. What you're saying must be true, but when I read Milton it's just words. I'd never think about President Reagan if I read *Paradise Lost* a hundred times. I don't think about anything. It's just words, words, words. Piles of word I don't understand and never will.

Milton's not easy for anyone. And you're only responsible for the thirty or so pages in the anthology.

I mean, you know, if you can just tell me in a couple minutes what it's all about, why should I blow a night plowing through that stuff. You said its a classic and all but what good's it going to do me when I get out of here. If I ever do. You know. Who cares if Milton's on my transcript.

Milton Berle. Milton Bradley. Comics. Games. Milton Eisenhower. Ike's little bro. Little Milton. Blues harmonica playing fool. She feels like a straight man in a situation comedy. Her students reduce her to this role constantly. She knows what they're going to ask. They know what she's going to reply. They deadpan through the script. Nobody thinks anything's funny. Going through the motions, the parts they've learned so well they can perform them in their sleep.

You little blond, blue-eyed devil. Was it Malcolm who'd first called them that. Devils. Peeked the ground-zero menace in their blue eyes. This white boy bothering her, because his goddamn culture doesn't work. Like she's a plumber or the one who jerry-rigged the shaky thing together in the first place. Don't hassle me. I just work here. Doing my job. Following orders, you little Hun. Speak to my department head, the dean, the trustees, the governor. Mr. Reagan's CIA bagman occupying the White House now.

Rebel angels. I could hip you to some true rebel carrying on, child. Martin. Malcolm. Mandela. Saint Douglas. Saint Harriet. No, not Ozzie's wife, cracker. Ms. Tubman to you. If the syllabus of Western Civ ever tilted my way. Which it don't, boy. So ask your mama to apologize. Not me. She married the boss. Raised you. I was just someone to fetch his slippers. Iron his pants. A little action on the side.

Mr. Beausolay. Pretty Sunshine. Whatever you call yourself. I suggest going slowly. A bit at a time. Look up words you don't understand. Read passages aloud. To yourself or to someone else. Ask a friend to read to you. Relax. Enjoy the sound. Don't mean a thing if it ain't got that swing. *Paradise Lost* is a poem. The old, blind bastard's trying to sing to you. Listen, as the Isley Brothers say, to the music. You must learn to do that before you can expect to understand. Slowly. Slowly. A few licks at a time. Or chuck the goddamn book— Oedipus to Eliot—in the pond on the green. Feed it to the ducks, Mr. Goldenrod, for all I care.

Gooey stuff from her exploded head sticks to the ceiling. Viscous, elongated drops plop down onto the desk. Drip-drop. Drippity-drop.

Out the window bells and children playing the waddle of web-footed birds walking across water.

I know it's not easy, Bobby Baby. See these wounds in my palms. If I unbuttoned this desk from my waist and let it float down around my slim ankles and lifted my naked foot for you to inspect you'd find a ten-penny nail hole bored through my instep. Of all people I know how easy it's not.

For instance, Mr. B, there's this letter I wrote once to myself. I'll quote just a verse or two: Dear Mom, The professor returned my first paper. A big red *X* across page one. Giant red question mark on the last sheet of my 1000 word essay. I cried, Mama. For two days and nights I cried. Couldn't go back to that professor's class for a week. Those marks he put on my paper, Mama, it was as if he'd tattooed my body. Scarlet slashes on my chest. Rusty iron hook in my back. Felt like I was walking around naked and everybody could see. Everybody knew. This nigger gal don't belong here. She ain't worth the time of day. Doesn't write or speak our language. We gotta use signs to communicate with her. An *X* like her daddy signed on the dotted line when he sold her. I can't come home, Mama. Can't stay here. I'm so sorry. I'm scared, Mama.

LAST NIGHT HOME she'd bathed herself in the huge tub which was her favorite place in her dead mother's house. Warm water lapped and purled the tub's cool sides as she slowly opened and closed her steepled knees. Her will, her pleasure animated a universe in whose center she sat, toes splayed on a faucet, twisting it, brown toes interlaced with antique white knobs, subtly adjusting the water's temperature till what was inside and outside perfectly merge. Monkey toes.

Pale underneath, then her color darkens the sides and top of each digit, color starting there and spreading everywhere. Nails painted a hussy shade of scarlet. For those days when her feet are bare and she will clack across campus in Greek sandals with straps like serpents coiled around her ankles. Daring anyone to notice, not to notice. Clammy days. Days when anybody stuck outdoors for a few minutes between air-conditioned buildings is uncomfortable under their clothes, days she will claim, a tall, big-boned woman with dainty hands and feet, sailing past in bold African prints. On her final night home before the first semester in her new school she had settled deeper till water floated her breasts. Fantasized a lover entering her life, a face, hands, eyes hungry for her, a lover with the power to change the way she looked at herself. A lover with her in her dead mother's bathroom that was mostly tub. Enjoying a vision of herself through her lover's eyes. Her aloneness heightened, sharpened but also less alone, better somehow. When she'd touched herself, it was with anticipation not resignation. Two pairs of eyes working to resolve the dark mass of flesh within the water into woman-shape.

Instead of a lover at school, the signs had begun appearing. Like the marks on her paper, but different and worse. Signs telling her story as if she'd never had another.

When she'd seen the first sign, a piece of cardboard thumbtacked to a door, she'd thought it was a joke, poor, poor taste, but a joke nonetheless, the *Whites Only* sign stuck to the communal bathroom door of a grad dorm on an integrated campus in the post-emancipation, post-riots, post–civil rights, post–equal opportunity, post-modern last decade of the twentieth century. Unfunny, but some unreconstructed asshole's idea of humor. Or a campy, hip, slip-the-yoke turn-the-joke installation mounted by one of those odd black guys who talked kiss-my-ass street tough but sneaked off and wrote scared-rabbit essays. She'd considered that second possibility, perpetrator or perpetrators of her own race only later in her bed, the night of the day the sign had appeared, when the silly sign had robbed her of sleep. She hadn't ever suspected a woman, white or black. No. Clearly the handiwork of that extra, mean, male chromosome.

The morning it had greeted her she'd stared at it, unsure what she was looking at, trying to place it, to connect it, the way her aunts said the newly dead inspect the body they've left behind. She'd almost left it hanging. The damned thing had nothing to do with her. She was Kendra Crawley, wooed by this institution and others, gratefully, graciously embraced here when she'd finally informed the English Department she'd accept their grad fellowship. Deal included a double room for herself, with a lovely view of campus and now sure enough she'd awakened in that very room, as close to *hers* as she could transform it with her things—tapes, records, posters, her grubby stuffed bear—awakened, and as she did each morning, shuffled half-awake down the hall, needing to pee, needing to begin to order her day, arrange and parse the hours to fit in the impossibility of everything she needed to accomplish. A normal, usual trip first thing to do her business and what in the world is this. Who stuck a sign on the door. As she gets closer her panicked kidneys squeal like James Brown *please please* don't be out of order.

When she reads the two words, she's stunned, but they're also irrelevant to who she is, where she is, what she intends to do with her day, her life so she almost ignores the sign, nearly pushes through into the bathroom. Almost but not quite an irrelevancy so she doesn't ignore it and push through the whiny door. She snatches the sign down. A tack pops out and pings against the tiled floor. She hears it and knows someone's bare foot could snag on it, but doesn't give a damn. Cardboard in hand she slams through the swinging door, rips the sign into pieces. Crushes the pieces and dumps them in the bin under the sink. Why is she ashamed as they drop from her fingers. Why do her hands tremble. Whose mess, whose dirty secret is she hiding. In the speckled mirror over the sink, the mirror a colored cleaning woman polishes every afternoon, the pained expression—alert and absent, forgetting and remembering—that would have been there if she'd left the damned sign undisturbed where she'd found it, stared back at her.

You couldn't just breeze by it. No more than you could breeze by an old lover in the cafeteria in the morning having coffee with another woman. You were entangled. Like her toes in the faucet. Whatever you did, you were affecting the temperature of the water. Toes twisting or toes frozen, you were implicated.

If it was one of the black guys who'd stuck up the sign, why here, why now. None of them chose to live on campus. Too tame, too bourgie, too white for them. No. They roomed in town where they could cop to their heart's content, tame, bourgie, white pussy in private. Why didn't they stick cute little signs on their own doors. *Whites Only.* The men were all in Comp Lit, anyway. Three black men, a Barbadian woman writing about a Portuguese Renaissance poet, and herself, the only people of color in the graduate Lit program. And this school patting itself on the back because it's recruiting more blacks than its peers. How long. How long. But in her heart of hearts the black men weren't to blame. Not for the sign, not for the shitty system that turned them inside out and rarefied their cropped heads. One named for a defect. The other for a city. One whose name she never could recall or hadn't ever learned. Nubby and Dee Cee and Whatchamicallit, when she described them to her aunts at home. In Cambodia when they started offing people who wore eyeglasses, those boys wouldn't have lasted a hot minute. They avoided her strategically with a kind of stiff suspicious deference or smirking conspiratorial nods. As if she were a whole bunch of babes who sat around playing whist, scheming to trap brothers into marriage. Then there was the Mr. Pitiful look: You think you got it bad, sister. What about us.

IN A DREAM her mother visits wearing a floppy-brimmed hat, her arms full of roses, her face hidden by the hat except for her mouth, a lipsticked oval singing a note in a song, holding it perfectly, molded by its shape. A song of smoke rings, silent oval within oval issuing from her mouth, rings rising, decaying soundlessly. Then the roses turn to big behinds, a bouquet of jiggling backsides that spill from the cradle of her mother's arms and split and bleed sticky red juice and black roachy seeds.

THE SECOND SIGN was slipped under her door. Since she was the sole nonwhite in the dorm the first sign had been intended for her, but this one in its envelope with her name typed on the outside was more personal. Cheap white envelope, unsealed, a ruled sheet of yellow tablet paper folded within: *Nig bitch go home.* In a dumb spy novel she'd read, the gimmick was poisoned paper that kills on contact. Her hand shuddered, she scanned the paper for telltale spots, but she couldn't turn the yellow paper loose till she read it twice. Once more for good measure then note and envelope mashed into a ball. *Two,* she said. Fuck you, and two points in your face when she shot it swish into the trash can next to her desk.

What annoyed her most about the third sign, giant triple *K*'s scrawled with chalk on her door, was the difficulty of determining how long the letters had been on display. Could she have missed something so big and ugly when she'd left for the library that morning. Does she always slam doors behind herself without looking back. The sign couldn't have been on her door when she'd entered last night. No way. Even in the semidark, weary as she'd been, she'd have noticed. Which meant the door probably was defaced at night. Typical cowardly nightcrawling sneaky Klan style. Shadowy figures tiptoeing up the stairs, down the hall, convening outside her room. Many nights afterward she'll listen for them listening for her. Huddle of masked men crouched with ears bent to the door. Next time they'll use paint. She'll hear paint sloshing. Spattering the tiles, the slap drag of brush against wood. If the chalked letters had been screaming all day long, why hadn't someone rubbed them off. Is that what she wished had happened. Another secret, another insult hoarded by her neighbors. What did they think when they strolled by and saw KKK on a black woman's door. Who would they blame. Who was incriminated. Not one of them she wouldn't feel embarrassed asking. That also vexed her. Why hadn't one of them come forward. I saw that shit on your door. Some real Neanderthals on campus. Have you seen anybody suspicious lurking around here lately. Townspeople. Workmen. Outside agitators. A band of crackers on horseback in flowing white robes and hoods over their heads. If they burn a cross outside your door, the fire might spread. Roast us all in our sleep. Maybe we should demand a guard. Or arm ourselves, patrol the floor at night. Vigilantes. White Panthers. Lynch the rotten bastards ruining our sleep.

A wet towel erased the letters quite easily. No trace. Except some cleaner swipes on the door. Maybe the marks never existed. What matters now is the clean slate, starting fresh. She wrings out her baby blue hand towel, discards it where she'd dropped the ripped cardboard.

THREE WEEKS OF incidents, ten signs, a dozen, she'd lost count, wasn't certain whether some things that occurred were part of an assault focused on her or belonged with the general, everyday nonsense, the poison she'd been wading through all her life, what fell like rain, the gray drizzle you got used to, even expected if you were black. The mumbling, clumsy, dangerous beast carried off more than a few souls every day, but that was part of the rain, too, and survivors taught themselves to live with those losses, too, to be grateful they weren't the one grabbed and gone. Three weeks of signs, and without really knowing why, really knowing better, she phoned to ask for an appointment with her dean.

He is a pipe smoker who's kicked the habit. For health reasons. I still crave it, he confesses. Every day, many times a day I want to light up. In his office he surrounds himself with a pipe smoker's paraphernalia. Before she saw the pipe racks and elegant tools, the exotic tobacco tins shelved behind his desk, before he'd recited for her the sad tale of his unrequited romance with tobacco, when she'd first heard his voice on the phone extolling the virtues of his school, the region, the transcendent pleasures and worth of academic life, she would have bet he was a man who owned a velvet smoking jacket, ascots, red leather slippers, armchair and matching ottoman. How he yearned to have her enter the inner sanctum where he'd been hiding out while the world went haywire. She couldn't decide whether to hate him or laugh at him as he offered all the wrong enticements over the phone. He was blind past the point of hypocrisy. Too dangerous to be called anything less than a liar. Yet his lies were about such silly, worthless things. Nothing that mattered to most people anymore, puny, petty, transparent falsehoods that once had been essential links in a network of grand deceptions, a trick bag slick enough and big enough to entrap a good percentage of the world's peoples and resources. Now his lies served mainly to keep this fool and others like him on the sidelines, trussed up in a self-spun web of pretension and inconsequence.

The only surprise when she met him face-to-face was his age. The dean was barely forty. Beard, pipe, yellow teeth, clunky clothing, the stale smell that clung to him, were props of age. He'd long ago decided to be an old man, and snuggled down in his baggy tweeds and corduroys.

What he'd smothered in himself, he certainly didn't appreciate in her. The dean sat behind his forty acres of polished walnut (or was she behind the desk, the blue-eyed devil soliciting her) already crossed over to the promised land. That dead, ironic tic of a twinkle in his eye welcomed and dismissed her. Nobody's effort, his, hers, anybody's made a speck of difference. Point was not how you got over, but being safe on the far side where the ones in control sit.

It's sick. Really disgusting. I don't know what to say, Professor Crawley. Of course you have my deepest sympathy. I've never understood people who do those kinds of things. Yet they've always been with us. Whether we like it or not, we can't legislate change in people's hearts. A certain element—and believe me, I have no patience, make no apology for them—but that element is bent on tearing down what others of goodwill are attempting to build. You are situated better than most to understand and appreciate the university's commitment. I can't pretend to fathom how shocking this harassment must be to you, but I assure you, your friends won't waver in their determination to stand behind you.

I'll convey this conversation to the chief of campus security. We'll start an investigation immediately. And please. Let's keep this matter within the university family. The naysayers would love to get hold of this and carry it to the press. We owe it to ourselves, to the seriousness of our commitment, to proceed in a fashion benefiting all parties. For the meantime, if there are any new developments, let me know instantly. I'm here to help.

IN HER DREAM he is hydra-headed. She allows each head bobbing on the end of its stalk to say one word before she lops it off.

. . .

LESS THAN AN HOUR after she leaves his office—in the time it took to sign a tax-exemption voucher in the administrative building, scarf down an egg salad on pita and can of orange-pineapple juice in the building's minicafeteria, grab her mail on her way up to her office where she intended to review Keats' *Ode on a Grecian Urn* in the ten minutes remaining before class—she finds in a sheaf of flyers and mimeos snatched from her mailbox, another sign, magic-markered on the back of an old departmental stencil: *Nig whore—Your box stinks. Ha. Ha.*

Because it arrived so quickly on the heels of her visit to the dean's office, she knew this sign was meant to remind her who was actually in charge. Her mailbox had been empty earlier in the day. No. Not mailbox. Her *Nig whore's* box. The rippling letters looked as if they might still be damp. Perhaps she's being followed. Perhaps in the busy lobby, she'd bumped the one who'd stuffed this present in her mailbox. But even if she'd been shadowed to the dean's door, how would anyone know what had been discussed beyond it. Unless they listened from the hall. Unless the dean himself was in league with the pigs.

Her box. A stranger's dirty hand poking around in her mailbox. The outrageous, obscene pun dogged her. She couldn't help staring down at herself, *box,* ready to brush away an imaginary hand. Laughing at herself. At what was funny. Ha. Ha. What wasn't, ha, ha. Take my hand, precious lord. My doomsday lover, my king. My breathy-voiced Lucifer: *Hello you nappy-head liver-lipped cunt bitch. Just in case you can't read I'm telling you in plain English. Get the fuck away from here before something real bad happens to you. Go home, bitch, or the next time you hear my voice will be in hell.*

She sought patterns. As if generating a theory might distance what was happening, defang it, achieve order out of chaos. She was trained to decipher texts of all kinds. Good at theory. She'd been praised, encouraged. Did regular intervals occur between signs. How did the context of their presentation vary. The medium vary. Was the space between delivery and reception significant. Were events in her private (private?) life linked somehow to the timing and content of the messages or were the links random. If she could answer any or all of her queries, would the answers change anything. Would a theory supplant her persistent, perverse fantasy that a lover, a powerful, savage, mad lover was exploding into her life, taking it over.

Under the microscope of her inquiry, everything about her mattered. She became more attentive to herself. Pampered herself. Magnified the importance of her actions, reactions. The same sort of exaggerated importance her fellow sufferers in the grad program squandered upon the subjects of their dissertations. An obscure poet touted as the key to unlocking the whole sweep of Western literature. Would she wind up like them, foggy, distracted, head in the sand, bare behind exposed to the air?

A ROSE is a rose is a rose is an asshole.

Today is Friday dear diary dear invisible friend who listens but does not tell. No classes to teach or take till Monday. For once I'm almost caught up. As caught up as I ever can be on a treadmill that never stops just burps everynowandthen, shifts gears and loses a beat and for a millisecond I'm free free at last free long enough to grab a deep breath and try to remember what people do when they escape for a minute from what must be done. I can afford an afternoon, stretch it maybe to an afternoon and early evening (though I'll pay dearly) doing my own thing. A long walk. Listen to music. Rap with you, dear diary. Browse a bookstore or record shop, stock up on good stuff I might get to when I'm finally rich, famous and retired. Maybe I'll just go outdoors. Enjoy the beauty of this place now that spring has settled— its smells, the gush of flowering things. People changing color, showing off flesh, bodies stretched everywhere there is a patch of green peace. Shade trees a black rhythm dappling the lawns. Frat houses, every door and window flung wide open, exorcising winter ghosts, blasting the sidewalks with music that sounds like the hour before feeding time at the zoo. I sort through what I might wear on my stroll. What his reaction might be to various outfits I could style together. Is there a chance I'd actually run into him. Him. The one who's taken over. Whom I shed my clothes for. Dress for. Will he call his buddies to the window when I stroll past. Jeer me. Invite me in for tea. Signify about what's up under my clothes. Any woman passing gets what she deserves. In the men's eyes. Fraternity row two blocks long and I've seen women weeping by the end of the gauntlet. Other chicks give the righteous finger, ogle back and trade insults, a high old time enjoyed by all. Frat rats close to naked, sprawl on steps, roofs, dangle from windows, throw footballs, Frisbees, baseballs, kick around Foosballs on stomped-down front yards while the ladies parade past. I remember this same spring thing on the black campus near home. Why had it seemed less evil there. In my heart of hearts I know he's waiting for me in one of those huge, crooked mansions on frat row. Daring me. Teasing me. That's where I will find him, confront him. Leave me alone. Leave me alone, you goddamn bastard. That's where he's waiting, certain I won't come.

And he's correct. I nod and he nods back, his head inside mine, mine inside his. This is how we achieve intimacy. Mind fuck each other to exhaustion.

Perhaps, Mom, I should go to the duck pond behind the lab building. In my white pants too tight in the butt for Aunt Ethel's taste. When I wish to be attractive, am I really wishing to be you, playing with the possibility of becoming you if I pick the proper foxy outfit for each occasion. For strolling on this lovely spring afternoon somewhere I won't feel or look like a fool. No, Mama. Not your blackness. I'm not ashamed of color, of your gift of glorious color running in my blood, the precious little of you I mirror (Aunt Ethel says your nose and lips, says mine are identical, and your flawless skin though I've been careless enough to go far in ruining that, too). What I don't want anyone to witness is how my blackness is treated. Yes, I'm ashamed of how I'm treated. I can't stay here. Can't leave. Same dumb helpless mess since the day I arrived. I've allowed myself to be treated in a fashion I'm ashamed of. A subtle corruption, Mama. They do certain things to me, then I do them to myself. I make exceptions. I tolerate. I endure. I'll probably wind up at the duck pond because on a fine weekend like this one only a few others will. A poet maybe, or a pair of lovers, people with no real destination who will hang out a minute or two, daydreaming away from the crowd. If I'm spotted at the pond, what will I be a symbol of. Think of it, Mama. You who have been dead all these years I've been alive. Does anything change. I will be seen willy-nilly no thanks to what I am or am not. I'll be a slate and they can write any name they want, outcast, misfit, stuck-up bitch, racist shunning white people, lost soul. The blues. There goes a black lady with the blues, Mummy. See her. Can I feed her some of the bread we brought for the ducks. Do they eat bread, Mummy.

I'll probably walk to the pond, anyway. Wearing these whorish white toreadors only a mother would love. Do you. Do you.

Those are willows. Those are reeds. Ducks and geese today floating on the pond. More than one variety of duck. Or is it gender difference. Bright ones and dull ones. Males with iridescent neck feathers, bandit eye patches. I know the answers, I'm simply making conversation. They've done that to me, too.

A date. *Date,* Mother? Dates are those sickly sweet sticky gooey gritty middle-eastern snacks. Or blank squares on a calendar. Or when a paper or a baby is due. Due date. With whom. Why.

Yes. I admit I dread the coming of weekends. I may even go out of my way to fill every second of my time so I won't have to consider what a weekend could be in another place, another life. I write with invisible ink in my dear invisible diary for the same reason. I don't want evidence to pile up against me. I'd be tempted to go back and read, double, triple the heartbreak. Who needs it. Instead, I talk, diary listens. I empty myself. Diary remembers everything. Never speaks till I speak first. We do our Bell and Ethel routine. Rubber and glue. Oil and water. Indispensable to each other.

I don't want anyone to see how my blackness is treated. My role in the conspiracy shames me. Stuffing myself in ridiculous white pants, smuggling myself to the duck pond. As if my desires, my needs are best served by doing exactly the opposite of what any sensible human being would do. I want to touch and be touched, smile at somebody, hear them say nice things about me, cute little passing things about lights flashing in my eyes, *Uh huh, you got it girl,* a nod of agreement when I find just the right words to express an idea. Instead of giving myself a chance, I obey the signs. Or worse. Half obey the signs. I don't leave, but I go away. I don't run, but I hide. I contradict myself. My solitude amens the sermon the signs preach.

Mother: You died before I could fight you, forget you, become you. I am beautiful only when I am you, but I can't remember your face.

I miss church, Mama. Church sitting where it always has, the corner of Chestnut and Prescott, Ebenezer Baptist where they buried you, Mother, where your father and mother were married, where I felt tiny as a seed, squeezed between the mountain of Aunt Bell, the mountain of Aunt Ethel, every Sunday of my childhood. Led through the door of Ebenezer, safe, my hand clasped in one of their's, Aunt Bell or Aunt Ethel, they took turns, fought some Sundays outside the church door, over whose turn it was to lead me by the hand safely in. Safe, huddled between them when the service moaned of toil and snare, when the sick, dying and dead perfumed the air with the heaviness of their dark robes, rotting flowers, safe when I heard you, Mother, calling in the hymns, Mother, summoning me to a shadowed place, a valley, a house with many rooms of furniture all draped in sheets and dust and spiderwebs and no one lived there anymore, broken windows, spooky doors that creaked in the wind, a house I must dwell in if I answer your sweet voice calling. Safe from saying yes or no when I could not stay and couldn't go, safe to shuffle down the carpeted aisle and drop pennies in the gold plate, drop down on my knees with Aunt Ethel and Aunt Bell, their wheezing, their old bones cracking like Fourth of July, to taste the blood and body, safe between them to gaze down into a casket and say good-bye. Not god's church. Ebenezer belonged to Aunt Ethel and Aunt Bell. They carried its building blocks in their bulky bosoms and behinds. Each brick lifted by their voices rising from the songbooks. Aunt Ethel's finger stutters along the hymnal, tapping the words, teaching me to read as she taught me to sing, verse after verse of an old anthem, the endless choruses where I'm always safe. If it was god's church, he owned it only because they loved him and loved his son, Jesus, and forgave him for killing you, their sister's child, my mother, and loved me too, bringing me by the hand each Sunday morning, squeezed between them, their soprano voices a starry roof over my head.

A WEEK AFTER the dean's office she returns from the library at 10 P.M. to find her stuffed bear pushed back against her pillow, its stubby legs in the air and between them a pencil jammed in the smooth emptiness where genitals could be. The bear's throat is slashed, its mouse-eared head dangles crazily to one side held by a flap of skin. Beside the bear a note, red ink this time: *You next bitch.*

She collapses onto the foot of the bed. Wraps herself in her own arms and cries quietly till the shaking stops, till she's ready to turn and pat the bear's ear, a spot rubbed bare from years of petting, grooming, rocking the bear that's older than she is. She used to hold him while she sucked her thumb, rubbing his ear against her nose, lost in his secret smells, layers of spit and sweat, her stink ground into the grubby pelt. Her aunts had threatened to throw out Teddy the Bear if she didn't stop that nasty habit, but she knew they were only trying to scare her. Her mother had left her the bear and that meant no one on earth had the right to take it. The bear was from a time before memory. Those days when her mother was alive to speak, give her things, when she was her mama's baby and no one in the world besides the two of them. Who could tell her different, who would know better than she did the origin of this stuffed creature she hugged and sniffed, this bear with her mother's sweet funk in his nappy fur, a lost world, a found world, herself curled and safe in the soft dream of this animal who must be beside her every night before she can fall to sleep.

SHE ATTENDS a lecture. The speaker is an exiled South African, a member of the ANC on tour to raise financial and moral support for the freedom struggle. Vincent Mahlangu has been detained, jailed, tortured, banned. She thinks of chains, sirens, gunfire, bruises, blood, yet this small brown man, soft-spoken, impeccable in his gray double-breasted suit is CEO clean, cordial and convincing. He's based in an office in D.C. She imagines Frederick Douglass at a United Airlines counter. Sharp suit, expensive briefcase, chatting with other execs as he waits in line for yet another jet to fly him to yet another rally, meeting, rendezvous, crisscrossing the country, the horrors of the slave trade a slide show stored in his brain. Houselights go out and beams from his eyes burn pictures onto a blank wall. Observe my brothers and sisters being beaten, shot, hanged. Soweto, Crossroads, South Bronx, Philadelphia, Brixton, Dallas. Mr. Mahlungu answers a question about necklacing, the terrible wrath of the people visited upon collaborators, informers. You must understand the crucial role informers play. Our country is a vast prison. The security forces are everywhere. The existence of even one informer breeds a worm of doubt, means you can't ever be sure whom to trust. When the people cannot speak freely to one another without fear, when they mistrust one another, they aid the oppressor in his dirty work. Informers give the police eyes everywhere. Even in our own minds. These traitorous eyes must be torn out.

Does she inform on herself. Does a traitor lurk in her heart passing on her secrets to the authorities. The fear of one shuts down trust. If she cannot trust herself, is she fatally divided. Which voice the traitor—the one keeping her here at school or the one calling her home. What's being betrayed—her wish to be a person the signs can't turn around, or is the person holding on, fighting for a place in this wilderness betraying the one who knows good and well being here is wrong. She understands precisely what the speaker from South Africa is saying. Uncontrollable rage exploding when you discover the enemy outside is also inside. The urge to root out, to maim, smash, purify, exorcise, burn. Logic of a gasoline-soaked tire, a lynch rope, a fiery cross.

SOMEBODY SAYS, Bet the campus cops storm in here any minute. Yeah. All us coloreds in one place at one time. Must be up to no good, right. Fomenting a riot. Unlawful assembly. Cafeteria takeover. Shame it takes something negative like this to get us all sitting down at a table together. One bomb take everybody out. Ha. Ha. C'mon youall, stop the fooling. Let's get down to business. I called this meeting. Hey, wait a minute. This is Sister Crawley's jam. She should speak first. All youall already spoke first. That's the problem. Always has been. Black race got all chiefs no indins. Look who's talking. Big Chief Crazy Horse Geronimo Osceola hisself. Cool it, man. Let's be real. This sister out here fighting a righteous fight and we got to get behind her. Why don't you let Sister Crawley say where she wants us to get. Uh huh. She's the one got these honkies by the tail. We know that, brother. We're all here cause Sister Crawley got this mess started.

Nobody's trying to steal her thunder but I'm the one called a meeting so we could hash out some things, organize around the issue, connect what's going down to other issues so we don't lose an opportunity to work some fundamental mojo on this institution. Ain't but one issue. Get the crackers off the sister's back. Hey, macho man. We know you lettered in J.V. football in that jive prep school in Vermont. We know you can whip tons of crackers wit your bare hands. But hold on, dude. Let's act not react. Let's go in wit a total program, you dig. Excuse me, Mr. Trotsky, Gramsci, Karl Marx steely-eyed intellectual. What we got here is an incident. A racial incident, blood. You remember those. Ole time nigger baiting and lots of folks are mighty upset about it. Bush and them honkies trying to turn back the clock. This the kind of thing the brothers on the corner will hip-hop right up here on campus behind. Buses from the City. TV and press conferences. Stir up shit while folks still hot. This sister opened the door. We can sit around bullshucking or march on through. March. Did I hear you say march. Where you been. What decade you in, home. What century. Dubois said fifty years ago that the struggle was past the marching stage and old W.E.B. a day late then. *March.* Who march. Where. For what, bruh. I still ain't heard a word from the sister. From neither sister. How somebody spozed to get a word in edgewise you cats arguing since we sat down here. People staring at us like we crazy. I don't give a dime fuck about them people, man. Them people is the problem. You the problem. Paying attention to what they be thinking about you. You should know by now what they always be thinking when they look at you. Ain't nothing new, they want you gone. Damn. This shit's getting on my nerves now. I thought it might be useful for us to meet and rap. No agenda. No party line. No ego. Just reason together. By the way, sister, I admire what you're doing. I mean you've exposed them. What you said in the newspaper was brilliant.

The article didn't reflect my conversation with the reporter very accurately. In fact I was quite disappointed. What I wanted to say, what I thought I did say was just about totally lost in what the newspaper printed.

Those bastards. That's how they do us. One time at Cornell, remember the cafeteria strike, the guns. I was an undergrad then, into a real confrontational in-your-face thing then, so me and my home-boys, shit wasn't about five or six of us, we armed ourselves and started raising hell, turned out the whole johnson.

DEAR DIARY. In the end it doesn't matter. Let them believe I did it to myself. Everybody's off the hook. A plausible explanation. With deniability built in so no one finally is held responsible. Unverifiable as a dream. The silliness of it all came crashing down on me when I received the phone call about my aunts. Both dead when the van carrying them to the senior citizens' center rammed by a trailer truck. The final sign. The one I heeded.

The day before I left for the funeral I called the dean's office and confessed.

Yes, that's correct. I made it all up. I'm responsible for the signs. No one else but me involved. No. I don't know why I did it. I just did it. Perhaps pressure, strain. I can't really say. Can't think anymore about it now. I'm exhausted. As far as I'm concerned the matter is closed. No more signs will appear, I assure you. If not healed, I'm cured. Say what you need to say to the press. I'm not available for comment. I'm leaving tomorrow on personal business and I won't speak of the matter in public ever again. This is the last you'll hear of it from me. I regret causing anyone any trouble. I may or may not return in the fall. If I do, I can guarantee there will be no problem.

She could have been the one. As she thinks back she acknowledges access to most of the guilty materials—yellow tablet, red ink, cardboard, Magic Marker, chalk, plain white envelope, pencils. The ugly words were all words she knew, words she'd employed at one time or another. But how could she have spoken to herself on the phone. Of course the call could have been dreamed or imagined. She has learned she possesses an enormous capacity for self-deception. Wouldn't have required much, after all, in the heat of that tortured affair to conjure a voice, husky, menacing, crawling out of the receiver into her ear. Crawling. Creepy. Creepy Crawley. The more she thinks about the call the less real it becomes. A hallucinatory quality about it. Possessed by a voice, raped by it. She remembers heavy breathing, obscenities, then a sequence of rasping static, the frantic scramble of a million insect feet maneuvering, commandeering their queen's naked body deeper into the tunnels where they feed and breed.

what he saw

I have a photo of a man whose name I don't know. A black South African man, gut-shot, supported on either side by women, large, turbaned black women whose dark faces bear the man's pain, the shock of his sudden, senseless injury as clearly as they carry the weight of his body slumped against them. A black and white picture. The light is flat and merciless. Distorted by the angle at which the camera was held to snap this image, the man's face dominates. A lean face, though the elongated forehead bulges, again an effect of camera position. The brow of a Benin bronze mask, one might say of it, swollen as a sail full of wind. A comparison like that might be appropriate if the man weren't dying, if his dazed expression and vacant eyes, the women's sorrow and fear, weren't real, a few feet away from the van in which we are sitting.

In this settlement called Crossroads some streets are wide for the same reason they say the boulevards of Paris are broad and straight. Within the grid of highway-sized main drags, an aimless, endless sprawl of dwellings. Acres of shanties, shacks, lean-tos, tents, shelters so mean and bizarre they take me back to the vacant lots of Pittsburgh, the clubhouses my gang of ten-year-olds jerry-rigged from whatever materials we could scavenge and steal. Only these habitations stretching as far as I could see in every direction were not the playhouses of kids acting out fantasies of escape and independence. In this jumble whole families slept in makeshift shelters, woke up every morning, concocted meals, moved their bowels, made love, watched one another, separated only by inches, day after day performing the primal tasks that enable a unit of human beings to survive.

Wide streets with little or no traffic. But we were lost. Our driver had pulled off on a shoulder, out of the way of the nonexistent vehicles this street or highway or whatever was built to accommodate. Our van and another following us had been separated from the press caravan inspecting Crossroads. We decided to stay put while the second van backtracked. We didn't know whether the way out of the settlement was ahead or behind us, right or left at the next yawning intersection.

The scale of this so-called squatter's camp had struck me first. Then the permanence of the roads that cordoned and defined it. Tarmac the last solid surface beneath your feet if you stepped from these runways onto the areas where people lived. Clatter and crunch of gravel then the pitch and slippage of loose, rutted earth under the van's tires after the lead car had diverted the caravan onto a side road. At first this byway had seemed as deserted as the main arteries. Then children began appearing. You saw them in groups of two or three in front of you or along the sides of the path. A scattering of curious kids checking out this invasion of their turf. Then I happen to glance out the back windows and see we'd gathered a crowd, hundreds of young people had materialized in our wake, the brothers and sisters of the bold ones whose stares had met us first. Empty. Full. A country immense enough to try and hide its secrets. Millions of black people who don't seem to be around until the whites summon them by ones or twos or a handful when there's a job to be done. Until—and this is a phenomenon mirroring the unpredictability of the land itself where you never know what's coming next, veldt or mountainscape, forest or desert—you turn a bend and you're surrounded by all the missing people, the black sea always more and less than the next step away.

Vehicles ahead of us had stopped in an open area and we pulled up next to them and parked. Barely a quarter mile from the turnoff, but no doubt we were in a different world. Row after row of dwellings with footpaths in between meandered in every direction. No discernible plan, no logic except the contours of the land, an eroded gully or outcropping of naked rock, the fact that a spot was already occupied, had dictated where the next dwelling would be erected. A crazy quilt patchwork of sculpted carpet spreading over the ground, covering, burying the earth. A dense fabric changing texture square by square. Or segment by segment since there were no straight lines, no right angles anywhere. Houses supporting one another, fragile embellishments of porch, roof, fenced yards all leaning against an adjacent structure and that structure leaning on its neighbor and the neighbor sharing an arrangement of stakes and ropes that shore up a common wall, the common wall at one end abutting a sheet of corrugated tin siding, vaguely perpendicular, that holds the wall's weight while wall sustains tin's verticality. A good wind and whole blocks would topple like dominos. I'd watched footage of a bulldozer scraping away a squatter camp. Plowing straight ahead, little or no resistance offered by the dozens of shelters it levels in a single charge. An hour or so and all that remains a pall of dust and mounds of rubble neatly heaped at measured intervals. Full. Empty. Before the smashing starts black people slip away, disappear into the immensity of the land, travel secret routes as ancient and deeply understood in the blood as the instinctual knowledge of migrating birds. Moving where they must, how they must, to satisfy imperatives of survival, renewal. Keeping on keeping on we called it at home. If you start with nothing you have nothing to lose and you keep losing it but you keep starting again and carry that nothing, burden and gift, with you on the journey that is all the life you have. In Georgia, Mississippi, South Carolina uprooted even after we're dead. Blades dig up our ancestor's bones, crush them, scatter our cemeteries to clear the way for shopping malls, parking lots.

I hang back. There is smoke in my eyes. Coal burned here for cooking and heat. A thousand points of light. Fires kept alive in perforated oil drums. Smouldering fires, fire that leaps and dances and throws off sparks. Small children ring the women who tend the fire drums, women with babies slung on their backs, bellies, hips, shoulders, like the cameras and battery packs girding the European women in our party. Laughter, the babble of many excited languages in these dusty streets when the vans spill their cargo. Ground the color of thorns. Rocks everywhere. A munitions dump of rocks. Dogs, chickens, children underfoot. Houses on either side of the footpath are protected by exotic fences. Any material will do for fencing—boards, chicken wire, concrete blocks, string, brick, aluminum siding, pipe, plywood panels, bottles, broken bits of furniture, whatever can be combined, aligned, stuck in the ground to suggest the ancient idea of the African compound, preserve the sacred space of family, the fences a link with the ways of the ancestors in this shriven place that devours everything. Memory in these fences and skimpy yards, a conscious or unconscious continuity with the past and also the practical, immediate necessity of protection. Gangs prey on the weak, the isolated, the stray. Thieves on everyone. Precious little new wealth comes into the community so what exists must be cycled and recycled ingeniously, brutally, till it's exhausted, tossed on the trash heap. True of things, of people.

An old woman sweeping the stones in front of the canvas flap door of her dwelling tells me how sorry she is for the newcomers in the low-lying areas whose tents are inundated by red rivers of mud when it rains. How blessed she feels, how happy to share her dry space with a family from over there when they must flee to higher ground. A comrade pulls me aside, complains in a whisper about dope dealers operating in broad daylight, cops white and black on the take, kids addicted, violence intensified as the trade spreads.

I imagine night falling, a foul night wind. Shit, piss, rancid garbage, acrid smoke. Loud talk, the inevitable squabbles and pitched fights. Night noises magnified by a tin roof buckling in a gust of wind. Walls flutter, doors, when there is a door, flap, wind shuttles through chinks and cracks, whining, whistling. The crackle of fire, a dream of awakening in the middle of a furnace. Dogs howl, babies shriek, chickens cackle. A mad rooster announces dawn every hour. Blazing midday light now but I can't help envisioning darkness at its center.

We stroll and gawk and snap. Some visitors pat the shaved heads of the children. Peer into the dark interiors of their homes. One is open for inspection. A government official supervises the photo opportunity. Only room inside for four camera people at a time. The official clocks each group. Smiles as he counts down the last ten seconds, 3 . . . 2 . . . 1. That's all folks. Hurries in the next crew.

Towards the far end of the footpath an invisible barrier none of the journalists crosses. I watch a number of them approach it and retreat. Beyond the barrier the path's deserted. No one's tempted to retrieve the story that might be lurking there. We understand we must not spread ourselves too thin. A fragile strength in numbers. Perhaps we're already infected by the laager mentality. Circle the wagons. Move in a swarm. The heat and noise of each of us exciting, emboldening the others. But beyond that knot in which we are casual and self-assured, another world begins. A larger, threatening presence palpable as the sullen coal smoke that poisons the air. The presence is barely a whisper when the faces are like your face, the voices your voice, the words in your language, the clothes purchased from stores where you bought yours, a whisper then, a murmur defeated by the buzzing certainty of your kind. But the whisper explodes to a shout, a deafening roar—*Go back, go back; you do not belong here*—the instant you stray one inch beyond the safety zone. An invisible line cuts you off. On one side a whisper. On the other side a wind hurling you back. I pretend the color of my skin grants me license to pass beyond the point my colleagues stop.

To my left and slightly behind, a horse-drawn wagon trundles into view, stops on a vacant rise in front of crowded ranks of tents. Gunnysacks of coal stacked on the wagon. Coal dust has blackened its slatted sides. The horse's ribs sooty and distinct as the slats. The bare-chested, coveralled driver sootier. Kids try to climb up where the driver sits. He shoos them. They squeal at him. He hoots back, shakes his fist, but everybody's smiling. Where there should be a slit of gleaming white in the man's grimy face are dark gums, a cavernous emptiness. His body is taut and lean, wide shoulders bulk under his over-all's loose straps. Not more than twenty, a young man with an old man's mouth, he grins, toothless pied piper to the drove of kids who have been prancing behind his wagon, surrounding him and his horse now that the wagon's halted. More kids flying from everywhere, drawn by the shouting, the coal vendor's chant, the playful threats. Doesn't take much to make the young ones happy. Split high in the crotch, they gallop, dance. Quarter-miler's strides. Streamlined to black splinters of elegant bone. Cropped, round heads like fists on stalks. Stick drawings animated. The gait of antelopes. Nervous as sparrows.

I stroll two hundred yards or so further, beyond the invisible barrier, towards a distant glint on the horizon that turns out to be railroad tracks. A kind of shallow valley lushly green dips between the rail embankment and parched plain on which Crossroads has formed. What pulled me down the path, beyond the corridor of houses, many no wider across than the span of my arms, no deeper than three medium strides, down through the phantasmagoric architecture of yards, fences, second stories, porches, towards the emptiness on the far side of the invisible wall was the great, booming, explosion of a tree, or island of trees, whose arching crowns towered at least a hundred feet over the broken horizon line of roofs. Trees the oldest living things around. Green, enduring. How had they survived whatever was imposing itself on the land, whatever was draining life out of the soil, the people. A green shock in the sky, a place I could fix my eyes upon, my thoughts, and vault over the question of what the hell were we doing here, tourists and squatters, visitors and prisoners.

A softness, a lushness at the base of these giant trees, a reminder of what Africa may have been once. Thick grass, grazing animals. From the minivalley's floor, a man climbs towards a ridge where another ragged screen of shanties begins.

I was cheating, romanticizing this green remnant while Crossroads howled at my back for attention. The man climbed slowly, absorbed in what he was doing. A long stick in his hand he planted like a Swiss mountaineer, boosting himself up the slope. A few hairy, miniature, water buffalo–looking creatures with fluted horns nuzzled each other on the valley bottom, ghostly where the grass was thickest. I picked out three spotted goats, a horse, wondered if they belonged to the climber, wondered if anybody remembered this African postcard here, right next door to the desolation my colleagues were documenting.

Crossroads today. Yesterday Soweto. The grand tour. Rolling into Soweto in a column of combies trailing a gold, bulletproof Mercedes. Have you ever seen a car window two inches thick. Armor plating sinks the Mercedes low on its springs. It drags over the smallest bumps, groans like a wounded animal. What is our business. What in the world are we doing here. Later that night after the Soweto rally, the rowdy dinner, a sobering interview with one of the detainees freed after twenty-two years in prison, we tried to figure it out. At the top of the Carlton, Jo'burg's international hotel where white and black have been permitted to fraternize long before the current relaxation of apartheid, we had tried to begin at the beginning. Discussed our introduction to Soweto. A kid shitting, staring into the road that runs past the garbage-strewn berm which he'd chosen as a private place. Which suddenly wasn't as our convoy steamed past.

The question we bounced back and forth over our last drinks that evening in the very English, very Victorian, clubby, clubby Clubroom Bar of the Carlton was this: Why did some people shoot the boy and some not. Hey, I got him good. I saw the shot, too, dude. Everybody saw it, but I didn't take it. I could have, but I didn't. You make me feel good about you, man. I mean, you know, you had the sensitivity in a split second to decide not to shoot. I like that in you. I didn't really think about it. Saw him. Knew the picture was there. He was mine if I wanted him, but I didn't pull the trigger. Could you say why, now. Was it privacy. You didn't want to violate his privacy. Something like that. Privacy, dignity. But not exactly. Just knew I didn't want the picture. Something was wrong. I disagree. To me the kid said it all. Soweto. Goddamn Soweto. Little kid having to creep outside, over the hill through all that filth to do his business. These people don't have anything. Nothing, man. We got to tell their story. The dirty drawers got to me. Coal black. Least he had drawers. Lots don't. You dudes should have just left the little guy alone. How'd you feel trying to take a crap and half the press corps of Southern Africa clicking away at you.

Let me propose something, gents. The speaker was a good kid, a relative of one of the trip's organizers and full of vodka so we let him go on. We have a print journalist, photographers, a video person, a fiction writer. I'd like to hear how each of you folks come at this from the perspective of your art.

We half-ass attempted to sort it out, but without much energy or luck. It was late. We wandered off into abstractions then silliness, teasing, flirting with the one woman present, something about different folks and different strokes degenerating into swimming against the tide, breast strokes. We were growing tired of one another's company. Needed the people at home we were missing. It had been a long day. With an early rise next morning. And each of us a little tired of himself, herself. We couldn't make sense of the boy. Emblem. Symbol. Mirror. Ourselves. What the hell were we doing.

Full. Empty. The African trick of disappearing a means perhaps of reclaiming the land. Of being present when not seen. Of being everywhere that is just out of view. Around a bend, folded into the cleft of a valley, concealed in high wavering grass, in a dark alleyway between tall buildings, lurking in the dreamscape that materializes once the eyes close for sleep. Everywhere. And just in case you forget, or don't believe they're out there anymore, the unexpected popping up of one leads your eyes to another, another, and then the whole noisy trekking multitude swarming. Like that marching fence of young people toi-toi-ing, singing the throat-deep tribal war songs, bodies stretched across the horizon, darkening it, animating it as they danced closer towards you, engulfing the narrow dirt path in Soweto where you and your colleagues were stopped short by this tidal wave of chanting, fist-thrusting, hip-hopping Africans that seemed for a righteous moment coming not to greet you, welcome you, but to sweep this bad joke of a place for human habitation away. And you with it.

We are lost. Lost in that moment when the wave blocked the path, cresting, gathering force for the fatal blowout. Lost now at the edge of this landing strip roadway, our last companion van gone. Guts of this settlement as foreign, after all, to our colored drivers as to us. We'd heard gunfire just moments before. Single shots followed by the popping of automatic weapons. Not a soul visible in the melee of houses recessed fifty yards or so from the road's edges. Does everyone except us know the bulldozers are coming. Or the helicopter gunships and paratroopers dropping from the sky. Or the rockets and bombs.

The shots had come from behind us, the direction the other van was backtracking for a way out. Finney was up on his knees, his video camera trained through the rear window, his face pressed into the eyepiece. As far as I could see down the road, nothing was moving. Only heat devils shimmering at the vanishing point of the flat, flat expanse. Unless those colors bleeding into the bluish shimmer were people darting across the road, fleeing gunfire.

What can you see, Finney.

Not much, man. Not much. But those were AK-47 sounds a minute ago. Beirut. Heard enough of them pop pop pop motherfuckers last me a lifetime.

Uh huh. No mistaking that sound.

All you guys are vets and war heroes, I know. But I'm scared. I ain't never heard nothing but my very own little Lone Ranger cap pistol.

Pam. You OK, Pam.

I'm OK. I just don't think we ought to be here.

Calvin the driver is sidesaddle in his seat. Speaking back at us. Pam's right. This is just the kind of business we hoped to avoid. We should have stuck with the caravan.

Loverboy here said turn left. A shortcut. Some fucking shortcut.

Well, now we have to wait for Erroll's van. We agreed we'd stick together. They'll return here looking for us.

We don't know where they are or what happened to them.

They've only been gone five minutes.

Don't even want to think about those shots, man. That's the way Erroll and them went. Where those shots came from.

They may have run into some bad shit and split.

Erroll wouldn't abandon us.

Well, he may not have had a choice. Who knows who was shooting at what.

If anything's happened to the other van, that's even more reason to stay put. Where would we go anyway. The reason we stopped is we don't know the way out.

Hey, man. Following any one of these big streets to the end's bound to get us out.

But where? Didn't you hear the dude say some go for miles. End in the middle of nowhere.

Listen, everybody. Even if I knew the way, I wouldn't desert the other van.

You're responsible for us, too.

I know. I know. And I'm terribly sorry I've lost us.

People coming this way. Whole mess of people haul-assing.

I can barely make them out. Distinct bits of color, dark flashes. Pop pop popping again and the road's wiped clean.

A few still coming. Slowly. I think somebody's hurt. Yeah. They're carrying a wounded guy. Bunch of women and a wounded man.

The tableau wobbles into focus. I see them clearly, then the image is smeared intermittently as they weave in and out of what seems to be sheets of flame leaping from the surface of the tarmac.

Let me look through the zoom.

Pam repeats to us what Finney has been relaying. He shoos her and jams the machine into his forehead again.

I'm getting some amazing shit, man. Hot. Hot. The guy's bleeding. Blood all over his shirt.

A white shirt crackling in the heat haze.

Snatches of moaning reach us, the women's voices shredded, detached fragments in the heat-driven wind, so we hear them before we can really listen to whatever it is they might be saying. If it's words they're saying. Are they crying out for help. Or injured, too, in ways we can't tell.

We sure can't leave now.

No way. This is network shit, man. Six o'clock national news.

Please. I'm responsible for your safety.

This is our job.

Van wasn't going nowhere anyway, right. White and Cheers are loading up. Cheers festooned with cameras and film cartridges in belts that crisscross and circle his body like bandoliers. White wears a camouflage tunic with a thousand bulging pockets. Cheers has declared at least five times in my hearing, I'm gonna get me one of those. Or steal yours. They are scrambling, clanking out the van's sliding door. Calvin's arm waves at them, miming a gesture that could be barring or locking the door, though he's really not attempting to reach it. White and Cheers hit the tarmac running. In a second Finney's humping his gear through the door, getting it balanced on his shoulder in a wobbly little hitch as he lands and straightens up. A few bounds and he's caught the others. Three blind mice, I think, each one with a camera stuck in front of his face.

Those fools are crazy.

Probably no safer in here than out there.

You mean you're going, too. If you do, you're crazy, too. And don't even have the excuse of a camera.

We should all stay in the combi. First rule is stay with the vehicle in an emergency.

I miss the second rule. Yell over my shoulder. I'll try to bring them back. Keep them close at least.

Though she is only a few yards away I still can't decipher what the woman is saying. She's speaking more than one language. From the evidence confronting us, the cries and gestures, what's happened is clear. Shots fired into the crowd after the rally ended, after guest celebrity, news cameras and foreigners had split. Many wounded and down. They were trying to find help for this victim. He's in shock, White said. White had seen shock before. Wagged his head like poor bastard's not going to make it. Half the white shirt dyed black. Light stunning away color. Preparing me for the photo Cheers would send later. Black and white, stark contrast, no middle ground. Black face, black blood. Shirt blazing as if it has been scrubbed and scrubbed to the threshold of incandescence. This photo in my hand today. That day an exact copy of the representation Cheers captured. The glare causing him he said to see nothing for a second. A blind plunge into the machine's vision. Arm extended overhead, he snapped what he didn't see. The day screaming in, streaming out the lens.

Calvin assumes authority again. Corrals us closer to the van. I climb in. Pam, nearly in tears, squeezes my hand. The women, who are all that remain of the cortege, gather alongside the van. The man reclines against two of them. Another leans over his face, cooing, fanning. The fourth woman converses with Calvin. Calvin fills us in. He's slid over to the passenger's seat, talking out the window. Translates back to us the language scatted like reggae, studded with almost familiar words. No way, no way he says he can take responsibility for transporting the man to hospital. You are foreigners. You don't understand. I must live here after you've gone home to America. No, no, no. No way. None of us should interfere. We would be committing serious crimes. Be arrested. His first duty is to us. The struggle. And to his family. We must understand his position. He is no coward, but we must let these people go their way. Larger issues at stake. The woman must have been made to understand this also because she breaks off abruptly, points to the intersection, a flatbed cart halted on the near corner. All four women begin shouting to get the cart driver's attention. The speaker double-times, squat and efficient, towards the corner and the others drape the man as best, as gently as they can, so his limp body is a litter now in their grasp as they inch forward.

Was the man a son, a brother, husband, father, lover of one of the women. Did they all belong to one family, one clan. I'd studied them through the van's open door. The women were approximately the same age. What exact age, I had no clue. Not young, not old. Their deep black skin suffered no aging in this light. Round, broad faces. High cheekbones. A tarry sheen, plushness and resiliency. Thick, work-hardened women, but supple, light on their feet. I'd thought of Slavic peasants. Women similarly featured, stamped from the same sturdy mould. Wearing babushkas. We used to call them hunkies. Eastern European women picking through secondhand clothes when I was a boy and tagged along with my mother and aunts to the rummage sales on Homewood Avenue. These South African women also had their heads wrapped, turbans, kerchiefs. Strong, bulky in the shoulders, wide-keeled, unbowed by the man's weight they eased towards the intersection.

The picture takers had fastened themselves again to the wounded man and his rescuers. Cheers whipped ahead of everybody. In the lead now, backpedaling. His shots would catch the whole party. Africans, the black video guy and still cameramen. Pictures of their picture-taking. A frame. A statement.

He never saw the hole that took him down. Clean as a bullet between the eyes. One second he's cock of the walk, high on the advantage he'd gained over the other photographers, busily scooting side to side to orchestrate them into what he was shooting, in front, in command, backing towards the corner. Then he disappears. Lucky he didn't break his neck. A hole cut out of the road, no warning posted, a neat, shallow rectangular ditch and he'd tumbled backwards into it.

Did one of the other photographers catch the surprise on his face. The astonished sayonara as Cheers suddenly backflipped off the edge of the world. Would we all giggle one day at the Kilroy snapshot of him, embarrassed, pants down, sheepishly existing the hole. Would Finney or White digress a moment to document Cheers' writhing, the sickening angle of one leg bent under him, buried in a ditch like pharaoh with his ten thousand dollars' worth of equipment scattered around him. No. The luck of innocents and babes was with Cheers. He refused the hands stretched out to help, emerged sputtering, wiping himself off, frowning, checking his stuff, motioning ahead to the women, who had detoured the hole and him in it without losing a step, the real story we all pursued. Lucky as a sleepwalker.

Light pools on black faces, drips in glistening claw marks. Black skin absorbs the sun and radiates warmth long after nightfall from soft bosoms and cheeks, the muscled, high butts. Each bearer everywoman to the man. Daughter mother wife. Safer to view them that way. Not give them names, ages. In a few moments they'd be gone. The man would live or die. The women would mourn him or nurse him back to health. I'd be oceans away. Receive one day in the mail this black and white photo from Cheers. A black South African man lifted down off his cross by his women. The sorrowful progress stopped in time, emptied of time, time painted over by an image that proclaims nothing else will happen, this moment is all that matters.

A military-looking canvas-covered snub-backed truck blocks the intersection. Disgorges a squad of black boys in slouch hats, blue coveralls. The ghetto comrades call them *instant cops.* Ignorant kids recruited from the poorest, rawest quarters, their loyalty purchased by three square meals a day, a barracks roof over their heads, coveralls, boots, two weeks of indoctrination that transforms them from street punks going nowhere to bullies with guns and power who can push other black people around. I'd seen these paramilitary keepers of order before. Always in pairs or groups. In kiosk checkpoints along the wide streets. I knew they patrolled here. Which meant sauntering along the bare peripheries of the settlement, gun cradled in one arm, hat cocked at a hip angle. They bother the girls, I'd been told. Harass comrades. Shoot when they feel like shooting. We kill them when we can. All the above flashing back as I stop beside the booby trap that had upended Cheers. Wonder about its utility as a foxhole when the shooting starts. Because the procession is frozen as I am in its tracks. The instant cops have formed into a phalanx blockading the road. Rifles up and trained at our hearts. I want to believe I will have time to react once the firing commences. Plenty of targets between me and guns. Should I drop into the hole. Try to sprint back to the van. Would the van be safe. Isn't it as much the enemy as I am.

An officer leaps from the truck's cab and screams a command. Rifle butts thump the ground. I'm grateful for the two weeks of training. The men relax into a kind of shambling, shifty-eyed parade rest alert. I'm close enough to see they're scared, too. And that scares me more.

The officer beckons the women and their burden forward. I begin to retreat, slowly, hoping no one is paying attention to me. Hoping the officer's orders didn't include me, remembering Cheers poleaxed, dropping out of sight, expecting a land mine under my heels, the earth to open and swallow me whole. But determined to back away, back, back.

Right on time the women explode in a volley of shouts, cries, pleadings, outrage. Beat their chests, pull at turbaned hair. One is doubled over, pounds the ground as if she, too, is afflicted with a grievous stomach wound. One points to the wounded man. Flails at heaven, then, head bowed, folds her arms across her chest, swaying, moaning. I can't be sure what anything means. Are the women attacking, begging, demanding. Whatever else it accomplishes, the storm they crank up allows me to sidle more quickly to the van and slip into the open door. Cheers, White and Finney aren't too far behind. I'd seen the officer karate-chop the air. Cheers, White and Finney aren't completely nuts. They'd instantly obeyed his unambiguous signal to cease and desist, dropped cameras to their sides, retreated. Guilty schoolboys.

Those motherfuckers weren't playing, man.

That was close, real close. Could have gone either way. I don't think those cats decided till the last minute whether they were going to cap us or not.

Let's hope they keep deciding not to.

I believe it's over. They're letting them lay him on the cart.

Still leaves *us*. We's a whole nother story, man.

The police won't want an incident. Not with foreign press involved. If we just sit tight, they'll probably bugger off and we'll be okay.

You're the man, Calvin.

They may come confiscate your film.

Naw. Not my pictures. I'll fight those assholes for my pictures.

You and what army, fool.

Finney be all up in the dude's face in a minute. Here, Cap'n Boss. Take my tape and the camera, too. I didn't mean no harm. Lemme do a picture of you in your nice uniform for your wife and kiddies.

What do you think will happen to the wounded man.

They'll let him go to hospital, probably. What will happen then is anybody's guess. The hospital here is very poor. And the unlucky devil seems seriously hurt.

Be gone before dark.

You still determined to wait for the other van.

Things are different now. We don't want the police to think we're skulking about. We'd better leave right after they do. We'll just have to feel our way out.

Try the first left, Calvin.

Shut up, man. You the one fucked us up with your shortcut.

Just didn't go far enough. We needed to drive a little farther and I would have recognized the way out. Guarantee it.

I wonder where the others are.

They may have been escorted out. The police are about now. They'll be clearing the area. Impose an early curfew. You won't see anyone. When the shooting starts these people know to hide.

But the rally was peaceful. It was over. Who was shooting.

Of course I'm not positive. But most likely blue behinds like these. Letting people know the rally annoyed them. They didn't approve of the rally so they killed a few who attended.

That's horrible, Calvin.

We're working to change things in my country. I'll continue the fight after you leave. I know the police. I'm not afraid of them, but I must answer to them in ways you don't. That's why you must listen to me.

Sorry, Calvin. But we got a job, too. You know. In a couple hours, if we ever get out of here, this shit I copped be on TV all over the world.

Shooting people minding their own business. People trying to go home. Damn.

Home. You call this junkyard home.

White's got his camera up, shielded by his body. A sneak thief furtively snapping something he's seen down the long, flat road. Twisting heat mirages. An abandoned dugout and the scrap of rag on a stick that must have once been its roof. The dust-colored dog rooting in gravel. I wonder what's caught his attention. If he copped it. If I'll open an envelope one day and it will all unfurl again again and again.

▨ a voice foretold*

I follow the photographer up the stairs. He is a white boy from another country, with a braided beard down to his navel. I try not to hate him as we climb, one flight and then another and another, stopping on each landing to catch a breath where the narrow stairwell opens two directions to flats on either side.

He smells as if he sleeps in his clothes, so I keep my distance batting up narrow steps behind him, wondering if someone loves him and how long it takes to get past the stink, if stink still stinks after you live with it and you're part of what's high and rotten in his clownish drawers. He clanks. Like he's wearing armor under his baggy shirt and baggy pants. The strap of his camera is beaded many bright colors— cherry red, blue, yellow, black, green. A Native American design I think, the heads of snakes or fish or birds repeated. And we are single file, Indian style. Barely room for that up these steps. One, two, three

*The title and other italicized lines in the text are from a section called (Prayer) in *The Gospel at Colonus,* a musical play adapted by Lee Bruer and Bob Telson from various translations of Sophocles.

landings, where we pause and listen, count to ourselves so we don't make a mistake.

A deep sigh on each floor, a heartbeat's pause to check out halls where scarred, unnumbered doors are sealed tight. October, but summer heat's still bottled up inside the building. Old heat. Ripe heat. I remember the stifling basements of my childhood, carrying my brothers' and sisters' dirty diapers down into the cellar to soak them in tin tubs, wet wash hanging, the funky skins of dead animals I had to duck and drag my face through. Ammonia smell so strong my eyes watered. Sweat dripping as soon as I begin wringing the diapers. I hope I'll be surprised on one of these floors by the odors of good food cooking. Somebody's dinner simmering to drown out the stink. His. Mine. All the bodies that have penetrated the front door and pounded up these steps, scuffing off layers of skin that decompose and hover in the hot air.

The photographer's my guide because he's the one who first thought of coming here, questioned the little boys on the front stoop who shook their heads, each head crowned with a different hippy-dip cap, no, they didn't know what shooting he was talking about here in this building, but pointed across the street where two dudes was wasted last week.

No. No. Here. On floor number five. In this building, where it turns out one of the boys lives, but they don't know. They forget the photographer instantly, busy again with each others' eyes, gestures. One smiles, giggles. His hand flies up to cover his mouth. Then they are perfect see no, hear no, speak no evil monkeys, frozen on the steps till the weather of this strange white man passes. Among the things they don't see is me, invisible, trailing behind him.

He is killed here. They shoot Lester on floor five. You live here and know nothing?

Huh uh. They don't know nothing, mister, and dropped their eyes as if they're ashamed of him for asking again.

The photographer's a tall ship listing, swaying, sea-smacked, driven by crazy winds. He's my leader. A rock I want to squeeze till blood runs out. He knew about this place, about the murder here. Now, because of him, I know. Proof in his pictures. The picture book/diary

I began to leaf through, then couldn't let go, needed to squeeze till the blood ran out.

He asks the boys if they want their picture taken. Without answering they draw together in a pose. For the mirror of the camera they make themselves sullen old men, dare it to come one inch closer. Before I can warn them, he's snapped, click, click, click. He thanks them, waves good-bye and bounds past them into the dark vestibule.

Should I believe what he says? That he hitchhikes north and south, east and west, crisscrossing the country without a penny in his pocket, somehow managing to eat, find places to sleep, buy film for his camera. By any and all means possible. Dependent on the goodness, the evil in his fellowmen. Vagabonding, the photographer calls it. Like ancient, raggedy Oedipus with his swollen feet wandering the land, seeking sanctuary. How long has he been on the road? His funk says years. A lifetime ripening.

When a car stops for me I get in. No matter who is driver. How many in car. If they stop, I get in. Rich, poor, young, old, man, woman, black, white. All stop. With all I ride. Sometime they offer smoke, drink, food, maybe place to stay few days. I take. Sometime they ask me to do things. Some things not so nice, but I do what they ask. You know, man. Saves trouble, man. You know. Not always so nice. Maybe not what I want, but I survive. I am still here. I learn much about your country this way.

But this is not a story about him. His Ingmar Bergman accent, the black lilt, slur, lisp, and dance he mimics in his speech, his walk. That I mimic now. His *American Pictures* brought me here. I'm behind him. In his debt. I try not to hate that either. He swaggers the way he may think Buddy Bolden or Big Bill Broonzy swaggered, but he is a pirate ship with the blues, patched canvas, filthy rigging, rotten wood, a shabby thief lurking, tilting, as if this stairwell is a secret cove from which he can pounce on his prey.

Mounting the stairs, I come to a busted window that allows me a view down to the air shaft's pit where garbage is heaped. On top of the refuse a snow of newspapers bleached white as bone. Is the debris thick enough to cushion a fall from this height? From heaven?

I, too, am seeking sanctuary, a resting place, my father's house. *Pity a man's poor carcass and his ghost/For Oedipus is not the strength he was.* This building, these stairs are in East Harlem, where the streets are gold. No one wants to stay indoors in the summer. But even in the sweet heat, if you listen, you can hear winter swirling beneath the sidewalks. A woman imprisoned under asphalt wailing, scratching, refusing to die until she climbs out and faces those who've consumed her children's flesh. Her eyes say she'll survive as long as it takes, and when she emerges into the light of day, she'll ask no questions, take no prisoners.

At last we reach the apartment the photographer brought me here to see. Corinne and Lester's place, gaping open and empty now. I notice bullet holes right away. Like gigantic nails have been ripped from the plaster. No bloodstains. No other visible signs of violence. Just the palpable emptiness of a lived-in space that has been recently, suddenly vacated. Not quite as empty as it seemed at first glance. I imagine other tenants sorting through Corinne and Lester's possessions, tossing what's useless out the apartment's one window. Hear the couple's things splashing in the air shaft's maw. A few items probably salvaged, clothes mainly, perhaps Corinne's saved for her by a friend, perhaps a pocked, cherrywood bureau that once belonged to the people Lester's mother worked for, dragged across the hall, jimmied down two flights of steps, maybe rabbit ears torn from atop a shattered TV before it's heaved where everything else is going. The apartment stripped nearly to the bone, except as I lean closer, adjust my reading glasses on the wings of my nose, pick through the 5 × 7 photo hungrily, with the rummage-sale connoisseurship, diligence, and studied nonchalance of the mob of neighbors looting Corinne and Lester's bullet-riddled love nest, I notice a clothes rack, one wheel and leg missing, collapsed in the corner of a closet, hangers adangle where they've slipped to an end of the pole, one of those ubiquitous kitchen chairs of bent aluminum tubing, its vinyl seat and backrest gashed, leaking grayish stuffing. On the linoleum, scattered sheets of newspaper, miscellaneous boxes, papers too tiny to read no matter how close I get. A thick board that must have been wedged under the knob of the front door for safety lies splintered where it landed when the cops brammed down the door. I know that's the purpose of the board because my father uses one just like it and half a dozen other contraptions to seal himself in every night. One busted screen, a radiator, a slashed blind drooling off its shaft somebody stood in a corner by the window then forgot to toss. Oh abundance. Oh sad toys. When their stuff was raining from the window the sound must have been like fire crackling in the pit.

The photographer said they were lovers. Lester and Corinne lived here two years, working together in a kosher restaurant, partying together in the Bandbox Bar and Grill. Everybody called them the Two Musketeers. If you saw one on the street you were sure to see the other. They say Corinne's grief drove her insane. Cops might as well have shot them both the night they broke open this door still crooked in its frame. A mistake. Wrong address. Shooting first. Too late for questions later. Years since the shooting and the photographer continues to make inquiries about Corinne, in the kosher restaurant, the street, questioning, when his travels bring him back to the scene of the crime, the grandmother he discovered after he learned the story and took his pictures and couldn't shake the fate of the "ghetto lovers," as he dubbed them, from his mind.

I share his hurt, his compassion, curiosity, the weight of memory he wears around his neck on a strap. Angry I needed him to find this place, this broken promise, angry to be trapped five stories up, at the threshold of the apartment where Lester and Corinne lived.

The lighting of the picture is dismal, severe and vacant as the colorless paint of interior walls and ceiling.

We remain outside, staring in. Him first, then I stand where he stood, in painted footprints, peering over his shoulder, through his skull. His shaggy mane erratically braided like the Rasta beard he wears to his waist. Neighbors sprout like a knot on a wound as soon as cops, wagon, ambulance depart. They mill about, surly, pissed-off, injured, snubbed. Is this always how love ends? They had observed only one rubber-shrouded stretcher loaded into the meat wagon. Corinne half-dressed, half-led, half-carried down. In shock, her naked legs buckling, her eyes unfocused so she stumbled rather than walked, faltering on each landing, fighting the cops who pinned her arms into theirs. Not crazy, not screaming. Her eyes dry and wild. A little scuffle, predictable after a while, on each landing, as she fought to pull away and they fought to hold her. It's as if she's forgotten something crucial, left it behind in the apartment and was remembering on each landing she must return up the stairs to get it. But the commotion lessens with each repetition. The caravan—a cop on each arm, camouflaged SWAT cops behind, uniformed officers and plainclothes detectives in the lead, nobody had ever seen so many official people all at once, no progress so elaborate as that 3:30 A.M. parade carting poor Corinne away—doesn't hesitate, doesn't change pace or direction. Down, down. Corinne sewed up tight in their midst, in their business that left absolutely no room for hers.

Mize well have shot her, too. Poor child. For all she was worth afterwards.

That black, bowlegged man was her life. When they murdered Lester, they murdered Corinne. Could have pitched her out the window for all she cared. She was dead the second them bullets stole her man. Shame to see a nice young woman like Corinne let herself go like she did. So fast, so fast. Seemed like wasn't but a couple weeks and she's walking the streets like one them pitiful bag people.

What makes it so bad they ain't never done nothing to nobody. Happy living together up in that apartment. Make you feel good when you see them on the street. One day in the prime of life. Next day those dogs come and both them children gone. People in there like roaches cleaning out the place.

I watch Corinne's screaming fill the room. Wave after wave of bullets smack her man back down on the bed. She crouches over him, shielding him. Both hands dig under his belly, trying to turn him, rouse him. She screams one last time. It rises, circles, climbs higher, takes him, takes her spirit with it, leaves her body stretched on a rack of silent mourning. Silence heavy as heat. Strong as stink. Rioting in its invisibleness. A burst of gunfire and her man's gone. Only a bloody mess left on the bed. By the time the cops snatch her off him, her screaming's over. Her grief something quiet, private she will pick up and finger the way her neighbors inspect the things that used to belong to her and Lester.

The photographer disappears inside his camera. To take its picture. A picture of its picture taking. I am alone now, facing a vacant room. I list its contents. Itemize what's missing. How had they furnished this space? A lamp. Where? Bed. Where? A table. Where? TV. Where? In two years they must have accumulated lots of stuff. New and used. Emblems of their fabled love.

After climbing many flights, pausing on many landings, I'm tired. The air feels weighted and thin. Both. Yes. Both. The steps are hard, steep, my heart heaves, pain binds my chest, sticks in my throat. I'm afraid now, with the white boy gone, everybody gone, afraid of what I'll find if I step alone into these tiny, stale, heat-choked, ransacked, death-haunted rooms. I will find my father there. And his father before him. Both alone at the end. At the top of many lonely stairs. Was this the resting place they'd suffered to find. Sanctuary at last. *Portents, he said, would make me sure of this.*

Have you ever heard your grandfather talk about elevators? How you ride alone in a piss-smelling box and when the door glides open you never know what will be there to greet you. Who will leap in for a joyride. What knife or gun or cruelty waits to spring on you when the door rattles open and he enters or they enter and take over the space, wild boy kings of the elevators, junkie emperors of the old folk in the senior citizens' high-rise, old folks who must ride up and down now that gimpy limbs and frail hearts are failing them, who must push buttons and pray their worst dreams will not jump into the car when the door slides back, will not be waiting in ambush when you step out and the door seals itself behind you, delivering you to your fate. Who wants to hold their breath as the elevator passes each floor, who can resist a gasp or cringe every time the car stops at night and the door sighs open. Who wants to ride with that lung-pinching terror or the terror of exposed blind-cornered outdoor walkways many stories up with only a waist-high guardrail the drugged, crazy ones will pitch you over. My father's father spent his last days in rooms like these and his son, my father, lives solitary, two floors above a shoemaker, in rooms like the ones in this photo I scan, scoured of love.

A voice foretold/Where I shall die. Think of our great cities. Towers of silk and gold and sounding brass as they rise and shimmer in the best light at the best hour of the day for photographing giant splendor and endless allure. These cities, these treasures heaped so high we must erect transparent elevator tubes, spiraling staircases to wind our way to the top, for the best view, pearly bubbles of car, gleaming, free-floating slabs of stair and banister curling, rising. We mount intricately and with awe. Up and up till we are thin as the thin air we must breathe at the mountainous heights we've achieved. Below us the fruited plain. The amber waves. Beams of light so powerful they are visible in daytime, cross and crisscross, fingers searching the sky, tracking it for signs of life, or perhaps lost themselves, programmed to describe lazy, random arcs horizon to horizon over and over again.

Think of the Lone Ranger. The clattering hooves of his mighty white stallion descending nude, hysterical, down, down the many floors, negotiating this narrow, nasty-smelling stairwell at an impossible, bone-busting gallop. And the masked man slumped half on a landing, half on the stairs, bleeding profusely from multiple wounds, every silver bullet spent, six-shooter cool in its holster, ten-gallon Stetson still stuck on his head, boots spit-shined, eyes shut behind the slits in the black cloth that camouflages his identity.

Think of endless traffic up and down the stairs, night and day, up and down, wearing out the stairs, the building, the city, the land.

Think of up and down and paths crossing and crossing roads and crossroads and traffic and what goes up must come down and heaven's gate and what goes 'round comes 'round.

Think of what is unseen till strangers come to take it away.

newborn thrown
in trash and dies

They say you see your whole life pass in review the instant before you die. How would *they* know. If you die after the instant replay, you aren't around to tell anybody anything. So much for they and what they say. So much for the wish to be a movie star for once in your life because I think that's what people are hoping, what people are pretending when they say you see your life that way at the end. Death doesn't turn your life into a five-star production. The end is the end. And what you know at the end goes down the tube with you. I can speak to you now only because I haven't reached bottom yet. I'm on my way, faster than I want to be traveling and my journey won't take long, but I'm just beginning the countdown to zero. Zero's where I started also so I know a little bit about zero. Know what they say isn't necessarily so. In fact the opposite's true. You begin and right in the eye of that instant storm your life plays itself out for you in advance. That's the theater of your fate, there's where you're granted a preview, the coming attractions of everything that must happen to you. Your life rolled into a ball so dense, so superheavy it would drag the universe down to hell if this tiny, tiny lump of whatever didn't dissipate as quickly as it formed. Quicker. The weight of it is what you recall some infinitesimal fraction of when you stumble and crawl through your worst days on earth.

Knowledge of what's coming gone as quickly as it flashes forth. Quicker. Faster. Gone before it gets here, so to speak. Any other way and nobody would stick around to play out the cards they're dealt. No future in it. You begin forgetting before the zero's entirely wiped off the clock face, before the next digit materializes. What they say is assbackwards, a saying by the way, assbackwards itself. Whether or not you're treated to a summary at the end, you get the whole thing handed to you, neatly packaged as you begin. Then you forget it. Or try to forget. Live your life as if it hasn't happened before, as if the tape has not been prepunched full of holes, the die cast.

I remember because I won't receive much of a life. A measure of justice in the world, after all. I receive a compensatory bonus. Since the time between my wake-up call and curfew is so cruelly brief, the speeded-up preview of what will come to pass, my life, my portion, my destiny, my career, slowed down just enough to let me peek. Not slow enough for me to steal much, but I know some of what it contains, its finality, the groaning, fatal weight of it around my neck.

Call it a trade-off. A standoff. Intensity for duration. I won't get much and this devastating flash isn't much either, but I get it. Zingo.

But the future remains mysterious. Even if we all put our heads together and became one gigantic brain, a brain lots smarter than the sum of each of our smarts, an intelligence as great as the one that guides ants, whales or birds, because they're smarter, they figure things out not one by one, each individual locked in the cell of its head, its mortality, but collectively, doing what the group needs to do to survive, relate to the planet. If we were smarter even than birds and bees, we'd still have only a clue about what's inside the first flash of being. I know it happened and that I receive help from it. Scattered help. Sometimes I catch on. Sometimes I don't. But stuff from it's being pumped out always. I know things I have no business knowing. Things I haven't been around long enough to learn myself. For instance, many languages. A vast palette of feelings. The names of unseen things. Nostalgia for a darkness I've never experienced, a darkness another sense I can't account for assures me I will enter again. Large matters. Small ones. Naked as I am I'm dressed so to speak for my trip. Down these ten swift flights to oblivion.

Floor Ten. Nothing under the sun, they say, is new. This time they're right. They never stop talking so percentages guarantee they'll be correct sometimes. Especially since they speak out of both sides of their mouths at once: *Birds of a feather flock together. Opposites attract.* Like the billion billion monkeys at typewriters who sooner or later will bang out this story I think is uniquely mine. Somebody else, a Russian, I believe, with a long, strange-sounding name, has already written about his life speeding past as he topples slow-motion from a window high up in a tall apartment building. But it was in another country. And alas, the Russian's dead.

Floor Nine. In this building they shoot craps. One of many forms of gambling proliferating here. Very little new wealth enters this cluster of buildings that are like high-rise covered wagons circled against the urban night, so what's here is cycled and recycled by games of chance, by murder and other violent forms of exchange. Kids do it. Adults. Birds and bees. The law here is the same one ruling the jungle, they say. They say this is a jungle of the urban asphalt concrete variety. Since I've never been to Africa or the Amazon I can't agree or disagree. But you know what I think about what they say.

Seven come eleven. Snake eyes. Boxcars. Fever in the funkhouse searching for a five. Talk to me, baby. Talk. Talk. Please. Please. Please.

They cry and sing and curse and pray all night long over these games. On one knee they chant magic formulas to summon luck. They forget luck is rigged. Some of the men carry a game called Three Card Monte downtown. They cheat tourists who are stupid enough to trust in luck. Showmen with quick hands shuffling cards to a blur, fast feet carrying them away from busy intersections when cops come to break up their scam or hit on them for a cut. Flimflam artists, con men who daily use luck as bait and hook, down on their knees in a circle of other men who also should know better, trying to sweet-talk luck into their beds. Luck is the card you wish for, the card somebody else holds. You learn luck by its absence. Luck is what separates you from what you want. Luck is always turning its back and you lose.

Like other potions and powders they sell and consume here luck creates dependency. In their rooms people sit and wait for a hit. A yearning unto death for more, more, more till the little life they've been allotted dies in a basket on the doorstep where they abandoned it.

The Floor of Facts. Seventeen stories in this building. The address is 2950 West 23rd Street. My mother is nineteen years old. The trash chute down which I was dropped is forty-five feet from the door of the apartment my mother was visiting. I was born and will die Monday, August 12, 1991. The small door in the yellow cinder block wall is maroon. I won't know till the last second why my mother pushes it open. In 1990 nine discarded babies were discovered in New York City's garbage. As of August this year seven have been found. 911 is the number to call if you find a baby in the trash. Ernesto Mendez, forty-four, a Housing Authority caretaker, will notice my head, shoulders and curly hair in a black plastic bag he slashes open near the square entrance of the trash compactor on the ground floor of this brown-brick public housing project called the Gerald J. Carey Gardens. Gardens are green places where seeds are planted, tended, nurtured. The headline above my story reads "Newborn Is Thrown in Trash and Dies." The headline will remind some readers of a similar story with a happy ending that appeared in March. A baby rescued and surviving after she was dropped down a trash chute by her twelve-year-old mother. The reporter, a Mr. George James who recorded many of the above facts, introduced my unhappy story in the Metro Section of the *New York Times* on Wednesday, August 14, with this paragraph: "A young Brooklyn woman gave birth on Monday afternoon in a stairwell in a Coney Island housing project and then dropped the infant down a trash chute into a compactor ten stories below, the police said yesterday." And that's about it. What's fit to print. My tale in a nutshell followed by a relation of facts obtained by interview and reading official documents. Trouble is I could not be reached for comment. No one's fault. Certainly no negligence on the reporter's part. He gave me sufficient notoriety. Many readers must have shaken their heads in dismay or sighed or blurted Jesus Christ, did you see this, handing the Metro Section across the breakfast table or passing it to somebody at work. As grateful as I am to have my story made public you should be able to understand why I feel cheated, why the newspaper account is not enough, why I want my voice to be part of the record. The awful silence is not truly broken until we speak for ourselves. One chance to speak was snatched away. Then I didn't cry out as I plunged through the darkness. I didn't know any better. Too busy thinking to myself, *This is how it is, this is how it is, how it is* . . . accustoming myself to what it seemed life brings, what life is. Spinning, tumbling, a breathless rush, terror, exhilaration and wonder, wondering is this it, am I doing it right. I didn't know any better. The floors, the other lives packed into this building were going on their merry way as I flew past them in the darkness of my tunnel. No one waved. No one warned me. Said hello or good-bye. And of course I was too busy flailing, trying to catch my breath, trying to stop shivering in the sudden, icy air, welcoming almost the thick, pungent draft rushing up at me as if another pair of thighs were opening below to replace the ones from which I'd been ripped.

In the quiet dark of my passage I did not cry out. Now I will not be still.

A Floor of Questions. Why.

A Floor of Opinions. I believe the floor of fact should have been the ground floor, the foundation, the solid start, the place where all else is firmly rooted. I believe there should be room on the floor of fact for what I believe, for this opinion and others I could not venture before arriving here. I believe some facts are unnecessary and that unnecessary borders on untrue. I believe facts sometimes speak for themselves but never speak for us. They are never anyone's voice and voices are what we must learn to listen to if we wish ever to be heard. I believe my mother did not hate me. I believe somewhere I have a father, who if he is reading this and listening carefully will recognize me as his daughter and be ashamed, heartbroken. I must believe these things. What else do I have. Who has made my acquaintance or noticed or cared or forgotten me. How could anyone be aware of what hurtles by faster than light, blackly, in a dark space beyond the walls of the rooms they live in, beyond the doors they lock, shades they draw when they have rooms and the rooms have windows and the windows have shades and the people believe they possess something worth concealing.

In my opinion my death will serve no purpose. The streetlamps will pop on. Someone will be run over by an expensive car in a narrow street and the driver will hear a bump but consider it of no consequence. Junkies will leak out the side doors of this gigantic mound, nodding, buzzing, greeting their kind with hippy-dip vocalizations full of despair and irony and stylized to embrace the very best that's being sung, played and said around them. A young woman will open a dresser drawer and wonder whose baby that is sleeping peaceful on a bed of dishtowels, T-shirts, a man's ribbed sweat socks. She will feel something slither through the mud of her belly and splash into the sluggish river that meanders through her. She hasn't eaten for days, so that isn't it. Was it a deadly disease. Or worse, some new life she must account for. She opens and shuts the baby's drawer, pushes and pulls, opens and shuts.

I believe all floors are not equally interesting. Less reason to notice some than others. Equality would become boring, predictable. Though we may slight some and rattle on about others, that does not change the fact that each floor exists and the life on it is real, whether we pause to notice or not. As I gather speed and weight during my plunge, each floor adds its share. When I hit bottom I will bear witness to the truth of each one.

Floor of Wishes. I will miss Christmas. They say no one likes being born on Christmas. You lose your birthday, they say. A celebration already on December 25 and nice things happen to everyone on that day anyway, you give and receive presents, people greet you smiling and wish you peace and goodwill. The world is decorated. Colored bulbs draped twinkling in windows and trees, doorways hung with wild berries beneath which you may kiss a handsome stranger. Music everywhere. Even wars truced for twenty-four hours and troops served home-cooked meals, almost. Instead of at least two special days a year, if your birthday falls on Christmas, you lose one. Since my portion's less than a day, less than those insects called ephemera receive, born one morning dead the next, and I can't squeeze a complete life cycle as they do into the time allotted, I wish today were Christmas. Once would be enough. If it's as special as they say. And in some matters we yearn to trust them. Need to trust something, someone, so we listen, wish what they say is true. The holiday of Christmas seems to be the best time to be on earth, to be a child and awaken with your eyes full of dreams and expectations and believe for a while at least that all good things are possible—peace, goodwill, love, merriment, the raven-maned rocking horse you want to ride forever. No conflict of interest for me. I wouldn't lose a birthday to Christmas. Rather than this smoggy heat I wish I could see snow. The city, this building snug under a blanket of fresh snow. No footprints of men running, men on their knees, men bleeding. No women forced out into halls and streets, away from their children. I wish this city, this tower were stranded in a gentle snowstorm and Christmas happens day after day and the bright fires in every hearth never go out, and the carols ring true chorus after chorus, and the gifts given and received precipitate endless joys. The world trapped in Christmas for a day dancing on forever. I wish I could transform the ten flights of my falling into those twelve days in the Christmas song. *On the first day of Christmas my true love said to me* . . . angels, a partridge in a pear tree, ten maids a milking, five gold rings, two turtledoves. I wish those would be the sights greeting me instead of darkness, the icy winter heart of this August afternoon I have been pitched without a kiss through a maroon door.

Floor of Power. El Presidente inhabits this floor. Some say he owns the whole building. He believes he owns it, collects rent, treats the building and its occupants with contempt. He is a bold-faced man. Cheeks slotted nose to chin like a puppet's. Chicken lips. This floor is entirely white. A floury, cracked white some say used to gleam. El Presidente is white also. Except for the pink dome of his forehead. Once, long ago, his flesh was pink head to toe. Then he painted himself white to match the white floor of power. Paint ran out just after the brush stroke that permanently sealed his eyes. Since El Presidente is cheap and mean he refused to order more paint. Since El Presidente is vain and arrogant he pretended to look at his unfinished self in the mirror and proclaimed he liked what he saw, the coat of cakey white, the raw, pink dome pulsing like a bruise.

El Presidente often performs on TV. We can watch him jog, golf, fish, travel, lie, preen, mutilate the language. But these activities are not his job; his job is keeping things in the building as they are, squatting on the floor of power like a broken generator or broken furnace or broken heart, occupying the space where one that works should be.

Floor of Regrets. One thing bothers me a lot. I regret not knowing what is on the floors above the one where I began my fall. I hope it's better up there. Real gardens perhaps or even a kind of heaven for the occupants lucky enough to live above the floors I've seen. Would one of you please mount the stairs, climb slowly up from floor ten, examine carefully, one soft, warm night, the topmost floors and sing me a lullaby of what I missed.

Floor of Love. I'm supposed to be sleeping. I could be sleeping. Early morning and my eyes don't want to open and legs don't want to push me out of bed yet. Two rooms away I can hear Mom in the kitchen. She's fixing breakfast. Daddy first, then I will slump into the kitchen Mom has made bright and smelling good already this morning. Her perkiness, the sizzling bacon, water boiling, wheat bread popping up like jack-in-the-box from the shiny toaster, the Rice Krispies crackling, fried eggs hissing, the FM's sophisticated patter and mincing string trios would wake the dead. And it does. Me and Daddy slide into our places. Hi, Mom. Good morning, Dearheart. The day begins. Smells wonderful. I awaken now to his hand under the covers with me, rubbing the baby fat of my tummy where he's shoved my nightgown up past my panties. He says I shouldn't wear them. Says it ain't healthy to sleep in your drawers. Says no wonder you get those rashes. He rubs and pinches. Little nips. Then the flat of his big hand under the elastic waistband wedges my underwear down. I raise my hips a little bit to help. No reason not to. The whole thing be over with sooner. Don't do no good to try and stop him or slow him down. He said my Mama knows. He said go on fool and tell her she'll smack you for talking nasty. He was right. She beat me in the kitchen. Then took me in to their room and he stripped me butt-naked and beat me again while she watched. So I kinda hump up, wiggle, and my underwear's down below my knees, his hand's on its way back up to where I don't even understand how to grow hairs yet.

The Floor That Stands for All the Other Floors Missed or Still to Come. My stepbrother Tommy was playing in the schoolyard and they shot him dead. Bang. Bang. Gang banging and poor Tommy caught a cap in his chest. People been in and out the apartment all day. Sorry. Sorry. Everybody's so sorry. Some brought cakes, pies, macaroni casseroles, lunch meat, liquor. Two Ebony Cobras laid a joint on

Tommy's older brother who hadn't risen from the kitchen chair he's straddling, head down, nodding, till his boys bop through the door. They know who hit Tommy. They know tomorrow what they must do. Today one of those everybody-in-the-family-and-friends-in-dark-clothes-funeral days, the mothers, sisters, aunts, grandmothers weepy, the men motherfucking everybody from god on down. You can't see me among the mourners. My time is different from this time. You can't understand my time. Or name it. Or share it. Tommy is beginning to remember me. To join me where I am falling unseen through your veins and arteries down down to where the heart stops, the square opening through which trash passes to the compactor.

welcome

At this time of the year she could not help thinking of the daughter given then so quickly taken away. Not daughter. She didn't think daughter. She thought Njeri. Who had been her, living inside her, unseparate, her blood breath and heart beating then Njeri for a spring summer and fall and then when the streets again were full of snow not full really but rags and tags of old snow everywhere and blistered skins of ice and the hawk under your clothes the instant you step out the door, then in a haze of sedation that quieted the howling pain Njeri had slipped away, her own pain an afterthought recalled days years later howling as if God or the Devil himself were entering or leaving her Njeri's breathing something she could watch but could not do yes it was that simple you could not do it for her that simple you lay down one day and just about died and then a child was born and you were in two places two pieces always the inside outside outside inside the cold raw your skin cracks and shatters the whole world one crisp frozen sheet of glass a strong wind could break everything the lighted windows like ornaments hung on buildings the music in the aisles of department stores this season fresh each time it comes she comes the first time again dancing her brother Njeri in his arms to the Brothers

Johnson *I'll be good to you good to you good to you* beside a glittering tree and then the next Christmas Njeri is gone. She cannot help thinking and then she sees through the lines of the carols, the songs that always were to her packages wrapped neatly, carefully, lovingly wrapped in beautiful paper, stars, bells, trees, stripes of luminous ribbon, swirls of ribbon flowers, someone had spent hours decorating what was precious inside to save it, give it away, those carols each held Njeri, her smell, her eyes, the words she'd begun to chatter.

She would be twelve now. A dozen candles on the cake to count. 1—2—3—4—5 . . . and her chipmunk cheeks bell to puff them all out in a single breath. No one had said one word last birthday. She'd waited for her mother to call and when she finally did neither of them mentioned the day, the day Njeri had come here or the day one year plus eleven days more when she'd left. She tried to remember what they did say. What else could they have talked about? Her mother knew the birth day, the death day. How in this season those days would drop like something heavy shot from the sky. A soundless explosion, the sky screams, the earth buckles as something that had been flying lands with all the weight of things broken that will not rise again. Perhaps they'd talked about the grandkids, what each one wanted, what they were going to get and not get. Lines in the stores. Layaways. Snapshots with tacky Santas the wrong color. Dolls that pee. Machines that talk and count and shoot and how many batteries needed to make them run. How much it cost and how in God's name was anybody ever going to pay for it all in January when the bills came due. What else could they have talked about? And had her mother sighed after she hung up the phone, happy or not happy she'd avoided mentioning Njeri? Had her mother been trying to take all the weight upon herself the way she decided sometimes to spare her children and be the strong one, the one who could bear the suffering meant for all of them, willing herself to stand alone in the rain, as if she could will the rain to fall on her and no one else? How much had her mother wanted to say Njeri's name? How many times did her mother need to say it to herself as she gripped the phone and said other words into it? She had not said Njeri either. Always other things to talk about. Sometimes on the phone with her mother she wouldn't know who was doing the talking and who the listening. Conversation weaves back and forth. Whose turn to answer? Whose turn to start a new topic? Or listen? Who'd attended the Community Council meeting Tuesday night at the center? Was she there or had her mother told her about it and who'd heard Delia Goins tell that big lie on Willa Mae who'd never even been to Cleveland? Or did Willa follow her up and down the aisles of the A&P whispering in her ear and then she passed Willa's tale to her mother and she could tell her mother was nodding uh huh, uh huh at the other end of the line, hold on a minute water's boiling and in the quiet, the crackle of the wait, Njeri's name over and over as if they both understood space must be allowed for it so something would say it get it over with and say it again and again since they wouldn't since they couldn't bring themselves to say it, they must make space to let something else say it so both of them could stop holding their breath, let it out, the sinus bursting pressure in ears and throat and behind the eyes, let it out.

I put water on for coffee before I dialed you. Can't keep anything in my brain anymore. Afraid I'm going to leave the stove on when I go to bed one night and burn down the house.

Always terrible fires around Christmas. Every Christmas you hear about babies and old folks burning up. Whole families.

Dry trees and hot lights. Kids playing around all those wires. Do you have your tree yet?

Mom. You know we don't get trees anymore.

Of course I do. Talking to myself, I guess. I've been putting off and putting off getting a tree. What it is I think I don't really want the bother. Nobody here now but me. What do I need with a Christmas tree?

She could hear how the talk went but could not remember really whether it was last year or any particular year. Two women talking. During the holiday season. One was her mother. She was the other. The woman's daughter who was now a woman herself. Who'd had children of her own. Children getting big now who she'd make Kwansa for. Grandchildren. Faces and names more familiar than her own. Not separate from her own. Their sicknesses. Their smiles. Shopping to find a gift for Grandma. A daughter. She was her mother's daughter and her kids were gifts, her children herself returning to her mother's house for an old-fashioned Christmas. Bright boxes under the tree. One missing. One lost. But let's not talk about that this afternoon. Even if it just about kills us both.

Hello hi good morning how are you haven't heard from you oh I'm fine everybody here's OK on my way to Homewood Avenue to get some last minute shopping done how you doing same ole same ole I you she said did you hear . . .

Have you talked to Tom lately?

He's on the road. I worry so when he's on the road.

Mom, you worry when he's sitting at the dinner table beside you.

I know. I know. I'm terrible.

No. You're not terrible. Worrying's your job. Wouldn't be you if you weren't lying in bed with one eye open waiting for whichever one of us out partying to come tipping up the stairs. I knew you'd be awake. Whatever time I dragged in. Why'd I always try to creep up those big-mouth steps. Like they wouldn't moan and groan no matter how quiet I tried to be. Like you wouldn't be in your room listening, waiting. Zat you, Sis.

Your brother's changed.

She sees him in a plane over New York City. It is Sunday morning, early. She looks down on bridges, highways, houses laid out like a crowded cemetery. Haze hangs over the skyline. Flat low-lying stretches of land are sweat-stained where the ocean has come and gone. Most of the sky a blue sigh. Except for brown smearing the tops of the tallest buildings. Except for snowy swipes of cloud here and there that help her know how high she is, how far she can see. He is over New York or some other city she's met only in movies or in her dream of escape. She knows he's flying to some fabulous place and knows he won't stay long. He'll be home for the holidays. He'll tell her it's best here at home when the family's all together. When you travel to a place and don't really know anybody there, it gets old pretty quick. I used to love it, he says, but now I think of myself falling down in the street. Strangers stepping past and stepping over and a cold white room with no visitors, no one who understands I wasn't always the wreck they see now. She listens and thinks how impossible it is to be in another place, how difficult it is to imagine herself landing in another place, visiting, staying, having another life. She envies her brother. She's glad he does what he does so she doesn't need to bother.

From some faraway city he'd sent them that nice card the Christmas Njeri came.

Thou were born of a mayden mylde
Uppon a day, so it befelle
There fore we say, bothe man and childe
"Thou arte welcum with us to dwelle."

He's older. We're all older, Mom. All changed.

Yes. God knows that's true, but he's different, changed in ways that make me worry about him.

After all that's happened these past few years, it's a wonder he's not crazy. Wonder we're not all stone crazy.

Sometimes I believe we're being tested.

Well, I wish whoever's conducting the damned test would get it the hell over with. Enough's enough.

You sound like him now.

He's my brother.

And my son. Youall are what I live for now. The only thing that keeps me going.

C'mon, lady. Don't talk that mess. Make yourself sound like some dried-up prune piece of something.

Listen at you. Listen how you talk to your poor sick pitiful old mother.

We're all poor. But I ain't buying the rest. You heard what the doctor said. You're a healthy woman with lots of life left.

Except.

We're taking care of the except. And you're coming along just fine.

It's a pretty big except. Big. Big. All my hair's gone. And how those treatments make me feel is a long way from fine, but let's leave the doctors out of this. I'm not the one I'm worried about now. I'm worried about Tom.

Looked good to me last time he was home. Same old big brother as far as I could tell. A little thinner maybe, but still eats like a horse. Nothing wrong with that man's appetite. And he still loves to tease.

He's not himself.

What do you expect, Mom? Nobody could live through what he did, what we all did, and not come out changed.

I know what it is.

What?

It hasn't hit him yet. Not really. He's walking around talking and doing what he thinks he needs to do and I don't believe he's let it hit him yet. He thinks he's faced it down and now he's going on with his life, but it's still out there somewhere waiting and he won't be ready, he won't know what to do when it hits him.

Mom.

You were that way with Njeri, bless her soul. Youall are my children and I know how you are. My Hard-Hearted Hannah pour water on a drowning man. But then she goes off somewhere and drowns her own self.

He's been through a lot. He's coping the best he can. Better than most people would as far as I can tell.

Oh. He's tough, all right. You're all tough. My tough-as-nails children. Tell me about it. I got the scars to prove it. But each and every one has that soft spot, too. Under all the ice. Deep under there, deep, deep, but not so deep it can't be reached. I've seen that, too. Got the scars behind that, too.

She tells a story about her brother. An old one she doesn't have to work too hard at. One her mother can jump in and finish with her. Then a tidbit about Keesha, the youngest, the last gift, not to replace Njeri but give her lost daughter another chance, this time in the strong brown arms and legs and healthy lungs of her sister, baby sister who knows Njeri as a photograph on the mantel. That's Njeri, baby, your sister. Yes, she used to live here. She still lives here in Mama's heart. Yes. Inside. You can't see her but she's there. Always. Beside you and Staci and Tanya. Yes. Plenty room for all of you, don't worry. You can't touch her or see her, but here's what she looked like. Her picture. You would be her little sister. Uh huh. That's right. Yes. She's a baby still in the picture because she didn't have a chance to grow up and be a big girl like you. Mama's big girl. But she's here. You're both here. All my babies, all my big girls.

Faver. You know how Keesh says father. Faver, I don't care if it good I'm not going to drink this goddamn juice. And Faver just about fell out his chair. Trying his best not to laugh. Hand all up in front of his mouth. Bout strangled hisself. Coughing, you know. Trying not to laugh.

What did you say? Still had his hand up. You know. He could barely talk. Trying to get together his proper father voice.

Where'd you hear that word, young lady?

What goddamn word, Faver?

Then I'm rolling. I had to leave the table. Let Faver handle this one, I'm thinking. I'm out of here. Time to go to work.

She stares at the phone. Her mother's voice no longer in there. A little death. If she lifts the receiver it will buzz and then a voice comes on and then it will beep and then silence. Not her mother's voice. A woman's voice but no woman she knows. Once she'd been sure she'd never touch a phone again. Not after she'd called her mother and cried into the receiver and couldn't say one word except Mom . . . Mom. Three times if she's remembering right, standing at a bank of phones in the hospital lobby, reading numbers and messages scratched on the partition that screened her face but not her voice from the caller next to her. How could you do so many things at once? Dial and read and say Mom three times and hate to be where you are so public and so sorry sorry you are hurting your mother and making a fool of yourself sobbing like a baby and none of it does a damn bit of good because you can also hang like a spider from the dirty ceiling and pity yourself and see none of it doing any good because your baby is still dead upstairs on a metal cart wrapped up in hospital blankets wherever they'd taken her.

You could lose a child in an instant that way and for a long time after feel each lurch forward of the hands of the clock, as if you were stuck there like a naked chicken turning on a spit but you didn't turn you ticked one click at a time so time didn't change night into day one hour into the next one minute passing to another minute, time stopped then had to start up again, again and again. You wondered why anybody wanted to continue, how others could pretend to keep going. Your children. Why were they such noisy survivors? As if only she could remember. Till their eyes, their demands shocked her into speeding up again, matching herself to the business around her so she can step again into the frantic pace of those who were not skewered as she was, who were not clicking as she was, miles between clicks, lifetimes between each tiny lunge forward.

You could lose a child like that, once and for always in an instant and walk around forever with a lump in your throat, with the question of *what might have been* weighing you down every time you measure the happiness in someone else's face. Or you could lose a child and have him at the same time and how did this other way of losing a child in prison for life change her brother.

Her brother had said: No matter how much you love them you only get one chance, so if something happens and you lose one, no matter how, no matter who's to blame, you're guilty forever because you had that one chance, that precious life given to you to protect, and you blew it. I know you must understand, Sis. And she did and didn't and reached out to touch him, but he wasn't asking for that. His eyes in another country that quick.

She feels the pull of that slow slow time on her shoulders. Shrugs it off and squeezes her arms into her coat. I could stand here all day, she thinks, and says aloud Huh uh to the silence in the empty house as she slams the door behind her and steps into the winter street.

Tom, Tom the piper's son / Stole a pig and away he run.

She is staring at her boots. Hears tinkling of a bell. The old man's propped on a box on a grate just beyond the corner of Hamilton and Homewood in front of the little store where people are lined up to buy lottery tickets. The man's beard is not white. He's not wearing a red suit trimmed in milky white fur. No shiny black leather boots on his feet but on his head an elf's tassel cap, many colors, earflaps like those Eskimo reindeer people wear. The jingle bell, then rattle of change in his tin cup. People in the store bob up and down, blow on their hands and hug themselves and shiver as if it's just as cold inside as outside. She can only see them from the shoulders up in the partially painted-over window. They are real now. Like fish constantly swimming in their glass tanks, they must move to live. They are bumping into each other. Huddling. Exchanging news, lies, yesterday's numbers. She didn't believe in luck. If she was supposed to win some huge pot of money, she'd know it, she'd be told when, where and how to collect it. It wouldn't just happen. Nothing just happened. It was already out there waiting. She hadn't known she was staring at her feet until she heard the bell and saw the old man staring at his crusty hi-top sneakers. One reason he was over that grate begging pennies was so she could see his old face, remember her grandfather's in it, her brother's in that. Another reason was to chase her eyes from the pavement, remind her she could not walk these Homewood streets in a dream.

He was blind. Blind. Old crippled blind Solomon. She needed to say the word before she could remember he was blind as a stone. And there were no legs in that mound of rags draping the crate. No feet in his used-to-be sky blue Connies. Someone had pulled him in a kid's wagon to this warm spot over the grate. Wagon nowhere in sight. Probably hauling groceries home for the shoppers at the A&P. Same one who pulled Solomon here be hustling groceries now. She can hear the wagon wheels bumping over the broken streets. She's digging in her purse for a quarter. Maybe two quarters since it's the holiday season. To give a boy who sets her bags on the stoop. To drop in Solomon's tin cup. She studies the lines of his face, thinks of swirls of barbed wire that would tear up your hand if you tried to pat his cheeks.

Her grandfather shaved clean everyday, chin clean as his clean bald head till his heart stopped the first time and he was a prisoner in the big chair in the living room. When their father left them they'd stay at Grandma's house and play around their grandfather's feet and he'd cough into his huge red handkerchief the only sound from him for days except sometimes when they were in the middle of a game his voice would begin a conversation with nobody they could see and the words float down to the floor so they'd stop what they were doing, freeze and listen to words only half understood, half hummed, whistled, whispered, Sunshine you are my sunshine or Froggy went a courtin and he did ride or Tom Tom the piper's son the song with his name a name they never called him everybody called him DaddyTom except Grandma who said Thomas, Thomas, and shook his arm when the snoring got too loud she couldn't hear her stories on the radio or when she took the snot rag from his hand all nasty and bloody in two fingers the way Mom would carry traps with mouse crushed in them when we lived in that basement on Bellefonte Street Tom Tom he'd sing little half songs and we'd be down there nailed to the floor wondering what he might say next and who was up there with him talking back. Little pickaninnies he'd call us and pat our heads and tickle us with his funny-looking nub of crooked thumb and find us pennies in the pocket of his flannel shirt and then he'd be gone again days and days no sound but the coughing till spooky talk begins again out of nowhere and we'd pay attention as if our lives depended on not missing one word. After his heart stopped the second time bristle grew on his cheeks, all the color drained from him but his cheeks turned comic book hairy blue and lines like blind Solomon's deep black cut the dough of his skin into a thousand pieces. Coughing and snoring and the bad smell of his feet, he spent most days in bed but when he's downstairs we'd play a little further away from his chair than we used to, further from his silence, his wordlessness except once or twice as if we all heard a signal we'd scoot closer, stop and listen even though we knew DaddyTom was finished long ago saying whatever it was he needed to tell us. DaddyTom didn't look back when we looked at him. His noises made him wet. Grandma wiped him with towels. Solomon lets me study his face. Then does something he shouldn't be able to do. Returns my stare so I know he knows I'm there in front of him and he also lets me know enough's enough he's tired of me leaning my eyeballs on him so I'm a little ashamed when I turn away until I remember what he's sitting there for. Not to be worn out by my staring, but to be a way I can begin to learn my brother's pain.

My brother who is Tom. Named for our grandfather. My brother Tom who named his lost son after Will, our handsome father who shaved every morning and sang, too. Crooned gospel songs and love songs before he deserted us. Sweet music at the mirror Sunday morning while he shaved and dressed.

When people come out the store they are smiling. A few drop coins in Solomon's cup for luck. Luck no one should believe they can beg or buy. Not with buckets of tears or shovelfuls of gold dumped in a cup big enough to hold Solomon and his box and the whole damn corner store. Luck is what you wish for. And as long as you're wishing you sure don't have it. So you sure should shut up and go on about your business and something will tell you soon enough what happens next. What always happens next in its own peculiar way in its own sweet time because there's nothing else. Only that.

Doctor said there's nothing else we can do, Mrs. Crawford. I'm sorry, Mrs. Crawford. And he was. A sorry-ass bringer of bad news and nothing else he could do. Nobody to blame. Just that sorry moment when he said Njeri had to die and nobody's fault nobody could do anything more and because he was sorry there in front of her bringing the sorry news why shouldn't she strike him down tear up his sorry white ass just because there was nothing else she could do nobody could do nobody to blame just knock him down and stomp on his chest and grind those coke bottle glasses into his soft sorry face.

Sunshine. My only sunshine.

She'll say it's good to see you. And her brother will grin back at her. Hug each other close as they've learned to do these last dozen years. How are you?

Kiss. Kiss me. My cheeks. My lips. Do it. Don't say a word.

I'm fine. Everybody's fine.

The lives we live lead to this. You are my brother. I'm your sister. We will spend most of our time apart then on holidays we'll hug, cling. When we let go, what I'll truly want to know is everything about you.

Do you remember DaddyTom singing?

Did you hold your breath the whole time like I did? Did it snow while we were holding our breath? Did the seasons change? Did Christmas come?

I'm ok. Terry and the kids send love.

Too bad they couldn't make it.

They're very disappointed. But Terry had to stay close to her father, sick as he is. So it's just me. In and out quick. I want to be back with Terry and the kids Christmas morning. Maybe we can all get here Easter.

I feel so badly for her father. He's a good man. A year since youall've been here, I bet. Kids grow so fast. I won't recognize your youngest.

She's prettier every day. Like your Keesha.

Hey Keesha. Look at you. You're getting tall, girl. Come over here and give your uncle some sugar, sugar pie.

It doesn't take long, does it?

In his face I see whatever he's put there for me. I will let him go. The moment will pass. He will bend down to kiss Keesha, then lift her high in his arms. He asks about my whole life as I ask about his in the singsong questions. If he stays long enough to catch him a second time, alone, then's when I'll ask about my nephew, his son, who's not dead and gone in an instant, but who's lost to him, to us in ways none of us knows words for. None of us can say except in the silence this old toothless man was set on a corner to break with his cup his bell his silence all of him that's missing under rags that are blankets blankets blankets.

WHEN I DO finally catch him he tells me how hard it is to face these Homewood streets. Like the world is washed fresh after rain, right, and when you step out in the sunshine everything is different, Sis, anything seems possible, well, think of just the opposite. Of flying or driving for hours on the turnpike and getting off in Monroeville then the Parkway and already the dread starting, the little-boy feeling of fear I used to have when I'd leave home to deliver newspapers in Squirrel Hill and all the houses up there big and set back from the curb and wide spaces between them and green lawns, fat trees and nothing but white people in those huge houses. I'd walk softly no place up there really to put my feet afraid my big black footprints would leave a trail anywhere I stepped. That kind of uneasiness, edginess till the car crosses Braddock Avenue. Then blam. The whole thing hits me. I'm home again and it's the opposite of a new shiny world because I feel everything closing down. Blam. I know nothing has changed and never will these streets swallow me alive and hate everybody and that's how it's going to be. Takes me a day at least to get undepressed behind that feeling of being caught up again and unable to breathe and everybody I love in some kind of trouble that is past danger worse than danger a state I don't want to give a name to, can't say because I don't want to hear it. Then I sort of gradually settle in. Youall remind me of what's good here. Why I need to come back. How this was home first and always will be.

Last night I was driving to cop some chicken wings you know how

I love them salty and greasy as they are I slap on extra hot sauce and pop a cold Iron City pour it over ice hog heaven you know so I'm on my way to Woodside Bar-B-Que and I see a man and a little boy on the corner at the bus stop on Frankstown at the bottom of the hill across from Mom's street. It's cold cold cold. I'm stopped at the light. So I can see the little boy's upset and crying. His father's standing there looking pissed off, helpless and lost. Staring up the hill for a bus that probably ain't coming for days this late on a weekend. Daddy a kid himself and somehow he finds himself on a freezing night with an unhappy little boy on a black windy corner and no bus in sight no soul in sight like it's the end of the world and I think Damn why are they out there in this arctic-ass weather, the kid shivering and crying in a skimpy K Mart snowsuit, the man not dressed for winter either, a hooded sweatshirt under his shiny baseball jacket and I see a woman somewhere, the mother, another kid really, already split from this young guy, a broken home, the guy's returning the boy to his mother, or her mother or his and this is the only way, the best he can do and the wind howls the night gets blacker and blacker they'll find the two of them, father son man and boy frozen to death, icicles in the morning on the corner.

I think all that in a second. The whole dreary story line. Characters and bad ending waiting for the light to change on my way for chicken wings. On my way back past that same corner I see the father lift his son and hug him. No bus in sight and it's still blue cold but the kid's not fidgeting and crying anymore he's up in his daddy's arms and I think Fuck it. They'll make it. Or if they don't somebody else will come along and try. Or somebody else try. To make kids. A home. A life. That's all we can do. Any of us. And that's why Homewood's here, because lots of us won't make it but others will try and keep on keeping on. And if I'd had just one wish in the world then, it would have been to be that father or that son hugging that moment when nothing could touch them.

One more thing and then I'll shut up. But I need to tell you one more thing because that's how it happened. Just little things one after another prying me open. Tears in my eyes when I got back to that corner because there was this fat girl in the Woodside. No, not fat. A big girl, solid, pretty, light on her feet, a large pretty big-eyed brown girl thirteen or fourteen with black crinkly hair and smooth kind of round chubby cheek babydoll face who served me my chicken wings through the iron bars they have on the counter at the Woodside. And while she was using tongs to dig my dozen wings out the bin she was singing. Singing while she wrapped them in wax paper and stuffed them in a bag. Bouncing on her toes and in the sweetest, purest, trilling soprano singing little riffs in another language of something for this time of year, something old like Bach with Christ's name in it and hallelujah hallelujah you know and it sounded so fine I hoped she'd never stop singing and my eyes clouded up for no good reason right there standing in the Woodside. I'm no crier, Sis. You know me. But I couldn't stop all the way home till I saw those two on the corner again and knew how much I was missing Will, and then I had to cry some more.

PART II

fever

1 9 8 9

doc's story

He thinks of her small, white hands, blue veined, gaunt, awkwardly knuckled. He'd teased her about the smallness of her hands, hers lost in the shadow of his when they pressed them together palm to palm to measure. The heavy drops of color on her nails barely reached the middle joints of his fingers. He'd teased her about her dwarf's hands but he'd also said to her one night when the wind was rattling the windows of the apartment on Cedar and they lay listening and shivering though it was summer on the brass bed she'd found in a junk store on Haverford Avenue, near the Woolworth's five-and-dime they'd picketed for two years, that God made little things closer to perfect than he ever made big things. Small, compact women like her could be perfectly formed, proportioned, and he'd smiled out loud running his hand up and down the just-right fine lines of her body, celebrating how good she felt to him.

She'd left him in May, when the shadows and green of the park had started to deepen. Hanging out, becoming a regular at the basketball court across the street in Regent Park was how he'd coped. No questions asked. Just the circle of stories. If you didn't want to miss anything good you came early and stayed late. He learned to wait, be patient. Long hours waiting were not time lost but time doing nothing because there was nothing better to do. Basking in sunshine on a stone bench, too beat to play any longer, nowhere to go but an empty apartment, he'd watch the afternoon traffic in Regent Park, dog strollers, baby carriages, winos, kids, gays, students with blankets they'd spread out on the grassy banks of the hollow and books they'd pretend to read, the black men from the neighborhood who'd search the park for braless young mothers and white girls on blankets who didn't care or didn't know any better than to sit with their crotches exposed. When he'd sit for hours like that, cooking like that, he'd feel himself empty out, see himself seep away and hover in the air, a fine mist, a little, flattened-out gray cloud of something wavering in the heat, a presence as visible as the steam on the window as he stares for hours at winter.

He's waiting for summer. For the guys to begin gathering on the court again. They'll sit in the shade with their backs against the Cyclone fencing or lean on cars parked at the roller-coaster curb or lounge in the sun on low, stone benches catty-corner from the basketball court. Some older ones still drink wine, but most everybody cools out on reefer, when there's reefer passed along, while they bullshit and wait for winners. He collects the stories they tell. He needs a story now. The right one now to get him through this long winter because she's gone and won't leave him alone.

In summer fine grit hangs in the air. Five minutes on the court and you're coughing. City dirt and park dust blowing off bald patches from which green is long gone, and deadly ash blowing over from New Jersey. You can taste it some days, bitter in your spit. Chunks pepper your skin, burn your eyes. Early fall while it's still warm enough to run outdoors the worst time of all. Leaves pile up against the fence, higher and higher, piles that explode and jitterbug across the court in the middle of a game, then sweep up again, slamming back where they blew from. After a while the leaves are ground into coarse, choking powder. You eat leaf trying to get in a little hoop before the weather turns, before those days when nobody's home from work yet but it's dark already and too cold to run again till spring. Fall's the only time sweet syrupy wine beats reefer. Ripple, Manischewitz, Taylor's Tawny Port coat your throat. He takes a hit when the jug comes round. He licks the sweetness from his lips, listens for his favorite stories one more time before everybody gives it up till next season.

His favorite stories made him giggle and laugh and hug the others, like they hugged him when a story got so good nobody's legs could hold them up. Some stories got under his skin in peculiar ways. Some he liked to hear because they made the one performing them do crazy stuff with his voice and body. He learned to be patient, learned his favorites would be repeated, get a turn just like he got a turn on the joints and wine bottles circulating the edges of the court.

Of all the stories, the one about Doc had bothered him most. Its orbit was unpredictable. Twice in one week, then only once more last summer. He'd only heard Doc's story three times, but that was enough to establish Doc behind and between the words of all the other stories. In a strange way Doc presided over the court. You didn't need to mention him. He was just there. Regent Park stories began with Doc and ended with Doc and everything in between was preparation, proof the circle was unbroken.

They say Doc lived on Regent Square, one of the streets like Cedar, dead-ending at the park. On the hottest afternoons the guys from the court would head for Doc's stoop. Jars of ice water, the good feeling and good talk they'd share in the shade of Doc's little front yard was what drew them. Sometimes they'd spray Doc's hose on one another. Get drenched like when they were kids and the city used to turn on fire hydrants in the summer. Some of Doc's neighbors would give them dirty looks. Didn't like a whole bunch of loud, sweaty, half-naked niggers backed up in their nice street where Doc was the only colored on the block. They say Doc didn't care. He was just out there like everybody else having a good time.

Doc had played at the University. Same one where Doc taught for a while. They say Doc used to laugh when white people asked him if he was in the Athletic Department. No reason for niggers to be at the University if they weren't playing ball or coaching ball. At least that's what white people thought, and since they thought that way, that's the way it was. Never more than a sprinkle of black faces in the white sea of the University. Doc used to laugh till the joke got old. People freedom-marching and freedom-dying, Doc said, but some dumb stuff never changed.

He first heard Doc's story late one day, after the yellow streetlights had popped on. Pooner was finishing the one about gang warring in North Philly: Yeah. They sure nuff lynched this dude they caught on their turf. Hung him up on the goddamn poles behind the backboard. Little kids found the sucker in the morning with his tongue all black and shit down his legs, and the cops had to come cut him down. Worst part is them little kids finding a dead body swinging up there. Kids don't be needing to find nothing like that. But those North Philly gangs don't play. They don't even let the dead rest in peace. Run in a funeral parlor and fuck up the funeral. Dumping over the casket and tearing up the flowers. Scaring people and turning the joint out. It's some mean shit. But them gangs don't play. They kill you they ain't finished yet. Mess with your people, your house, your sorry-ass dead body to get even. Pooner finished telling it and he looked round at the fellows and people were shaking their heads and then there was a chorus of You got that right, man. It's a bitch out there, man. Them niggers crazy, boy, and Pooner holds out his hand and somebody passes the joint. Pooner pinches it in two fingers and takes a deep drag. Everybody knows he's finished, it's somebody else's turn.

One of the fellows says, I wonder what happened to old Doc. I always be thinking about Doc, wondering where the cat is, what he be doing now . . .

Don't nobody know why Doc's eyes start to going bad. It just happen. Doc never even wore glasses. Eyes good as anybody's far as anybody knew till one day he come round he got goggles on. Like Kareem. And people kinda joking, you know. Doc got him some goggles. Watch out, youall. Doc be skyhooking youall to death today. Funning, you know. Cause Doc like to joke and play. Doc one the fellas like I said, so when he come round in goggles he subject to some teasing and one another thing like that cause nobody thought nothing serious wrong. Doc's eyes just as good as yours or mine, far as anybody knew.

Doc been playing all his life. That's why you could stand him on the foul line and point him at the hoop and more times than not, Doc could sink it. See he be remembering. His muscles know just what to do. You get his feet aimed right, line him up so he's on target, and Doc would swish one for you. Was a game kinda. Sometimes you get a

sucker and Doc win you some money. Swish. Then the cat lost the
dough start crying. He ain't blind. Can't no blind man shoot no pill.
Is you really blind, brother? You niggers trying to steal my money,
trying to play me for a fool. When a dude start crying the blues like
that Doc wouldn't like it. He'd walk away. Wouldn't answer.

Leave the man lone. You lost fair and square. Doc made the basket
so shut up and pay up, chump.

Doc practiced. Remember how you'd hear him out here at night
when people sleeping. It's dark but what dark mean to Doc? Blacker
than the rentman's heart but don't make no nevermind to Doc, he be
steady shooting fouls. Always be somebody out there to chase the ball
and throw it back. But shit, man. When Doc into his rhythm, didn't
need nobody chase the ball. Ball be swishing with that good backspin,
that good arch bring it back blip, blip, blip, three bounces and it's
coming right back to Doc's hands like he got a string on the pill.
Spooky if you didn't know Doc or know about foul shooting and
understand when you got your shit together don't matter if you
blindfolded. You put the motherfucker up and you know it's spozed
to come running back just like a dog with a stick in his mouth.

Doc always be hanging at the court. Blind as wood but you couldn't
fool Doc. Eyes in his ears. Know you by your walk. He could tell if
you wearing new sneaks, tell you if your old ones is laced or not.
Know you by your breath. The holes you make in the air when you
jump. Doc was hip to who fucking who and who was getting fucked.
Who could play ball and who was jiving. Doc use to be out here every
weekend, steady rapping with the fellows and doing his foul-shot thing
between games. Every once in a while somebody tease him, Hey, Doc.
You want to run winners next go? Doc laugh and say, No, Dupree
. . . I'm tired today, Dupree. Besides which you ain't been on a winning
team in a week have you, Du? And everybody laugh. You know, just
funning cause Doc one the fellas.

But one Sunday the shit got stone serious. Sunday I'm telling youall
about, the action was real nice. If you wasn't ready, get back cause the
brothers was cooking. Sixteen points, rise and fly. Next. Who got
next? . . . Come on out here and take your ass kicking. One them good
days when it's hot and everybody's juices is high and you feel you
could play till next week. One them kind of days and a run's just over.

Doc gets up and he goes with Billy Moon to the foul line. Fellas hanging under the basket for the rebound. Ain't hardly gon be a rebound Doc get hisself lined up right. But see, when the ball drop through the net you want to be the one grab it and throw it back to Billy. You want to be out there part of Doc shooting fouls just like you want to run when the running's good.

Doc bounce the ball, one, two, three times like he does. Then he raise it. Sift it in his fingers. You know he's a ballplayer, a shooter already way the ball spin in them long fingers way he raises it and cocks his wrist. You know Doc can't see a damn thing through his sunglasses but swear to God you'd think he was looking at the hoop way he study and measure. Then he shoots and ain't a sound in whole Johnson. Seems like everybody's heart stops. Everybody's breath behind that ball pushing it and steadying it so it drops through clean as new money.

But that Sunday something went wrong. Couldna been wind cause wasn't no wind. I was there. I know. Maybe Doc had playing on his mind. Couldn't help have playing on his mind cause it was one those days wasn't nothing better to do in the world than play. Whatever it was, soon as the ball left his hands, you could see Doc was missing, missing real bad. Way short and way off to the left. Might hit the backboard if everybody blew on it real hard.

A young boy, one them skinny, jumping-jack young boys got pogo sticks for legs, one them kids go up and don't come back down till they ready, he was standing on the left side the lane and leap up all the sudden catch the pill out the air and jams it through. Blam. A monster dunk and everybody break out in Goddamn. Do it, Sky, and Did you see that nigger get up? People slapping five and all that mess. Then Sky, the young boy they call Sky, grinning like a Chessy cat and strutting out with the ball squeezed in one hand to give it to Doc. In his glory. Grinning and strutting.

Gave you a little help, Doc.

Didn't ask for no help, Sky. Why'd you fuck with my shot, Sky?

Well, up jumped the Devil. The joint gets real quiet again real quick. Doc ain't cracked smile the first. He ain't playing.

Sorry, Doc. Didn't mean no harm, Doc.

You must think I'm some kind of chump fucking with my shot that way.

People start to feeling bad. Doc is steady getting on Sky's case. Sky just a young, light-in-the-ass kid. Jump to the moon but he's just a silly kid. Don't mean no harm. He just out there like everybody else trying to do his thing. No harm in Sky but Doc ain't playing and nobody else says shit. It's quiet like when Doc's shooting. Quiet as death and Sky don't know what to do. Can't wipe that lame look off his face and can't back off and can't hand the pill to Doc neither. He just stands there with his arm stretched out and his rusty fingers wrapped round the ball. Can't hold it much longer, can't let it go.

Seems like I coulda strolled over to Doc's stoop for a drinka water and strolled back and those two still be standing there. Doc and Sky. Billy Moon off to one side so it's just Doc and Sky.

Everybody holding they breath. Everybody want it over with and finally Doc says, Forget it, Sky. Just don't play with my shots anymore. And then Doc say, Who has next winners?

If Doc was joking nobody took it for no joke. His voice still hard. Doc ain't kidding around.

Who's next? I want to run.

Now Doc knows who's next. Leroy got next winners and Doc knows Leroy always saves a spot so he can pick up a big man from the losers. Leroy tell you to your face, I got my five, man, but everybody know Leroy saving a place so he can build him a winner and stay on the court. Leroy's a cold dude that way, been that way since he first started coming round and ain't never gon change and Doc knows that, everybody knows that but even Leroy ain't cold enough to say no to Doc.

I got it, Doc.

You got your five yet?

You know you got a spot with me, Doc. Always did.

Then I'ma run.

Say to myself, Shit . . . Good God Almighty. Great Googa-Mooga. What is happening here? Doc can't see shit. Doc blind as this bench I'm sitting on. What Doc gon do out there?

Well, it ain't my game. If it was, I'd a lied and said I had five. Or maybe not. Don't know what I'da done, to tell the truth. But Leroy didn't have no choice. Doc caught him good. Course Doc knew all that before he asked.

Did Doc play? What kinda question is that? What you think I been talking about all this time, man? Course he played. Why the fuck he be asking for winners less he was gon play? Helluva run as I remember. Overtime and shit. Don't remember who won. Somebody did, sure nuff. Leroy had him a strong unit. You know how he is. And Doc? Doc ain't been out on the court for a while but Doc is Doc, you know. Held his own . . .

If he had tried to tell her about Doc, would it have made a difference? Would the idea of a blind man playing basketball get her attention or would she have listened the way she listened when he told her stories he'd read about slavery days when Africans could fly, change themselves to cats and hummingbirds, when black hoodoo priests and conjure queens were feared by powerful whites even though ordinary black lives weren't worth a penny. To her it was folklore, superstition. Interesting because it revealed the psychology, the pathology of the oppressed. She listened intently, not because she thought she'd hear truth. For her, belief in magic was like belief in God. Nice work if you could get it. Her skepticism, her hardheaded practicality, like the smallness of her hands, appealed to him. Opposites attracting. But more and more as the years went by, he'd wanted her with him, wanted them to be together . . .

They were walking in Regent Park. It was clear to both of them that things weren't going to work out. He'd never seen her so beautiful, perfect.

There should have been stars. Stars at least, and perhaps a sickle moon. Instead the edge of the world was on fire. They were walking in Regent Park and dusk had turned the tree trunks black. Beyond them in the distance, below the fading blue of sky, the colors of sunset were pinched into a narrow, radiant band. Perhaps he had listened too long. Perhaps he had listened too intently for his own voice to fill the emptiness. When he turned back to her, his eyes were glazed, stinging. Grit, chemicals, whatever it was coloring, poisoning the sky, blurred his vision. Before he could blink her into focus, before he could speak, she was gone.

If he'd known Doc's story he would have said: *There's still a chance.*
There's always a chance. I mean this guy, Doc. Christ. He was stone
blind. But he got out on the court and played. Over there. Right over
there. On that very court across the hollow from us. It happened. I've
talked to people about it many times. If Doc could do that, then
anything's possible. We're possible . . .

If a blind man could play basketball, surely we . . . If he had known
Doc's story, would it have saved them? He hears himself saying the
words. The ball arches from Doc's fingertips, the miracle of it sinking.
Would she have believed any of it?

the statue of liberty

One of the pleasures of jogging in the country is seeing those houses your route takes you past each day and wondering who lives in them. Some sit a good distance from the road, small, secluded by trees, tucked in a fold of land where they've been sheltered thousands of years from the worst things that happen to people. A little old couple lives in this kind. They've raised many children and lost some to the city but the family name's on mailboxes scattered up and down the road, kids and grandkids in houses like their folks', farmers like them, like more generations than you'd care to count back to England and cottages that probably resemble these, Capes, with roofs pulled down almost to the ground the way the old man stuffs on a wool cap bitter February days to haul in firewood from the shed. There are majestic hilltop-sitters with immaculate outbuildings and leaded glass and fine combed lawns sloping in every direction, landmarks you can measure your progress by as you reel in the countryside step by step jogging. I like best those ramshackle outfits—you can tell it's an old farm two young people from the city have taken over with their city dreams and city habits because it's not a real farm anymore, more somebody's idea of what living in the country should be at this day

154

and time. A patched-together look, a corniness and coziness like pictures in a child's book, these city people have a little bit of everything growing on their few acres, and they keep goats, chickens, turkeys, ducks, geese, one cow—a pet zoo, really, and a German shepherd on a chain outside the trailer they've converted to a permanent dwelling. You know they smoke dope and let their kids run around naked as the livestock. They still blast loud city music on a stereo too big for the trailer and watch the stars through a kind of skylight contraption rigged in the tin roof and you envy them the time they first came out from the city, all those stars and nobody around but the two of them, starting out fresh in a different place and nothing better to do than moon up at the night sky and listen to the crickets and make each other feel nice in bed. Those kinds of houses must have been on your jogging route once. You look for them now beneath overloaded clotheslines, beyond rusted-out car stumps, in junk and mess and weeds, you can't tell what all's accumulated in the front yard from where you pass on the road.

A few houses close to the road. Fresh paint and shutters and shrubs, a clean-cut appearance and you think of suburbs, of neat house after house exactly alike, exactly like this one sitting solitary where it doesn't fit into the countryside. Retired people. Two frail old maids on canvas folding chairs in the attached garage with its wizard door rolled up and a puffy, ginger-colored cat crossing from one lady's stockinged feet to the other lady's stockinged feet like a conversation you can't hear from the road. Taking the air in their gazebo is what they're thinking in that suburban garage with its wide door open.

In the window of another one only a few yards from the road you can't tell if there's a person in the dark looking out because the panes haven't been washed in years. A house wearing sunglasses. You have a feeling someone very very old is still alive inside watching you, watching everything that passes, a face planted there in the dark so long, so patient and silent it scares you for no good reason. A gray, sprawled sooty clapboard swaybacked place a good wind could knock over but that wind hasn't blown through yet, not in all the time it's taken the man and woman who live here to shrivel up and crack and curl like the shingles on their steep roof that looks like a bad job of trying to paint a picture of the ocean, brushstrokes that don't become stormy ocean waves but stay brushstrokes, separate, unconnected, slapped on one after another in a hurry-up, hopeless manner that doesn't fool anyone.

A dim-shouldered, stout woman in a blue housedress with a lacy dirty white collar is who I imagine staring at me when I clomp-clomp-clomp by, straining on the slight grade that carries me beyond this house and barn people stopped painting fifty years ago, where people stopped living at least that long ago but they're too old now to die.

Once I thought of an eye large enough to fill the space inside those weather-beaten walls, under that slapdash roof. Just an eye. Self-sufficient. Enormous. White and veiny. Hidden in there with nothing else to do but watch.

Another way jogging pleasures me is how it lets me turn myself into another person in another place. The city, for instance. I'm small and pale running at night in a section of town I've been warned never to enter alone even in daylight. I run burning with the secret of who I am, what I'm carrying, what I can do, secrets no one would guess just watching me jog past, a smallish, solitary white woman nearly naked on dangerous streets where she has no business being. She's crazy, they think. Or asking for it. But no one knows I can kill instantly, efficiently, with my fingers, toes and teeth. No one can see the tiny deadly weapons I've concealed on my person. In a wristband pouch. Under a Velcro flap in my running shorts. Nor would anyone believe the speed in my legs. No one can catch me unless I want to be caught.

When the huge black man springs from the shadows I let him grapple me to the ground. I tame him with my eyes. Instantly he understands. Nothing he could steal from me, throwing me down on the hard cement, hurting me, stripping me, mounting me with threats and his sweaty hand in my mouth so I won't scream, none of his violence, his rage, his hurry to split me and pound himself into me would bring the pleasure I'm ready to give of my own free will. I tell him with my eyes that I've been running to meet him. I jog along his dangerous streets because I'm prepared for him. He lets me undress him. I'm afraid for a moment his skin will be too black and I'll lose him in this dark alley. But my hands swim in the warmth of him. His smell, the damp sheen tells me he's been jogging too. It's peaceful where we are. We understand each other perfectly. Understand how we've been mistaken about each other for longer than we care to admit. Instead of destroying you, I whisper to him, I choose to win you with the gentleness in my eyes. Convert you. Release you. Then we can invent each other this quiet way, breath by breath, limb by limb, as if we have all the time in the world and our bodies are a route we learn jogging leisurely till the route's inside us, imagining us, our bodies carried along by it effortlessly. We stand and trot off shoulder to shoulder. He has Doberman legs. They twirl as if on a spit.

For weeks now they've been going by each morning. Crooker hears them first. Yapping and thrashing, running the length of her chain till it yanks her back to reality. A loud, stupid dog. I think she believes she's going to escape each time she takes a dash at her chain. She barks and snarls at them and I'd like to rubber-band her big mouth shut.

Quiet, Crooker. Hush.

Leave her be, Orland grumps to me. Barking's her job. She gets fed to bark.

We both know Crooker's useless as a watchdog. She growls at her reflection in the French doors. She howls at birds a mile away. A bug can start her yelping. Now she's carrying on as if the Beast from Babylon's slouching down the road to eat us all for breakfast and it's nobody but the joggers she's seen just like I've seen them every morning for a week. Passing by, shading to the other edge of the road because they don't want to aggravate a strange, large country dog into getting so frantic it just might snap its chain.

Nothing but those joggers she's barking at. Shut up, Crooker.

How do you know those people ain't the kind to come back snooping around here at night? Pacify the dog and them or others like them be right up on top of us before we know it.

Orland, please. What in the world are you grumbling about? You're as bad as she is.

I pay her to bark. Let her bark.

She's Crooker because at birth her tail didn't come out right. An accident in the womb. Her tail snagged on something and it's been crook-ended since. Poor creature couldn't even walk through the door of life right. But she was lucky too. Molly must have been spooked by the queerness of that tail. Must have been the humped tail because Molly ate every other pup in that litter. Ate them before we caught on and rescued this crook-tailed one.

When they pass by the window Orland doesn't even glance up. He doesn't know what he's missing. Usually he's gone long before they jog past. I forget what kept him late the morning I'm recalling. It's not that he's a hard worker or busy or conscientious. For years now the point's been to rise early and be gone. Gone the important part. Once he's gone he can figure out some excuse for going, some excuse to keep himself away. I think he may have another place where he sleeps. Tucks himself in again after he leaves my bed and dreams half the day away like a baby. Orland misses them. Might as well be a squirrel or moth riling Crooker. If he knew the woman looked as good as she does in her silky running shorts, he'd sure pay attention. If he knew the man was a big black man his stare would follow mine out the window and pay even more attention.

They seem to be about my age more or less. Woman rather short but firm and strong with tight tanned legs from jogging. She packs a bit more weight in the thighs than I do, but I haven't gained an inch anywhere nor a pound since I was a teenager. My face betrays me, but I was blessed with a trim, athletic high school beauty queen's figure. Even after the first two children Orland swore at me once when he pulled off my nightie, Damned Jailbait.

The man's legs from ankle to the fist of muscle before the knee are straight and hard as pipes, bony as dog's legs then flare into wedges of black thigh, round black man's butt. First morning I was with the kids in the front yard he waved. A big hello-how-are-you smiling-celebrity wave the way black men make you think they're movie stars or professional athletes with a big, wide wave, like you should know them if you don't and that momentary toothy spotlight they cast on you is something special from that big world where they're famous. He's waved every morning since. When I've let him see me. I know he looks for me. I wasn't wearing much more than the kids when he saw me in the yard. I know he wonders if I stroll around the house naked or sunbathe in the nude on a recliner behind the house in the fenced yard you can't see from the road. I've waited with my back close enough to the bedroom window so he'd see me if he was trying, a bare white back he could spot even though it's hard to see inside this gloomy house that hour in the morning. A little reward, if he's alert. I shushed Crooker and smiled back at him, up at him the first time, kneeling beside Billy, tying my Billyboy's shoe. We're complete smiling buddies now and the woman greets me too.

No doubt about it he liked what he saw. Three weeks now and they'd missed only two Sundays and an odd Thursday. Three times it had rained. I didn't count those days. Never do. Cooped up in the house with four children under nine you wouldn't waste your time or energy either, counting rainy, locked-in days like that because you need every ounce of patience, every speck of will, just to last to bedtime. Theirs. Which on rainy cooped-up days is followed immediately by yours because you're whipped, fatigued, bone and brain tired living in a child's world of days with no middle, end or beginning, just time like some Silly Putty you're stuck in the belly of. You can't shape it; it shapes you, but the shape is no real shape at all, it's the formlessness of no memory, no sleep that won't let you get a handle on anything, let you be anything but whatever it is twisted, pulled, worried. Three weeks minus three minus days that never count anyway minus one Thursday minus twice they perhaps went to church and that equals what? Equals the days required for us to become acquainted. To get past curiosity into *Hi there.* To follow up his presidential candidate's grin and high-five salute with my cheeriness, my punch-clock punctuality, springing tick-tock from my gingerbread house so I'm in sight, available, when they jog by. Most of the time, apparently. Always, if he takes the trouble to seek me out. As if the two of them, the tall black man and his shortish, tanned white lady companion, were yoked together, pulling the sun around the world and the two of them had been circling the globe forever, in step, in time with each other, round and round like the tiger soup in a Little Black Sambo book I read to my children, achieving a rhythm, a high-stepping pace unbroken and sufficient unto itself but I managed to blend in, to jog beside them invisible till I learned their pace and rhythm, flowing, unobtrusive, even when they both discovered me there, braced with them, running with them, undeniably part of whatever they think they are doing every morning when they pass my house and wave.

He liked what he saw because when they finally did stop and come in for the cool drinks I'd proposed first as a kind of joke, then a standing offer, seriously, no trouble, whenever, if ever, they choose to stop, then on a tray, two actual frosty tumblers of ice water they couldn't refuse without hurting my feelings, he took his and brushed my fingertips in a gesture that wasn't accidental, he wasn't a clumsy man, he took a glass and half my finger with it because he'd truly liked what he saw and admired it more close up.

Sweat sheen gleamed on him like a fresh coat of paint. He was pungent as tar. I could smell her mixed in with him. They'd made love before they jogged. Hadn't bothered to bathe before starting off on their route. She didn't see me remove my halter. He did. I sat him where he'd have to force himself to look away in order not to see me slip the halter over my head. I couldn't help standing, my arms raised like a prisoner of war, letting him take his own good time observing the plump breasts that are the only part of my anatomy below my neck not belonging to a fourteen-year-old girl. She did not see what I'd done till I turned the corner, but she seemed not to notice or not to care. I didn't need to use the line I'd rehearsed in front of the mirror, the line that went with my stripper's curtsy, with my arm stretched like Miss Liberty over my head and my wrist daintily cocked, dangling in my fingers the wisp of halter: We're very casual around here.

Instead, as we sit sipping our ice waters I laugh and say, This weather's too hot for clothes. I tease my lips with the tip of my tongue. I roll the frosted glass on my breasts. This feels so nice. Let me do you. I push up her tank top. Roll the glass on her flat stomach.

You're both so wet. Why don't you get off those damp things and sit out back? Cool off awhile. It's perfectly private.

I'll fetch us more drinks. Not too early for something stronger than water, is it?

They exchange easily deciphered looks. For my benefit, speaking to me as much as to each other. Who is this woman? What the hell have we gotten ourselves into?

I guide her up from the rattan chair. It's printed ruts across the backs of her thighs. My fingers are on her elbow. I slide open the screen door and we step onto the unfinished mess of flagstone, mismatched tile and brick Orland calls a patio. The man lags behind us. He'll see me from the rear as I balance on one leg then the other, stepping out of my shorts.

I point her to one of the lawn chairs.

Make yourself comfortable. Orland and the kids are gone for the day. Just the three of us. No one else for miles. It's glorious. Pull off your clothes, stretch out and relax.

I turn quickly and catch him liking what he sees, all of me naked, but he's wary. A little shocked. All of this too good to be true. I don't allow him time to think overly long about it.

You're joining us, aren't you? No clothes allowed.

After I plop down I watch out of the corner of my eye how she wiggles and kicks out of her shorts, her bikini underwear. Her elasti- cized top comes off over her head. Arms raised in that gesture of surrender every woman performs shrugging off what's been hiding her body. She's my sister then. I remember myself in the mirror of her. Undressing just a few minutes before, submitting, taking charge.

Crooker howls from the pen where I've stuffed her every morning since the first week. She'd been quiet till his long foot in his fancy striped running shoe touched down on the patio. Her challenge scares him. He freezes, framed a moment in the French doors.

It's OK. She's locked in her pen. All she'd do if she were here is try to lick you to death. C'mon out.

I smile over at the woman. Aren't men silly most of the time? Under that silence, those hard stares, that playacting that's supposed to be a personality, aren't they just chicken-hearted little boys most of the time? She knows exactly what I'm thinking without me saying a word. Men. Her black man no different from the rest.

He slams the screen door three times before it catches in the glides that haven't been right since Orland set them. The man can't wait to see the two of us, sisters again because I've assumed the same stiff posture in my lawn chair as she has in hers, back upright, legs extended straight ahead, ankles crossed. We are as demure as two white ladies can be in broad daylight displayed naked for the eyes of a black man. Her breasts are girlish, thumb nippled. Her bush a fuzzy creature in her lap. I'm as I promised. He'll like what he'll see, can't wait to see, but he's pretending to be in no hurry, undoing his bulky shoes lace by lace instead of kicking them off his long feet. The three chairs are arranged in a Y, foot ends converging. I steered her where I wanted her and took my seat so he'll be in the middle, facing us both, her bare flesh or mine everywhere he turns. With all his heart, every hidden fiber he wants to occupy the spot I've allotted for him, but he believes if he seems in too much of a rush, shows undue haste, he'll embarrass himself, reveal himself for what he is, what he was when Crooker's bark stopped him short.

He manages a gangly nonchalance, settling down, shooting out his legs so the soles of three pairs of feet would kiss if we inched just a wee bit closer to the bull's-eye. His shins gleam like black marble. When he's jogging he flows. Up close I'm aware of joints, angles, hinges, the struts and wires of sinew assembling him, the patchwork of his dark skin, many colors, like hers, like mine, instead of the tar-baby sleekness that trots past my window. His palms, the pale underpads of his feet have no business being the blank, clownish color they are. She could wear that color on her hands and feet and he could wear hers and the switch would barely be noticeable.

We're in place now and she closes her eyes, leans back her head and sighs. It is quiet and nice here. So peaceful, she says. This is a wonderful idea, she says, and teaches herself how to recline, levers into prone position and lays back so we're no longer three wooden Indians.

My adjustment is more subtle. I drop one foot on either side of my chair so I'm straddling it, then scoot the chair with me on it a few inches to change the angle the sun strikes my face. An awkward way to move, a lazy, stuttering adjustment useful only because it saves me standing up. And it's less than modest. My knees are spread the width of the lawn chair as I ride it to a new position. If the man has liked what he's seen so far, and I know he has, every morsel, every crumb, then he must certainly be pleased by this view. I let him sink deeper. Raise my feet back to the vinyl strips of the leg rest, but keep my knees open, yawning, draw them towards my chest, hug them, snuggle them. Her tan is browner than mine. Caramel then cream where a bikini shape is saved on her skin. I show him the bottom of me is paler, but not much paler than my thighs, my knees I peer over, knees like two big scoops of coffee ice cream I taste with the tip of my tongue.

I'm daydreaming some of the things I'll let them do to me. Tie my limbs to the bed's four corners. Kneel me, spread the cheeks of my ass. I'll suck him while her fingers ply me. When it's the black man's turn to be bondaged and he's trussed up too tight to grin, Orland bursts through the bedroom door, chain saw cradled across his chest. No reason not to let everything happen. They are clean. In good health. My body's still limber and light as a girl's. They like what they see. She's pretending to nap but I know she can sense his eyes shining, the veins thickening in his rubbery penis as it stirs and arches between his thighs he presses together so it doesn't rear up and stab at me, single me out impolitely when there are two of us, two women he must take his time with and please. We play our exchange of smiles, him on the road, me with Billy and Sarah and Carl and Augie at the edge of our corn patch. I snare his eyes, lead them down slowly to my pearly bottom, observe myself there, finger myself, study what I'm showing him so when I raise my eyes and bring his up with me again, we'll both know beyond a doubt what I've been telling him every morning when he passes is true.

No secrets now. What do you see, you black bastard? My pubic hair is always cropped close and neat, a perfect triangle decorates the fork of the Y, a Y like the one I formed with our lawn chairs. I unclasp my knees, let them droop languorously apart, curl my toes on the tubing that frames my chair. She may be watching too. But it's now or never. We must move past certain kinds of resistance, habits that are nothing more than habits. Get past or be locked like stupid baying animals in a closet forever. My eyes challenge his. Yes those are the leaves of my vagina opening. Different colors inside than outside. Part of what's inside me unfolding, exposed, like the lips of your pouty mouth.

The petals of my vagina are two knuckles spreading of a fist stuck in your face. They are the texture of the softest things you've ever touched. Softer. Better. Fleece bedding them turns subtly damp. A musk rises, gently, magically, like the mist off the oval pond that must be included in your route if you jog very far beyond my window. But you may arrive too late or too early to have noticed. About a half mile from here the road climbs as steeply as it does in this rolling country-side. Ruins of a stone wall, an open field on the right, a ragged screen of pine trees borders the other side and if you peer through them, green of meadow is broken just at the foot of a hill by a black shape difficult to distinguish from dark tree trunks and their shadows, but search hard, it rests like a mirror into which a universe has collapsed. At dawn, at dusk the pond breathes. You can see when the light and air are right, something rare squeezed up from the earth's center, hanging over this pond. I believe a ghost with long, trailing hair is marooned there and if I ever get my courage up, I've promised myself I'll go jogging past at night and listen to her sing.

valaida

Whither shall I go from thy spirit?
Or whither shall I flee from thy presence?

Bobby tell the man what he wants to hear. Bobby lights a cigarette. *Blows smoke and it rises and rises to where I sit on my cloud overhearing everything. Singing to no one. Golden trumpet from the Queen of Denmark across my knees. In my solitude. Dead thirty years now and meeting people still. Primping loose ends of my hair. Worried how I look. How I sound. Silly. Because things don't change. Bobby with your lashes a woman would kill for, all cheekbones, bushy brows and bushy upper lip, ivory when you smile. As you pretend to contemplate his jive questions behind your screen of smoke and summon me by rolling your big, brown-eyed-handsome-man eyeballs to the ceiling where smoke pauses not one instant, but scoots through and warms me where I am, tell him, Bobby, about "fabled Valaida Snow who traveled in an orchid-colored Mercedes-Benz, dressed in an orchid suit, her pet monkey rigged out in an orchid jacket and cap, with the chauffeur in orchid as well." If you need to, lie like a rug, Bobby. But don't waste the truth, either. They can't take that away from me. Just be cool. As always. Recite those countries and cities we played. Continents we conquered. Roll those faraway places with strange-sounding names around in your sweet mouth. Tell him they loved me at home too, a downhome girl*

165

from Chattanooga, Tennessee, who turned out the Apollo, not a mumbling word from wino heaven till they were on their feet hollering and clapping for more with the rest of the audience. Reveries of days gone by, yes, yes, they haunt me, baby, I can taste it. Yesteryears, yesterhours. Bobby, do you also remember what you're not telling him? Blues lick in the middle of a blind flamenco singer's moan. Mother Africa stretching her crusty, dusky hands forth, calling back her far-flung children. Later that same night both of us bad on bad red wine wheeling round and round a dark gypsy cave. Olé. Olé.

Don't try too hard to get it right, he'll never understand. He's watching your cuff links twinkle. Wondering if they're real gold and the studs real diamonds. You called me Minnie Mouse. But you never saw me melted down to sixty-eight pounds soaking wet. They beat me, and fucked me in every hole I had. I was their whore. Their maid. A stool they stood on when they wanted to reach a little higher. But I never sang in their cage, Bobby. Not one note. Cost me a tooth once, but not a note. Tell him that one day I decided I'd had enough and walked away from their hell. Walked across Europe, the Atlantic Ocean, the whole U.S. of A. till I found a quiet spot put peace back in my soul, and then I began performing again. My tunes. In my solitude. And yes. There was a pitiful little stomped-down white boy in the camp I tried to keep the guards from killing, but if he lived or died I never knew. Then or now. Monkey and chauffeur and limo and champagne and cigars and outrageous dresses with rhinestones, fringe and peekaboo slits. That's the foolishness the reporter's after. Stuff him with your MC b.s., and if he's still curious when you're finished, if he seems a halfway decent sort in spite of himself, you might suggest listening to the trumpet solo in My Heart Belongs to Daddy, *hip him to* Hot Snow, *the next to last cut, my voice and Lady Day's figure and ground, ground and figure* Dear Lord above, send back my love.

HE HEARD HER in the bathroom, faucets on and off, on and off, spurting into the sink bowl, the tub. Quick burst of shower spray, rain sound spattering plastic curtain. Now in the quiet she'll be polishing. Every fixture will gleam. *Shine's what people see. See something shiny, don't look no further, most people don't.* If she's rushed she'll wipe and polish faucets, mirrors, metal collars around drains. Learned that trick when she first came to the city and worked with gangs of girls in big downtown hotels. *Told me, said, Don't be fussing around behind in there or dusting under them things, child. Give that mirror a lick. Rub them faucets. Twenty more rooms like this one here still to do before noon.* He lowers the newspaper just enough so he'll see her when she passes through the living room, so she won't see him looking unless she stops and stares, something she never does. She knows he watches. Let him know just how much was enough once upon a time when she first started coming to clean the apartment. Back when he was still leaving for work some mornings. Before they understood each other, when suspicions were mutual and thick as the dust first time she bolted through his doorway, into his rooms, out of breath and wary-eyed like someone was chasing her and it might be him.

She'd burst in his door and he'd felt crowded. Retreated, let her stake out the space she required. She didn't bully him but demanded in the language of her brisk, efficient movements that he accustom himself to certain accommodations. They developed an etiquette that spelled out precisely how close, how distant the two of them could be once a week while she cleaned his apartment.

Odd that it took him years to realize how small she was. Shorter than him and no one in his family ever stood higher than five foot plus an inch or so of that thick, straight, black hair. America a land of giants and early on he'd learned to ignore height. You couldn't spend your days like a country lout gawking at the skyscraper heads of your new countrymen. No one had asked him so he'd never needed to describe his cleaning woman. Took no notice of her height. Her name was Clara Jackson and when she arrived he was overwhelmed by the busyness of her presence. How much she seemed to be doing all at once. Noises she'd manufacture with the cleaning paraphernalia, her humming and singing, the gum she popped, heavy thump of her heels even though she changed into tennis sneakers as soon as she crossed the threshold of his apartment, her troubled breathing, asthmatic wheezes and snorts of wrecked sinuses getting worse and worse over the years, her creaking knees, layers of dresses, dusters, slips whisper-ing, the sighs and moans and wincing ejaculations, addresses to invisi-ble presences she smuggled with her into his domain. *Yes, Lord. Save me, Jesus. Thank you, Father.* He backed away from the onslaught, the clamorous weight of it, avoided her systematically. Seldom were they both in the same room at the same time more than a few minutes because clearly none was large enough to contain them and the distance they needed.

She was bent over, replacing a scrubbed rack in the oven when he'd discovered the creases in her skull. She wore a net over her hair like serving girls in Horn and Hardart's. Under the webbing were clumps of hair, defined by furrows exposing her bare scalp. A ribbed yarmulke of hair pressed down on top of her head. Hair he'd never imagined. Like balled yarn in his grandmother's lap. Like a nursery rhyme. *Black sheep. Black sheep, have you any wool?* So different from what grew on his head, the heads of his brothers and sisters and mother and father and cousins and everyone in the doomed village where he was born, so different that he could not truly consider it hair, but some ersatz substitute used the evening of creation when hair ran out. Easier to think of her as bald. Bald and wearing a funny cap fashioned from the fur of some swarthy beast. Springy wires of it jutted from the netting. One dark strand left behind, shocking him when he discovered it marooned in the tub's gleaming, white belly, curled like a question mark at the end of the sentence he was always asking himself. He'd pinched it up in a wad of toilet paper, flushed it away.

Her bag of fleece had grayed and emptied over the years. Less of it now. He'd been tempted countless times to touch it. Poke his finger through the netting into one of the mounds. He'd wondered if she freed it from the veil when she went to bed. If it relaxed and spread against her pillow or if she slept all night like a soldier in a helmet.

When he stood beside her or behind her he could spy on the design of creases, observe how the darkness was cultivated into symmetrical plots and that meant he was taller than Clara Jackson, that he was looking down at her. But those facts did not calm the storm of motion and noise, did not undermine her power any more than the accident of growth, the half inch he'd attained over his next tallest brother, the inch eclipsing the height of his father, would have diminished his father's authority over the family, if there had been a family, the summer after he'd shot up past everyone, at thirteen the tallest, the height he remained today.

Mrs. Clara. Did you know a colored woman once saved my life?

Why is she staring at him as if he's said, Did you know I slept with a colored woman once? He didn't say that. Her silence fusses at him as if he did, as if he'd blurted out something unseemly, ungentlemanly, some insult forcing her to tighten her jaw and push her tongue into her cheek, and taste the bitterness of the hard lump inside her mouth. Why is she ready to cry, or call him a liar, throw something at him or demand an apology or look right through him, past him, the way his mother stared at him on endless October afternoons, gray slants of rain falling so everybody's trapped indoors and she's cleaning, cooking, tending a skeletal fire in the hearth and he's misbehaving, teasing his little sister till he gets his mother's attention and then he shrivels in the weariness of those sad eyes catching him in the act, piercing him, ignoring him, the hurt, iron and distance in them accusing him. Telling him for this moment, and perhaps forever, for this cruel, selfish trespass, you do not exist.

No, Mistah Cohen. That's one thing I definitely did not know.

His fingers fumble with a button, unfastening the cuff of his white shirt. He's rolling up one sleeve. Preparing himself for the work of storytelling. She has laundered the shirt how many times. It's held together by cleanliness and starch. A shirt that ought to be thrown away but she scrubs and sprays and irons it; he knows the routine, the noises. She saves it how many times, patching, mending, snipping errant threads, the frayed edges of cuff and collar hardened again so he is decent, safe within them, the blazing white breast he puffs out like a penguin when it's spring and he descends from the twelfth floor and conquers the park again, shoes shined, the remnants of that glorious head of hair slicked back, freshly shaved cheeks raw as a baby's in the brisk sunshine of those first days welcoming life back and yes he's out there in it again, his splay-foot penguin walk and gentleman's attire, shirt like a pledge, a promise, a declaration framing muted stripes of his dark tie. Numbers stamped inside the collar. Mark of the dry cleaners from a decade ago, before Clara Jackson began coming to clean. Traces still visible inside the neck of some of his shirts she's maintained impossibly long past their prime, a row of faded numerals like those he's pushing up his sleeve to show her on his skin.

The humped hairs on the back of his forearm are pressed down like grass in the woods where a hunted animal has slept. Gray hairs the color of his flesh, except inside his forearm, just above his wrist, the skin is whiter, blue veined. All of it, what's gray, what's pale, what's mottled with dark spots is meat that turns to lard and stinks a sweet sick stink to high heaven if you cook it.

Would you wish to stop now? Sit down a few minutes, please. I will make a coffee for you and my tea. I tell you a story. It is Christmas soon, no?

She is stopped in her tracks. A tiny woman, no doubt about it. Lumpy now. Perhaps she steals and hides things under her dress. Lumpy, not fat. Her shoulders round and padded. Like the derelict women who live in the streets and wear their whole wardrobes winter spring summer fall. She has put on flesh for protection. To soften blows. To ease around corners. Something cushioned to lean against. Something to muffle the sound of bones breaking when she falls. A pillow for all the heads gone and gone to dust who still find ways at night to come to her and seek a resting place. He could find uses for it. Extra flesh on her bones was not excess, was a gift. The female abundance, her thickness, her bulk reassuring as his hams shrink, his fingers become claws, the chicken neck frets away inside those razor-edged collars she scrubs and irons.

Oh you scarecrow. Death's-head stuck on a stick. Another stick lashed crossways for arms. First time you see yourself dead you giggle. You are a survivor, a lucky one. You grin, stick out your tongue at the image in the shard of smoky glass because the others must be laughing, can't help themselves, the ring of them behind your back, peeking over your scrawny shoulders, watching as you discover in the mirror what they've been seeing since they stormed the gates and kicked open the sealed barracks door and rescued you from the piles of live kindling that were to be your funeral pyre. Your fellow men. Allies. Victors. Survivors. Who stare at you when they think you're not looking, whose eyes are full of shame, as if they've been on duty here, in this pit, this stewpot cooking the meat from your bones. They cannot help themselves. You laugh to help them forget what they see. What you see. When they herded your keepers past you, their grand uniforms shorn of buttons, braid, ribbons, medals, the twin bolts of frozen

lightning, golden skulls, eagles' wings, their jackboots gone, feet bare
or in peasant clogs, heads bowed and hatless, iron faces unshaven, the
butchers still outweighed you a hundred pounds a man. You could not
conjure up the spit to mark them. You dropped your eyes in embar-
rassment, pretended to nod off because your body was too weak to
manufacture a string of spittle, and if you could have, you'd have saved
it, hoarded and tasted it a hundred times before you swallowed the
precious bile.

A parade of shambling, ox-eyed animals. They are marched past
you, marched past open trenches that are sewers brimming with
naked, rotting flesh, past barbed-wire compounds where the living sift
slow and insubstantial as fog among the heaps of dead. No one
believes any of it. Ovens and gas chambers. Gallows and whipping
posts. Shoes, shoes, shoes, a mountain of shoes in a warehouse. Shit.
Teeth. Bones. Sacks of hair. The undead who huddle into themselves
like bats and settle down on a patch of filthy earth mourning their
own passing. No one believes the enemy. He is not these harmless
farmers filing past in pillaged uniforms to do the work of cleaning up
this mess someone's made. No one has ever seen a ghost trying to
double itself in a mirror so they laugh behind its back, as if, as if the
laughter is a game and the dead one could muster up the energy to join
in and be made whole again. I giggle. I say, Who in God's name would
steal a boy's face and leave this thing?

Nearly a half century of rich meals with seldom one missed but you
cannot fill the emptiness, cannot quiet the clamor of those lost souls
starving, the child you were, weeping from hunger, those selves, those
stomachs you watched swelling, bloating, unburied for days and you
dreamed of opening them, of taking a spoon to whatever was growing
inside because you were so empty inside and nothing could be worse
than that gnawing emptiness. Why should the dead be ashamed to eat
the dead? Who are their brothers, sisters, themselves? You hear the
boy talking to himself, hallucinating milk, bread, honey. Sick when the
spoiled meat is finally carted away.

Mistah Cohen, I'm feeling kinda poorly today. If you don mind
I'ma work straight through and and gwan home early. Got all my
Christmas still to do and I'm tired.

She wags her head. Mumbles more he can't decipher. As if he'd offered many times before, as if there is nothing strange or special this morning at ten forty-seven, him standing at the china cupboard prepared to open it and bring down sugar bowl, a silver cream pitcher, cups and saucers for the two of them, ready to fetch instant coffee, a tea bag, boil water and sit down across the table from her. As if it happens each day she comes, as if this once is not the first time, the only time he's invited this woman to sit with him and she can wag her old head, stare at him moon eyed as an owl and refuse what's never been offered before.

The tattoo is faint. From where she's standing, fussing with the vacuum cleaner, she won't see a thing. Her eyes, in spite of thick spectacles, watery and weak as his. They have grown old together, avoiding each other in these musty rooms where soon, soon, no way round it, he will wake up dead one morning and no one will know till she knocks Thursday, and knocks again, then rings, pounds, hollers, but no one answers and she thumps away to rouse the super with his burly ring of keys.

He requires less sleep as he ages. Time weighs more on him as time slips away, less and less time as each second passes but also more of it, the past accumulating in vast drifts like snow in the darkness outside his window. In the wolf hours before dawn this strange city sleeps as uneasily as he does, turning, twisting, groaning. He finds himself listening intently for a sign that the night knows he's listening, but what he hears is his absence. The night busy with itself, denying him. And if he is not out there, if he can hear plainly his absence in the night pulse of the city, where is he now, where was he before his eyes opened, where will he be when the flutter of breath and heart stop?

They killed everyone in the camps. The whole world was dying there. Not only Jews. People forget. All kinds locked in the camps. Yes. Even Germans who were not Jews. Even a black woman. Not gypsy. Not African. American like you, Mrs. Clara.

They said she was a dancer and could play any instrument. Said she could line up shoes from many countries and hop from one pair to the next, performing the dances of the world. They said the Queen of Denmark had honored her with a gold trumpet. But she was there, in hell with the rest of us.

A woman like you. Many years ago. A lifetime ago. Young then as you would have been. And beautiful. As I believe you must have been, Mrs. Clara. Yes. Before America entered the war. Already camps had begun devouring people. All kinds of people. Yet she was rare. Only woman like her I ever saw until I came here, to this country, this city. And she saved my life.

Poor thing.

I was just a boy. Thirteen years old. The guards were beating me. I did not know why. Why? They didn't need a why. They just beat. And sometimes the beating ended in death because there was no reason to stop, just as there was no reason to begin. A boy. But I'd seen it many times. In the camp long enough to forget why I was alive, why anyone would want to live for long. They were hurting me, beating the life out of me but I was not surprised, expected no explanation. I remember curling up as I had seen a dog once cowering from the blows of a rolled newspaper. In the old country lifetimes ago. A boy in my village staring at a dog curled and rolling on its back in the dust outside the baker's shop and our baker in his white apron and tall white hat striking this mutt again and again. I didn't know what mischief the dog had done. I didn't understand why the fat man with flour on his apron was whipping it unmercifully. I simply saw it and hated the man, felt sorry for the animal, but already the child in me understood it could be no other way so I rolled and curled myself against the blows as I'd remembered that spotted dog in the dusty village street because that's the way it had to be.

Then a woman's voice in a language I did not comprehend reached me. A woman angry, screeching. I heard her before I saw her. She must have been screaming at them to stop. She must have decided it was better to risk dying than watch the guards pound a boy to death. First I heard her voice, then she rushed in, fell on me, wrapped herself around me. The guards shouted at her. One tried to snatch her away. She wouldn't let go of me and they began to beat her too. I heard the thud of clubs on her back, felt her shudder each time a blow was struck.

She fought to her feet, dragging me with her. Shielding me as we stumbled and slammed into a wall.

My head was buried in her smock. In the smell of her, the smell of dust, of blood. I was surprised how tiny she was, barely my size, but strong, very strong. Her fingers dug into my shoulders, squeezing, gripping hard enough to hurt me if I hadn't been past the point of feeling pain. Her hands were strong, her legs alive and warm, churning, churning as she pressed me against herself, into her. Somehow she'd pulled me up and back to the barracks wall, propping herself, supporting me, sheltering me. Then she screamed at them in this language I use now but did not know one word of then, cursing them, I'm sure, in her mother tongue, a stream of spit and sputtering sounds as if she could build a wall of words they could not cross.

The kapos hesitated, astounded by what she'd dared. Was this black one a madwoman, a witch? Then they tore me from her grasp, pushed me down and I crumpled there in the stinking mud of the compound. One more kick, a numbing, blinding smash that took my breath away. Blood flooded my eyes. I lost consciousness. Last I saw of her she was still fighting, slim, beautiful legs kicking at them as they dragged and punched her across the yard.

You say she was colored?

Yes. Yes. A dark angel who fell from the sky and saved me.

Always thought it was just you people over there doing those terrible things to each other.

He closes the china cupboard. Her back is turned. She mutters something at the metal vacuum tubes she's unclamping. He realizes he's finished his story anyway. Doesn't know how to say the rest. She's humming, folding rags, stacking them on the bottom pantry shelf. Lost in the cloud of her own noise. Much more to his story, but she's not waiting around to hear it. This is her last day before the holidays. He'd sealed her bonus in an envelope, placed the envelope where he always does on the kitchen counter. The kitchen cabinet doors have magnetic fasteners for a tight fit. After a volley of doors clicking, she'll be gone. When he's alone preparing his evening meal, he depends on those clicks for company. He pushes so they strike not too loud, not too soft. They punctuate the silence, reassure him like the solid slamming of doors in big sedans he used to ferry from customer to customer. How long since he'd been behind the wheel of a car? Years, and now another year almost gone. In every corner of the city they'd be welcoming their Christ, their New Year with extravagant displays of joy. He thinks of Clara Jackson in the midst of her family. She's little but the others are brown and large, with lips like spoons for serving the sugary babble of their speech. He tries to picture them, eating and drinking, huge people crammed in a tiny, shabby room. Unimaginable, really. The faces of her relatives become his. Everyone's hair is thick and straight and black.

hostages

Her first husband, Ari, was darker than I am. Egyptian burnt toast with black beetle brows and sharp bones and hair tarry and straight as Geronimo's. I remembered him as fast and slick on the soccer field, a breakaway, one-on-one scorer with a rocket launcher of a foot. He played the game the way I imagined myself playing if I'd grown up in a soccer country, using my feet to catch and pass and shoot from distance, my feet as deadly as my hands that had learned their style on asphalt basketball courts in the city. Once I'd asked him about the constant fighting in the Middle East. He said he'd done his time in the Israeli army because all young men and women owed it. And said no, his squad had never been under fire, but close, and that was close enough for him. A black sky full of stars. The immensity of the open desert at night like a mirror so deep all those millions of stars got eaten and not a drop of light reflected from the sand. Close enough to know he never wanted closer to war than that field exercise near the border, so close that you weren't permitted to talk or light a cigarette after dark. A tomahawk of a face. All edges and thin, stark bone skittish under mahogany skin. To me he was the archetypal Arab, the swift bedouin horseman of the movies, so I was confused. Weren't Arabs enemies of the Jewish state? Years later when I questioned her about his dark skin, his accent, harsher, more guttural, more foreign than hers, she said, Yes, an Arab . . . he was an Arab.

And my family nearly disowned me when I married him. My mother hated Ari. Because he was irresponsible, she said. But really because he was poor and dark, as dark as you are. More eastern than European. A matter of class as much as race. My relatives from the old country told me my grandmother would break into hives if Yiddish was spoken around her. My mother barely escaped with her life from the Nazis. But even that experience didn't convince her she was a Jew. In Israel she remains a hostage, a queen in exile.

I hadn't seen her or her husband Ari for years so it was like a ghost asking after ghosts. She'd emigrated permanently from Israel, had another life, an American husband now. A good man. Their son Eli had dribbled apple juice from his bottle on my bare stomach as I bounced him on my knee. Her son and husband, my wife and kids were having lunch in the cottage. We'd stayed on the dock, enjoying the lake, a cloudless blue sky, the chance to reconnect. I'd asked about Ari because I wanted to remind her I knew some of her history, her loves and pain before this moment, this day we'd all seemed to emerge bright and flushed from an amusement park ride. Two couples and their children, families who'd never seen each other as families before so there were a thousand ways of saying nothing. Kid stories, stale news of shared acquaintances, endless chatty ways of squandering our chances to say something by saying nothing. Till this moment when just the two of us are sitting alone, quiet, gazing at the calm surface of the water, light shows beyond the cove where wind fans the lake into shimmering pools and I questioned her about Ari and wondered what had become of him, of us, of the ten or twelve years since I'd wondered about anything just this way.

I love my life. I'm very lucky. When Eli's a little older, perhaps I'll look for a teaching job. To get out of the house. Michael's away all day. And I don't have many friends. The women where we've moved are impossible. They do nothing. Absolutely nothing all day. It would drive me crazy.

What would have happened if you'd taken me home to your parents?

She smiles. Not easy. It wouldn't have been easy.

Do you think Ari ever noticed anything?

He was too sure of himself to be jealous.

Too bad we never gave him something to be jealous about. Very, very jealous.

I remember trying.

No. You flirted, that's all. You were just as chicken as I was. You flirted.

And you flirted back.

I didn't know we were allowed to go further.

Such an innocent.

We were young. Just starting out our marriages. We didn't know any better.

Live and learn, eh. And what have you learned? Is it better to sneak around?

Damned if you do. Probably if you don't.

Has that made you unhappy?

Unhappy. Happy. Who cares? What's happy or unhappy when things are as ugly as they are? The rich in a feeding frenzy. The poor gearing up to fight one another for leftovers. Race hate's respectable again.

She asks me how I can live here where people despise me because of the color of my skin. I ask her where else should I go? Would they love me in her old country?

How do you think Ari feels about the troubles on the West Bank? Soldiers shooting Arab children daily.

She sighs: I don't know.

But he's there, isn't he? In Israel?

He's an Israeli.

I'm an American.

I HEAR the others returning. Twist in my seat.

Did you bring bread for the ducks?

A bagful.

Eli will love the ducks. That mother and her babies come by every day. She started with ten. Down to seven little Indians now.

Every summer we see these strings of babies. About half survive. Towards the end of August the little ones are as big as the parents.

If you're still, they'll walk right up to your toes.

Yeah. You know they're really relaxed when they squat and shit on the ramp. See all those white freckles?

I watch bread crumbs strike the water. The ripples. The sallies of the birds. Their necks dart. A pecking order is maintained. Smallest last. They climb, half flying, half flutter and jump, onto the ramp. Waddle up burlap matting towards us. The mother remains in the lake, her yellow feet visible underwater, churning away. Seeing the busyness of her feet as she sits serene in the water, it's as if I'm privy to a secret, that I know something about her she doesn't know I know.

GUERRILLAS HAVE DEMANDED the release of fifty freedom fighters within twenty-four hours or they will begin executing hostages, one an hour till all ten are dead. No official response to their demand has been announced at this time.

We discuss the crisis. Everyone in a lounge chair except my boys, who are digging in the sand off to the left on a tiny horseshoe of beach and Eli sitting behind us on a blanket with a few of their old toys. Ducklings settle into tufted, downy balls, tuck their heads into fluff, seven of them parked midway up the ramp. Eli squeals. The mother duck squawks her homing squawk, curve of her neck and head craned like a periscope as she rotates 360 degrees then rises in the water beating her wings. The whole brood kicks towards open water.

Eli had strayed off the blanket we'd spread to save his bare feet from the hot deck. He sobs, tries to climb back up her arms as she sets him down again on the blanket. She points to the gleaming, painted boards. Hot. Hot. Mimics jerking her finger back from a flame. Wiggles it. Blows on it. Hot. Hot.

HOSTAGES ARE PEOPLE held for ransom. Someone must pay something to preserve a hostage's life. Hostages are detained by force, ripped from one world, plunged into the limbo of another. Other human beings assume godlike power over the lives of hostages. Being a hostage is a little like dying and awaiting resurrection. Hostages are commodities, their humanity put on hold while they serve as chips in a power game; they are also abstractions, symbols. Thus, the existence of hostages is paradoxically material and immaterial. Hostages are equally victims of those who love them and those who care nothing about them. Hostages are often blindfolded or beaten or stripped or raped to impress upon them their utter dependence and vulnerability, the absolute power of their captors. Sometimes hostages are displayed, photographed, paraded, videotaped, shown to be dupes, fools, proof of their captors' glory, the impotence of the violated.

THINK OF HOUSES set miles back from sidewalks, jowly houses with green bibs of lawn tucked tight under their chins. Houses no one lives in. Because the streets are so wide and quiet. Yet shrubs, grass and enormous trees are too well groomed to be natural so someone must tend them, swarthy foreigners with loud machines and rattletrap pickups who descend regularly like locusts and then disappear without a trace except the brutal square-cornered neatness they leave behind. No one lives in the houses, at least not anyone like you know, unless you yourself reside in one of these suburban castles and even then you must have your doubts. Mirrors, polished surfaces of wood, tile, porcelain and stainless steel gleam not so much to receive your image as to devour it. The scale of walls and stairs and hallways oppresses you. Exotic, imported ornaments recall lost souls, passing as you do through the emptiness, insinuating that you are always a stranger in this monument built for gods.

Think of owning this residence, the equivalent of a circus tent in square feet enclosed under various hipped and cantilevered roofs that stamp the silhouette of your dwelling each night against the backdrop of burning sky. Think of a child crying. A child's sleepscape shadowed by storm clouds till a peal of thunder cracks the sky and a finger of light stabs down to pluck out his eyes, pluck out his eyes. His first outcry is sudden. Then you hear heartbroken sobbing. He's been undone that quickly by the dream. And you dry your hands on a tea towel hanging by the kitchen sink, a towel pretending to be grapes, strawberries, apples, bananas, cherries, the ever ripe and perfect mood of bright fruit you chose to brighten your kitchen. Oh love, you think, your empty womb pushed up against teak cabinetry, squeezed there as if the room has slammed shut behind you. Warmth spreads below your waist, beginning and gone before you have a chance to acknowledge it, the subtle guilt and expectation shooed away as baby Eli weeps.

Think of being blindfolded. It's the price you pay for being alive. You open your eyes each morning and a guillotine crashes down, the dream ends. You are snatched into another version of reality. One voted upon, certified and practiced by consenting adults. You recognize your place in it as the furniture of your room eases into view. Like starting up a novel you closed the previous day, just before sleep. Nothing has intervened. Characters take up midsentence where you've left them when you grew drowsy and slipped under the covers and reached up to twist off a lamp. The story is comfortable, a page-turner. You know how it ends. But there are pages and pages to go, a best-seller thicker than your mattress, your fondest wishes.

Eli, Eli, darling. I'm coming, dear.

Your fingers are clean as a surgeon's. Why aren't they stained by the colors of strangled fruit? Why do I hesitate, staring at fingers as if I've never seen them before, one pale hand drawing the other when Eli needs me? Grief is swarming over him, dragging him back into that other world. His skull, his black bones shine through his skin.

He needs me. Why am I taking my time? Time that's not mine. Eli dear, will you still love me when I loom over your crib, my face bigger than the moon, my son, my stupid hands dropping into your bed, huge, awkward and dangerous as the weights at the end of chains wrecking the inner city whose ruins we must tour someday? Arm in arm, my son, we'll make a visit. I will be a frail, old lady with a hat tied under my chin. You will be my handsome Prince Charming. No one will wish us harm.

AFTER HE is diapered and fed and laid aside like a letter from someone at a great distance who is adored, she finishes as much as she remembers of what she was doing in the kitchen, then takes her spot at the upstairs window in the master bedroom. She recalls grooves scuffed inches deep into the granite floor of a guard post outside the gate of an ancient temple. She remembers her slow, rising horror—how many centuries, how many soft feet, how many hours shuffling and fretting had gouged these bruises and dents into the blackened stones. But she can't recall where she saw the footprints. Not in this infant nation. It must have been Greece or Turkey or Egypt or her own wounded country.

She finds herself asking other questions she can't answer. Which are more important, more *real,* omens or the events they portend. Today she believes it's omens. What happens, happens indiscriminately to everybody. The insult is universal, undistinguished. But the thrill, the dread of foreknowing rescues the seer from the numbing routine of events.

Tomorrow she'll fall on the other side of the argument. Events, with or without predictions, the steady day-by-day accumulation of the ordinary is what counts. Events without omens remain events, but what good are omens without the unraveling of what they predict?

But today she'll choose omens. Stirrings, presentiments in the cage of her skull. So what if nothing happens. So what if tomorrow comes or doesn't come. Omens have light and weight and spin. She relishes their luminous assurance that there's more to this life than meets the eye.

FROM THE SECOND-STORY WINDOW of the master bedroom she spies on black girls. Jamaican, Haitian, Puerto Rican, island girls in summer dresses, winter spring summer or fall. Colored girls in bright-colored dresses, rainbow blouses tucked into designer jeans. Emigrants like her. Women from warm countries who will always die a little when ice and snow cover this cold, adopted land. Their round, lively butts are balloons advertising themselves and the names of merchant princes. She envies the confidence of their buttocks. How do these maids, cooks, housecleaners and nannies afford designer jeans? Ari once described himself as *poor not cheap,* when she'd asked him why he'd spend money on a barber when she could trim his hair for him. She sees Ari wag his head, then grin and reach out to pat her hand, *poor not cheap.*

Is it Ari she's waiting for at the window this morning? Many mornings it was. Her Star. She called him that, *Star*, to tease him about his ambition to captain the national team, the six-pointed silver emblem he wore around his neck. He never grew older than the teenager he was when they first met in school. Slim and strong, like the boy Michelangelo discovered in a block of marble, only scrawnier, tougher, with a scrim of black hair webbing his dark skin. Ari running naked as a statue down the wide suburban sidewalks, his shadow bobbing on green lawns that reflect light in pools after automatic sprinklers spin their morning showers. Ari dressed like a cowboy strolling on the balls of his feet, ready to change pace or direction, hands poised above six-shooters crisscrossed low on his hips. Ari never troubles her broad street with its houses set back green miles from the curb except in her daydreams, her prophesies, and this morning at her post well before 9:00 A.M. with a whole day's shift still to pull, she isn't conjuring him, she's waiting for Eli's father to return in his purring German car.

Twenty minutes ago, twenty years ago she'd listened to the car, with her husband sealed inside, whine down the black strip of driveway, then roar into the gray street. He drives to the station, catches an early train to the city, leaves his sleek automobile with other sleek automobiles in the park-and-lock lot. She wishes he would invite her, just once, to ride with him to the station in the morning. She envies his car. She's jealous of its perfection, its sensuous leather upholstery, flashing digital lights. She'd crawl into the backseat after he boarded his train, tuck her legs under herself, doze through the day till another train brings him back. Like a pet. Like his faithful puppy automobile. All day long—heat or snow or rain—curled uncomplaining in the backseat. She'd enjoy weather against the roof. The rain's precise, military music. She'd be a piece of fruit ripening in a bell jar.

What if he forgot to retrieve her from those acres of expensive machines? Locked inside the car she'd shrivel like a raisin or turn to sticky, melted goo. Weeks later when he opens the driver's door, the putrid stench of her would embarrass him. Columns of sleek cars avert their eyes, turn up their noses as he stands stunned, the perfectly engineered handle in his hand. Guilt for a crime he didn't commit written on his face, reflected in the sticky puddle that stinks so badly his eyes water. Home again. Home again. She'd wait through storm and sun, the tease of express trains that never stop. She'll purr, she'll whine. Her doors will seal him safely in. Her wipers dry his tears.

SHE REMEMBERS two of her dreams: girls playing in a huge, manicured backyard. They are tickled by the coincidence of their names, the fact each contains *Van*—Vanita, Van Tyne, Vanessa, Vanna, Van de Meer, et cetera. They've just discovered this joke and it delights them, but very quickly the mood shifts. Giggles cease, longer and longer gaps of silence. They become aware of the size of the backyard. Its emptiness. There's really no one else to talk to as the identities of the group shrink to one girl. The silliness of the names is a mocking echo in her mind. The others have *van*ished. Far away, trailing the squeal and thunder of an old-fashioned engine, boxcars wobble along clickedy-click on toy wheels, like ducks bobbing, wise old heads nodding, sucking on pipes, puffing silent rings of smoke. She is weary and lonely. The jabbering of her friends, the syllable *Van* they shared are part of the weight this yard has accumulated. Its history bears down on her.

If she doesn't awaken from this next dream she'll be dead. But if she awakens, it will be two in the morning and worse than death. She will blunder around in the darkness, drink water, pop a pill, sit on the toilet. Sleep won't come again for hours. Her heart thumps and sputters. Not enough air. Her lungs ache. A bear scratches at the window. She's alert now. Resigned, she lifts the covers and cool, merciful air infiltrates the clamminess beneath the blankets she steeples with her knees. A slab of icy hip beside her. Someone naked and dead in her bed. She is afraid to move. She knows it's her body lying next to her and the thought of touching it again paralyzes her. She's soaked in her own sweat. Thick as blood or paint. She can't see its color but knows it's dark. The color of her lover, a man whose sweat turns her to a tar baby too, wet and black and sticky. She will die if she moves, if she doesn't. If she opens her eyes, the iridescent clock will say 2:00 A.M.

· · ·

DON'T LEAVE ME this morning. Take me with you. Did the car ever make demands? Hang on him like one of these island girls with a dancer's ass, a witch's long, vermilion fingernails. Please take me. I can't bear to be alone today.

They wouldn't whimper it like that, would they? In their island babble she can't understand there would be better ways of saying *don't go*. Sometimes they were squirrels chattering. Squirrel talk. Squirrel brains. But if they wanted a man to stay with them, they'd put music in their voices. Blue music. Old blue songs learned from their grandmothers, the wrinkled ones with shopping bags who waited at the station, too. Past their prime, but still waiting, still dangerous. Terrorists hiding bombs in their bags. The black girls whisper in husky, fruity warbles. Stay and love me, baby. Don't go, darling. They'd twist the keys from his fingers and lead him up the carpeted stairs. They'd fuck all day, not notice her standing at the window wishing him back when he only left twenty minutes ago.

THE LAMED-VOV are God's hostages. Without them humanity would suffocate in a single cry. She learned about them in a French novel that claimed they belong to ancient Talmudic legend. Lamed-Vov are sponges drawing mankind's suffering into themselves. She thought the dead photographer Diane Arbus might be one. A pampered rich girl escaping the suburbs, and wandering city streets, the city's misfits and lost ones her subjects—twins, midgets, corpses, derelicts, transvestites, giants, carny freaks, junkies, whores surrendering to her camera till the weight of it around her neck was too much and she slit her wrists and bled to death in the bathtub. According to the novel a thousand years is not long enough to thaw the agony each Lamed-Vov endures. When little Eli lay in an oxygen tent, racked by pneumonia, hollow-eyed, skeletal, too weak to cry or breathe or meet her eyes as she stared into his glass cage, she'd promised God that she'd be good, stop smoking, forfeit her life, do anything if her son was allowed to live. She begged the fever to leap from his chest to hers. The sneer, the nod dismissing, mocking her, was cold, cold. Why bargain if you held all the chips?

· · ·

WE HAVE SETTLED into the languor of a perfect Maine summer day. The loons were wild last night. Baying like dogs at the moon. They fractured sleep so it's easy to drowse away the day, sunbathing, cool dips in crisp lake water, then more sun and a few pages of a book, then more drowse. At about twelve we heard their car descending the gravel road behind our cottage. A new husband, new baby. It will be fun seeing her again. Meeting them.

GUERRILLAS HAVE DEMANDED the release of one hundred freedom fighters within twenty-four hours or they will begin executing hostages, one an hour till all ten are dead. No official response to their demand has been announced at this time.

Are guerrillas devaluing the currency of guerrilla lives, admitting one enemy life is worth ten of theirs? Isn't this reverse discrimination? Isn't this equation just what their enemies have been asserting all along? Who's responsible for calculating such odds? Do children under twelve count as fractions of lives? Will some patriot volunteer a son or daughter if half a life is needed to make a deal come out even? Is it possible to bank hostages against future needs? A stockpile available for potential negotiations. If a hostage dies in transit, does he or she retain value? Can the body be turned in for credit? Is being a hostage any less a vocation than sainthood? Are hostages called or do they choose their calling?

ONCE, WHEN I was a seed in my mother's womb, I overheard a gravelly voice threaten her with losing me if she didn't do exactly as the voice commanded. I'm here today telling the story so I must have survived, she must have paid.

In another version of the myth Adam weeps uncontrollably as Eve gives birth, a result neither had expected, another hostage in the garden.

BLACK GIRLS HAVE big teeth and laugh like squirrels. Their tails aren't bushy, but they're big, stamped with brand names like cattle. His dark three-piece suit for the next day hangs like a flayed skin in the closet behind her, which is larger than a room in most people's houses. If she turns from the window and walks into the closet and touches the suit, she will surely cry.

BLACK WOMEN SEEM fond of one another. They chatter endlessly. They touch one another constantly. Like her family's cook primped dough for the oven. She wishes they would talk to her but they fall silent when she approaches. Two of them are a crowd. Laughing, jostling, pulling faces, a choir of voices, astonished, pleased by each other, strangers, old, old comrades. If she didn't see them everyday after they finish their inside duties and take to the wide streets and the parklet at the end of the block with their white children, if she hadn't observed for hours from her solitary perch, she'd believe they were different girls each day and each day the new ones began fresh, innocent, reinventing those patterns, those intrigues she spied upon and registered in an empty book she thought she was saving for her own secrets.

ONE AFTERNOON in a dark room with shades drawn they were watching home movies, forty-year-old flicks filmed before she was born when her husband was the chubby baby of his family. He's dressed for the occasion in a sunsuit remembered as blue. For these family follies, this gray-toned frolic aged like fine wine in a family vault with no other purpose than to preserve a day in time, a perfect prosperous day collected so everyone might see it and say Yes, life was like that, we smiled and mugged for the camera and yes isn't that a gorgeous automobile, yes, we had firm flesh, fine clothes, jewelry and fun long before there was a Jewish state and Arabs worrying its borders, Arabs with their damp jackal snouts prying into our secret lives, our vaults, our bright day in time when your husband was our boy-king tasty and plump as linen-covered basketsful of lunch lined up on a picnic table on the huge lawn of the huge house where he carried you forty years later across the threshold to meet us. She meets them again, the dead, the living, his family then and now in a funny paper of a movie after temple and a drive in the countryside.

She said she could tell me everything because I was black. Because I was black, I would understand.

She whispers into the shadows rippling across her husband's face. What year were these taken?

He whispers back, half of him still entranced by the dreamy action on the screen, I'm three . . . so it's 1943.

My mother was a prisoner then. In Auschwitz. I say the terrible word louder. *Auschwitz.* So I'm certain. Hope no one else overhears. Hope he understands. I don't want to spoil the party.

IN ONE SCENE faces peer from a flat-topped touring sedan with a wire-spoked spare wheel inset behind the curl of its front fender. The photographer must be thinking of the circus in this shot. The magic car from which twenty clowns and a brace of dancing girls emerge, free at last after it wobbles down the midway. While the occupants are hidden from sight, nobody tattles, nobody lets out a peep. Then the cat springs from the bag. Joke's on everybody. A multitude stuffed like sardines in that tiny tin-can car with a calliope whistle. *Um pah. Um pah.* An astounded audience squeals as we unfold. That old circus scam is what the cinematographer must have had in mind as she sees his family packed in the car staring back at the camera.

SHE FEARS her husband might be hijacked on one of his business trips abroad. His grainy likeness appears on a tabloid's front page. He hasn't changed much. She recalls a sequence in the home movie. Or the movie triggers a flash-forward and she visualizes the kind of hostage he'd make. He's in a blue sunsuit, eating ice cream. He stops licking. A dreamy then blank, myopic stare held for a fraction of a second, long enough to register as a snapshot she glues in her secret, empty album. The picture's saved forty years. Long enough for the victim to be seen by millions. An exchange is being negotiated. She wonders how many dark lives must be sacrificed.

surfiction

Among my notes on the first section of Charles Chesnutt's *Deep Sleeper* there are these remarks:

Not reality but a culturally learned code—that is, out of the infinite number of ways one might apprehend, be conscious, be aware, a certain arbitrary pattern or finite set of indicators is sanctioned and over time becomes identical with reality. The signifier becomes the signified. For Chesnutt's contemporaries reality was *I* (eye) centered, the relationship between man and nature disjunctive rather than organic, time was chronological, linear, measured by man-made units—minutes, hours, days, months, etc. To capture this reality was then a rather mechanical procedure—a voice at the center of the story would begin to unravel reality: a catalog of sensuous detail, with the visual dominant, to indicate nature, *out there* in the form of clouds, birdsong, etc. A classical painting rendered according to the laws of perspective, the convention of the window frame through which the passive spectator observes. The voice gains its authority because it is literate, educated, perceptive, because it has aligned itself correctly with the frame, because it drops the cues, or elements of the code, methodically. The voice is reductive, as any code ultimately is; an implicit reinforcement occurs as the text elaborates itself through the voice: the voice gains authority because things are in order, the order gains authority because it is established by a voice we trust. For example the opening lines of *Deep Sleeper* . . .

It was four o'clock on Sunday afternoon, in the month of July. The air had been hot and sultry, but a light, cool breeze had sprung up; and occasional cirrus clouds overspread the sun, and for a while subdued his fierceness. We were all out on the piazza—as the coolest place we could find—my wife, my sister-in-law and I. The only sounds that broke the Sabbath stillness were the hum of an occasional vagrant bumblebee, or the fragmentary song of a mockingbird in a neighboring elm . . .

Rereading, I realize my *remarks* are a pastiche of received opinions from Barthes, certain cultural anthropologists and linguistically oriented critics and Russian formalists, and if I am beginning a story rather than an essay, the whole stew suggests the preoccupations of Borges or perhaps a footnote in Barthelme. Already I have managed to embed several texts within other texts, already a rather unstable mix of genres and disciplines and literary allusion. Perhaps for all of this, already a grim exhaustion of energy and possibility, readers fall away as if each word is a well-aimed bullet.

More Chesnutt. This time from the text of the story, a passage unremarked upon except that in the margin of the Xeroxed copy of the story I am copying this passage from, several penciled comments appear. I'll reproduce the entire discussion.

Latin: secundus-tertius-quartus-quintus.

"Tom's gran'daddy wuz name' Skundus," he began. "He had a brudder name' Tushus en' ernudder name' Squinchus." The old man paused a moment and gave his leg another hitch.

"drawing out Negroes"—custom in old south, new north, a constant in America. Ignorance of one kind delighting ignorance of another. Mask to mask. The real joke.

My sister-in-law was shaking with laughter. "What remarkable names!" she exclaimed. "Where in the world did they get them?"

Naming: plantation owner usurps privilege of family. Logos. Word made flesh. Power. Slaves named in order of appearance. Language masks joke. Latin opaque to blacks.

Note: last laugh. Blacks (mis)pronounce secundus. *Secundus = Skundus. Black speech takes over—opaque to white—subverts original purpose of name. Language (black) makes joke. Skundus has new identity.*

"Dem names wuz gun ter 'em by ole Marse Dugal' McAdoo, w'at I use' ter b'long ter, en' dey use' ter b'long ter. Marse Dugal' named all de babies w'at wuz bawn on de plantation. Dese young un's mammy wanted ter call 'em sump'n plain en' simple, like *Rastus* er *Caesar* er *George Wash'n'ton,* but ole Marse say no, he want all de niggers on his place ter hab diffe'nt names, so he kin tell 'em apart. He'd done use' up all de common names, so he had ter take sump'n else. Dem names he gun Skundus en' his brudders is Hebrew names en' wuz tuk out'n de Bible."

I distinguish remarks from footnotes. Footnotes clarify specifics; they answer simple questions. You can always tell from a good footnote the question which it is answering. For instance: *The Short Fiction of Charles W. Chesnutt,* edited by Sylvia Lyons Render (Washington, D.C.: Howard University Press, 1974), 47. Clearly someone wants to know, Where did this come from? How might I find it? Tell me where to look. OK. Whereas remarks, at least my remarks, the ones I take the trouble to write out in my journal,* which is where the first long cogitation appears/appeared [the ambiguity here is not intentional but situational, not imposed for irony's sake but necessary because the first long cogitation—*my remark*—being referred to both *appears* in the sense that every time I open my journal, as I did a few moments ago, as I am doing NOW to check for myself and to exemplify for you the accuracy of my statement—the remark *appears* as it does/did just now. (Now?) But the remark (original), if we switch to a different order of time, treating the text diachronically rather than paradigmatically, the remark *appeared;* which poses another paradox. How lan-

Journal unpaginated. In progress. Unpublished. Many hands.

guage or words are both themselves and *Others,* but not always. Because the negation implied by *appearance,* the so-called "shadow within the rock," is *disappearance.* The reader correctly anticipates such an antiphony or absence suggesting presence (shadow play) between the text as realized and the text as shadow of its act. The dark side paradoxically is the absence, the nullity, the white space on the white page between the white words not stated but implied. Forever], are more complicated.

The story, then, having escaped the brackets, can proceed. In this story, *Mine,* in which Chesnutt replies to Chesnutt, remarks, comments, asides, allusions, footnotes, quotes from Chesnutt have so far played a disproportionate role, and if this sentence is any indication, continue to play a grotesquely unbalanced role, will roll on.

It is four o'clock on Sunday afternoon, in the month of July. The air has been hot and sultry, but a light, cool breeze has sprung up; and occasional cirrus clouds (?) overspread the sun, and for a while subdue his fierceness. We were all out on the piazza (stoop?)—as the coolest place we could find—my wife, my sister-in-law and I. The only sounds that break the Sabbath stillness are the hum of an occasional bumblebee, or the fragmentary song of a mockingbird in a neighboring elm . . .

The reader should know now by certain unmistakable signs (codes) that a story is beginning. The stillness, the quiet of the afternoon tells us something is going to happen, that an event more dramatic than birdsong will rupture the static tableau. We expect, we know a payoff is forthcoming. We know this because we are put into the passive posture of readers or listeners (consumers) by the narrative unraveling of a reality which, because it is unfolding in time, slowly begins to take up our time and thus is obliged to give us something in return; the story enacts word by word, sentence by sentence in *real* time. Its moments will pass and our moments will pass simultaneously, hand in glove if you will. The literary, storytelling convention exacts this kind of relaxation or compliance or collaboration (conspiracy). Sentences slowly fade in, substituting fictive sensations for those which normally constitute our awareness. The shift into the fictional world is made easier because the conventions by which we identify the real world are conventions shared

with and often learned from our experience with fictive reality.
What we are accustomed to acknowledging as awareness is actually
a culturally learned, contingent condensation of many potential
awarenesses. In this culture—American, Western, twentieth-century
—an awareness that is eye centered, disjunctive as opposed to organic, that responds to clock time, calendar time more than biologi-
cal cycles or seasons, that assumes nature is external, acting on us
rather than through us, that tames space by manmade structures and
with the *I* as center defines other people and other things by the
nature of their relationship to the *I* rather than by the independent
integrity of the order they may represent.

An immanent experience is being prepared for, is being framed. The
experience will be real because the narrator produces his narration
from the same set of conventions by which we commonly detect
reality—dates, buildings, relatives, the noises of nature.

All goes swimmingly until a voice from the watermelon patch
intrudes. Recall the dialect reproduced above. Recall Kilroy's phallic
nose. Recall Earl and Cornbread, graffiti artists, their spray-paint cans
notorious from one end of the metropolis to the other—from Society
Hill to the Jungle, nothing safe from them and the artists uncatchable
until hubris leads them to attempt the gleaming virgin flanks of a 747
parked on runway N-16 at the Philadelphia International Airport.
Recall your own reflection in the fun house mirror and the moment
of doubt when you turn away and it turns away and you lose sight of
it and it naturally enough loses sight of you and you wonder where
it's going and where you're going and the wrinkly reflecting plate still
is laughing behind your back at someone.

The reader here pauses	Picks up in mid-
stream a totally irrelevant conversation: ... by accident twenty-seven double-columned pages by acci-dent?	
	I mean it started that way
started yeah I can see starting curiosity whatever staring over	

somebody's shoulder or a letter
maybe you think yours till you see
not meant for you at all

I'm not trying to excuse just understand it was not premedi-
tated your journal is your journal
that's not why I mean I didn't
forget your privacy or lose respect
on purpose

it was just there and, well we seldom talk and I was desperate we
haven't been going too well for a
long time

and getting worse getting finished when shit like this comes
down

I wanted to stop but I needed
something from you more than
you've been giving so when I saw
it there I picked it up you understand not to read but because it
was you you and holding it was all
a part of you

you're breaking my heart

please don't dismiss

dismiss dismiss what I won't dismiss your prying how you defiled
how you took advantage

don't try to make me a criminal
the guilt I feel it I know right
from wrong and accept whatever
you need to lay on me but I had
to do it I was desperate for something, anything, even if the cost

was rifling my personal life searching through my guts for ammuni-
tion and did you get any did you
learn anything you can use on me
Shit I can't even remember the

whole thing is a jumble I'm blocking it all out my own journal and
I can't remember a word because
it's not mine anymore

I'm sorry I knew I shouldn't as
soon as I opened it I flashed on the
Bergman movie the one where
she reads his diary I flashed on
how underhanded how evil a thing
she was doing but I couldn't stop

A melodrama a god damned
Swedish subtitled melodrama
you're going to turn it around
aren't you make it into

The reader can replay the tape at leisure. Can amplify or expand. There is plenty of blank space on the pages. A sin really given the scarcity of trees, the rapaciousness of paper companies in the forests which remain. The canny reader will not trouble him/herself trying to splice the tape to what came before or after. Although the canny reader would also be suspicious of the straightforward, absolute denial of relevance dismissing the tape.

Here is the main narrative again. In embryo. A professor of litera-ture at a university in Wyoming (the only university in Wyoming) by coincidence is teaching two courses in which are enrolled two students (one in each of the professor's seminars) who are husband and wife. They both have red hair. The male of the couple aspires to write novels and is writing fast and furious a chapter a week his first novel in the professor's creative writing seminar. The other redhead, there are only two redheads in the two classes, is taking the professor's seminar in Afro-American literature, one of whose stars is Charlie W. Chesnutt. It has come to the professor's attention that both husband and wife are inveterate diary keepers, a trait which like their red hair distin-guishes them from the professor's other eighteen students. Something old-fashioned, charming about diaries, about this pair of hip graduate students keeping them. A desire to keep up with his contemporaries (almost wrote *peers* but that gets complicated real quick) leads the professor, who is also a novelist, or as he prefers novelist who is also a professor, occasionally to assemble large piles of novels which he reads with bated breath. The novelist/professor/reader bates his breath because he has never grown out of the awful habit of feeling praise bestowed on someone else lessens the praise which may find its way to him (he was eldest of five children in a very poor family—not an excuse—perhaps an extenuation—never enough to go around breeds a fierce competitiveness and being for four years an only child breeds a selfishness and ego-centeredness that is only exacerbated by the shocking arrival of contenders, rivals, lower than dogshit pretenders to what is by divine right his). So he reads the bait and nearly swoons when the genuinely good appears. The relevance of this to the story is that occasionally the professor reads systematically and because on this occasion he is soon to appear on a panel at a neighboring university (Colorado) discussing *Surfiction* his stack of novels was culled from the latest, most hip, most avant-garde, new *Tel Quel* chic, anti, non-novel bibliographies he could locate. He has determined at least three qualities of these novels. *One*—you can stack ten in the space required for two traditional novels. *Two*—they are *au rebours* the present concern for ecology since they sometimes include as few as no words at all on a page and often no more than seven. *Three*—without authors whose last names begin with *B*, surfiction might not exist. *B* for Beckett, Barth, Burroughs, Barthes, Borges, Brautigan, Barthelme . . . (Which list further discloses a startling coincidence or perhaps the making of a scandal—one man working both sides of the Atlantic as a writer and critic explaining and praising his fiction as he creates it: *Barth Barthes Barthelme.*)

The professor's reading of these thin (not necessarily a dig—thin pancakes, watches, women for instance are *à la mode*) novels suggests to him that there may be something to what they think they have their finger on. All he needs then is a local habitation and some names. Hence the redheaded couple. Hence their diaries. Hence the infinite layering of the fiction he will never write (which is the subject of the fiction which he will never write). Boy meets Prof. Prof reads boy's novel. Girl meets Prof. Prof meets girl in boy's novel. Learns her pubic hair is as fiery red as what she wears short and stylish, flouncing just above her shoulders. (Of course it's all fiction. The fiction. The encounters.) What's real is how quickly the layers build, how like a spring snow in Laramie the drifts cover and obscure silently.

Boy keeps diary. Girl meets diary. Girl falls out of love with diary (his), retreats to hers. The suspense builds. Chesnutt is read. A conference with Prof in which she begins analyzing the multilayered short story *Deep Sleeper* but ends in tears reading from a diary (his? hers?). The professor recognizes her sincere compassion for the downtrodden (of which in one of his fictions he is one). He also recognizes a fiction in her husband's fiction (when he undresses her) and reads her diary. Which she has done previously (read her husband's). Forever.

The plot breaks down. It was supposed to break down. The characters disintegrate. Whoever claimed they were whole in the first place? The stability of the narrative voice is displaced into a thousand distracted madmen screaming in the dim corridors of literary history. Whoever insisted it should be more ambitious? The train doesn't stop here. Mistah Kurtz he dead. Godot ain't coming. Ecce Homo. Dat's all, folks. Sadness.

And so it goes.

rock river

Main Street out of Rock River narrows abruptly into a two-lane and in twenty-five minutes you are in the middle of nowhere. Past a couple clumps of buildings that used to be towns and one that might still be, then a railroad embankment's on your left for a while till it veers off over the plains, a spine of mountains to the right, blue in the distance, miles of weather-cracked wasteland stretching to foothills hunkered like a pack of gray dogs at the base of the mountains. Moonscape till you turn off at the Bar-H gate on the dirt track under the power line and follow it through a pass, along a ridge and then things get brown, green some, not exactly a welcome mat rolled out but country you could deal with, as long as you don't decide to stay. Trees can tunnel out of thickets of boulders, grass can root in sand and shale, the river you can't find most summers in its seamed bed manages to irrigate a row of dwarf cottonwoods whose tops, situated as they are, higher than anything else around, black-green silhouettes orderly on the horizon, remind you that even the huge sky gives way to something, sometimes, that its weight can be accommodated by this hard ground, that the rooster tail of dust behind your pickup will dissipate, rise and settle.

The road twists and bumps and climbs, curves back on itself, almost disappears totally in a circus of ruts, gouges and tire-size stones, dropping steadily while it does whatever else it's doing, shaking the pickup to pieces, steering it, tossing it up and catching it like a kid warming up a baseball. No seat belt and your head would squash on the roof of the cab. Last few miles the steepest. Then this fold of land levels, meadows and thick, pine woods, sudden outcroppings of aspen, hillocks, mini-ravines, deer country, a greenness and sweet smell of water cutting the sage, a place nothing most of the trip here would have suggested you'd find.

I am alone. My job is to clean up Rick's truck, get it ready to bring back to town. They said that would be all right now. The police have finished their investigation. Tomorrow I'll come back with Stevenson. He can drive my truck and I'll drive Rick's. But today I want to do what I have to do by myself. I expect it will be a mess. He stood outside, but the blast carried backwards to the open window of the truck. They warned me, then they said the gas is OK. Better take jumper cables, though, Quinson said. As if any fool wouldn't know that. Cops were making arrangements to tow it to town. I thought I'd rather drive it. Clean it up first. Then me and Stevenson come out and I'll bring it in.

I have old towels. Two five-gallon cans of water. Upholstery cleaner. Brillo. Spot remover. Mr. Clean, sponges, rags, Windex, all the tools on my knife, heavier gear like shovel, ax and rope that's always stowed in the truck box. I think I have enough. Mary Ellen said, Take this, holding out a can of Pine Sol spray deodorant. I hadn't thought of that and was surprised she did and didn't know what to say when she held it out to me.

I shook my head no, but she didn't take it back. Didn't push it on me but she didn't pull it away either.

I think to myself. Can't hurt, can it? There's room. So I took it.

She nodded. Rick got on her nerves. He liked her. He reminded her of her father. Hopeless. Hopeless. Hopeless. You had to smile and be nice to him he was so hopeless. She'd never neglect the small kindnesses to him she said because you'd never want him to feel you'd given up on him. But he could try your patience. Try a saint's. He couldn't count the times she'd said in private she'd given up on Rick.

Don't bring him around here anymore, she'd say. I'm sick and tired of that man, she'd say. But then she'd always hug Rick or cry on his shoulder or say something awful and provoking to let him know she was very well aware of how hopeless he was, and let him know he'd never force her to give up on him.

Mary Ellen.

It's been a week. They probably locked it and shut the windows to keep out the rain. They'd want to protect a brand-new vehicle like that.

Almost new.

Looked new. He was so cockeyed proud of it.

I doubt Sarah will want to keep it. Either way if it's cleaned up, that's one thing she won't have to bother with.

Will you be all right?

There's room. Won't hurt to take it. They probably did close up the windows.

I HAVE RICK's extra set of keys. Went by his house to get them. Here's what I saw.

A tall woman. Sarah, Rick's wife. In blue jeans sitting at a table with a look I'd seen somewhere before, a picture of a Sioux Indian in a long line of Indians staring at the camera and it was hard to tell whether male or female, the photo was old and brown, the face I remembered round and the hood of dark hair could be a woman or a long-haired Indian man.

Sarah never wore blue jeans. Dresses almost always. If pants, they were slacks with sewn-in creases. You could never guess what she might say or do but her clothes wasn't the place that she showed she was different. I liked her a whole lot less than I liked Rick. Nobody talked more than Rick once he'd had his few drinks but you knew Rick didn't mean anything by it. When Rick talked you could tell he was talking just to keep himself from sinking down. If he stopped talking, he'd be in trouble, worse trouble than anything he might say would get him in. He needed to keep talking so he could sit there with you and play liar's poker or watch a campfire burn or just drink on Friday afternoon at the Redbird where we all did to forget the week that was. He'd make people mad who didn't know him because he was subject to say anything about anybody, but after a while, if you were around Rick any amount of time at all you knew it was foolish to take what he said seriously, personally. Rick was just riding along on this stream of words, merrily, merrily riding along and you could ride it too or pay it no mind, cause he wasn't really either.

Sarah on the other hand couldn't be any way but personal. She couldn't say Howdy-do without an edge to it. Like she's reminding you she had spoke first, giving you a lesson in manners and too bad you weren't raised right. I think the woman just couldn't help it. Something about growing up in too holy a house. Like the best anybody could do would never be good enough. And somebody had to take the job of reminding people of that fact. So here's Sarah. Eagle eyed and cat quick to pounce on universal slovenliness and your particular personal peccadilloes any hour of night or day. In blue jeans. Looking, as you might suspect, as if she's sleeping poorly or not at all, on the losing side force-marched by cavalry back to the reservation and mug shot. A drink on the kitchen table and offering me one even though we both know it's barely ten o'clock in the morning and that's not what I came for, reminding me, her lips pursed tight, that I'm in no position to judge her, in fact just the opposite case, because when she stares up at me red eyed there's just a little silliness, a little judgmentalness, a little I-know-better-than-you this is not the right thing to be doing but we've both started drinking earlier of a morning, you many more mornings than I, and you with Rick nonstop so morning, afternoon or night left far behind.

I better not stop now.

Didn't think you would.

Better get this done while I'm feeling up to it.

Why don't you let the police handle it?

It's just something I thought I could do. Ease a little of the burden.

You've done enough already. We're all grateful for what you've done for us.

They were going to tow it. Makes more sense to drive it. They said if it was all right with you, it was all right with them. I'm happy to help out if it's OK with you.

There the keys are on the table.

I won't be bringing it back today. Thought I'd just go up today and see what had to be done. Get it ready and tomorrow Stevenson said he would ride up with me and drive my truck back.

Don't bring it here.

You want me to park it at my place?

I don't care where you park it. It's Rick's truck. He won't be needing it. His brains were all over the seat. He drove away from us in that cute little shiny red truck and I don't care if I never see it again.

It's almost new. Rick talked himself up on a real bargain. Probably get most of what he paid if you sell it.

You've been a great help. Keep the truck. He'd want you to have it.

I couldn't do that.

I have some other stuff of his you might want as well. To remember him by. You can have his shotgun if the cops return it.

If you want me to take care of selling the truck I'd be happy to try. I'm sure it will bring a good price. From the outside it seemed in decent shape. Police sealed it and roped off the clearing where it was parked but as far as I could tell from where they kept us standing, everything was fine. Quinson told me it has plenty of gas, that I should bring cables just in case. I guess he thought I was born yesterday.

Simon?

Yes.

Do you miss him?

I'm real sorry. My heart goes out to you and your fine boys.

I can't miss him. He was gone too long.

Still in a state of shock, I guess. I sat there at the funeral still hoping Rick would change his mind.

He left while I was sleeping. I didn't get worried till the third day. I woke up early, early that morning and decided I'd call you. Ask if you'd seen him. Begin the whole humiliating routine. Has anybody seen my husband wandering around town? Blue eyes, blond, slightly balding, eyeglasses, middle-aged but boyish face, till he's acutely sloshed, then he resembles his grandfather's corpse. Tame when sober, answers to the name Rick. Please call 545-6217 if you've seen this individual. No reward. Except knowing you've saved a happy home.

I'd made up my mind to begin phoning around and you of course were at the top of the list, but the cops called me first.

What I saw was she looked like parts of this town, skimpy as it is, I haven't seen for years. Below Second Street, near the railroad tracks where there are storage bins for rent. It's a ragtag, helter-skelter whole lot of nothing dead end. Nobody lives there. Nobody's ever going to or ever has. You can hear sixteen-wheelers humping on the interstate, trains rattle across the overpass. It's the kind of hardscrabble little patch of concrete and gravel and cinders and corrugated tin-roofed sheds that will always be at the edge of towns on the prairie and outlast the rest—downtown, the nice neighborhoods—be here when no one's left to listen to coyotes howling, the sage running, wind at night screaming in as many voices as there's stars.

What I saw was her eyes on a level only slightly below mine, fixing me, daring me to ignore them. The last party at their house is what I saw. Rick was chef. Spaghetti sauce from ground antelope. Elk liver pâté. Neatly wrapped packages from his game locker that I'd seen thawing, blooding in his refrigerator when I'd popped in for a Bud the afternoon before. Sarah's eyes told me Rick probably hadn't been to bed or stopped drinking before he started up for this party. He'd been telling the story of how he'd tracked the wily elk whose liver was being nibbled as an hors d'oeuvre on Ritz crackers. No one was listening so Rick was telling it softly, slouched down in an armchair, telling again what he'd related at least three times to every single one of us that evening, mumbled quietly, one more time, his gestures slow motion as somebody underwater, his eyes invisible behind his bifocals, his drink glass abiding on the chair's mashed-potato arm, sunken as deeply, as permanent as Rick is in its lap. You pass by and think that man's not moving soon, nor his drink, and wonder how they ended up that way and wonder if they'd ever get unstuck from the tacky fruit-and-flower print slipcover that couldn't hide the fact that easy chair had seen better days.

Eye to eye with Sarah and she winks at me, even though both of us long past having fun at this party. But she's sloshed and I'm two sheets and that's why we both came so I wink back and hear the banjo and fiddle and whiny hill voices from the next room, the slapping of knees, whooping and stomping. It's getting good to itself in there. Dancing usually means wee hours before you can squeeze everybody out the door. It's what we've come for. To stay late. To holler a little bit and grab ass and thump a little on one another. I look back but Sarah's gray eyes are gone in the direction of the music, but music's not what's in them. I know by the set of her jaw what's in them. If I was close enough so her breath would ripple my lashes, that close but invisible so I wouldn't spoil her view, what I'd see would be two little Ricks, one in each gray globe of her eyes, two Ricks the stereo in her brain turns to one in three dimensions, real as things get in a kitchen at 11:00 P.M. when a full-scale party's raging.

Sure enough what I see is him stumbling into the kitchen this morning, hitting both sides of the doorframe before he gets through. He tries one more step. More lurch than step. As if his dancing partner has fooled him. He reaches for her hand and she whirls away laughing and he's caught with his weight on the wrong foot and almost falls on his nose after her. But he respects the quickness, the cunning, the spinning sexy grace in her, and forgives and catches himself with a little clumsy half skip, half shuffle, do-si-do, it's just a thing that happens. Hi. Hi. Hi. All. He catches me red-handed sliding the keys off the vinyl tablecloth. There are too many to close in my fist. She didn't separate the truck keys from the rest, twelve, thirteen, fifteen keys in my fist. I could shake them and make a mighty noise, shake them to the beat of that dancing music from the next room.

Where you going with ma keys, Simon? Simon-Simon. What you doing wit ma fucking keys, boyo? Ho. Ho. Don't touch that dial.

He glides in slow. The tempo has changed. He clamps one hand on Sarah's shoulder. Twirls her so she lands smack up against his chest. Then they are both gliding cheek to cheek and the song is waltz time, but they two-step it, hitch around the kitchen graceful as Arthur Murray and Ginger Rogers on stilts. Don't stop when Rick's elbow chops a whole row of empty beer bottles off the counter and they tumble and break and scatter and the worst godawful racket in the world does not attract one interested or curious face from the party in the other room.

▊ when it's time to go

Peace, my brother. Those hills on the horizon give up the golden light and we won't have it to worry about no more. I'm just as tired as you are. I know it's late. But sleep's like pussy. And pussy like meat on the bone. You can worry it or leave it alone. So don't you go yet, brother. Hold on least till I finish my story.

I click my glass on his and he starts.

Once upon a time was this little blind boy. He lived in Alabam boom bang a langa. His mama was named Clara and his daddy one those no-name shadows drop like a icy overcoat on you when you ain't looking. You be standing in the sun, happy as a tick on a bloody bug all the sudden it's black as night and you shivering like cold's a knife slicing your liver. Why? Cause that shadow got you. Done dropped out of nowhere and got you good, that's why. Little boy's daddy was a shadow like that and he told Clara he loved her and gave her a baby behind him swearing how beautiful she was and how much he loved her and rubbing her big butt and telling her he'd stay with her always. Well, he came up a little short on the always. Had him a young girl the whole time Clara carrying his son and woulda been long gone before the little bun popped out the oven if Clara hadn't turned him to a stone, a stone black as pitch-black night and cold as white people's lies. So the little blind boy, little Sambo was born with magic on one side and night on the other. No wonder there was a caul over his head. It turned him blue, just about strangled him. They buried it under a tree so it wouldn't come back like a sneaky cat trying to steal his breath.

Well, it wasn't long before the lil fella could talk. Chatter like a treeful of ravens and the lil thing ain't no bigger than a minute, ain't nine months old and got a mouth on him tell you more than you care to know. Folks could see from the beginning he was something special. Look what his mama was. Look who they think was his daddy. And look at the shopping bag he came here in. And them eyes. Them long eyes look right through you but can't see a thing. Some say they was green and some say they was lavender. Some say you could hear that child's eyes crackle you get close enough. Like the dust cooking on a light bulb some people swore they heard it and that's what the sound was. Or a moth circling something hot that's gon kill it sooner or later.

Was a time he could see just like you or me. Born blind but after a while you wave something in front his eyes they'd follow it back and forth, back and forth so you knew he knew something was there. Got so he would reach out his hand and find what you was dangling. Like keys, or a watch, or a earring, whatever shiny a person shake at him to catch his eyes. He got better and better and we thought Praise the Lord he's gon have eyes like the rest us.

So once upon a time he could see the light. Least we thought he could. That's a blessing cause how you spozed to tell anybody been in dark all they life about sunshine? How you gon say red or green or blue if all they know is the black black at the heart of black? So he knew about light, about mist in the morning, and sparrows breaking across a blue sky and leaves turning and all the colors niggers be wearing in they skins. Which depending on how you see it is better or worse once the light start to failing. I mean maybe you don't miss what you never had. Maybe never having nothing is a blessing in disguise. On the other hand if you seen the light once, then you got it inside where can't nobody take it. Even if somebody steal it from the world and it's gone forever you got that memory. You got it to fall back on don't matter they bury you ten miles underground and stack another mile of rocks on top you still got the memory down there in that black hole with you.

He was round about nine or ten when it start happening again. When the dark start closing in again. He said, Mama, the hills keep getting closer. I sits still but the hills keep sliding closer, picking up speed, getting taller and wider and the green trees covering them black as tar. Moving towards him fast as his daddy moves away in his dream. His dream of a father striding bandy-legged faster and faster, kicking up dust in the twisting road till he ain't nothing but a speck and a feather of smoke.

They couldn't go to the doctor treated only white folks and the one treated anybody he got that whiskey on his breath and them yellow-cake teeth people got to turn they face away and he's thinking like it's respect or some dumb scared rabbit coons fraid to look him in the eye. Ol Mr. Shitbreath Doctor, he don't know squat. Say: Peel that crust in the morning. Say: Hot rags, hot as he can stand, and peel that crust away.

His mama Clara listens, stares down at her bad feet in tennis sneakers with open toes so her corns can breathe. If her feet wasn't hurting so bad this morning she'd stomp a hole in the nasty floor. She can see where somebody skimmed a mop through the dirt. Like somebody grabbed the ankles of his skinny nurse and turned her upside-down and dragged her witchy hair across the linoleum. Stomp a hole clean through and let the whole dirty office slide back where it came from. Let the white table and his squeaky spinning stool and pills and bottles and needles and sticks and those rubber gloves he rolls on to stick his finger up your ass, let it all gurgle down the hole like dishwater draining out the sink.

Got to peel it, baby. I know it hurts but I got to get it all off.

Some call Clara a witch. They remember Clyde McDonald spinning like a roach what got that Kills-em-Dead all over his eight feet, spinning like a crazy top and roaring like he's on fire till he dropped dead in front of Minnie Washington's porch and Min she just sitting there rocking, rocking and watching him spin faster and faster till he bright as a light bulb about to pop, till he did pop and laid there curled dead as the dust at her feet. Told you so, Min said. She fixed him sure enough. Min the one sicced Clara on his trifling behind and told everybody she did it and would do it again, a thousand times again he hurt her so bad he ain't nothing but a dog and a coward and a baby-killing rat. Min never said hello or good-bye to Clyde McDonald just watched him spinning and watched him drop and ain't never missed a beat in her rocker. So people knew Clara was a witch. Much witch as she wanted to be even though it was a long time ago she did that business for Min. Some the younger sassy ones asking if Clara so bad why don't she cure her blind child her own bad self. Why she trotting way down the road to that whiskey-head quack she so bad. Well, there's some people you can't tell nothing to anyway. Mize well save your breath cause ignorant's the way they born, the way they gon stay till the day they die. Ain't no sense trying to tell them nothing so you just shake your head and remember Clyde spinning through the dust. It's more than one kind of power in the world. Ain't no kind of power can win all the time. If one thing don't work don't be too proud to try something else. Clara loved her boy. Maybe she loved him so much she touch him and ain't no magic in her hands ain't nothing but a natural woman when she touch him cause she love him so much.

Be that as it may the light steady failing her boy. Thick crust over his eyes every morning. Like the hills and the trees sneaking up on him at night, like they creeping closer all the time and he's always picking pieces of tree and dirt and dark off his eyelids. Getting closer every day. The place they call the horizon, where the sky stops being sky, where the edges of sky and ground make one long seam, that place is closing down like a scar over a wound.

Sambo wrings them boiling rags and lays them on his eyes. Hot as he can stand it, hot enough to suck all the color out his skin, so it's bleached like side meat been cooking all day. He a tough little monkey and scared too so he lays them on hot as he can stand it. Thinks of fire. Thinks he got to burn to see. His eyeballs burning like they up there in the sky, in the fire colors of sunset. He sits blind as a bat with them hot pads over his eyes and tries to think of things take his mind off the scalding, till the crust gets soft and sticky like candy. He sees the world turning, crackling like a piece of fish in a frying pan when you flip it over. One side brown and crispy, the other white as a ghost. He remembers the good times before he got here. Swimming round. Kicking his legs like a frog. Everything mellow like it is when you dive deep in the river and squeeze your eyes tight shut. He thinks if I do it right this time, if I push back the dark far enough this time, won't be crowding me tomorrow.

But he knows better. His mama told him better. Said the light's failing. Said it be worser and worser fore it get better. Nothing we can do but try to hold on to the little light you got. Fight for it every morning. Get them rags hot as you can stand it and fight that crust.

Sambo a good boy. Don't never sass. Always listen to his mama so he fought it every morning like she say. But one morning he got to dreaming behind those rags. Got to dreaming cause it's better than hurting and it was a dream he told his mama later, a dream of shedding them rags and getting up off his bed and walking out the door and starting down the road towards the hills where the sun rises every day God sends. He walks in his dream and the rags is gone and the fire is gone and he just goes about his business counting everything he sees. Trees, birds, squirrels, chipmunks and whatnot scooting and crawling through the weeds. Counts ants and blades of grass. Not missing a thing and counting everything at once cause that light feels so good, so easy and cool in his dream. Like the swimming time, the paddling time. Light carries him along. *Singing* is how he told it. Light was just singing to me, Mama, and telling me I didn't need no eyes. Wasn't no such a thing as eyes less you call your knees and hands and shoulders eyes cause everything you got can hear the light, or touch it and everything you got is something to see with. Told her it was a dream but then other folks said, I seen your boy, Clara. Sure was in a hurry to get somewhere, the other morning. Must be all better now, ain't he? Walking and whistling by, ain't never said howdy-do, good morning or good-bye, but he was steady trucking somewhere.

And that's the kinda thing make his mama scared. Cause she was a witch and knew about power and knew about turning to air, about rushing through your own bones, about running like sweet marrow and leaving your bones hollow as a reed. About being in two places at once. So you can mind your mama, so you can lay on your bed with hot rags on your eyes and at the same time, be running around the countryside. Dreaming one place while you supposed to be in another and the power lets you be in both. One man can watch you snoring and another swear you was in his henhouse stealing eggs. Clara scared cause if the boy had power, he had to pay the piper. And the piper kept her lonely and a fool all the days of her life. Made her wrap her legs round his daddy and holler hallelujah. Made her bow down when he reared up over her. Made her be mare to his stallion when it shoulda been her riding him till wasn't nothing left but bloody nubs where his arms and legs supposed to be.

Yeah, they might could have saved my sight. Ain't never gon forgive them that. Number-one cracker didn't treat colored so wasn't nowhere else to go but down the road to the whiskey head that did. My mama took off work one morning and carried me down there but the old bad-breath turkey couldn't do no good. So here I sit behind these shades blind as a rock.

Must have been twelve or thirteen years old when I left home. Gripping the handles of my shopping bag so tight it put a crease in my hand I can feel today. Tear my whole arm out the socket only way you get that bag with everything I owned away from me. Mama told the bus driver. Leave him be. Let him find the steps his ownself. Mama was like that. Had to be. Other folks treat me like I was blind but she know better. She the one let me fall on my face. Let me slam my shins, ride my bike, let me cross the road by myself and walk on down to the store. She said if he don't do it hisself, he ain't never gon learn. Be crippled for sure if he always waiting till somebody else do for him.

So I was steady gripping my shopping bag and listening at that bus motor humming. There's a place where the door be breathing. You know. A place like a mouth where the inside air leaving and outside air pushing in and it's warmer, it's got a different smell, that's how you find a open door. Motor sound tells me it's a big bus so I know I got to step up on it but I don't get situated quite right and bang my ankle and I'm seeing fire and gripping my bag and thinking, Shit, I can't even step up in this damn bus how I'ma get around when it stop a thousand miles away in some damn place I never been before. But I hear Mama say, Leave him be, Mr. Driver. He'll find it all right.

And you know I been bumping my shins and tripping over things and falling flat on my face ever since but I ain't never considered turning back. Ain't never felt sorry for myself neither cause my mama never did and I know she love me better than I love my ownself.

That's what little Sambo said, a grown man sitting on a barstool in the Crawford Grill in the Hill District in Pittsburgh, Pennsylvania. How do I know that? Well, I was on another stool and it was after the last set and the bartender had locked the door so it was just us and quiet. Us locked in and everybody else locked out while Raymond the bartender went about his business closing down the bar. Just Raymond and me and Sambo and Marylou, the waitress, cleaning off the booths and tables. Just her shuffling slow-motion on tired feet and the tinkle of glasses gathered, washed, stacked. Raymond humming a low-down bluesy something while he wipes and stashes things away. Nobody exactly a stranger to nobody. You know. We all just out there at the end of the night, in the early morning if the truth be told, out there after most people have gone about their business, home sleeping in their beds if they got good sense, but we're holding on, holding out after the music's over and the night's over and in a hour or two if we keep on hanging on it's light when you step outside. So what you are saying you sort of say to anybody who cares to listen because you're saying it mostly to yourself. Hey. You know what I mean. You been there, ain't you, sisters and brothers. In the Crawford Grill at three-thirty in the morning on barstools rapping.

Sambo talking slow and easy as molasses. Yeah. Left the country with everything I had in a shopping bag. Didn't know where in hell I was going. New Orleans nothing but a name to me. But I knew I could play. Knew they had pianos in New Orleans and if I could find me one and sit down and get my fingers on them keys, somebody would listen.

Been on the road ever since. Finding pianos and playing and paying my way. One place get just the same as another afterwhile. Be worse if I had eyes. When you got eyes it's too easy to forget. I mean you can get around and don't have to pay attention to nothing. Eyes get to be like them dogs lead blind people around. They do the seeing and you just follow along behind. You forget the light. You steady losing the light and don't even know it's gone.

So that's about all of it, my friends. Sambo could sure nuff play. I'm a witness. Yes I am. Point of the story, I guess, if it has one, I guess, if it got to, is look down at your hands. Look at the blood in the ropes in the backs of your hands. Think of that blood leaving you and running up in somebody else's arms, down into somebody's fingers black or brown or ivory just like yours. And listen to those hands playing music. Now shut your eyes. Shut them for good. And ask yourself if anything's been lost, if something's been taken away or something given. Then try to remember the color of light.

■ concert

Death drapes the stage like all those things you know you must do when the performance is over.

Buck called.

Your mother, man. It's your mother . . .

Shit, Buck. Don't say it. Buck your magic twanger.

Everybody in the auditorium on their feet now. Putting their hands together. You'll catch the first fast train out of here. The piano man and bass player wink, nod and mouth words at each other like lovers across a crowded room. You hear again the groan of him slicing the bow across the fat belly of the bass. Screeching halt. A trolley stop when the treacly ballad threatened to la-di-da forever and with one throaty gasp, one pen stroke the bassist ended it. One man, one vote. Everybody out. You consider the formality of their dress. Tux. Black tie. How the starched white shirtfronts sever their dark heads. Cannonballs dropped in the snow. You commiserate. Monkey suits. Monkeyshines. How many one-night stands in front of all these strangers. Who listen. Who applaud. What. Inside the elevator of their music. Going up. Down. The brothers too smooth to move. Wearing refrigerators. Laid out ice elegant on cooling boards. Got a letter this morning,

213

how do you reckon it read? How do you reckon it read? That letter. This morning.

Can you hear me? Lots of static on the line. I can barely . . .

Why are they costumed as pallbearers? Why the morticians' manners? Have they been pulling legs so long they don't have one left to stand on? You think of Africans down on their knees scrabbling for grains of wheat dribbling from gunnysacks slabbed on a U.N. relief truck. You imagine those skeletons inside these formal suits. The high-butt shuffle of the xylophone man tells you which corner and which year and which city he hails from. Surely as the zebra's wobbly gait in his zoo pen recalls haul-assing across a Serengeti plain. The thinnest note's too heavy for these African ghosts to bear. They shiver in the shivering heat and expire. You are left alone shimmering till he bops the metal plate again. Bell ringer. Stinger. Big Bopper. Word Dropper. Quells the vibrations with his padded mallet.

One last tune. From our latest album. Available now at your record store. That was, by the way, a commercial, ha, ha. A composition we've entitled . . .

Buck, Buck.

It's ten here. Two hours difference.

If I hurry home, it won't have happened yet.

Do you remember driving into the City? From Philly over the bridges into Jersey. Flat out up the pike then the tunnel. Didn't it seem everybody going our way, headed for the same place? All those cars and trucks and buses, man. Planes in the air. Trains. Close to Newark you could even see ocean liners. Every damn form of transportation known to man, man. And every kind of high. All making it to the City. Unanimous. The people's choice. And you were there in that number. Doing it, boy. Shoom. Kicking the Jersey turnpike. Pedal to the metal. Radio already there and sending back waves. Chasing. Chased. Won't it be something when all these folks pour down through the tunnel and we're each and all of us packed into the same tight squeeze of our destination. The Five Spot. Lintons. The Village Gate. Miracle of planes trains buses cars ships arriving and checking in and checking out the scene. I can't wait. Nobody can. Ghosts boogie through the marshes. A nasty KKK greeting scrawled in four-foot-tall letters on an overpass. We see city lights braced for us. A line of hostiles on the horizon deciding whether they'll let us pass or swoop down and burn the wagons. How long ago was that, Buck? I haven't forgotten any of it. Not that long ago, really. I was in college, first in my family, first splib this and that, the early sixties first time I checked these guys out. Now the bass player's head is bowed, his eyes closed. Is he remembering my dream? Piano man, bottom lip belled, sputters like a trumpet as he gazes down at the intricate journeying of his long fingers. I notice the bass man's hair is thinning, even worse than mine, over the crown of his skull. Brown skin dropped over his eyes blinds him. Two sightless bubbles transfix the audience. When he can't sleep he counts the fences his four fingers have jumped over, his dangling thumb along for the ride. Oh, it's a long way from May to December. So willow. Willow weep for me. I think *Ashanti* describes the bass man because the word sounds spare, sparse, taut. Quiver attached to the fiddle holds an arrow he will shoot into someone's heart. Wheels turning behind his blind eyes choose the victim. *Ashanti* because he's a warrior. Hard. Pitiless. His eyes rolled back into his skull. Madness. Ecstasy. The blank mask surveys us. Choosing a target. Nothing reveals what the hidden eyes think of us yet we know our measure is being taken, know that part of us begs to be seen by someone else in order to be real. We're in mortal danger if no mirror remembers us, reminds us what to do next.

Buck. Buck.

Listen, man. I got something important to tell you. Your mother, man.

Wait. Let me tell you this dream I've been scoping lately. See, you call me on the phone. I'm sitting in a theater. Not a movie theater. A theater theater. Phone rings. I'm aware as I start to answer it that I'm listening to music. Jazz. Chamber ensemble jazz. Like a string quartet. You dig. Like maybe the M.J.Q. Phone rings but I don't want to miss the music. I hesitate. Or maybe I already have the phone at my ear. I'm unhappy because I'm about to miss the concert, but, you know, once I answered or decided to answer I wasn't hearing the music anyway, so shit. I say hello. Hello who is it? Kind of in a hurry. Annoyed you know because I've been interrupted. Then you come on.

Buck. Buck, is that you?

She's gone, man.

Buck your magic twanger.

Then I look at the stage. The musicians are in tuxedos. You know. Like penguins. And the darkness is not behind them. Darkness is this crisp sharp hard kind of foreground and the stage is behind it. I think maybe a steel curtain is pulled in front of the four players, four of them, a quartet. I think that's what's strange, different about the way the four of them look. They are marooned far away behind this darkness. The black curtain has been scissored precisely to surround each silhouette, then seamlessly each player's been sewn into the fabric. But a curtain wouldn't hang that way. A curtain has drapes and folds, people need room to move and breathe so what I saw was crazy. Something inside of me says no. I can't be seeing what I'm seeing, what I think I see. My eyes readjust. Do a double take, you know. Figure-ground reversal. Fish become birds, or birds fish. Except once you make up your mind which it is, ain't no going back. You say, Show me something else, this doesn't make sense. Then you're stuck with what you got. The paper-thin men and thin paper cut-out black screen come together in another way so I can deal with what was up there on the stage.

It happened much quicker than I can tell it. I never heard words, myself talking to myself. Just that blink. That click. Before I can say, Hey, wait a minute. This ain't right. Click. It's back to normal. I'm holding the phone. It's you. The players are three-dimensional again. Onstage. Not projected on a screen. Not millions of white specks and black specks floating, dancing. Their suits are not the curtain. Faces not holes punched in the snow. The stage is not wearing them any-more. I'm getting all that mess resolved in my mind. La-di-da. But it's costing me. I can't go back. Dizzy almost. My heart's thumping. I worry about everybody in the family's high blood pressure. And there's still you on the phone.

Buck. Are you there? Zat you?

I'm scared to pick up the receiver. I've already been through the conversation and I don't want to hear bad news again. The phone rings and rings but I don't hear a thing. I can't hang up. Because I haven't picked up yet. The piece playing I know the title of because the xylophone man just said it. Or part of the title. Europe's in it. Milan. Streets of Milano. Or Milano Afternoon. I heard it announced. Before.

When I was paying attention. Before you rang. Before I started getting sick inside my self and looking for an exit.

Did you ever think of titles as premonitions? Threats. Destiny. Most come after I've written or told a story many times but occasionally the first words name everything else that follows. And stop me when I've said enough. A threat. A destination. I might as well say it all. A title can be like death. Like dying and being born at the same time.

The audience begins to file out. Some people stand at their seats clapping but when it becomes clear the musicians aren't going to play anymore no matter how long or loud we applaud, the trick of slapping one hand against the other, like hundreds of trained seals, starts to feel, first to one, then another and finally to the entire group like a silly way to behave. One hand continues clapping in the void but all the rest split, leaving me stuck with the phone in mine, unplayed and exhausted passages of concert in my brain, a fear, a withering godawful fright that something terrible has happened or was going to happen.

Ping. Ping. The Chinese water torture drop of the phone no one is left to answer but me in the bright hall.

On the other hand some tunes need no introduction.

presents

I *stood on the bank ...*

Oh yes, she said. Oh yes and I did not know what she was yessing any more than I know how her voice, her yes reaches from wherever she is to wherever I am now, except it's like the ships seen from the bank of Jordan in that song sailing on, sailing on from there to here quietly as dream.

Big Mama. Big Mama. Doubling her not because she is not real enough once but because her life takes up so much space. I stare at her afraid to look away. Scared she'll be gone if I do. Scared I'll be gone.

Baby, you listen to your Big Mama now. Listen cause I ain't got nothing but mouth and time and hardly none that left.

He is saucer-eyed. Awkward. A big, nappy head.

She pats each nap and each awakes. A multitude stirring as she passes her old hand once in the air over the crown of his skull.

Love Jesus and love yourself and love those who love you, sugar. Those who don't love you don't love theyselves and shame on them. Nobody but Jesus can save their sorry souls.

She purses her lips. Her tongue pushes that hard-as-the-world bitter

218

lemon into one cheek. She sucks on it. All the sour of it smears her old lips. She is Big Mama. No bones in her body. Even now, even this Christmas so close to death the bones cannot claim her. Nothing will crack or snap or buckle in her. In her lap he will curl and sleep and always find soft room to snuggle deeper. To fall. To sleep.

He remembers being big enough to crawl alone under her bed and little enough, little sweet doodlebug, you come on over here gimme some sugar, to sit upright and his head just grazes the beehive network of springs. Hiding under her bed and playing with the dust and light he raises and the tasseled knots of fringed chenille bedspread. Bed so high so you had to *climb* up on it. Mind you don't roll off, boy. He did not think *throne* but he knew her bed was raised high to be a special place, to be his Big Mama's bed.

So when she kneels beside the bed he hears the sigh of the room rushing together again over her head, sigh as the fist of her heart, the apron pocket of her chest empties and fills, the grunt and wheeze of his Big Mama dropping to one knee and lifts the spread and her arm disappears as if she's fishing for him under there. Come out, you little doodlebug rascal. I know you hiding in there. Boogeyman get you you don't come from under there. Her arm sweeps and he can see her fingers under the edge of the bed, inside the cave, though he is outside now and it's like being two places at once, hiding and looking for his ownself, watching her old hand, the fingers hooked, beckoning. C'mon out, you monkey you, sweeping a half inch off the floor, precisely at the level of the unfailing, fringed spread hanging off the side of the bed.

What she drags forth this Christmas Eve afternoon as he watches her kneeling beside the bed is wrapped in a blanket. Not him this time, but something covered with a sheet and swaddled in a woolly blanket. Shapeless. Then Big Mama digs into folds and flaps, uncovers woman curves, the taut shaft. There are long strings and a hole in the center. Gently as she goes she cannot help accidents that trick stirrings from the instrument. A bowl of jelly quivering. Perhaps all it needs is the play of her breath as she bends over it, serious and quiet as a child undressing a doll. Or the air all by its ownself is enough to agitate the strings when Big Mama finally has it laid bare across her bed.

The story as he's preached it so many times since is simple. A seven-year-old boy makes his grandmother a song. He intends to sing it for her Christmas Day but Christmas Eve afternoon she calls him into her bedroom and kneels and pulls a guitar wrapped in rags and blankets from under her bed. He is mesmerized and happy. He hugs his Big Mama and can't help telling her about the love song he's made up for her Christmas present. She says you better sing it for me now, baby, and he does and she smiles the whole time he sings. Then she lays out the sad tale of his life as a man. He'll rise in the world, sing for kings and queens but his gift for music will also drag him down to the depths of hell. She tells it gently, he is only a boy, with her eyes fixed on the ceiling and they fill up with tears. Oh yes. Oh yes, yes. Yes, Jesus. The life he must lead a secret pouring out of her. Emptying her. Already she's paying for the good and evil in him. Yes. Yes. She's quiet then. Still. They sit together on the side of her high bed till it's dark outside the window. He can't see snow but smells it, hears how silently it falls. She asks him, Sing my song one more time. His little Christmas gift song because he loves to sing and make rhymes and loves his Big Mama and the grace of sweet Jesus is heavy in this season of his birth. By the next morning his Big Mama is dead. The others come for Christmas Day, discover her. He's been awake since dawn, learning to pick out her song quietly on his new guitar. His mother and the rest of them bust in, stomp their snowy shoes in the hallway and Merry Christmas and where's Big Mama? They find her dead in bed and he's been playing ever since. Everything she prophesied right on the money, honey. To this very day. He's been up and he's been down and that's the way she told him it would be all the days of his life. Amen.

Each time in the middle of the story he thinks he won't ever need to tell it again. Scooted up under the skirt of Big Mama's bed. His mother comes over to visit and she fusses at him. You're too big a boy to be hiding go seek under Mama's bed. Don't let him play under there, Mama. Don't baby him. Time he start growing up.

His mother visits and takes a bath in Big Mama's iron tub. He sees her bare feet and bare ankles, her bare butt as he holds his breath and quiet as a spider slides to the edge and peeks up through the fringy spread. He lifts the covering to see better. Inch by inch. Quiet as snow. She has a big, round behind with hairs at the bottom. He thinks of watermelons and can't eat that fruit without guilt ever after. He watches her as she stands in front of the mirror of his grandmother's chiffonier. His heart beats fast as it can. He's afraid she'll hear it, afraid she'll turn quickly and find his eye peeking up from under the covers at her. But when she does turn, it's slowly, slowly so he hears the rub of her bare heel on the linoleum where the rug doesn't stretch to where she's standing. He drops the window of his hiding place. He's spared a vision of the front of her. Titties. Pussycat between her legs. Just ankles and bare feet till she's finished and wrapped in one Big Mama's housecoats and asking for him in the other room.

You been in here all this time? You been hiding under there while I was dressing? Why didn't you say something, boy?

The story has more skins than an onion. And like an onion it can cause a grown man to cry when he starts to peeling it.

Or else it can go quick. Big Mama said, That's the most beautiful song in the world. Thank you, precious. Thank you and thank Jesus for bringing such a sweet boy to this old woman.

Will you teach me how to play?

Your old grandmama don't know nothing bout such things. She's tired besides. You learn your ownself. Just beat on it like a drum till something come out sound good to you.

The music's in the box like the sword in the stone. Beat it. Pound it. Chisel away. Then one day it gon sound good. Gon slide loose easy as it slided in. Then it's smooth as butter. Then it sings God's praise. Oh yes. Oh yes.

She gave him the guitar in Jesus' name. Amened it. Prayed over it with him that Christmas Eve afternoon how many years ago. Well, let's see. I was seven then and I'm an old man now so that's how long it's been, that's how many times I've preached the story.

My grandmother believed in raising a joyful noise unto the Lord. Tambourines and foot stomping and gut-bucket piano rolls and drums and shouts and yes if you could find one a mean guitar rocking like the ark in heavy seas till it gets good to everybody past the point of foot patting and finger popping in your chair past that till the whole congregation out they seats dancing in the air.

Something born that day and something died. His fate cooked up for him like a mess of black-eyed peas and ham hocks and he's been eating at the table of it ever since. Lean days and fat days.

Where did she find a guitar? Who'd played the instrument before it was his? Could it ever be his if other fingers had plucked the strings, run up and down the long neck? Grease and sweat ground into its wood, its metal strings. When he was at last alone with the gift she'd given him and told him not to play till Christmas, he'd peered into the hole in its belly. Held it by its fat hips and shook it to hear if anybody'd left money in there. If the right sound won't come out plucking it, there was always the meaty palm of his hand to knock sense in it.

How long did he hide in the church before he carried his box out on the street corner? How long for the Lord, how many licks for the Devil? How long before you couldn't tell one from the other? Him the last to know. Always.

A boy wonder. An evil hot blood Buddy Bolden Willie the Lion Robert Johnson wild man boy playing the fool and playing the cowboy fool shit out that thang, man. Yes. Oh yes.

And one day Praise God I said, Huh uh. No more. Thank you Jesus and broke it over my knee and cried cause I'd lost my Big Mama.

Atlantic City. Niggers pulling rickshaws up and down the Boardwalk. Naw. If I'm lying, I'm flying. They did, boy. Yes they did. Drugging white folks around behind them in these big carts. Like in China, man. Or wherever they keep them things. Saw that shit on the Boardwalk in Atlantic City, U.S. of A. Yeah. And niggers happy to be doing it. Collecting fabulous tips, they say. Hauling peckerwoods around. Not me. See, I knew better. I'd seen the world. Had me a gig in one those little splib clubs on Arctic Avenue. Enough to keep me in whiskey. Didn't need no pad. It was summer. Sleep on the beach. Or sleep with one the ladies dig my playing. A real bed, a shower every few days to scald the sand out my asshole. Living the life, partner. Till I woke up one morning in the gutter. Stone gutter, man. Like a dead rat. Head busted. Vomit all on my clothes. In broad daylight I'm lolling in the gutter, man. Said, Huh uh. No indeed. These the bonds of hell. Done fell clean off the ladder and I'm down in the pit. The goddamn gutter floor of the pit's bottom. I'm lost. Don't a living soul give one dime fuck about me and I don't neither.

That's when I hollered, Get me up from here, Big Mama. You said I'd rise and I did. You prophesied I'd fall and here I am. Now reach down and help me up. Gimme your soft silk purse old woman's hand and lift this crusty burden off the street. Take me back to your bosom. Rise and fall, you said. Well, I can't fall no further so carry me on up again. Please. Please. Big Mama. Reach down off the high side of your bed and bring me back.

Her fingers hooked like a eagle's beak. Holding a cloak of feathers fashioned from wings of fallen angels. Where you find this, Big Mama? How'm I spozed to play this thing? Beat it, you say. Pound it like a drum. Just step out in the air with it round your shoulders. Let the air take you and fly you on home. Squeeze it till it sound like you need it to sound. Good. Giant steps ain't nothing if they ain't falling up and falling down and carrying you far from this place to another.

Sailing. To meet me in the morning. On Jordan one day. Singing, Yes. Oh yes.

I stood on the bank . . .

And my neck ached like I'd been lynched. Like I'd been laid out for dead and hard rock was my pillow and cold ground my bed.

Hard rock my pillow and help me today, Lord. Help me tell it. I scrambled to my feet and shook the sooty graveclothes and sand and scales and dust and feathers and morning blood off my shoulders. Skinny as a scarecrow. Funky as toejam. My mouth dry and my eyes scored by rusty razors, my tongue like a turtle forgot how to poke his head out his shell. Scrambled to my aching feet and there it was spread out over me the city of my dreams, Philadelphia all misbegotten and burnt crisp and sour sour at the roots as all my bad teefs.

Play it, son.

Bucka do. Bucka do little dee.

Black as sugar burnt to the bottom of a pan. And Big Mama told me. She said, Squeeze it to the last drop.

A simple story. Easy to tell to a stranger at the bar who will buy you a drink. Young boy and old woman. Christmastime. Reading each other's minds. Exchanging gifts of song. His fortune told. The brief, bright time of his music. How far it took him, how quickly gone. The candle flaring up, guttering, gone. He'd told it many times. Risen. Fallen. Up. Down. Rubs his crusty eyes and peers into a honey-colored room with no walls, feet scurry past his head, busy going every which way, sandals and brogans and sneakers and shiny Stacy-Adamses and pitter-pat of high-stepper high heels on the pavement as he lifts his head and goes over the whole business again, trying to settle once and for all who he must be and why it always ends this way his head on the hard rock of curbstone, the ships sailing on, sailing on.

The river is brass or blood or mud depending on the day, the season, the hour. Big Mama is where she is. He is here. Her voice plain as day in his ear. He wishes someone would pat him on his head and say everything's gon be all right.

the tambourine lady

Now *I lay me down to sleep* . . . there will be new shoes in the morning. New shoes and an old dress white as new. Starched white and stiff with petticoats whispering like angel wings and hair perfect as heat and grease can press it. There will be hands to shake as she rises from the curb onto the one broad step that took you off Homewood Avenue, which was nowhere, to the red doors of the church that were wide enough to let the whole world in but narrow too, narrower than your narrow hips, child, eye of the needle straight and narrow, don't make no mistake. Hands to help her across the threshold, through the tall red doors, from hard pavement that burned in summer, froze in winter, to the deep cushion of God's crimson carpet. She's unsteady as she passes to His world. Like that first step from moving stairs downtown in Kaufmann's Department Store when you always think you're falling, pitched down and about to be cracked to pieces on the shiny checkerboard floor rushing up to mire your feet. At the church door her mother's hand, the gloved hand of Miss Payton to help her through. Miss Payton all in white, white veil, white gloves, white box tied over her hair with a silky white bandage. Breath might catch in her throat, her heart stutter but she wouldn't fall. She'd catch hold to

225

old Miss Payton's hand, soft and white as a baby rabbit. Miss Payton smelling like Johnson's baby powder, who'd say, Bless you, sweet darling daughter, so the step up did not trip you, the wide doors slam in your face.

New shoes pinched your feet. Too big, too small, too much money, too ugly for anybody to be caught dead in. The white ladies who sold them would stick any old thing on your feet and smile at your mama and say, Just right. But sometimes when her feet in new shoes she'd forget how they felt, and she'd float. Couldn't take her eyes off them, stepping where she stepped, she follows them everywhere they go, click-clack cleats on the bottoms to save the heels and soles. They are new and shiny and for a while she's brand-new and shiny in them. Now she's nobody, nowhere, kneeled down beside her bed, remembering into the silence of God's ear a little girl in new shoes that didn't belong to her, that wouldn't fit. Her toes are drawn up curly, black against pink underskin. She dreams white anklets with a lacy band around the top. Dreams meat on her bones so socks don't slip down to her shoe tops.

If you polished old shoes, you could see your face inside. New ones come with your face in them. In the morning she'd take them out the box polish them anyway and then wash and dry her face and clean her hands and tug the purple Buds of Promise sash straight. Make sure of everything in the mirror. On the threshold of the African Methodist Episcopal Zion Church there will be a mirror in the gray sky, a mirror in the brick walls, a mirror in her mother's eyes and in the hand of Miss Payton reaching for hers, patting her ashy skin, promising she will not fall.

She closes her eyes and hears tambourines. Crashing like a pocketful of silver in her daddy's pants when he stuck in his hand and rummaged round, teasing out a piece of change for her. Like somebody saying dish dish dish dish and every dish piled high with something good to eat.

Dish. Dish.

And if I die . . . before I wake. You walk funny because more crack than sidewalk some places on the way home from school. You sneak out into Hamilton Avenue to get past the real bad busted-up part where sidewalk's in little pieces like a broken jar.

You looked both ways up and down Hamilton Avenue but you know you might die. *A thousand times. I've told you a thousand times to stay out of Hamilton Avenue, girl.* But if the sidewalk looked like a witch's face you'd rather get runned over than step on a crack and break your mama's back. So you looked both ways up and down the street like Mama always said. You looked and listened and hoped you wouldn't get hit like little fat Angela everybody called Jelly who was playing in Cassina Way and the car mashed her up against the fence where you can still see the spot to this day.

She feels mashed like Jelly when Tommy Bonds pushes her down. He laughs and calls her crybaby. Says, You ain't hurt and runs away. But she ain't no crybaby over no little blood snot on her knee. She cries cause he hurt her mama. Pushed her into the spider web of cracks cause he knew what she was playing. She'd told him her secret because she thought they were friends. But he never really was. He hates her and pushes her right dead down in a whole mess of snakes. She cries cause she's trapped, can't get out without stepping on more. Every crack a bone in her mama's back. He hates her. He follows her after school and calls her nasty stuck-up bitch till she stops, hands on hips, and hollers. Boy, I ain't studying you. You ain't nothing, Tommy Bonds, and wiggles her butt at him, then she is running, tearing down the sidewalk, scared and happy to have him after her again no matter what he wants to do. She would forgive him. Forgive his bad words, forgive his lies, forgive him for telling her secrets to everybody. She is forgiving, forgetting everything as he flies down Hamilton after her. She knows he can't catch her if she doesn't want to be caught. Says to herself, See what he wants now. Stops, hands on hips, at the edge of the worst busted-up place. *Girl, don't you dare set foot in that traffic on Hamilton Avenue.* And all he wants is to shove her down. Kill her mama.

She'd told Tommy Bonds her secret. He'd sneaked out into the street with her. Played her game and the cars whipping past on Hamilton Avenue had never been louder, closer, their wind up under her clothes as they ran the twenty steps past Wicked Witch Face City. And never had she cared less about getting mashed because who ever heard of a car killing two at a time.

Tommy, Tommy, Tommy *Bonds.* If she didn't duck just in time the rope would cut off her neck. If she didn't bounce high enough there go her cut-off feet hopping down the street all by they ownselves. Say it, girl. Say it. *Bonds* was when the rope popped the ground. *Tommy* three fast times while the loop turned lazy in the air.

Shake it to the east, Shake it to the west. Now tell the one you love the best. Say it loud and proud, girl. We ain't turning for nothing.

Tommy-Tommy-Tommy *Bonds.*

She is not crying because it hurts. A little snotty-looking blood. Scab on her knee next day. That's all. That's not why I'm crying, Mister Smarty-pants. Mister Know-it-all. But she can't say his name, can't say what she's thinking because the tears in her nose and ears and mouth might come crashing down and she'd be a puddle. Nasty brown puddle in the middle of the street.

Pray the Lord my soul to take.

The lady who beat the tambourine and sang in church was a Russell. Tomorrow was church so she'd see the Russells, the Strothers, Bells, Frenches, Pattersons, Whites, Bonds. Tomorrow was church so this was Saturday night and her mama ironing white things in the kitchen and her daddy away so long he mize well be dead and the new patent-leather shoes in their box beneath her side of the bed be worn out before he sees them. She thinks about how long it takes to get to the end of your prayers, how the world might be over and gone while you still saying the words to yourself. Words her mama taught her, words her mama said her mother had taught her so somebody would always be saying them world without end amen. So God would not forget His children. Saying the words this Saturday night, saying them tomorrow morning so He would not forget. Tommy Tommy Tommy Bonds. Words like doors. You open one wide and peek inside and everybody in there, strolling up and down the red aisles, singing, shaking hands. People she wanted to see and people she didn't know and the ones she'd been seeing all her life. People she hates. *God bless* ... Words like the rope right on time slapping the pavement, snapping her heart. Her feet in new shoes she knows better than to be wearing outside playing in the street girl and they break and she falls and falls and if she had one wish it would be let me hear the lady sing her tambourine song tomorrow morning in church.

little brother

for Judy

Penny, don't laugh. Come on now, you know I love that little critter. And anyway, how you so sure it didn't work?

Tylenol?

Yep. Children's liquid Tylenol. The children's formula's not as strong and he was only a pup. Poured two teaspoons in his water dish. I swear it seemed to help.

Children's Tylenol.

With the baby face on it. You know. Lapped it up like he understood it was good for him. He's alive today, ain't he? His eye cleared up, too.

You never told me this story before.

Figured you'd think I was crazy.

His eye's torn up again.

You know Little Brother got to have his love life. Out tomcatting around again. Sticking his nose in where it don't belong. Bout once a month he disappears from here. Used to worry. Now I know he'll be slinking back in three or four days with his tail dragging. Limping around spraddle-legged. Sleeping all day cause his poor dickie's plumb wore out.

Geral.

It's true. Little Brother got it figured better than most people. Do it till you can't do it no more. Come home half dead and then you can mind your own business for a while.

Who you voting for?

None of them fools. Stopped paying them any mind long time ago.

I hear what you're saying, but this is special. It's for president.

One I would have voted for. One I would have danced for buck naked up on Homewood Avenue, is gone. My pretty preacher man's gone. Shame the way they pushed him right off the stage. The rest them all the same. Once they in they all dirty dogs. President's the one cut the program before I could get my weather stripping. Every time the kitchen window rattles and I see my heat money seeping out the cracks, I curse that mean old Howdy Doody turkey-neck clown.

How's Ernie?

Mr. White's fine.

Mama always called him Mr. White. And Ote said *Mr. White* till we shamed him out of it.

I called Ernie that too before we were married. When he needed teasing. Formal like Mama did. *Mr. White.* He was *Mr. White* to her till the day she died.

But Mama loved him.

Of course she did. Once she realized he wasn't trying to steal me away. Thing is she never had that to worry about. Not in a million years. I'd have never left Mama. Even when Ote was alive and staying here. She's been gone all these years but first thing I think every morning when I open my eyes is, You OK, Mama? I'm right here, Mama. Be there in a minute, to get you up. I still wake up hoping she's all right. That she didn't need me during the night. That I'll be able to help her through the day.

Sometimes I don't know how you did it.

Gwan, girl. If things had been different, if you didn't have a family of your own, if I'd had the children, you would have been the one to stay here and take care of Mama.

I guess you're right. Yes. I would.

No way one of us wouldn't have taken care of her. You. Ote. Sis or me. Made sense for me and Ote to do it. We stayed home. If you hadn't married, you'd have done it. And not begrudged her one moment of your time.

Ote would have been sixty in October.

I miss him. It's just Ernie and me and the dogs rattling around in this big house now. Some things I have on my mind I never get to say to anybody because I'm waiting to tell them to Ote.

He was a good man. I can still see Daddy pulling him around in that little wagon. The summer Ote had rheumatic fever and the doctor said he had to stay in bed and Daddy made him that wagon and propped him up with pillows and pulled him all over the neighborhood. Ote bumping along up and down Cassina Way with his thumb in his mouth half sleep and Daddy just as proud as a peacock. After three girls, finally had him a son to show off.

Ote just about ran me away from here when I said I was keeping Little Brother. Two dogs are enough, Geraldine. Why would you bring something looking like that in the house? Let that miserable creature go on off and find a decent place to die. You know how Ote could draw hisself up like John French. Let you know he was half a foot taller than you and carrying all that John French weight. Talked like him, too. *Geraldine,* looking down on me saying all the syllables of my name like Daddy used to when he was mad at me. *Geraldine.* Run that miserable thing away from here. When it sneaks up under the porch and dies, you won't be the one who has to get down on your hands and knees and crawl under there to drag it out.

But he was the one wallpapered Little Brother's box with insulation, wasn't he? The one who hung a flap of rug over the door to keep out the wind.

The one who cried like a baby when Pup-pup was hit.

Didn't he see it happen?

Almost. He was turning the corner of Finance. Heard the brakes screech. The bump. He was so mad. Carried Pup-pup and laid him on the porch. Fussing the whole time at Pup-pup. You stupid dog. You stupid dog. How many times have I told you not to run in the street. Like Pup-pup could hear him. Like Pup-pup could understand him if he'd been alive. Ote stomped in the house and up the stairs. Must have washed his hands fifteen minutes. Running water like we used to do when Mama said we better not get out of bed once we were in the bed so running and running that water till it made us pee one long last time before we went to sleep.

What are you girls doing up there wasting all that water? I'ma be up there in ten minutes and you best be under the covers.

Don't be the last one. Don't be on the toilet and just starting to pee good and bumpty-bump here she comes up the steps and means what she says. Uh ohh. It's Niagara Falls and you halfway over and ain't no stopping now. So you just sit there squeezing your knees together and work on that smile you don't hardly believe and she ain't buying one bit when she brams open the door and Why you sitting there grinning like a Chessy cat, girl. I thought I told youall ten minutes ago to get in bed.

Ote washed and washed and washed. I didn't see much blood. Pup-pup looked like Pup-pup laid out there on the porch. Skinny as he was you could always see his ribs moving when he slept. So it wasn't exactly Pup-pup because it was too still. But it wasn't torn up bloody or runned-over looking either.

Whatever Ote needed to wash off, he took his time. He was in the bathroom fifteen minutes, then he turned off the faucets and stepped over into his room and shut the door but you know how the walls and doors in this house don't stop nothing so I could hear him crying when I went out in the hall to call up and ask him if he was all right, ask him what he wanted to do with Pup-pup. I didn't say a word. Just stood there thinking about lots of things. The man crying on his bed was my baby brother. And I'd lived with him all my life in the same house. Now it was just the two of us. Me in the hall listening. Him on his bed, a grown man sobbing cause he's too mad to do anything else. You and Sis moved out first. Then Daddy gone. Then Mama. Just two of us left and two mutts in the house I've lived in all my life. Then it would be one of us left. Then the house empty. I thought some such sorrowful thoughts. And thought of poor Pup-pup. And that's when I decided to say yes to Ernie White after all those years of no.

Dan. If you want a slice of this sweet potato pie you better come in here now and get it. It's leaving here fast. They're carting it away like sweet potato pie's going out of style.

It's his favorite.

That's why I bake one every time old Danny boy's home from school.

Did he tell you he saw Marky at Mellon Park?

No.

Dan was playing ball and Marky was in a bunch that hangs around on the sidelines. He said Marky recognized him. Mumbled hi. Not much more than that. He said Marky didn't look good. Not really with the others but sitting off to the side, on the ground, leaning back against the fence. Dan went over to him and Marky nodded or said hi, enough to let Danny know it really was Marky and not just somebody who looked like Marky, or Marky's ghost because Dan said it wasn't the Marky he remembered. It's the Marky who's been driving us all crazy.

At least he's off Homewood Avenue.

That's good I suppose.

Good and bad. Like everything else. He can move hisself off the Avenue and I'm grateful for that but it also means he can go and get hisself in worse trouble. A healthy young man with a good head on his shoulders and look at him. It's pitiful. Him and lots the other young men like zombies nodding on Homewood Avenue. Pitiful. But as long as he stays on Homewood the cops won't hassle him. What if he goes off and tries to rob somebody or break in somebody's house? Marky has no idea half the time who he is or what he's doing. He's like a baby. He couldn't get away with anything. Just hurt hisself or hurt somebody trying.

What can we do?

We kept him here as long as we could. Ernie talked and talked to him. Got him a job when he dropped out of school. Talked and talked and did everything he could. Marky just let hisself go. He stopped washing. Wore the same clothes night and day. And he was always such a neat kid. A dresser. Stood in front of the mirror for days arranging himself just so for the ladies. I don't understand it. He just fell apart, Penny. You've seen him. You remember how he once was. How many times have I called you and cried over the phone about Marky? Only so much any of us could do, then Ernie said it was too dangerous to have him in the house. Wouldn't leave me here alone with Marky. I about went out my mind then. Not safe in my own house with this child I'd taken in and raised. My husband's nephew who'd been like my own child, who I'd watched grow into a man. Not safe. Nothing to do but let him roam the streets.

None of the agencies or programs would help. What else could you do, Geral?

They said they couldn't take him till he did something wrong. What kind of sense does that make? They'll take him after the damage is done. After he freezes to death sleeping on a bench up in Homewood Park. Or's killed by the cops. Or stark raving foaming at the mouth. They'll take him then. Sorry, Mrs. White, our hands are tied.

Sorry, Mrs. White. Just like the receptionist at Dr. Franklin's. That skinny, pinched-nosed *sorry, Mrs. Whatever-your-name-is* cause they don't give a good goddamn they just doing their job and don't hardly want to be bothered, especially if it's you, and you're black and poor and can't do nothing for them but stand in line and wait your turn and as far as they're concerned you can wait forever.

Did I tell you what happened to me in Dr. Franklin's office, Penny? Five or six people in the waiting room. All of them white. Chattering about this and that. They don't know me and I sure don't know none of them but cause they see my hair ain't kinky and my skin's white as theirs they get on colored people and then it's niggers after they warm up awhile. Ain't niggers enough to make you throw up? Want everything and not willing to work a lick. Up in your face now like they think they own the world. Pushing past you in line at the A&P. Got so now you can't ride a bus without taking your life in your hands. This city's not what it used to be. Used to be a decent place to live till they started having all those nigger babies and now a white person's supposed to grin and bear it. It's three women talking mostly and the chief witch's fat and old as I am. And listen to this. She's afraid of being raped. She hears about white women attacked every day and she's fed up. Then she says, It's time somebody did something, don't you think? Killing's too good for those animals. Looking over at me with her head cocked and her little bit of nappy orange hair got the nerve to google at me like she's waiting for me to wag my head and cluck like the rest of those hens. Well I didn't say a word but the look I gave that heifer froze her mouth shut and kept it shut. Nobody uttered a word for the half hour till it was my turn to see Dr. Franklin. Like when we were bad and Mama'd sit us down and dare us to breathe till she said we could. They're lucky that's all I did. Who she think want to rape her? What self-respecting man, black, white, green or polka dot gon take his life in his hands scuffling with that mountain of blubber?

Geral.

Don't laugh. It wasn't funny. Rolling her Kewpie-doll eyes at me. Ain't niggers terrible? I was about to terrible her ass if I heard *nigger* one more time in her mouth.

Listen at you. Leave that poor woman alone. How old's Little Brother now?

We've had him nine years. A little older than that. Just a wee thing when he arrived on the porch. *Geraldine.* You don't intend bringing that scrawny rat into the house, do you?

And the funny thing is Little Brother must have heard Ote and been insulted. Cause Little Brother never set foot inside the front door. Not in the whole time he's lived here. Not a paw. First he just made a bed in the rags I set out by the front door. Then the cardboard box on the front porch. Then when he grew too big for that Ote built his apartment under the porch. I just sat and rocked the whole time Ote hammering and sawing and cussing when the boards wouldn't stay straight or wouldn't fit the way he wanted them too. Using Daddy's old rusty tools. Busy as a beaver all day long and I'm smiling to myself but I didn't say a mumbling word, girl. If I had let out so much as one signifying I-told-you-so peep, Ote woulda built another box and nailed me up inside. Little Brother went from rags to his own private apartment and in that entire time he's never been inside the house once. I coaxed him, Here, puppy, here, puppy, puppy, and put his food inside the hallway but that's one stubborn creature. Little Brother'd starve to death before he'd walk through the front door.

He about drove Pup-pup crazy. Pup-pup would sneak out and eat Little Brother's food. Drag his rags away and hide them. Snap and growl but Little Brother paid him no mind. Pup-pup thought Little Brother was nuts. Living outdoors in the cold. Not fighting back. Carrying a teddy bear around in his mouth. Peeing in his own food so Pup-pup wouldn't bother it. Pup-pup was so jealous. Went to his grave still believing he had to protect his territory. Pup-pup loved to roam the streets, but bless his heart, he became a regular stay-at-home. Figured he better hang around and wait for Little Brother to make his move. Sometimes I think that's why Pup forgot how to act in the street. In such a hurry to get out and get back, he got himself runned over.

That reminds me of Maria Indovina. Danny wanted me to walk around the neighborhood with him. He wanted to see the places we're always talking about. Mr. Conley's lot. Klein's store. Aunt Aida's. Hazel and Nettie's. Showed him the steps up to Nettie's and told him she never came down them for thirty years. He said, In youall's tales these sounded like the highest, steepest steps in creation. I said they were. Told him I'd follow you and Sis cause I was scared to go first. And no way in the world I'd be first coming back down. They didn't seem like much to him even when I reminded him we were just little girls and Aunt Hazel and Cousin Nettie like queens who lived in another world. Anyway, we were back behind Susquehanna where we used to play and there's a high fence back there on top of the stone wall. It's either a new fence or newly painted but the wall's the same old wall where the bread truck crushed poor Maria Indovina. I told him we played together in those days. Black kids and white kids. Mostly Italian then. Us and the Italians living on the same streets and families knowing each other by name. I told him and he said that's better than it is today. Tried to explain to him we lived on the same streets but didn't really mix. Kids playing together and Hello, how are you, Mr. So-and-so, Mrs. So-and-so, that and a little after-hours under-cover mixing. Only time I ever heard Mama curse was when she called Tina Sabettelli a whorish bitch.

John French wasn't nobody's angel.

Well, I wasn't discussing none of that with Dan. I did tell him about the stain on the wall and how we were afraid to pass by it alone.

Speaking of white people, how's your friend from up the street?

Oh, Vicki's fine. Her dresses are still too mini for my old fuddy-duddy taste. But no worse than what the other girls wearing. Her little girl Carolyn still comes by every afternoon for her piece of candy. She's a lovely child. My blue-eyed sweetheart. I worry about her. Auntie Gerry, I been a good girl today. You got me a sweet, Auntie

Gerry? Yes, darling, I do. And I bring her whatever we have around the house. She'll stand in line with the twins from next door, and Becky and Rashad. They're my regulars but some the others liable to drop by, too. Hi, Aunt Gerry. Can I have a piece of candy, please? When they want something they're so nice and polite, best behaved lil devils in Homewood.

Yes, my friend Vicki's fine. Not easy being the only white person in the neighborhood. I told Fletcher and them to leave her alone. And told her she better respect herself a little more cause they sure won't if she don't. Those jitterbugs don't mean any harm, but boys will be boys. And she's not the smartest young lady in the world. These slicksters around here, you know how they are, hmmph. She better be careful is what I told her. She didn't like hearing what I said but I've noticed her carrying herself a little different when she walks by. Saw her dressed up real nice in Sears in East Liberty last week and she ducked me. I know why, but it still hurt me. Like it hurts me to think my little sugar Carolyn will be calling people niggers someday. If she don't already.

Did you love Ernie all those years you kept him waiting?

Love?

You know what I mean. Love.

Love love?

Love love love. You know what I'm asking you.

Penny. Did you love Billy?

Five children. Twenty-seven years off and on before he jumped up and left for good. I must have. Some of the time.

Real love? Hootchy-gootchy cooing and carrying on?

What did you say? Hootchy-koo? Is that what you said? To tell the truth I can't hardly remember. I must of had an operation when I was about eleven or twelve. Cut all that romance mess out. What's love got to do with anything, anyway.

You asked me first.

Wish I'd had the time. Can you picture Billy and Ernie dancing the huckle-buck, doing the hootchy-koo?

Whoa, girl. You gonna start me laughing.

Hootchy-gootchy-koo. Wish I'd had the time. Maybe it ain't too late. Here's a little hootchy-gootchy-koo for you.

Watch out. You're shaking the table. Whoa. Look at my drink.

Can't help it. I got the hootchy-goos. I'm in love.

Hand me one of those napkins.

Gootchy-gootchy-goo.

Behave now. The kids staring at us. Sitting here acting like two old fools.

So you think I ought to try Tylenol?

Two things for sure. Didn't kill Little Brother. And Princess is sick. Now the other sure thing is it might help Princess and it might not. Make sure it's the baby face. Kids' strength. Try that first.

I just might.

No you won't. You're still laughing at me.

No I'm not. I'm smiling thinking about Ote hammering and sawing an apartment for Little Brother and you rocking on the porch trying to keep your mouth shut.

Like to bust, girl.

But you didn't.

Held it in to this very day. Till I told you.

Hey, youall. Leave a piece of sweet potato pie for your cousin, Dan. It's his favorite.

fever

To Mathew Carey, Esq., who fled Philadelphia in its hour of need and upon his return published a libelous account of the behavior of black nurses and undertakers, thereby injuring all people of my race and especially those without whose unselfish, courageous labours the city could not have survived the late calamity.

Consider Philadelphia from its centrical situation, the extent of its commerce, the number of its artificers, manufacturers and other circumstances, to be to the United States what the heart is to the human body in circulating the blood.
Robert Morris, 1777.

He stood staring through a tall window at the last days of November. The trees were barren women starved for love and they'd stripped off all their clothes, but nobody cared. And not one of them gave a fuck about him, sifting among them, weightless and naked, knowing just as well as they did, no hands would come to touch them, warm them, pick leaves off the frozen ground and stick them back in place. Before he'd gone to bed a flutter of insects had stirred in the dark outside his study. Motion worrying the corner of his eye till he turned and focused where light pooled on the deck, a cone in which he could trap slants of snow so they materialized into wet, gray feathers that blotted against the glass, the planks of the deck. If he stood seven hours, dark would come again. At some point his reflection would hang in the glass, a ship from the other side of the world, docked in the ether. Days were shorter now. A whole one spent wondering what goes wrong would fly away, fly in the blink of an eye.

PERHAPS, *perhaps it may be acceptable to the reader to know how we found the sick affected by the sickness; our opportunities of hearing and seeing them have been very great. They were taken with a chill, a headache, a sick stomach, with pains in their limbs and back, this was the way the sickness in general began, but all were not affected alike, some appeared but slightly affected with some of these symptoms, what confirmed us in the opinion of a person being smitten was the colour of their eyes.*

VICTIMS IN THIS low-lying city perished every year, and some years were worse than others, but the worst by far was the long hot dry summer of '93, when the dead and dying wrested control of the city from the living. Most who were able, fled. The rich to their rural retreats, others to relatives and friends in the countryside or neighboring towns. Some simply left, with no fixed destination, the prospect of privation or starvation on the road preferable to cowering in their homes awaiting the fever's fatal scratching at their door. Busy streets deserted, commerce halted, members of families shunning one another, the sick abandoned to suffer and die alone. Fear ruled. From August when the first cases of fever appeared below Water Street, to November when merciful frosts ended the infestation, the city slowly deteriorated, as if it, too, could suffer the terrible progress of the disease: fever, enfeeblement, violent vomiting and diarrhea, helplessness, delirium, settled dejection when patients *concluded they must go (so the phrase for dying was), and therefore in a kind of fixed determined state of mind went off.*

IN SOME *it raged more furiously than in others—some have languished for seven and ten days, and appeared to get better the day, or some hours before they died, while others were cut off in one, two or three days, but their complaints were similar. Some lost their reason and*

raged with all the fury madness could produce, and died in strong
convulsions. Others retained their reason to the last, and seemed rather
to fall asleep than die.

YELLOW FEVER: an acute infectious disease of subtropical and tropical
New World areas, caused by a filterable virus transmitted by a mosquito of the genus *Aëdes* and characterized by jaundice and dark
colored vomit resulting from hemorrhages. Also called *yellow jack.*

Dengue: an infectious, virulent tropical and subtropical disease
transmitted by mosquitos and characterized by fever, rash and severe
pains in the joints. Also called *breakbone fever, dandy.* [Spanish, of
African origin, akin to Swahili *kindinga.*]

CURLED IN THE black hold of the ship he wonders why his life on solid
green earth had to end, why the gods had chosen this new habitation for
him, floating, chained to other captives, no air, no light, the wooden
walls shuddering, battered, as if some madman is determined to destroy
even this last pitiful refuge where he skids in foul puddles of waste,
bumping other bodies, skinning himself on splintery beams and planks,
always moving, shaken and spilled like palm nuts in the diviner's fist,
and Esu casts his fate, constant motion, tethered to an iron ring.

In the darkness he can't see her, barely feels her light touch on his
fevered skin. Sweat thick as oil but she doesn't mind, straddles him,
settles down to do her work. She enters him and draws his blood up
into her belly. When she's full, she pauses, dreamy, heavy. He could
kill her then; she wouldn't care. But he doesn't. Listens to the whine
of her wings lifting till the whimper is lost in the roar and crash of
waves, creaking wood, prisoners groaning. If she returns tomorrow
and carries away another drop of him, and the next day and the next,
a drop each day, enough days, he'll be gone. Shrink to nothing, slip
out of this iron noose and disappear.

AËDES AEGYPTI: a mosquito of the family *Culicidae*, genus *Aëdes* in
which the female is distinguished by a long proboscis for sucking

blood. This winged insect is a vector (an organism that carries pathogens from one host to another) of yellow fever and dengue. [New Latin *Aëdes,* from Greek *aedes,* unpleasant: *a* −, not + *edos,* pleasant …]

ALL THINGS ARRIVE in the waters and waters carry all things away. So there is no beginning or end, only the waters' flow, ebb, flood, trickle, tides emptying and returning, salt seas and rivers and rain and mist and blood, the sun drowning in an ocean of night, wet sheen of dawn washing darkness from our eyes. This city is held in the water's palm. A captive as surely as I am captive. Long fingers of river, Schuylkill, Delaware, the rest of the hand invisible; underground streams and channels feed the soggy flesh of marsh, clay pit, sink, gutter, stagnant pool. What's not seen is heard in the suck of footsteps through spring mud of unpaved streets. Noxious vapors that sting your eyes, cause you to gag, spit and wince are evidence of a presence, the dead hand cupping this city, the poisons that circulate through it, the sweat on its rotting flesh.

No one has asked my opinion. No one will. Yet I have seen this fever before, and though I can prescribe no cure, I could tell stories of other visitations, how it came and stayed and left us, the progress of disaster, its several stages, its horrors and mitigations. My words would not save one life, but those mortally affrighted by the fever, by the prospect of universal doom, might find solace in knowing there are limits to the power of this scourge that has befallen us, that some, yea, most will survive, that this condition is temporary, a season, that the fever must disappear with the first deep frosts and its disappearance is as certain as the fact it will come again.

They say the rat's-nest ships from Santo Domingo brought the fever. Frenchmen and their black slaves fleeing black insurrection. Those who've seen Barbados's distemper say our fever is its twin born in the tropical climate of the hellish Indies. I know better. I hear the drum, the forest's heartbeat, pulse of the sea that chains the moon's wandering, the spirit's journey. Its throb is source and promise of all things being connected, a mirror storing everything, forgetting nothing. To explain the fever we need no boatloads of refugees, ragged and wracked with killing fevers, bringing death to our shores. We have bred the affliction within our breasts. Each solitary heart contains all the world's tribes, and its precarious dance echoes the drum's thunder. We are our ancestors and our children, neighbors and strangers to ourselves. Fever descends when the waters that connect us are clogged with filth. When our seas are garbage. The waters cannot come and go when we are shut off one from the other, each in his frock coat, wig, bonnet, apron, shop, shoes, skin, behind locks, doors, sealed faces, our blood grows thick and sluggish. Our bodies void infected fluids. Then we are dry and cracked as a desert country, vital parts wither, all dust and dry bones inside. Fever is a drought consuming us from within. Discolored skin caves in upon itself, we burn, expire.

I regret there is so little comfort in this explanation. It takes into account neither climatists nor contagionists, flies in the face of logic and reason, the good doctors of the College of Physicians who would bleed us, purge us, quarantine, plunge us in icy baths, starve us, feed us elixirs of bark and wine, sprinkle us with gunpowder, drown us in vinegar according to the dictates of their various healing sciences. Who, then, is this foolish, old man who receives his wisdom from pagan drums in pagan forests? Are these the delusions of one whose brain the fever has already begun to gnaw? Not quite. True, I have survived other visitations of the fever, but while it prowls this city, I'm in jeopardy again as you are, because I claim no immunity, no magic. The messenger who bears the news of my death will reach me precisely at the stroke determined when it was determined I should tumble from the void and taste air the first time. Nothing is an accident. Fever grows in the secret places of our hearts, planted there when one of us decided to sell one of us to another. The drum must pound ten thousand thousand years to drive that evil away.

FIRES BURN on street corners. Gunshots explode inside wooden houses. Behind him a carter's breath expelled in low, labored pants warns him to edge closer to housefronts forming one wall of a dark, narrow, twisting lane. Thick wheels furrow the unpaved street. In the fire glow the cart stirs a shimmer of dust, faint as a halo, a breath smear on a mirror. Had the man locked in the traces of the cart cursed him or was it just a wheeze of exertion, a complaint addressed to the unforgiving weight of his burden? Creaking wheels, groaning wood, plodding footsteps, the cough of dust, bulky silhouette blackened as it lurches into brightness at the block's end. All gone in a moment. Sounds, motion, sight extinguished. What remained, as if trapped by a lid clamped over the lane, was the stench of dead bodies. A stench cutting through the ubiquitous pall of vinegar and gunpowder. Two, three, four corpses being hauled to Potter's Field, trailed by the unmistakable wake of decaying flesh. He'd heard they raced their carts to the burial ground. Two or three entering Potter's Field from different directions would acknowledge one another with challenges, raised fists, gather their strength for a last dash to the open trenches where they tip their cargoes. Their brethren would wager, cheer, toast the victor with tots of rum. He could hear the rumble of coffins crashing into a common grave, see the comical chariots bouncing, the men's legs pumping, faces contorted by fires that blazed all night at the burial ground. Shouting and curses would hang in the torpid night air, one more nightmare troubling the city's sleep.

He knew this warren of streets as well as anyone. Night or day he could negotiate the twists and turnings, avoid cul-de-sacs, find the river even if his vision was obscured in tunnel-like alleys. He anticipated when to duck a jutting signpost, knew how to find doorways where he was welcome, wooden steps down to a cobbled terrace overlooking the water where his shod foot must never trespass. Once beyond the grand houses lining one end of Water Street, in this quarter of hovels, beneath these wooden sheds leaning shoulder to shoulder were cellars and caves dug into the earth, poorer men's dwellings under these houses of the poor, an invisible region where his people burrow, pull earth like blanket and quilt round themselves to shut out cold and dampness, sleeping multitudes to a room, stacked and crosshatched and spoon fashion, themselves the only fuel, heat of one body passed to others and passed back from all to one. Can he blame the lucky ones who are strong enough to pull the death carts, who celebrate and leap and roar all night around the bonfires? Why should they return here? Where living and dead, sick and well must lie face to face, shivering or sweltering on the same dank floor.

Below Water Street the alleys proliferate. Named and nameless. He knows where he's going but fever has transformed even the familiar.

He'd been waiting in Dr. Rush's entrance hall. An English mirror, oval framed in scalloped brass, drew him. He watched himself glide closer, a shadow, a blur, then the shape of his face materialized from silken depths. A mask he did not recognize. He took the thing he saw and murmured to it. Had he once been in control? Could he tame it again? Like a garden ruined overnight, pillaged, overgrown, trampled by marauding beasts. He stares at the chaos until he can recall familiar contours of earth, seasons of planting, harvesting, green shoots, nodding blossoms, scraping, digging, watering. Once upon a time he'd cultivated this thing, this plot of flesh and blood and bone, but what had it become? Who owned it now? He'd stepped away. His eyes constructed another face and set it there, between him and the wizened old man in the glass. He'd aged twenty years in a glance and the fever possessed the same power to alter suddenly what it touched. This city had grown ancient and fallen into ruin in two months since early August, when the first cases of fever appeared. Something in the bricks, mortar, beams and stones had gone soft, had lost its permanence. When he entered sickrooms, walls fluttered, floors buckled. He could feel roofs pressing down. Putrid heat expanding. In the bodies of victims. In rooms, buildings, streets, neighborhoods. Membranes that preserved the integrity of substances and shapes, kept each in its proper place, were worn thin. He could poke his finger through yellowed skin. A stone wall. The eggshell of his skull. What should be separated was running together. Threatened to burst. Nothing contained the way it was supposed to be. No clear lines of demarcation. A mongrel city. Traffic where there shouldn't be traffic. An awful void opening around him, preparing itself to hold explosions of bile, vomit, gushing bowels, ooze, sludge, seepage.

Earlier in the summer, on a July afternoon, he'd tried to escape the heat by walking along the Delaware. The water was unnaturally calm, isolated into stagnant pools by outcroppings of wharf and jetty. A shelf of rotting matter paralleled the river edge. As if someone had attempted to sweep what was unclean and dead from the water. Bones, skins, entrails, torn carcasses, unrecognizable tatters and remnants broomed into a neat ridge. No sigh of the breeze he'd sought, yet fumes from the rim of garbage battered him in nauseating waves, a palpable medium intimate as wind. Beyond the tidal line of refuge, a pale margin lapped clean by receding waters. Then the iron river itself, flat, dark, speckled by sores of foam that puckered and swirled, worrying the stillness with a life of their own.

Spilled. Spoiled. Those words repeated themselves endlessly as he made his rounds. Dr. Rush had written out his portion, his day's share from the list of dead and dying. He'd purged, bled, comforted and buried victims of the fever. In and out of homes that had become tombs, prisons, charnel houses. Dazed children wandering the streets, searching for their parents. How can he explain to a girl, barely more than an infant, that the father and mother she sobs for are gone from this earth? Departed. Expired. They are resting, child. Asleep forever. In a far, far better place, my sweet, dear suffering one. In God's bosom. Wrapped in His incorruptible arms. A dead mother with a dead baby at her breast. Piteous cries of the helpless offering all they own for a drink of water. How does he console the delirious boy who pummels him, fastens himself on his leg because he's put the boy's mother in a box and now must nail shut the lid?

Though light-headed from exhaustion, he's determined to spend a few hours here, among his own people. But were these lost ones really his people? The doors of his church were open to them, yet these were the ones who stayed away, wasting their lives in vicious pastimes of the idle, the unsaved, the ignorant. His benighted brethren who'd struggled to reach this city of refuge and then, once inside the gates, had fallen, prisoners again, trapped by chains of dissolute living as they'd formerly been snared in the bonds of slavery. He'd come here and preached to them. Thieves, beggars, loose women, debtors, fugitives, drunkards, gamblers, the weak, crippled and outcast with nowhere else to go. They spurned his church so he'd brought church to them, preaching in gin mills, whoring dens, on street corners. He'd been jeered and hooted, spat upon, clods of unnameable filth had spattered his coat. But a love for them, as deep and unfathomable as his sorrow, his pity, brought him back again and again, exhorting them, setting the gospel before them so they might partake of its bounty, the infinite goodness, blessed sustenance therein. Jesus had toiled among the wretched, the outcast, that flotsam and jetsam deposited like a ledge of filth on the banks of the city. He understood what had brought the dark faces of his brethren north, to the Quaker promise of this town, this cradle and capital of a New World, knew the misery they were fleeing, the bright star in the Gourd's handle that guided them, the joy leaping in their hearts when at last, at last the opportunity to be viewed as men instead of things was theirs. He'd dreamed such dreams himself, oh yes, and prayed that the light of hope would never be extinguished. He'd been praying for deliverance, for peace and understanding when God had granted him a vision, hordes of sable bondsmen throwing off their chains, marching, singing, a path opening in the sea, the sea shaking its shaggy shoulders, resplendent with light and power. A radiance sparkling in this walkway through the water, pearls, diamonds, spears of light. This was the glistening way home. Waters parting, glory blinking and winking. Too intense to stare at, a promise shimmering, a rainbow arching over the end of the path. A hand tapped him. He'd waited for it to blend into the vision, for its meaning to shine forth in the language neither word nor thought, God was speaking in His visitation. Tapping became a grip. Someone was shoving him. He was being pushed off his knees, hauled to his feet. Someone was snatching him from the honeyed dream of salvation. When his eyes popped open he knew the name of each church elder manhandling him. Pale faces above a wall of black cloth belonged to his fellow communicants. He knew without looking the names of the men whose hands touched him gently, steering, coaxing, and those whose hands dug into his flesh, the impatient, imperious, rough hands that shunned any contact with him except as overseer or master.

Allen, Allen. Do you hear me? You and your people must not kneel at the front of the gallery. On your feet. Come. Come. Now. On your feet.

Behind the last row of pews. There ye may fall down on your knees and give praise.

And so we built our African house of worship. But its walls could not imprison the Lord's word. Go forth. Go forth. And he did so. To this sinful quarter. Tunnels, cellars and caves. Where no sunlight penetrates. Where wind off the river cuts like a knife. Chill of icy spray channeled here from the ocean's wintry depths. Where each summer the brackish sea that is mouth and maw and bowel deposits its waste in puddles stinking to high heaven.

Water Street becomes what it's named, rises round his ankles, soaks his boots, threatens to drag him down. Patrolling these murky depths he's predator, scavenger, the prey of some dagger-toothed creature whose shadow closes over him like a net.

When the first settlers arrived here they'd scratched caves into the soft earth of the riverbank. Like ants. Rats. Gradually they'd pushed inland, laying out a geometrical grid of streets, perpendicular, true angled and straight edged, the mirror of their rectitude. Black Quaker coats and dour visages were remembrances of mud, darkness, the place of their lying in, cocooned like worms, propagating dreams of a holy city. The latest comers must always start here, on this dotted line, in this riot of alleys, lanes, tunnels. Wave after wave of immigrants unloaded here, winnowed here, dying in these shanties, grieving in strange languages. But white faces move on, bury their dead, bear their children, negotiate the invisible reef between this broken place and the foursquare town. Learn enough of their new tongue to say to the blacks they've left behind, *thou shalt not pass.*

I WATCHED HIM bring the scalding liquid to his lips and thought to myself that's where his color comes from. The black brew he drinks every morning. Coloring him, changing him. A hue I had not considered until that instant as other than absence, something nonwhite and therefore its opposite, what light would be if extinguished, sky or sea drained of the color blue when the sun disappears, the blackness of cinders. As he sips, steam rises. I peer into the cup that's become mine, at the moon in its center, waxing, waning. A light burning in another part of the room caught there, as my face would be if I leaned over the cup's hot mouth. But I have no wish to see my face. His is what I study as I stare into my cup and see not absence, but the presence of wood darkly stained, wet plowed earth, a boulder rising from a lake, blackly glistening as it sheds crowns and beards and necklaces of water. His color neither neglect nor abstention, nor mystery, but a swelling tide in his skin of this bitter morning beverage it is my habit to imbibe.

We were losing, clearly losing the fight. One day in mid-September fifty-seven were buried before noon.

He'd begun with no preamble. Our conversation taken up again directly as if the months since our last meeting were no more than a cobweb his first words lightly brush away. I say conversation but a better word would be soliloquy because I was only a listener, a witness learning his story, a story buried so deeply he couldn't recall it, but dreamed pieces, a conversation with himself, a reverie with the power to sink us both into its unreality. So his first words did not begin the story where I remembered him ending it in our last session, but picked up midstream the ceaseless play of voices only he heard, always, summoning him, possessing him, enabling him to speak, to be.

Despair was in my heart. The fiction of our immunity had been exposed for the vicious lie it was, a not so subtle device for wresting us from our homes, our loved ones, the afflicted among us, and sending us to aid strangers. First they blamed us, called the sickness Barbados fever, a contagion from those blood-soaked islands, brought to these shores by refugees from the fighting in Santo Domingo. We were not welcome anywhere. A dark skin was seen not only as a badge of shame for its wearer. Now we were evil incarnate, the mask of long agony and violent death. Black servants were discharged. The draymen, carters, barbers, caterers, oyster sellers, street vendors could find no custom. It mattered not that some of us were born here and spoke no language but the English language, second-, even third-generation African Americans who knew no other country, who laughed at the antics of newly landed immigrants, Dutchmen, Welshmen, Scots, Irish, Frenchmen who had turned our marketplaces into Babel, stomping along in their clodhopper shoes, strange costumes, haughty airs, Lowlander gibberish that sounded like men coughing or dogs barking. My fellow countrymen searching everywhere but in their own hearts, the foulness upon which this city is erected, to lay blame on others for the killing fever, pointed their fingers at foreigners and called it Palatine fever, a pestilence imported from those low countries in Europe where, I have been told, war for control of the sea-lanes, the human cargoes transported thereupon, has raged for a hundred years.

But I am losing the thread, the ironical knot I wished to untangle for you. How the knife was plunged in our hearts, then cruelly twisted. We were proclaimed carriers of the fever and treated as pariahs, but when it became expedient to command our services to nurse the sick and bury the dead, the previous allegations were no longer mentioned. Urged on by desperate counselors, the mayor granted us a blessed immunity. We were ordered to save the city.

I swear to you, and the bills of mortality, published by the otherwise unreliable Mr. Carey, support my contention, that the fever dealt with us severely. Among the city's poor and destitute the fever's ravages were most deadly and we are always the poorest of the poor. If an ordinance forbidding ringing of bells to mourn the dead had not been passed, that awful tolling would have marked our days, the watches of the night in our African American community, as it did in those environs of the city we were forbidden to inhabit. Every morning before I commenced my labors for the sick and dying, I would hear moaning, screams of pain, fearful cries and supplications, a chorus of lamentations scarring daybreak, my people awakening to a nightmare that was devouring their will to live.

The small strength I was able to muster each morning was sorely tried the moment my eyes and ears opened upon the sufferings of my people, the reality that gave the lie to the fiction of our immunity. When my duties among the whites were concluded, how many nights did I return and struggle till dawn with victims here, my friends, parishioners, wandering sons of Africa whose faces I could not look upon without seeing my own. I was commandeered to rise and go forth to the general task of saving the city, forced to leave this neighborhood where my skills were sorely needed. I nursed those who hated me, deserted the ones I loved, who loved me.

I RECITE the story many, many times to myself, let many voices speak to me till one begins to sound like the sea or rain or my feet those mornings shuffling through thick dust.

WE ARRIVED at Bush Hill early. To spare ourselves a long trek in the oppressive heat of day. Yellow haze hung over the city. Plumes of smoke from blazes in Potter's Field, from fires on street corners curled above the rooftops, lending the dismal aspect of a town sacked and burned. I've listened to the Santo Domingans tell of the burning of Cap François. How the capital city was engulfed by fires set in cane fields by the rebelling slaves. Horizon in flames all night as they huddled offshore in ships, terrified, wondering where next they'd go, if any port would permit them to land, empty-handed slaves, masters whose only wealth now was naked black bodies locked in the hold, wide-eyed witnesses of an empire's downfall, chanting, moaning, uncertain as the sea rocked them, whether or not anything on earth could survive the fearful conflagration consuming the great city of Cap François.

Dawn breaking on a smoldering landscape, writhing columns of smoke, a general cloud of haze the color of a fever victim's eyes. I turn and stare at it a moment, then fall in again with my brother's footsteps trudging through untended fields girding Bush Hill.

FROM A PRISONER-OF-WAR SHIP in New York harbor where the British had interned him he'd seen that city shed its graveclothes of fog. Morning after morning it would paint itself damp and gray, a flat sketch on the canvas of sky, a tentative, shivering screen of housefronts, sheds, sprawling warehouses floating above the river. Then shadows and hollows darkened. A jumble of masts, spars, sails began to sway, little boats plied lanes between ships, tiny figures inched along wharves and docks, doors opened, windows slid up or down, lending an illusion of depth and animation to the portrait. This city infinitely beyond his reach, this charade other men staged to mock him, to mark the distance he could not travel, the shore he'd never reach, the city, so to speak, came to life and with its birth each morning dropped the palpable weight of his despair. His loneliness and exile. Moored in pewter water, on an island that never stopped moving but never arrived anywhere. The city a mirage of light and air, chimera of paint, brush and paper, mattered naught except that it was denied him. It shimmered. Tolled. Unsettled the watery place where he was sentenced to dwell. Conveyed to him each morning the same doleful tidings: *The dead are legion, the living a froth on dark, layered depths. But you are neither, and less than both.* Each night he dreamed it burning, razed the city till nothing remained but a dry, black crust, crackling, crunching under his boots as he strides, king of the nothing he surveys.

WE PASSED HOLES dug into the earth where the sick are interred. Some died in these shallow pits, awash in their own vomited and voided filth, before a bed in the hospital could be made ready for them. Others believed they were being buried alive, and unable to crawl out, howled till reason or strength deserted them. A few, past caring, slept soundly in these ditches, resisted the attendants sent to rouse them and transport them inside, once they realized they were being resurrected to do battle again with the fever. I'd watched the red-bearded French doctor from Santo Domingo with his charts and assistants inspecting this zone, his *salle d'attente* he called it, greeting and reassuring new arrivals, interrogating them, nodding and bowing, hurrying from pit to pit, peering down at his invisible patients like a gardener tending seeds.

An introduction to the grave, a way into the hospital that prefigured the way most would leave it. That's what this bizarre rite of admission had seemed at first. But through this and other peculiar stratagems, Deveze, with his French practice, had transformed Bush Hill from lazarium to a clinic where victims of the fever, if not too weak upon arrival, stood a chance of surviving.

The cartman employed by Bush Hill had suddenly fallen sick. Faithful Wilcox had never missed a day, ferrying back and forth from town to hospital, hospital to Potter's Field. Bush Hill had its own cemetery now. Daily rations of dead could be disposed of less conspicuously in a plot on the grounds of the estate, screened from the horror-struck eyes of the city. No one had trusted the hospital. Tales of bloody chaos reigning there had filtered back to the city. Citizens believed it was a place where the doomed were stored until they died. Fever victims would have to be dragged from their beds into Bush Hill's cart. They'd struggle and scream, pitch themselves from the rolling cart, beg for help when the cart passed a rare pedestrian daring or foolish enough to be abroad in the deadly streets.

I wondered for the thousandth time why some were stricken, some not. Dr. Rush and this Deveze dipped their hands into the entrails of corpses, stirred the black, corrupted blood, breathed infected vapors exhaled from mortified remains. I'd observed both men steeped in noxious fluids expelled by their patients, yet neither had fallen prey to the fever. Stolid, dim Wilcox maintained daily concourse with the sick and buried the dead for two months before he was infected. They say a woman, undiscovered until boiling stench drove her neighbors into the street crying for aid, was the cause of Wilcox's downfall. A large woman, bloated into an even more cumbersome package by gases and liquids seething inside her body, had slipped from his grasp as he and another had hoisted her up into the cart. Catching against a rail, her body had slammed down and burst, spraying Wilcox like a fountain. Wilcox did not pride himself on being the tidiest of men, nor did his job demand one who was overfastidious, but the reeking stench from that accident was too much even for him and he departed in a huff to change his polluted garments. He never returned. So there I was at Bush Hill, where Rush had assigned me with my brother, to bury the flow of dead that did not ebb just because the Charon who was their familiar could no longer attend them.

THE DOCTORS BELIEVE they can find the secret of the fever in the victims' dead bodies. They cut, saw, extract, weigh, measure. The dead are carved into smaller and smaller bits and the butchered parts studied but they do not speak. What I know of the fever I've learned from the words of those I've treated, from stories of the living that are ignored by the good doctors. When lancet and fleam bleed the victims, they offer up stories like prayers.

IT WAS A jaunty day. We served our white guests and after they'd eaten, they served us at the long, linen-draped tables. A sumptuous feast in the oak grove prepared by many and willing hands. All the world's eyes seemed to be watching us. The city's leading men, black and white, were in attendance to celebrate laying the cornerstone of St. Thomas Episcopal African Church. In spite of the heat and clouds of mettlesome insects, spirits were high. A gathering of whites and blacks in good Christian fellowship to commemorate the fruit of shared labor. Perhaps a new day was dawning. The picnic occurred in July. In less than a month the fever burst upon us.

WHEN YOU OPEN the dead, black or white, you find: the dura mater covering the brain is white and fibrous in appearance. The leptomeninges covering the brain are clear and without opacifications. The brain weighs 1,450 grams and is formed symmetrically. Cut sections of the cerebral hemispheres reveal normal-appearing gray matter throughout. The white matter of the corpus callosum is intact and bears no lesions. The basal ganglia are in their normal locations and grossly appear to be without lesions. The ventricles are symmetrical and filled with crystal-clear cerebrospinal fluid.

The cerebellum is formed symmetrically. The nuclei of the cerebellum are unremarkable. Multiple sections through the pons, medulla oblongata and upper brain stem reveal normal gross anatomy. The cranial nerves are in their normal locations and unremarkable.

The muscles of the neck are in their normal locations. The cartilages of the larynx and the hyoid bone are intact. The thyroid and parathyroid glands are normal on their external surface. The mucosa of the larynx is shiny, smooth and without lesions. The vocal cords are unremarkable. A small amount of bloody material is present in the upper trachea.

The heart weighs 380 grams. The epicardial surface is smooth, glistening and without lesions. The myocardium of the left ventricle and septum are of a uniform meaty-red, firm appearance. The endocardial surfaces are smooth, glistening and without lesions. The auricular appendages are free from thrombi. The valve leaflets are thin and delicate, and show no evidence of vegetation.

The right lung weighs 400 grams. The left lung 510 grams. The pleural surfaces of the lungs are smooth and glistening.

The esophageal mucosa is glistening, white and folded. The stomach contains a large amount of black, noxious bile. A veriform appendix is present. The ascending, transverse and descending colon reveal hemorrhaging, striations, disturbance of normal mucosa patterns throughout. A small amount of bloody, liquid feces is present in the ano-rectal canal.

The liver weighs 1,720 grams. The spleen weighs 150 grams. The right kidney weighs 190 grams. The left kidney weighs 180 grams. The testes show a glistening white tunica albuginea. Sections are unremarkable.

DR. RUSH and his assistants examined as many corpses as possible in spite of the hurry and tumult of never-ending attendance on the sick. Rush hoped to prove his remedy, his analysis of the cause and course of the fever correct. Attacked on all sides by his medical brethren for purging and bleeding patients already in a drastically weakened state, Rush lashed back at his detractors, wrote pamphlets, broadsides, brandished the stinking evidence of his postmortems to demonstrate conclusively how the sick drowned in their own poisoned fluids. The putrefaction, the black excess, he proclaimed, must be drained away, else the victim inevitably succumbs.

Dearest:
I shall not return home again until this business of the fever is terminated. I fear bringing the dread contagion into our home. My life is in the hands of God and as long as He sees fit to spare me I will persist in my labors on behalf of the sick, dying and dead. We are losing the battle. Eighty-eight were buried this past Thursday. I tremble for your safety. Wish the lie of immunity were true. Please let me know by way of a note sent to the residence of Dr. Rush that you and our dear Martha are well. I pray every hour that God will preserve you both. As difficult as it is to rise each morning and go with Thomas to perform our duties, the task would be unbearable if I did not hold in my heart a vision of these horrors ending, a blessed shining day when I return to you and drop this weary head upon your sweet bosom.

Allen, Allen, he called to me. Observe how even after death, the body rejects this bloody matter from nose and bowel and mouth. Verily, the patient who had expired at least an hour before, continued to stain the cloth I'd wrapped round him. We'd searched the rooms of a regal mansion, discovering six members of a family, patriarch, son, son's wife and three children, either dead or in the last frightful stages of the disease. Upon the advice of one of Dr. Rush's most outspoken critics, they had refused mercury purges and bleeding until now, when it was too late for any earthly remedy to preserve them. In the rich furnishings of this opulent mansion, attended by one remaining servant whom fear had not driven away, three generations had withered simultaneously, this proud family's link to past and future cut off absolutely, the great circle broken. In the first bedroom we'd entered we'd found William Spurgeon, merchant, son and father, present manager of the family fortune, so weak he could not speak, except with pained blinks of his terrible golden eyes. Did he welcome us? Was he apologizing to good Dr. Rush for doubting his cure? Did he fear the dark faces of my brother and myself? Quick, too quickly, he was gone. Answering no questions. Revealing nothing of his state of mind. A savaged face frozen above the blanket. Ancient beyond years. Jaundiced eyes not fooled by our busy ministrations, but staring through us, fixed on the eternal stillness soon to come. And I believe I learned in that yellow cast of his eyes, the exact hue of the sky, if sky it should be called, hanging over the next world where we abide.

Allen, Allen. He lasted only moments and then I wrapped him in a sheet from the chest at the foot of his canopied bed. We lifted him into a humbler litter, crudely nailed together, the lumber still green. Allen, look. Stench from the coffin cut through the oppressive odors permeating this doomed household. See. Like an infant the master of the house had soiled his swaddling clothes. Seepage formed a dark river and dripped between roughly jointed boards. We found his wife where she'd fallen, naked, yellow above the waist, black below. As always the smell presaged what we'd discover behind a closed door. This woman had possessed closets of finery, slaves who dressed, fed, bathed and painted her, and yet here she lay, no one to cover her modesty, to lift her from the floor. Dr. Rush guessed from the discoloration she'd been dead two days, a guess confirmed by the loyal black maid, sick herself, who'd elected to stay when all others had deserted her masters. The demands of the living too much for her.

She'd simply shut the door on her dead mistress. No breath, no heartbeat, Sir. I could not rouse her, Sir. I intended to return, Sir, but I was too weak to move her, too exhausted by my labors, Sir. Tears rolled down her creased black face and I wondered in my heart how this abused and despised old creature in her filthy apron and turban, this frail, worn woman, had survived the general calamity while the strong and pampered toppled round her.

I wanted to demand of her why she did not fly out the door now, finally freed of her burden, her lifelong enslavement to the whims of white people. Yet I asked her nothing. Considered instead myself, a man who'd worked years to purchase his wife's freedom, then his own, a so-called freeman, and here I was following in the train of Rush and his assistants, a functionary, a lackey, insulted daily by those I risked my life to heal.

Why did I not fly? Why was I not dancing in the streets, celebrating God's judgment on this wicked city? Fever made me freer than I'd ever been. Municipal government had collapsed. Anarchy ruled. As long as fever did not strike me I could come and go anywhere I pleased. Fortunes could be amassed in the streets. I could sell myself to the highest bidder, as nurse or undertaker, as surgeon trained by the famous Dr. Rush to apply his lifesaving cure. Anyone who would enter houses where fever was abroad could demand outrageous sums for negligible services. To be spared the fever was a chance for anyone, black or white, to be a king.

SO WHY DO YOU follow him like a loyal puppy, you confounded black fool? He wagged his finger. *You...* His finger a gaunt, swollen-jointed, cracked-bone, chewed thing. Like the nose on his face. The nose I'd thought looked more like finger than nose. *Fool. Fool.* Finger wagging, then the cackle. The barnyard braying. Berserk chickens cackling in his skinny, goiter-knobbed throat. You are a fool, you black son of Ham. You slack-witted, Nubian ape. You progeny of Peeping Toms and orangutans. Who forces you to accompany that madman Rush on his murderous tours? He kills a hundred for every one he helps with his lamebrain, nonsensical, unnatural, Sangrado cures. Why do you tuck your monkey tail between your legs and skip after that butcher? Are you his shadow, a mindless, spineless black puddle of slime with no will of its own?

You are a good man, Allen. You worry about the souls of your people in this soulless wilderness. You love your family and your God. You are a beacon and steadfast. Your fatal flaw is narrowness of vision. You cannot see beyond these shores. The river, that stinking gutter into which the city shovels its shit and extracts its drinking water, that long-suffering string of spittle winds to an ocean. A hundred miles downstream the foamy mouth of the land sucks on the Atlantic's teat, trade winds saunter and a whole wide world awaits the voyager. I know, Allen. I've been everywhere. Buying and selling everywhere.

If you would dare be Moses to your people and lead them out of this land, you'd find fair fields for your talent. Not lapdogging or doggy-trotting behind or fetch doggy or lie doggy or doggy open your legs or doggy stay still while I beat you. Follow the wound that is a river back to the sea. Be gone, be gone. While there's still time. If there is time, *mon frère.* If the pestilence has not settled in you already, breathed from my foul guts into yours, even as we speak.

HERE'S A MASTER for you. A real master, Allen. The fever that's supping on my innards. I am more slave than you've ever been. I do its bidding absolutely. Cough up my lungs. Shit hunks of my bowel. When I die, they say my skin will turn as black as yours, Allen.

Return to your family. Do not leave them again. Whatever the Rushes promise, whatever they threaten.

ONCE, ten thousand years ago I had a wife and children. I was like you, Allen, proud, innocent, forward looking, well-spoken, well-mannered, a beacon and steadfast. I began to believe the whispered promise that I could have more. More of what, I didn't ask. Didn't know, but I took my eyes off what I loved in order to obtain this more. Left my wife and children and when I returned they were gone. Forever lost to me. The details are not significant. Suffice to say the circumstances of my leaving were much like yours. Very much like yours, Allen. And I lost everything. Became a wanderer among men. Bad news people see coming from miles away. A pariah. A joke. I'm not black like you, Allen. But I will be soon. Sooner than you'll be white. And if you're ever white, you'll be as dead as I'll be when I'm black.

Why do you desert your loved ones? What impels you to do what you find so painful, so unjust? Are you not a man? And free?

Her sleepy eyes, your lips on her warm cheek, each time may be the last meeting on this earth. The circumstances are similar, my brother. My shadow. My dirty face.

THE DEAD are legion, the living a froth on dark, layered depths.

MASTER ABRAHAM. There's a gentleman to see you, Sir. The golden-haired lad bound to me for seven years was carted across the seas, like you, Allen, in the bowels of a leaky tub. A son to replace my son his fathers had clubbed to death when they razed the ghetto of Antwerp. But I could not tame the inveterate hate, his aversion and contempt for me. From my aerie, at my desk secluded among barrels, bolts, crates and trunks of the shop's attic, I watched him steal, drink, fornicate. I overheard him denounce me to a delegate sent round to collect a tithe during the emergency. 'Tis well known in the old country that Jews bring the fever. Palatine fever that slays whole cities. They carry it under dirty fingernails, in the wimples of lizardy private parts. Pass it on with the evil eye. That's why we hound them from our towns, exterminate them. Beware of Master Abraham's glare. And the black-coated vulture listened intently. I could see him toting up the account in his small brain. Kill the Jew. Gain a shop and sturdy prentice, too. But I survived till fever laid me low and the cart brought me here to Bush Hill. For years he robbed and betrayed me and all my revenge was to treat him better. Allow him to pilfer, lie, embezzle. Let him grow fat and careless as I knew he would. With a father's boundless kindness I destroyed him. The last sorry laugh coming when I learned he died in agony, fever shriven, following by a day his Water Street French whore my indulgence allowed him to keep.

. . .

IN AMSTERDAM I sold diamonds, Allen. In Barcelona they plucked hairs from my beard to fashion charms that brought ill fortune to their enemies. There were nights in dungeons when the mantle of my suffering was all I possessed to wrap round me and keep off mortal cold. I cursed God for choosing me, choosing my people to cuckold and slaughter. Have you heard of the Lamed-Vov, the Thirty-six Just Men set apart to suffer the reality humankind cannot bear? Saviors. But not Gods like your Christ. Not magicians, not sorcerers with bags of tricks, Allen. No divine immunities. Flesh and blood saviors. Men like we are, Allen. If man you are beneath your sable hide. Men who cough and scratch their sores and bleed and stink. Whose teeth rot. Whose wives and children are torn from them. Who wander the earth unable to die, but men always, men till God plucks them up and returns them to His side where they must thaw ten centuries to melt the crust of earthly grief and misery they've taken upon themselves. Ice men. Snowmen. I thought for many years I might be one of them. In my vanity. My self-pity. My foolishness. But no. One lifetime of sorrows enough for me. I'm just another customer. One more in the crowd lined up at his stall to purchase his wares.

You do know, don't you, Allen, that God is a bookseller? He publishes one book—the text of suffering—over and over again. He disguises it between new boards, in different shapes and sizes, prints on varying papers, in many fonts, adds prefaces and postscripts to deceive the buyer, but it's always the same book.

YOU SAY you do not return to your family because you don't want to infect them. Perhaps your fear is well-founded. But perhaps it also masks a greater fear. Can you imagine yourself, Allen, as other than you are? A free man with no charlatan Rush to blame. The weight of your life in your hands.

You've told me tales of citizens paralyzed by fear, of slaves on shipboard who turn to stone in their chains, their eyes boiled in the sun. Is it not possible that you suffer the converse of this immobility?

You, sir, unable to stop an endless round of duty and obligation. Turning pages as if the next one or the next will let you finish the story and return to your life.

Your life, man. Tell me what sacred destiny, what nigger errand keeps you standing here at my filthy pallet? Fly, fly, fly away home. Your house is on fire, your children burning.

I HAVE LIVED to see the slaves free. My people frolic in the streets. Black and white. The ones who believe they are either or both or neither. I am too old for dancing. Too old for foolishness. But this full moon makes me wish for two good legs. For three. Straddled a broomstick when I was a boy. Giddy-up, Giddy-up. Galloping m'lord, m'lady, around the yard I should be sweeping. Dust in my wake. Chickens squawking. My eyes everywhere at once so I would not be caught out by mistress or master in the sin of idleness. Of dreaming. Of following a child's inclination. My broom steed snatched away. Become a rod across my back. Ever cautious. Dreaming with one eye open. The eye I am now, old and gimpy limbed, watching while my people celebrate the rumor of Old Pharaoh's capitulation.

I've shed this city like a skin, wiggling out of it tenscore and more years, by miles and els, fretting, twisting. Many days I did not know whether I'd wrenched freer or crawled deeper into the sinuous pit. Somewhere a child stood, someplace green, keeping track, waiting for me. Hoping I'd meet him again, hoping my struggle was not in vain. I search that child's face for clues to my blurred features. Flesh drifted and banked, eroded by wind and water, the landscape of this city fitting me like a skin. Pray for me, child. For my unborn parents I carry in this orphan's potbelly. For this ancient face that slips like water through my fingers.

Night now. Bitter cold night. Fires in the hearths of lucky ones. Many of us still abide in dark cellars, caves dug into the earth below poor men's houses. For we are poorer still, burrow there, pull earth like blanket and quilt round us to shut out cold, sleep multitudes to a room, stacked and crosshatched and spoon fashion, ourselves the fuel, heat of one body passed to others and passed back from all to one. No wonder then the celebration does not end as a blazing chill sweeps off the Delaware. Those who leap and roar round the bonfires are better off where they are. They have no place else to go.

GIVEN THE DERIVATION of the words, you could call the deadly, winged visitors an *unpleasantness from Egypt.*

PUTRID STINK rattles in his nostrils. He must stoop to enter the cellar. No answer as he shouts his name, his mission of mercy. Earthen floor, ceiling and walls buttressed by occasional beams, slabs of wood. Faint bobbing glow from his lantern. He sees himself looming and shivering on the walls, a shadowy presence with more substance than he feels he possesses at this late hour. After a long day of visits, this hovel his last stop before returning to his brother's house for a few hours of rest. He has learned that exhaustion is a swamp he can wade through and on the far side another region where a thin trembling version of himself toils while he observes, bemused, slipping in and out of sleep, amazed at the likeness, the skill with which that other mounts and sustains him. Mimicry. Puppetry. Whatever controls this other, he allows the impostor to continue, depends upon it to work when he no longer can. After days in the city proper with Rush, he returns to these twisting streets beside the river that are infected veins and arteries he must bleed.

At the rear of the cave, so deep in shadow he stumbles against it before he sees it, is a mound of rags. When he leans over it, speaking down into the darkness, he knows instantly this is the source of the terrible smell, that something once alive is rotting under the rags. He thinks of autumn leaves blown into mountainous, crisp heaps, the north wind cleansing itself and the city of summer. He thinks of anything, any image that will rescue him momentarily from the nauseating stench, postpone what he must do next. He screams no, no to himself as he blinks away his wife's face, the face of his daughter. His neighbors had promised to check on them, he hears news almost daily. There is no rhyme or reason in whom the fever takes, whom it spares, but he's in the city every day, exposed to its victims, breathing fetid air, touching corrupted flesh. Surely if someone in his family must die, it will be him. His clothes are drenched in vinegar, he sniffs the nostrum of gunpowder, bark and asafetida in a bag pinned to his coat. He's prepared to purge and bleed himself, he's also ready and quite willing to forgo these precautions and cures if he thought surrendering his life might save theirs. He thinks and unthinks a picture of her hair, soft against his cheek, the wet warmth of his daughter's backside in the crook of his arm as he carries her to her mother's side where she'll be changed and fed. No. Like a choking mist, the smell of decaying flesh stifles him, forces him to turn away, once, twice, before he watches himself bend down into the brunt of it and uncover the sleepers.

Two Santo Domingan refugees, slave or free, no one knew for sure, inhabited this cellar. They had moved in less than a week before, the mother huge with child, man and woman both wracked by fever. No one knows how long the couple's been unattended. There was shame in the eyes and voices of the few from whom he'd gleaned bits and pieces of the Santo Domingans' history. Since no one really knew them and few nearby spoke their language, no one was willing to risk, et cetera. Except for screams one night, no one had seen or heard signs of life. If he'd been told nothing about them, his nose would have led him here.

He winces when he sees the dead man and woman, husband and wife, not entwined as in some ballad of love eternal, but turned back to back, distance between them, as if the horror were too visible, too great to bear, doubled in the other's eyes. What had they seen before they flung away from each other? If he could, he would rearrange them, spare the undertakers this vision.

Rat feet and rat squeak in the shadows. He'd stomped his feet, shooed them before he entered, hollered as he threw back the covers, but already they were accustomed to his presence, back at work. They'd bite indiscriminately, dead flesh, his flesh. He curses and flails his staff against the rags, strikes the earthen floor to keep the scavengers at bay. Those sounds are what precipitate the high-pitched cries that first frighten him, then shame him, then propel him to a tall packing crate turned on its end, atop which another crate is balanced. Inside the second wicker container, which had imported some item from some distant place into this land, twin brown babies hoot and wail.

WE ARE PASSING over the Dismal Swamp. On the right is the Appalachian range, some of the oldest mountains on earth. Once there were steep ridges and valleys all through here but erosion off the mountains created landfill several miles deep in places. This accounts for the rich loamy soil of the region. Over the centuries several southern states were formed from this gradual erosion. The cash crops of cotton and tobacco so vital to southern prosperity were ideally suited to the fertile soil.

YEAH, I nurse these old funky motherfuckers, all right. White people, specially old white people, lemme tell you, boy, them peckerwoods stink. Stone dead fishy wet stink. Talking all the time bout niggers got BO. Well, white folks got the stink and gone, man. Don't be putting my hands on them, neither. Never. Huh uh. If I touch them, be wit gloves. They some nasty people, boy. And they don't be paying me enough to take no chances wit my health. Matter of fact they ain't paying me enough to really be expecting me to work. Yeah. Starvation wages. So I ain't hardly touching them. Or doing much else either. Got to smoke a cigarette to get close to some of them. Piss and shit theyselves like babies. They don't need much taking care anyway. Most of them three-quarters dead already. Ones that ain't is crazy. Nobody don't want them round, that's why they here. Talking to theyselves. Acting like they speaking to a roomful of people and not one soul in the ward paying attention. There's one old black dude, must be a hundred, he be muttering away to hisself nonstop everyday. Pitiful, man. Hope I don't never get that old. Shoot me, bro, if I start to getting old and fucked up in body and mind like them. Don't want no fools like me hanging over me when I can't do nothing no more for my ownself. Shit. They ain't paying me nothing so that's what I do. Nothing. Least I don't punch em or tease em or steal they shit like some the staff. And I don't pretend I'm God like these so-called professionals and doctors flittin round here drawing down that long bread. Naw. I just mind my own business, do my time. Cop a little TV, sneak me a joint when nobody's around. It ain't all that bad, really. Long as I ain't got no ole lady and crumb crushers. Don't know how the married cats make it on the little bit of chump change they pay us. But me, I'm free. It ain't that bad, really.

BY THE TIME his brother brought him the news of their deaths . . .

ALMOST AN AFTERTHOUGHT. The worst, he believed, had been overcome. Only a handful of deaths the last weeks of November. The city was recovering. Commerce thriving. Philadelphia must be revictualed, refueled, rebuilt, reconnected to the countryside, to markets foreign and domestic, to products, pleasures and appetites denied during the quarantine months of the fever. A new century would soon be dawning. We must forget the horrors. The Mayor proclaims a new day. Says let's put the past behind us. Of the eleven who died in the fire he said extreme measures were necessary as we cleansed ourselves of disruptive influences. The cost could have been much greater, he said I regret the loss of life, especially the half dozen kids, but I commend all city officials, all volunteers who helped return the city to the arc of glory that is its proper destiny.

WHEN THEY CUT him open, the one who decided to stay, to be a beacon and steadfast, they will find: liver (1,720 grams), spleen (150 grams), right kidney (190 grams), left kidney (180 grams), brain (1,450 grams), heart (380 grams) and right next to his heart, the miniature hand of a child, frozen in a grasping gesture, fingers like hard tongues of flame, still reaching for the marvel of the beating heart, fascinated still, though the heart is cold, beats not, the hand as curious about this infinite stillness as it was about thump and heat and quickness.

notes

"Valaida"—Valaida Snow (c. 1900–1956), whose life and legend inspired this story, was a jazz trumpeteer, singer and dancer of immense talent. A short article about her appears in *Stormy Weather: The Music and Lives of a Century of Jazzwomen* (1984), by Linda Dahl, Pantheon Books, New York.

"Presents"—I first heard about a boy being given a guitar and prophecy by his grandmother on a recording by "Preacher" Solomon Burke.

"Little Brother"—My wife and love of my life, to whom this story is dedicated, suggested that my Aunt Geraldine's strange dog needed a biographer.

"Fever"—Absalom Jones and Richard Allen's "Narrative" (1794); Gary B. Nash's *Forging Freedom* (1988), Harvard University Press; and especially J. H. Powell's *Bring Out Your Dead* (1949), University of Pennsylvania Press, were useful sources for this meditation on history.

PART III

damballah

1 9 8 1

to robby

Stories are letters. Letters sent to anybody or everybody. But the best kind are meant to be read by a specific somebody. When you read that kind you know you are eavesdropping. You know a real person somewhere will read the same words you are reading and the story is that person's business and you are a ghost listening in.

Remember. I think it was Geral I first heard call a watermelon a letter from home. After all these years I understand a little better what she meant. She was saying the melon is a letter addressed to us. A story for us from down home. Down Home being everywhere we've never been, the rural South, the old days, slavery, Africa. That juicy, striped message with red meat and seeds, which always looked like roaches to me, was blackness as cross and celebration, a history we could taste and chew. And it was meant for us. Addressed to us. We were meant to slit it open and take care of business.

Consider all these stories as letters from home. I never liked watermelon as a kid. I think I remember you did. You weren't afraid of becoming instant nigger, of sitting barefoot and goggle-eyed and Day-Glo black and drippy-lipped on massa's fence if you took one bit of the forbidden fruit. I was too scared to enjoy watermelon. Too self-conscious. I let people rob me of a simple pleasure. Watermelon's still tainted for me. But I know better now. I can play with the idea even if I can't get down and have a natural ball eating a real one.

Anyway . . . these stories are letters. Long overdue letters from me to you. I wish they could tear down the walls. I wish they could snatch you away from where you are.

damballah

good serpent of the sky

"Damballah Wedo is the ancient, the venerable father; so ancient, so venerable, as of a world before the troubles began; and his children would keep him so; image of the benevolent, paternal innocence, the great father of whom one asks nothing save his blessing. . . . There is almost no precise communication with him, as if his wisdom were of such major cosmic scope and of such grand innocence that it could not perceive the minor anxieties of his human progeny, nor be transmuted to the petty precision of human speech.

"Yet it is this very detachment which comforts, and which is evidence, once more, of some original and primal vigor that has somehow remained inaccessible to whatever history, whatever immediacy might diminish it. Damballah's very presence, like the simple, even absent-minded caress of a father's hand, brings peace. . . . Damballah is himself unchanged by life, and so is at once the ancient past and the assurance of the future. . . .

"Associated with Damballah as members of the Sky Pantheon, are Badessy, the wind, Sobo and Agarou Tonerre, the thunder. . . . They seem to belong to another period of history. Yet precisely because these divinities are, to a certain extent, vestigial, they give, like Damballah's detachment, a sense of historical extension, of the ancient origin of the race. To invoke them today is to stretch one's hand back to that time and to gather up all history into a solid, contemporary ground beneath one's feet."

One song invoking Damballah requests that he "Gather up the Family."

Quotation and citation from Maya Deren's *Divine Horsemen: The Voodoo Gods of Haiti.*

a begat chart

1860s   Sybela and Charlie arrive in Pittsburgh; bring two children with them; eighteen more born in next twenty-five years.

1880s   Maggie Owens, oldest daughter of Sybela and Charlie, marries Buck Hollinger; bears nine children among whom are four girls—Aida, Gertrude, Gaybrella, Bess.

1900s   Hollinger girls marry—Aida to Bill Campbell; Gaybrella to Joe Hardin (three children: Fauntleroy, Ferdinand, Hazel); Bess to Riley Simpkins (one son: Eugene)—except Gert, who bears her children out of wedlock. Aida and Bill Campbell raise Gert's daughter, Freeda.

1920s   Freeda Hollinger marries John French; bears four children who survive: Lizabeth, Geraldine, Carl and Martha.

1940s   Lizabeth French marries Edgar Lawson; bears five children among whom are John, Shirley and Thomas.

1960s   Lizabeth's children begin to marry, propagate—not always in that order. John marries Judy and produces two sons

(Jake and Dan); Shirley marries Rashad and bears three daughters (Keesha, Tammy, and Kaleesha); Tommy marries Sarah and produces one son (Clyde); etc. . . .

FAMILY TREE

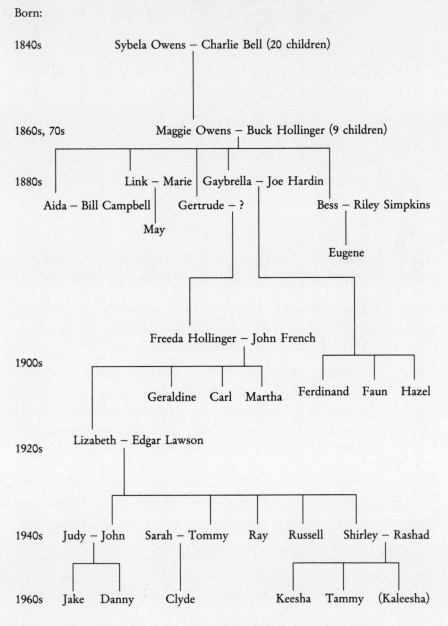

damballah

Orion let the dead, gray cloth slide down his legs and stepped into the river. He picked his way over slippery stones till he stood calf deep. Dropping to one knee he splashed his groin, then scooped river to his chest, both hands scrubbing with quick, kneading spirals. When he stood again, he stared at the distant gray clouds. A hint of rain in the chill morning air, a faint, clean presence rising from the far side of the hills. The promise of rain coming to him as all things seemed to come these past few months, not through eyes or ears or nose but entering his black skin as if each pore had learned to feel and speak.

He watched the clear water race and ripple and pucker. Where the sun cut through the pine trees and slanted into the water he could see the bottom, see black stones, speckled stones, shining stones whose light came from within. Above a stump at the far edge of the river, clouds of insects hovered. The water was darker there, slower, appeared to stand in deep pools where tangles of root, bush and weed hung over the bank. Orion thought of the eldest priest chalking a design on the floor of the sacred *obi*. Drawing the watery door no living hands could push open, the crossroads where the spirits passed between worlds. His skin was becoming like that in-between place the

275

priest scratched in the dust. When he walked the cane rows and dirt paths of the plantation he could feel the air of this strange land wearing out his skin, rubbing it thinner and thinner until one day his skin would not be thick enough to separate what was inside from everything outside. Some days his skin whispered he was dying. But he was not afraid. The voices and faces of his fathers bursting through would not drown him. They would sweep him away, carry him home again.

In his village across the sea were men who hunted and fished with their voices. Men who could talk the fish up from their shadowy dwellings and into the woven baskets slung over the fishermen's shoulders. Orion knew the fish in this cold river had forgotten him, that they were darting in and out of his legs. If the whites had not stolen him, he would have learned the fishing magic. The proper words, the proper tones to please the fish. But here in this blood-soaked land everything was different. Though he felt their slick bodies and saw the sudden dimples in the water where they were feeding, he understood that he would never speak the language of these fish. No more than he would ever speak again the words of the white people who had decided to kill him.

The boy was there again hiding behind the trees. He could be the one. This boy born so far from home. This boy who knew nothing but what the whites told him. This boy could learn the story and tell it again. Time was short but he could be the one.

"THAT RYAN, he a crazy nigger. One them wild African niggers act like he fresh off the boat. Kind you stay away from less you lookin for trouble." Aunt Lissy had stopped popping string beans and frowned into the boy's face. The pause in the steady drumming of beans into the iron pot, the way she scrunched up her face to look mean like one of the Master's pit bulls told him she had finished speaking on the subject and wished to hear no more about it from him. When the long green pods began to shuttle through her fingers again, it sounded like she was cracking her knuckles, and he expected something black to drop into the huge pot.

"Fixin to rain good. Heard them frogs last night just a singing at the clouds. Frog and all his brothers calling down the thunder. Don't rain soon them fields dry up and blow away." The boy thought of the men trudging each morning to the fields. Some were brown, some yellow, some had red in their skins and some white as the Master. Ryan black, but Aunt Lissy blacker. Fat, shiny blue-black like a crow's wing.

"Sure nuff crazy." Old woman always talking. Talking and telling silly stories. The boy wanted to hear something besides an old woman's mouth. He had heard about frogs and bears and rabbits too many times. He was almost grown now, almost ready to leave in the mornings with the men. What would they talk about? Would Orion's voice be like the hollers the boy heard early in the mornings when the men still sleepy and the sky still dark and you couldn't really see nobody but knew they were there when them cries and hollers came rising through the mist.

PINE NEEDLES CRACKLED with each step he took, and the boy knew old Ryan knew somebody spying on him. Old nigger guess who it was, too. But if Ryan knew, Ryan didn't care. Just waded out in that water like he the only man in the world. Like maybe wasn't no world. Just him and that quiet place in the middle of the river. Must be fishing out there, some funny old African kind of fishing. Nobody never saw him touch victuals Master set out and he had to be eating something, even if he was half crazy, so the nigger must be fishing for his breakfast. Standing there like a stick in the water till the fish forgot him and he could snatch one from the water with his beaky fingers.

A skinny-legged, black waterbird in the purring river. The boy stopped chewing his stick of cane, let the sweet juice blend with his spit, a warm syrup then whose taste he prolonged by not swallowing, but letting it coat his tongue and the insides of his mouth, waiting patiently like the figure in the water waited, as the sweet taste seeped away. All the cane juice had trickled down his throat before he saw Orion move. After the stillness, the illusion that the man was a tree rooted in the rocks at the riverbed, when motion came, it was too swift to follow. Not so much a matter of seeing Orion move as it was feeling the man's eyes inside him, hooking him before he could crouch lower in the weeds. Orion's eyes on him and through him boring a hole in his chest and thrusting into that space one word *Damballah*. Then the hooded eyes were gone.

ON A SPOON you see the shape of a face is an egg. Or two eggs because you can change the shape from long oval to moons pinched together at the middle seam or any shape egg if you tilt and push the spoon closer or farther away. Nothing to think about. You go with Mistress to the chest in the root cellar. She guides you with a candle and you make a pouch of soft cloth and carefully lay in each spoon and careful it don't jangle as up and out of the darkness following her rustling dresses and petticoats up the earthen steps each one topped by a plank which squirms as you mount it. You are following the taper she holds and the strange smell she trails and leaves in rooms. Then shut up in a room all day with nothing to think about. With rags and pieces of silver. Slowly you rub away the tarnished spots; it is like finding something which surprises you though you knew all the time it was there. Spoons lying on the strip of indigo: perfect, gleaming fish you have coaxed from the black water.

Damballah was the word. Said it to Aunt Lissy and she went upside his head, harder than she had ever slapped him. Felt like crumpling right there in the dust of the yard it hurt so bad but he bit his lip and didn't cry out, held his ground and said the word again and again silently to himself, pretending nothing but a bug on his burning cheek and twitched and sent it flying. Damballah. Be strong as he needed to be. Nothing touch him if he don't want. Before long they'd cut him from the herd of pickaninnies. No more chasing flies from the table, no more silver spoons to get shiny, no fat, old woman telling him what to do. He'd go to the fields each morning with the men. Holler like they did before the sun rose to burn off the mist. Work like they did from can to caint. From first crack of light to dusk when the puddles of shadow deepened and spread so you couldn't see your hands or feet or the sharp tools hacking at the cane.

He was already taller than the others, a stork among the chicks scurrying behind Aunt Lissy. Soon he'd rise with the conch horn and do a man's share so he had let the fire rage on half his face and thought of the nothing always there to think of. In the spoon, his face long and thin as a finger. He looked for the print of Lissy's black hand on his cheek, but the image would not stay still. Dancing like his face reflected in the river. Damballah. "Don't you ever, you hear me, ever let me hear that heathen talk no more. You hear me, boy? You talk Merican, boy." Lissy's voice like chicken cackle. And his head a barn packed with animal noise and animal smell. His own head but he had to sneak round in it. Too many others crowded in there with him. His head so crowded and noisy lots of time don't hear his own voice with all them braying and cackling.

ORION SQUATTED the way the boy had seen the other old men collapse on their haunches and go still as a stump. Their bony knees poking up and their backsides resting on their ankles. Looked like they could sit that way all day, legs folded under them like wings. Orion drew a cross in the dust. Damballah. When Orion passed his hands over the cross the air seemed to shimmer like it does above a flame or like it does when the sun so hot you can see waves of heat rising off the fields. Orion talked to the emptiness he shaped with his long black fingers. His eyes were closed. Orion wasn't speaking but sounds came from inside him the boy had never heard before, strange words, clicks, whistles and grunts. A singsong moan that rose and fell and floated like the old man's busy hands above the cross. Damballah like a drum beat in the chant. Damballah a place the boy could enter, a familiar sound he began to anticipate, a sound outside of him which slowly forced its way inside, a sound measuring his heartbeat then one with the pumping surge of his blood.

THE BOY HEARD part of what Lissy saying to Primus in the cooking shed: "Ryan he yell that heathen word right in the middle of Jim talking bout Sweet Jesus the Son of God. Jump up like he snake bit and scream that word so everybody hushed, even the white folks what came to hear Jim preach. Simple Ryan standing there at the back of the chapel like a knot poked out on somebody's forehead. Lookin like a nigger caught wid his hand in the chicken coop. Screeching like some crazy hoot owl while Preacher Jim praying the word of the Lord. They gon kill that simple nigger one day."

Dear Sir:

The nigger Orion which I purchased of you in good faith sight unseen on your promise that he was of sound constitution "a full grown and able-bodied house servant who can read, write, do sums and cipher" to recite the exact words of your letter dated April 17, 1852, has proved to be a burden, a deficit to the economy of my plantation rather than the asset I fully believed I was receiving when I agreed to pay the price you asked. Of the vaunted intelligence so rare in his kind, I have seen nothing. Not an English word has passed through his mouth since he arrived. Of his docility and tractability I have seen only the willingness with which he bares his leatherish back to receive the stripes constant misconduct earn him. He is a creature whose brutish habits would shame me were he quartered in my kennels. I find it odd that I should write at such length about any nigger, but seldom have I been so struck by the disparity between promise and performance. As I have accrued nothing but expense and inconvenience as a result of his presence, I think it only just that you return the full amount I paid for this flawed *piece of the Indies.*

You know me as an honest and fair man and my regard for those same qualities in you prompts me to write this letter. I am not a harsh master, I concern myself with the spiritual as well as the temporal needs of my slaves. My nigger Jim is renowned in this county as a preacher. Many say I am foolish, that the words of scripture are wasted on these savage blacks. I fear you have sent me a living argument to support the critics of my Christianizing project. Among other absences of truly human qualities I have observed in this Orion is the utter lack of a soul.

She said it time for Orion to die. Broke half the overseer's bones knocking him off his horse this morning and everybody thought Ryan done run away sure but Mistress come upon the crazy nigger at suppertime on the big house porch naked as the day he born and he just sat there staring into her eyes till Mistress screamed and run away. Aunt Lissy said Ryan ain't studying no women, ain't gone near to woman since he been here and she say his ain't the first black butt

Mistress done seen all them nearly grown boys walkin round summer in the onliest shirt Master give em barely come down to they knees and niggers man nor woman don't get drawers the first. Mistress and Master both seen plenty. Wasn't what she saw scared her less she see the ghost leaving out Ryan's body.

The ghost wouldn't steam out the top of Orion's head. The boy remembered the sweaty men come in from the fields at dusk when the nights start to cool early, remembered them with the drinking gourds in they hands scooping up water from the wooden barrel he filled, how they throw they heads back and the water trickles from the sides of they mouth and down they chin and they let it roll on down they chests, and the smoky steam curling off they shoulders. Orion's spirit would not rise up like that but wiggle out his skin and swim off up the river.

The boy knew many kinds of ghosts and learned the ways you get round their tricks. Some spirits almost good company and he filled the nothing with jingles and whistles and took roundabout paths and sang to them when he walked up on a crossroads and yoo-hooed at doors. No way you fool the haunts if a spell conjured strong on you, no way to miss a beating if it your day to get beat, but the ghosts had everything in they hands, even the white folks in they hands. You know they there, you know they floating up in the air watching and counting and remembering them strokes Ole Master laying cross your back.

THEY DRAGGED ORION across the yard. He didn't buck or kick, but it seemed as if the four men carrying him were struggling with a giant stone rather than a black bag of bones. His ashy nigger weight swung between the two pairs of white men like a lazy hammock but the faces of the men all red and twisted. They huffed and puffed and sweated through they clothes carrying Ryan's bones to the barn. The dry spell had layered the yard with a coat of dust. Little squalls of yellow spurted from under the men's boots. Trudging steps heavy as if each man carried seven Orions on his shoulders. Four grown men struggling with one string of black flesh. The boy had never seen so many white folks dealing with one nigger. Aunt Lissy had said it time to die and the boy wondered what Ryan's ghost would think dropping onto the dust surrounded by the scowling faces of the Master and his overseers.

One scream that night. Like a bull when they cut off his maleness. Couldn't tell who it was. A bull screaming once that night and torches burning in the barn and Master and the men coming out and no Ryan.

MISTRESS CRYING behind a locked door and Master messing with Patty down the quarters.

In the morning light the barn swelling and rising and teetering in the yellow dust, moving the way you could catch the ghost of something in a spoon and play with it, bending it, twisting it. That goldish ash on everybody's bare shins. Nobody talking. No cries nor hollers from the fields. The boy watched till his eyes hurt, waiting for a moment when he could slip unseen into the shivering barn. On his hands and knees hiding under a wagon, then edging sideways through the loose boards and wedge of space where the weathered door hung crooked on its hinge.

The interior of the barn lay in shadows. Once beyond the sliver of light coming in at the cracked door the boy stood still till his eyes adjusted to the darkness. First he could pick out the stacks of hay, the rough partitions dividing the animals. The smells, the choking heat there like always, but rising above these familiar sensations the buzz of flies, unnaturally loud, as if the barn breathing and each breath shook the wooden walls. Then the boy's eyes followed the sound to an open space at the center of the far wall. A black shape there. Orion there, floating in his own blood. The boy ran at the blanket of flies. When he stomped, some of the flies buzzed up from the carcass. Others too drunk on the shimmering blood ignored him except to join the ones hovering above the body in a sudden droning peal of annoyance. He could keep the flies stirring but they always returned from the recesses of the high ceiling, the dark corners of the building, to gather in a cloud above the body. The boy looked for something to throw. Heard his breath, heavy and threatening like the sound of the flies. He sank to the dirt floor, sitting cross-legged where he had stood. He moved only once, ten slow paces away from Orion and back again, near enough to be sure, to see again how the head had been cleaved from the rest of the body, to see how the ax and tongs, branding iron and other tools were scattered around the corpse, to see how one man's hat and another's shirt, a letter that must have come from someone's pocket lay about in a helter-skelter way as if the men had suddenly bolted before they had finished with Orion.

FORGIVE HIM, FATHER. I tried to the end of my patience to restore his lost soul. I made a mighty effort to bring him to the Ark of Salvation but he had walked in darkness too long. He mocked Your Grace. He denied Your Word. Have mercy on him and forgive his heathen ways as you forgive the soulless beasts of the fields and birds of the air.

SHE SAY MASTER still down slave row. She say everybody fraid to go down and get him. Everybody fraid to open the barn door. Overseer half dead and the Mistress still crying in her locked room and that barn starting to stink already with crazy Ryan and nobody gon get him.

And the boy knew his legs were moving and he knew they would carry him where they needed to go and he knew the legs belonged to him but he could not feel them, he had been sitting too long thinking on nothing for too long and he felt the sweat running on his body but his mind off somewhere cool and quiet and hard and he knew the space between his body and mind could not be crossed by anything, knew you mize well try to stick the head back on Ryan as try to cross that space. So he took what he needed out of the barn, unfolding, getting his gangly crane's legs together under him and shouldered open the creaking double doors and walked through the flame in the center where he had to go.

Damballah said it be a long way a ghost be going and Jordan chilly and wide and a new ghost take his time getting his wings together. Long way to go so you can sit and listen till the ghost ready to go on home. The boy wiped his wet hands on his knees and drew the cross and said the word and settled down and listened to Orion tell the stories again. Orion talked and he listened and couldn't stop listening till he saw Orion's eyes rise up through the back of the severed skull and lips rise up through the skull and the wings of the ghost measure out the rhythm of one last word.

Late afternoon and the river slept dark at its edges like it did in the mornings. The boy threw the head as far as he could and he knew the fish would hear it and swim to it and welcome it. He knew they had been waiting. He knew the ripples would touch him when he entered.

daddy garbage

"Be not dismayed
What ere betides . . ."

Daddy Garbage was a dog. Lemuel Strayhorn whose iceball cart is always right around the corner on Hamilton just down from Homewood Avenue is the one who named the dog and since he named him, claimed him, and Daddy Garbage must have agreed because he sat on the sidewalk beside Lemuel Strayhorn or slept in the shade under the two-wheeled cart or when it got too cold for iceballs, followed Strayhorn through the alleys on whatever errands and hustles the man found during the winter to keep food on the stove and smoke in the chimney of the little shack behind Dumferline. The dog was long dead but Lemuel Strayhorn still peddled the paper cups of crushed ice topped with sweet syrup, and he laughed and said, "Course I remember that crazy animal. Sure I do. And named him Daddy Garbage alright, but can't say now why I did. Must have had a reason though. Must been a good reason at the time. And you a French, ain't you? One of John French's girls. See him plain as day in your face, gal. Which one is you? Lemme see now. There was Lizabeth, the oldest, and Geraldine and one more . . ."

She answers: "Geraldine, Mr. Strayhorn."

285

"Sure you are. That's right. And you done brought all these beautiful babies for some ices."

"You still make the best."

"Course I do. Been on this corner before you was born. Knew your daddy when he first come to Homewood."

"This is his grandson, Lizabeth's oldest, John. And those two boys are his children. The girls belong to Lizabeth's daughter, Shirley."

"You got fine sons there, and them pretty little girls, too. Can hear John French now, braggin bout his children. He should be here today. You all want ices? You want big or small?"

"Small for the kids and I want a little one, please, and he'll take a big one, I know."

"You babies step up and tell me what kind you want. Cherry, lemon, grape, orange and tutti-frutti. Got them all."

"You remember Mr. Strayhorn. Don't you, John?"

"Uh huh. I think I remember Daddy Garbage too."

"You might of seen a dog around, son, but wasn't no Daddy Garbage. Naw, you way too young."

"Mr. Strayhorn had Daddy Garbage when I was a little girl. A big, rangy, brown dog. Looked like a wolf. Scare you half to death if you didn't know he was tame and never bothered anybody."

"Didn't bother nobody long as they didn't bother him. But that was one fighting dog once he got started. Dogs got so they wouldn't even bark when Daddy Garbage went by. Tore up some behinds in his day, yes, he did."

"Wish you could remember how he got that name."

"Wish I could tell you, too. But it's a long time ago. Some things I members plain as day, but you mize well be talking to a light post you ask me bout others. Shucks, Miss French. Been on this corner making iceballs, seem like four hundred years if it's a day."

"You don't get any older. And I bet you still remember what you want to remember. You look fine to me, Mr. Strayhorn. Look like you might be here another four hundred at least."

"Maybe I will. Yes mam, just might. You children eat them ices up now and don't get none on them nice clothes and God bless you all."

"I'm going to ask you about that name again."

"Just might remember next time. You ask me again."

"I surely will . . ."

SNOW FELL all night and in the morning Homewood seemed smaller. Whiteness softened the edges of things, smoothed out the spaces between near and far. Trees drooped, the ground rose up a little higher, the snow glare in your eyes discouraged a long view, made you attentive to what was close at hand, what was familiar, yet altered and harmonized by the blanket of whiteness. The world seemed smaller till you got out in it and understood that the glaze which made the snow so lustrous had been frozen there by the wind, and sudden gusts would sprinkle your face with freezing particles from the drifts as you leaned forward to get a little closer to the place you wanted to go, the place which from your window as you surveyed the new morning and the untouched snow seemed closer than it usually was.

The only way to make it up the alley behind Dumferline was to stomp right into the drifted snow as if the worn shoes on your feet and the pants legs pegged and tucked into the tops of your socks really kept out the snow. Strayhorn looked behind him at the holes he had punched in the snow. Didn't seem like he had been zigzagging that much. Looked like the tracks of somebody been pulling on a jug of Dago Red already this morning. The dog's trail wandered even more than his, a nervous tributary crossing and recrossing its source. Dog didn't seem to mind the snow or the cold, sometimes even seemed fool enough to like it, rolling on his side and kicking up his paws or bounding to a full head of steam then leaping and belly flopping splay-legged in a shower of white spray. Still a lot of pup in the big animal. Some dogs never lost those ways. With this one, this garbage-can-raiding champion he called Daddy Garbage, Strayhorn knew it was less holding on to puppy ways than it was stone craziness, craziness age nor nothing else ever going to change.

Strayhorn lifts his foot and smacks off the snow. Balances a second on one leg but can't figure anything better to do with his clean foot so plunges it again into the snow. Waste of time brushing them off. Going to be a cold, nasty day and nothing for it. Feet get numb and gone soon anyway. Gone till he can toast them in front of a fire. He steps through the crust again and the crunch of his foot breaks a stillness older than the man, the alley, the city growing on steep hills.

Somebody had set a lid of peeling wood atop a tin can. Daddy Garbage was up on his hind legs, pushing with his paws and nose against the snow-capped cover. The perfect symmetry of the crown of snow was the first to go, gouged by the dog's long, worrying snout. Next went the can. Then the lean-backed mongrel sprawled over the metal drum, mounting it and getting away from it simultaneously so he looked like a clumsy seal trying to balance on a ball. Nothing new to Strayhorn. The usual ungodly crash was muffled by the snow but the dog's nails scraped as loudly as they always did against garbage cans. The spill looked clean and bright against the snow, catching Strayhorn's eye for a moment, but a glance was all he would spare because he knew the trifling people living in those shacks behind Dumferline didn't throw nothing away unless it really was good for nothing but garbage. Slim pickins sure enough, and he grunted over his shoulder at the dog to quit fooling and catch up.

When he looked back again, back at his solitary track, at the snow swirls whipped up by the wind, at the thick rug of snow between the row houses, at the whiteness clinging to window ledges and doorsills and ragtag pieces of fence, back at the overturned barrel and the mess spread over the snow, he saw the dog had ignored him and stood stiff-legged, whining at a box disgorged from the can.

He cursed the dog and whistled him away from whatever foolishness he was prying into. Nigger garbage ain't worth shit, Strayhorn muttered, half to the dog, half to the bleakness and the squalor of the shanties disguised this bright morning by snowfall. What's he whining about and why am I going back to see. Mize well ask a fool why he's a fool as do half the things I do.

To go back down the alley meant walking into the wind. Wind cutting steady in his face and the cross drafts snapping between the row houses. He would snatch that dog's eyeballs loose. He would teach it to come when he called whether or not some dead rat or dead cat stuffed up in a box got his nose open.

"Daddy Garbage, I'm gonna have a piece of your skull." But the dog was too quick and Strayhorn's swipe disturbed nothing but the frigid air where the scruff of the dog's neck had been. Strayhorn tried to kick away the box. If he hadn't been smacking at the dog and the snow hadn't tricked his legs, he would have sent it flying, but his foot only rolled the box over.

At first Strayhorn thought it was a doll. A little dark brown doll knocked from the box. A worn out babydoll like he'd find sometimes in people's garbage too broken up to play with anymore. A little, battered, brown-skinned doll. But when he looked closer and stepped away, and then shuffled nearer again, whining, stiff-legged like the dog, he knew it was something dead.

"Aw shit, aw shit, Daddy Garbage." When he knelt, he could hear the dog panting beside him, see the hot, rank steam, and smell the wet fur. The body lay face down in the snow, only its head and shoulders free of the newspapers stuffed in the box. Some of the wadded paper had blown free and the wind sent it scudding across the frozen crust of snow.

The child was dead and the man couldn't touch it and he couldn't leave it alone. Daddy Garbage had sidled closer. This time the swift, vicious blow caught him across the skull. The dog retreated, kicking up a flurry of snow, snarling, clicking his teeth once before he began whimpering from a distance. Under his army greatcoat Strayhorn wore the gray wool hunting vest John French had given him after John French won all that money and bought himself a new leather one with brass snaps. Strayhorn draped his overcoat across the upright can the dog had ignored, unpinned the buttonless vest from his chest and spread it on the snow. A chill was inside him. Nothing in the weather could touch him now. Strayhorn inched forward on his knees till his shadow fell across the box. He was telling his hands what they ought to do, but they were sassing. He cursed his raggedy gloves, the numb fingers inside them that would not do his bidding.

The box was too big, too square shouldered to wrap in the sweater vest. Strayhorn wanted to touch only newspaper as he extricated the frozen body, so when he finally got it placed in the center of the sweater and folded over the tattered gray edges, the package he made contained half newspaper which rustled like dry leaves when he pressed it against his chest. Once he had it in his arms he couldn't put it down, so he struggled with his coat like a one-armed man, pulling and shrugging, till it shrouded him again. Not on really, but attached, so it dragged and flopped with a life of its own, animation that excited Daddy Garbage and gave him something to play with as he minced after Strayhorn and Strayhorn retraced his own footsteps, clutching the dead child to the warmth of his chest, moaning and blinking and tearing as the wind lashed his face.

AN HOUR LATER Strayhorn was on Cassina Way hollering for John French. Lizabeth shooed him away with all the imperiousness of a little girl who had heard her mama say, "Send that fool away from here. Tell him your Daddy's out working." When the girl was gone and the door slammed behind her, Strayhorn thought of the little wooden birds who pop out of a clock, chirp their message and disappear. He knew Freeda French didn't like him. Not anything personal, not anything she could change or he could change, just the part of him which was part of what drew John French down to the corner with the other men to talk and gamble and drink wine. He understood why she would never do more than nod at him or say *Good day, Mr. Strayhorn* if he forced the issue by tipping his hat or taking up so much sidewalk when she passed him that she couldn't pretend he wasn't there. *Mr. Strayhorn,* and he been knowing her, Freeda Hollinger before she was Freeda French, for as long as she was big enough to walk the streets of Homewood. But he understood and hadn't ever minded till just this morning standing in the ankle-deep snow drifted up against the three back steps of John French's house next to the vacant lot on Cassina Way, till just this moment when for the first time in his life he thought this woman might have something to give him, to tell him. Since she was a mother she would know what to do with the dead baby. He could unburden himself and she could touch him with one of her slim, white-woman's hands, and even if she still called him *Mr. Strayhorn,* it would be alright. A little woman like that. Little hands like that doing what his hands couldn't do. His scavenging, hard hands that had been everywhere, touched everything. He wished Freeda French had come to the door. Wished he was not still standing tongue-tied and ignorant as the dog raising his hind leg and yellowing the snow under somebody's window across the way.

"MAN SUPPOSED to pick me up first thing this morning. Want me to paper his whole downstairs. Seven, eight rooms and hallways and bathrooms. Big old house up on Thomas Boulevard cross from the park. Packed my tools and dragged my behind through all this snow and don't you know that white bastard ain't never showed. Strayhorn, I'm evil this morning."

Strayhorn had found John French in the Bucket of Blood drinking a glass of red wine. Eleven o'clock already and Strayhorn hadn't wanted to be away so long. Leaving the baby alone in that empty icebox of a shack was almost as bad as stuffing it in a garbage can. Didn't matter whose it was, or how dead it was, it was something besides a dead thing now that he had found it and rescued it and laid it wrapped in the sweater on the stack of mattresses where he slept. The baby sleeping there now. Waiting for the right thing to be done. It was owed something and Strayhorn knew he had to see to it that the debt was paid. Except he couldn't do it alone. Couldn't return through the snow and shove open that door, and do what had to be done by himself.

"Be making me some good money soon's I catch up with that peckerwood. And I'm gon spend me some of it today. Won't be no better day for spending it. Cold and nasty as it be outside, don't reckon I be straying too far from this stool till bedtime. McKinley, give this whatchamacallit a taste. And don't you be rolling your bubble eyes at me. Tolt you I got me a big money job soon's I catch that white man."

"Seems like you do more chasing than catching."

"Seems like you do more talking than pouring, nigger. Get your pop-eyed self on over here and fill us some glasses."

"Been looking for you all morning, man."

"Guess you found me. But you ain't found no money if that's what you looking for."

"Naw. It ain't that, man. It's something else."

"Somebody after you again? You been messing with somebody's woman? If you been stealin again or Oliver Edwards is after you again . . ."

"Naw, naw . . . nothing like that."

"Then it must be the Hell Hound hisself on your tail cause you look like death warmed over."

"French, I found a dead baby this morning."

"What you say?"

"Shhh. Don't be shouting. This ain't none McKinley's nor nobody else's business. Listen to what I'm telling you and don't make no fuss. Found a baby. All wrapped up in newspaper and froze stiff as a board. Somebody put it in a box and threw the box in the trash back of Dumferline."

"Ain't nobody could do that. Ain't nobody done nothing like that."

"It's the God awful truth. Me and Daddy Garbage on our way this morning up the alley. The dog, he found it. Turned over a can and the box fell out. I almost kicked it, John French. Almost kicked the pitiful thing."

"And it was dead when you found it?"

"Dead as this glass."

"What you do?"

"Didn't know what to do so I took it on back to my place."

"Froze dead."

"Laid in the garbage like wasn't nothing but spoilt meat."

"Goddamn . . ."

"Give me a hand, French."

"Goddamn. Goddamn, man. You seen it, sure nuff. I know you did. See it all over your face. God bless America . . . McKinley . . . Bring us a bottle. You got my tools to hold so just get a bottle on over here and don't say a mumbling word."

LIZABETH IS SINGING to the snowman she has constructed on the vacant lot next door to her home. The wind is still and the big flakes are falling again straight down and she interrupts her slow song to catch snow on her tongue. Other kids had been out earlier, spoiling the perfect whiteness of the lot. They had left a mound of snow she used to start her snowman. The mound might have been a snowman before. A tall one, taller than any she could build because there had been yelling and squealing since early in the morning which meant a whole bunch of kids out on the vacant lot and meant they had probably worked together making a giant snowman till somebody got crazy or evil and smacked the snowman and then the others would join in and snow flying everywhere and the snowman plowed down as they scuffled on top of him and threw lumps of him at each other. Till he was gone and then they'd start again. She could see bare furrows where they must have been rolling big snowballs for heads and bodies. Her mother had said: "Wait till some of those roughnecks go on about their business. Probably nothing but boys out there anyway." So she had rid up the table and scrubbed her Daddy's eggy plate and sat in his soft chair dreaming of the kind of clean, perfect snow she knew she wouldn't see by the time she was allowed out; dreaming of a ride on her Daddy's shoulders to Bruston Hill and he would carry her and the sled to a quiet place not too high up on the slope and she would wait till he was at the bottom again and clapping his hands and shouting up at her: "Go, go little gal."

"IF YOU GO to the police they find some reason put you in jail. Hospital got no room for the sick let alone the dead. Undertaker, he's gon want money from somebody before he touch it. The church. Them church peoples got troubles enough of they own to cry about. And they be asking as many questions as the police. It can't stay here and we can't take it back."

"That's what I know, John French. That's what I told you."

Between them the flame of the kerosene lamp shivers as if the cold has penetrated deep into its blue heart. Strayhorn's windowless shack is always dark except where light seeps through cracks between the boards, cracks which now moan or squeeze the wind into shrill whistles. The two men sit on wooden crates whose slats have been reinforced by stone blocks placed under them. Another crate, short-side down, supports the kerosene lamp. John French peers over Strayhorn's shoulder into the dark corner where Strayhorn has his bed of stacked mattresses.

"We got to bury it, man. We got to go out in this goddamn weather and bury it. Not in nobody's backyard neither. Got to go on up to the burying ground where the rest of the dead niggers is." As soon as he finished speaking John French realized he didn't know if the corpse was black or white. Being in Homewood, back of Dumferline wouldn't be anything but a black baby, he had assumed. Yet who in Homewood would have thrown it there? Not even those down home, country Negroes behind Dumferline in that alley that didn't even have a name would do something like that. Nobody he knew. Nobody he had ever heard of. Except maybe crackers who could do anything to niggers, man, woman or child don't make no difference.

Daddy Garbage, snoring, farting ever so often, lay next to the dead fireplace. Beyond him in deep shadow was the child. John French thought about going to look at it. Thought about standing up and crossing the dirt floor and laying open the sweater Strayhorn said he wrapped it in. His sweater. His goddamn hunting sweater come to this. He thought about taking the lamp into the dark corner and undoing newspapers and placing the light over the body. But more wine than he could remember and half a bottle of gin hadn't made him ready for that. What did it matter? Black or white. Boy or girl. A mongrel made by niggers tipping in white folks' beds or white folks paying visits to black. Everybody knew it was happening every night. Homewood people every color in the rainbow and they talking about white people and black people like there's a brick wall tween them and nobody don't know how to get over.

"You looked at it, Strayhorn?"

"Just a little bitty thing. Wasn't no need to look hard to know it was dead."

"Can't figure how somebody could do it. Times is hard and all that, but how somebody gon be so cold?"

"Times is surely hard. I'm out there every day scuffling and I can tell you how hard they is."

"Don't care how hard they get. Some things people just ain't supposed to do. If that hound of yours take up and die all the sudden, I know you'd find a way to put him in the ground."

"You're right about that. Simple and ungrateful as he is, I won't be throwing him in nobody's trash."

"Well, you see what I mean then. Something is happening to people. I mean times was bad down home, too. Didn't get cold like this, but the cracker could just about break your neck with his foot always on it. I mean I remember my daddy come home with half a pail of guts one Christmas Eve after he work all day killing hogs for the white man. Half a pail of guts is all he had and six of us pickaninnies and my mama and grandmama to feed. Crackers was mean as spit, but they didn't drive people to do what they do here in this city. Down home you knew people. And you knew your enemies. Getting so you can't trust a soul you see out here in the streets. White, black, don't make no difference. Homewood changing . . . people changing."

"I ain't got nothing. Never will. But I lives good in the summertime and always finds a way to get through winter. Gets me a woman when I needs one."

"You crazy alright, but you ain't evil crazy like people getting. You got your cart and that dog and this place to sleep. And you ain't going to hurt nobody to get more. That's what I mean. People do anything to get more than they got."

"Niggers been fighting and fussing since they been on earth."

"Everybody gon fight. I done fought half the niggers in Homewood, myself. Fighting is different. Long as two men stand up and beat on each other ain't nobody else's business. Fighting ain't gon hurt nobody. Even if it kill a nigger every now and then."

"John French, you don't make no sense."

"If I make no sense out no sense, I be making sense."

"Here you go talking crazy. Gin talk."

"Ain't no gin talking. It's me talking and I'm talking true."

"What we gon do?"

"You got a shovel round here?"

"Got a broken-handled piece of one."

"Well get it, and let's go on and do what we have to do."

"It ain't dark enough yet."

"Dark as the Pit in here."

"Ain't dark outside yet. Got to wait till dark."

John French reaches down to the bottle beside his leg. The small movement is enough to warn him how difficult it will be to rise from the box. Nearly as cold inside as out and the chill is under his clothes, has packed his bones in ice and the stiffness always in the small of his back from bending then reaching high to hang wallpaper is a little hard ball he will have to stretch out inch by painful inch when he stands. His fist closes on the neck of the bottle. Raises it to his lips and drinks deeply and passes it to Strayhorn. Gin is hot in John French's mouth. He holds it there, numbing his lips and gums, inhaling the fumes. For a moment he feels as if his head is a balloon and someone is pumping it full of gas and there is a moment when the balloon is either going to bust or float off his shoulders.

"Gone, nigger. Didn't leave a good swallow." Strayhorn is talking with his mouth half covered by coatsleeve.

"Be two, three hours before it's good and dark. Sure ain't sitting here that long. Ain't you got no wood for that fire?"

"Saving it."

"Let's go then."

"I got to stay. Somebody got to be here."

"Somebody got to get another taste."

"Ain't leaving no more."

"Stay then. I be back. Goddamn. You sure did find it, didn't you?"

When John French wrestles open the door, the gray light enters like a hand and grasps everything within the shack, shaking it, choking it before the door slams and severs the gray hand at the wrist.

IT IS the hottest time of a July day. Daddy Garbage is curled beneath the big wheeled cart, snug, regal in the only spot of shade on the street at one o'clock in the afternoon. Every once in a while his ropy tail slaps at the pavement. Too old for most of his puppy tricks but still a puppy when he sleeps, Strayhorn thinks, watching the tail rise up and flop down as if it measures some irregular but persistent pulse running beneath the streets of Homewood.

"Mr. Strayhorn." The young woman speaking to him has John French's long, pale face. She is big and rawboned like him and has his straight, good hair. Or the straight, good hair John French used to have. Hers almost to her shoulders but his long gone, a narrow fringe above his ears like somebody had roughed in a line for a saw cut.

"Have you seen my daddy, Mr. Strayhorn?"

"Come by here yesterday, Miss French."

"Today, have you seen him today?"

"Hmmm . . ."

"Mr. Strayhorn, he has to come home. He's needed at home right away."

"Well now . . . let me see . . ."

"Is he gambling? Are they gambling up there beside the tracks? You know if they're up there."

"Seems like I might have seen him with a few of the fellows . . ."

"Dammit, Mr. Strayhorn. Lizabeth's having her baby. Do you understand? It's time, and we need him home."

"Don't fret, little gal. Bet he's up there. You go on home. Me and Daddy Garbage get him. You go on home."

"NIGGER GAL, nigger gal. Daddy's sure nuff fine sweet little nigger gal." Lizabeth hears the singing coming closer and closer. Yes, it's him. Who else but him? She is crying. Pain and happiness. They brought the baby in for her to see. A beautiful, beautiful little boy. Now Lizabeth is alone again. Weak and pained. She feels she's in the wrong place. She was so big and now she can barely find herself in the immense whiteness of the bed. Only the pain assures her she has not disappeared altogether. The perfect white pain.

She is sweating and wishing for a comb even though she knows she should not try to sit up and untangle the mess of her hair. Her long, straight hair. Like her mama's. Her Daddy's. The hair raveled on the pillow beside her face. She is sweating and crying and they've taken away her baby. She listens for footsteps, for sounds from the other beds in the ward. So many swollen bellies, so many white sheets and names she forgets and is too shy to ask again, and where have they taken her son? Why is no one around to tell her what she needs to know? She listens to the silence and listens and then there is his singing. *Nigger gal. Sweet, sweet little nigger gal.* Her Daddy's drunk singing floating toward her and a nurse's voice saying *no,* saying *you can't go in there* but her Daddy never missing a note and she can see the nurse in her perfect white and her Daddy never even looking at her just weaving past the uniform and strutting past the other beds and getting closer and singing, singing an ignorant, darky song that embarrasses her so and singing that nasty word which makes her want to hide under the sheets. But it's him and he'll be beside her and he'll reach down out of the song and touch her wet forehead and his hand will be cool and she'll smell the sweet wine on his breath and she is singing silently to herself what she has always called him, always will, *Daddy John, Daddy John,* in time to the nigger song he chants loud enough for the world to hear.

"GOT TO SAY something. You the one likes to talk. You the one good with words." John French and Lemuel Strayhorn have been working for hours. Behind them, below them, the streets of Homewood are deserted, empty and still as if black people in the South hadn't yet heard of mills and mines and freedom, hadn't heard the rumors and the tall tales, hadn't wrapped packages and stuffed cardboard suitcases with everything they could move and boarded trains North. Empty and still as if every living thing had fled from the blizzard, the snow which will never stop, which will bury Dumferline, Tioga, Hamilton, Kelley, Cassina, Allequippa, all the Homewood streets disappearing silently, swiftly as the footprints of the two men climbing Bruston Hill. John French first, leaning on the busted shovel like it's a cane, stabbing the metal blade into the snow so it clangs against the pavement like a drum to pace their march. Strayhorn next, tottering unsteadily because he holds the bundle of rags and paper with both hands against his middle, thinking, when the wind gives him peace enough, of what he will say if someone stops him and asks him what he is carrying. Finally the dog, Daddy Garbage, trotting in a line straighter than usual, a line he doesn't waver from even though a cat, unseen, hisses once as the procession mounts higher toward the burying ground.

In spite of wind and snow and bitter cold, the men are flushed and hot inside their clothes. If you were more than a few feet away, you couldn't see them digging. Too much blowing snow, the night too black. But a block away you'd have heard them fighting the frozen earth, cursing and huffing and groaning as they take turns with the short-handled shovel. They had decided before they began that the hole had to be deep, six feet deep at least. If you had been close enough and watched them the whole time, you would have seen how it finally got deep enough so that one man disappeared with the tool while the other sat exhausted in the snow at the edge of the pit waiting his turn. You'd have seen the dark green bottle emptied and shoved neck first like a miniature headstone in the snow. You would have seen how one pecked at the stone hard ground while the other weaved around the growing mound of snow and dirt, blowing on his fingers and stomping his feet, making tracks as random as those of Daddy Garbage in the untouched snow of the cemetery . . .

"Don't have no stone to mark this place. And don't know your name, child. Don't know who brought you on this earth. But none that matters now. You your own self now. Buried my twins in this very place. This crying place. Can't think of nothing to say now except they was born and they died so fast too. But we loved them. No time to name one before she was gone. The other named Margaret, after her aunt, my little sister who died young too.

"Like the preacher say, May your soul rest in peace. Sleep in peace, child."

Strayhorn stands mute with the bundle in his arms. John French blinks the heavy snowflakes from his lashes. He hears Strayhorn grunt *amen* then Strayhorn sways like a figure seen underwater. The outline of his shape wiggles, dissolves, the hard lines of him swell and divide.

"How we gonna put it down there? Can't just pitch it down on that hard ground."

John French pulls the big, red plaid snot rag from his coat pocket. He had forgotten about it all this time. He wipes his eyes and blows his nose. Stares up into the sky. The snowflakes all seem to be slanting from one spot high over his head. If he could get his thumb up there or jam in the handkerchief, he could stop it. The sky would clear, they would be able to see the stars.

He kneels at the edge of the hole and pushes clean snow into the blackness. Pushes till the bottom of the pit is lined with soft, glowing fur.

"Best we can do. Drop her easy now. Lean over far as you can and drop her easy . . ."

lizabeth:
the caterpillar story

Did you know I tried to save him once myself. When somebody was dumping ashes on the lot beside the house on Cassina Way. Remember how mad Daddy got. He sat downstairs in the dark with his shotgun and swore he was going to shoot whoever it was dumping ashes on his lot. I tried to save Daddy from that.

It's funny sitting here listening at you talk about your father that way because I never thought about nobody else needing to save him but me. Then I hear you talking and think about John French and know there ain't no way he could have lived long as he did unless a whole lotta people working real hard at saving that crazy man. He needed at least as many trying to save him as were trying to kill him.

Knew all my life about what you did, Mama. Knew you punched through a window with your bare hand to save him. You showed me the scar and showed me the window. In the house we used to live in over on Cassina Way. So I always knew you had saved him. Maybe that's why I thought I could save him too.

I remember telling you the story.

And showing me the scar.

Got the scar, that's for sure. And you got the story.

301

Thought I was saving Daddy, too, but if you hadn't put your fist through that window I wouldn't have had a Daddy to try and save.

Had you in my lap and we were sitting at the window in the house on Cassina Way. You must have been five or six at the time. Old enough to be telling stories to. Course when I had one of you children on my lap, there was some times I talked just to hear myself talking. Some things couldn't wait even though you all didn't understand word the first. But you was five or six and I was telling you about the time your Daddy ate a caterpillar.

The one I ate first.

The very one you nibbled a little corner off.

Then he ate the rest.

The whole hairy-legged, fuzzy, orange and yellow striped, nasty rest.

Because he thought I might die.

As if my babygirl dead wouldn't be enough. Huh uh. He swallowed all the rest of that nasty bug so if you died, he'd die too and then there I'd be with both you gone.

So he was into the saving business, too.

Had a funny way of showing it but I guess you could say he was. Guess he was, alright. Had to be when I look round and see all you children grown up and me getting old as sin.

Nineteen years older than me is all.

That's enough.

I remember you telling me the caterpillar story and then I remember that man trying to shoot Daddy and then I remember Albert Wilkes's pistol you pulled out from under the icebox.

That's a whole lot of remembering. You was a little thing, a lap baby when that mess in Cassina happened.

Five or six.

Yes, you were. That's what you was. Had to be because we'd been on Cassina two, three years. Like a kennel back there on Cassina Way in those days. Every one of them shacks full of niggers. And they let their children run the street half-naked and those burr heads ain't never seen a comb. Let them children out in the morning and called em in at night like they was goats or something. You was five or six but I kept you on my lap plenty. Didn't want you growing up too fast.

Never did want it. With all you children I tried to keep that growing up business going slow as I could. What you need to hurry for? Where you going? Wasn't in no hurry to get you out my lap and set you down in those streets.

I remember. I'm sure I remember. The man, a skinny man, came running down the alley after Daddy. He had a big pistol just like Albert Wilkes. And you smashed your fist through the glass to warn Daddy. If I shut my eyes I can hear glass falling and hear the shots.

Never knew John French could run so fast. Thought for a moment one of them bullets knocked him down but he outran em all. Had to or I'd be telling a different story.

It's mixed up with other things in my mind but I do remember. You told me the story and showed me the scar later but I was there and I remember too.

You was there, alright. The two of us sitting at the front window staring at nothing. Staring at the quiet cause it was never quiet in Cassina Way except early in the morning and then again that time of day people in they houses fixing to eat supper. Time of day when the men come home and the children come in off the streets and it's quiet for the first time since dawn. You can hear nothing for the first time and hear yourself think for the first time all day so there we was in that front window and I was half sleep and daydreaming and just about forgot I had you on my lap. Even though you were getting to be a big thing. A five- or six-year-old thing but I wasn't in no hurry to set you down so there we was. You was there alright but I wasn't paying you no mind. I was just studying them houses across the way and staring at my ownself in the glass and wondering where John French was and wondering how long it would stay quiet before your sister Geraldine woke up and started to fuss and wondering who that woman was with a baby in her lap staring back at me.

And you told the caterpillar story.

Yes, I probably did. If that's what you remember, I probably did. I liked to tell it when things was quiet. Ain't much of a story if there's lots of noise around. Ain't the kind you tell to no bunch of folks been drinking and telling lies all night. Sitting at the window with you at the quiet end of the afternoon was the right time for that story and I probably told it to wake myself up.

. . .

JOHN FRENCH is cradling Lizabeth in one arm pressed against his chest. She is muttering or cooing or getting ready to throw up.

"What did she eat? What you saying she ate? You supposed to be watching this child, woman."

"Don't raise your voice at me. Bad enough without you frightening her."

"Give it here, woman."

His wife opens her fist and drops the fuzzy curled remnant of caterpillar in his hand. It lies there striped orange and yellow, dead or alive, and he stares like it is a sudden eruption of the skin of the palm of his hand, stares like he will stare at the sloppy pyramids of ash desecrating his garden-to-be. He spreads the fingers of the hand of the arm supporting the baby's back; still one minute, Lizabeth will pitch and buck the next. He measures the spiraled length of caterpillar in his free hand, sniffs it, strokes its fur with his middle finger, seems to be listening or speaking to it as he passes it close to his face. His jaws work the plug of tobacco; he spits and the juice sizzles against the pavement.

"You sure this the most of it? You sure she only ate a little piece?"

Freeda French is still shaking her head yes, not because she knows the answer but because anything else would be unthinkable. How could she let this man's daughter chew up more than a little piece of caterpillar. Freeda is crying inside. Tears glaze her eyes, shiny and thick as the sugar frosting on her Aunt Aida's cakes and there is too much to hold back, the weight of the tears will crack the glaze and big drops will steal down her cheeks. While she is still nodding yes, nodding gingerly so the tears won't leak, but knowing they are coming anyway, he spits again and pops the gaudy ringlet of bug into his mouth.

"I got the most of it then. And if I don't die, she ain't gonna die neither, so stop that sniffling." He chews two or three times and his eyes are expressionless vacant as he runs his tongue around his teeth getting it all out and down. . . .

SOMEONE HAD BEEN dumping ashes on the vacant lot at the end of Cassina Way. The empty lot had been part of the neighborhood for as long as anybody could remember and no one had ever claimed it until John French moved his family into the rear end of the narrow row house adjoining the lot and then his claim went no farther than a patch beside the end wall of the row houses, a patch he intended to plant with tomatoes, peppers and beans but never got around to except to say he'd be damned if he couldn't make something grow there even though the ground was more rock and roots than it was soil because back home in Culpepper, Virginia, where the soil so good you could almost eat it in handfuls scooped raw from the earth, down there he learned about growing and he was going to make a garden on that lot when he got around to it and fix it to look nearly as good as the one he had loved to listen to when he was a boy sitting on his back porch with his feet up on a chair and nobody he had to bother with from his toes to the Blue Ridge Mountains floating on the horizon.

Ashes would appear in gray, sloppy heaps one or two mornings a week. The shape of the mounds told John French they had been spilled from a wheelbarrow, that somebody was sneaking a wheelbarrow down the dark, cobbled length of Cassina Way while other people slept, smothering his dream of a garden under loads of scraggly ash. One afternoon when Lizabeth came home crying with ash in her hair, hair her mother had just oiled and braided that morning, John French decided to put a stop to the ash dumping. He said so to his wife, Freeda, while Lizabeth wept, raising his voice as Lizabeth bawled louder. Finally goddamned somebody's soul and somebody's ancestors and threatened to lay somebody's sorry soul to rest, till Freeda hollering to be heard over Lizabeth's crying and John French's cussing told him such language wasn't fit for a child's ears, wasn't fit for no place or nobody but the Bucket of Blood and his beer drinking, wine drinking, nasty talking cronies always hanging round there.

So for weeks Lizabeth did not sleep. She lay in her bed on the edge of sleep in the tiny room with her snoring sister, afraid like a child is afraid to poke a foot in bath water of an uncertain temperature, but she was frozen in that hesitation not for an instant but for weeks as she learned everything she could from the night sounds of Cassina Way, and then lay awake learning there was nothing else to learn, that having the nightmare happen would be the only way of learning, that after predictable grunts and alley clamors, the cobblestones went to sleep for the night and she still hadn't picked up a clue about what she needed to know, how she would recognize the sound of a wheelbarrow and find some unfrightened, traitorous breath in herself with which to cry out and warn the man who pushed the barrow of ashes that her father, John French, with his double-barrelled shotgun taller than she was, sat in ambush in the downstairs front room.

Even before she heard him promise to shoot whoever was dumping ashes she had listened for her Daddy to come home at night. He'd rummage a few minutes in the kitchen then she'd listen for the scrape of a match and count his heavy steps as he climbed to the landing; at *twelve* he would be just a few feet away and the candlelight would lurch on the wall and her father would step first to the girls' room, and though her eyes were squeezed as tightly shut as walnuts, she could feel him peering in as the heat of the candle leaned closer, feel him counting his daughters the way she counted the stairs, checking on his girls before he ventured the long stride across the deep well of the landing to the other side of the steps, the left turning to the room where her mother would be sleeping. Once in a while partying all by himself downstairs, he would sing. Rocking back and forth on a rickety kitchen chair his foot tapping a bass line on the linoleum floor, he'd sing, *Froggy went a courtin and he did ride, uh huh, uh huh.* Or the songs she knew came from the Bucket of Blood. His husky voice cracking at the tenor notes and half laughing, half swallowing the words in those songs not fit for any place but the Bucket of Blood.

Most times he was happy but even if she heard the icebox door slammed hard enough to pop the lock, heard his chair topple over and crash to the floor, heard the steps groan like he was trying to put his heel through the boards, like he was trying to crush the humpback of some steel-shelled roach with each stride, hearing even this she knew his feet would get quieter as she neared the end of her count, that no matter how long it took between steps when she could hear him snoring or shuffling back and forth along the length of a step like he had forgotten *up* and decided to try *sideways,* finally he would reach the landing and the staggering light from the candle her mother always set out for him on its dish beside the front door would lean in once then die with the bump of her parents' door closing across the landing.

Lizabeth could breathe easier then, after she had counted him safely to his bed, after the rasp of door across the landing and the final bump which locked him safely away. But for weeks she'd lain awake long after the house was silent, waiting for the unknown sound of the wheelbarrow against the cobblestones, the sound she must learn, the sound she must save him from.

"It got to be that bowlegged Walter Johnson cause who else be cleaning people's fireplaces round here. But I'll give him the benefit of the doubt. Every man deserves the benefit of the doubt so I ain't going to accuse Walter Johnson to his face. What I'm gon do is fill the next nigger's butt with buckshot I catch coming down Cassina Way dumping ash."

She knew her father would shoot. She had heard about Albert Wilkes so she knew that shooting meant men dead and men running away and never coming back. She could not let it happen. She imagined the terrible sound of the gun a hundred times each night. If she slept at all, she did not remember or could not admit a lapse because then the hours awake would mean nothing. Her vigilance must be total. If she would save her father from himself, from the rumbling cart and the gray, ashy faced intruder who would die and carry her father away with him in the night, she must be constant, must listen and learn the darkness better than it knew itself.

"DADDY." She is sitting on his knee. Her eyes scale her father's chest, one by one she climbs the black buttons of his flannel shirt until she counts them all and reaches the grayish neck of his long johns. Their one cracked pearl button showing below his stubbled chin.

"Daddy. I want to stay in your hat."

"What you talking about, little sugar?"

"I want to live in your hat. Your big brown hat. I want to live in there always."

"Sure you can. Yes indeed. Make you a table and some chairs and catch a little squirrel too, let him live in there with you. Now that sounds like a fine idea, don't it? Stay under there till you get too big for your Daddy's hat. Till you get to be a fine big gal."

Lizabeth lowers her eyes from his long jaw, from the spot he plumped out with his tongue. He shifted the Five Brothers tobacco from one cheek to the other, getting it good and juicy and the last she saw of his face before her eyes fell to the brass pot beside his chair was how his jaws worked the tobacco, grinding the wad so it came out bloody and sizzling when he spit.

She was already big enough for chores and hours beside her mother in the kitchen where there was always something to be done. But hours too on the three steps her Daddy had built from the crooked door to the cobbled edge of Cassina Way. Best in the summer when she could sit and get stupid as a fly in the hot sun after it rose high enough to crest the row houses across the alley. If you got up before everybody else summer mornings were quiet in Cassina, nothing moving until the quiet was broken by the cry of the scissors-and-knife man, a jingling ring of keys at his waist, and strapped across his back the flintstone wheel which he would set down on its three legs and crank so the sparks flew up if you had a dull blade for him to sharpen, or by the iceman who would always come first, behind the tired clomp of his horse's hooves striking Cassina's stones. The iceman's wagon was covered with gray canvas that got darker like a bandage on a wound as the ice bled through. *Ice. Ice. Any ice today, lady?* The iceman sang the words darkly so Lizabeth never understood exactly what he cried till she asked her mother.

"He's saying *Any ice today, lady,* least that's what he thinks he's saying. Least that's what I think he's saying," her mother said as she listened stock-still by the sink to make sure. For years the iceman was Fred Willis and Fred Willis still owned the horse which slept some people said in the same room with him, but now a scowling somebody whose name Lizabeth didn't know, who wore a long rubber apron the color of soaked canvas was the one talking the old gray horse down the alley, moaning *Ice, ice, any ice today, lady* or whatever it was she heard first thing behind the hollow clomp of the hooves.

Stupid as a fly. She had heard her Daddy say that and it fit just how she felt, sun-dazed, forgetting even the itchy places on her neck, the cries of the vendors which after a while like everything blended with the silence.

Stupid as a fly during her nightlong vigils when she couldn't learn what she needed to know but she did begin to understand how she

could separate into two pieces and one would listen for the wheelbarrow and the other part would watch her listening. One part had a
Daddy and loved him more than anything but the other part could see
him dead or dying or run away forever and see Lizabeth alone and
heartbroken or see Lizabeth lying awake all night foolish enough to
think she might save her Daddy. The watching part older and wiser
and more evil than she knew Lizabeth could ever be. A worrisome part
which strangely at times produced in her the most profound peace
because she was that part and nothing else when she sat sun-drugged,
stupid as a fly on the steps over Cassina Way.

BRACELETS OF GRAY soapsuds circled her mother's wrists as she lifted a
china cup from the sink, rinsed it with a spurt of cold water and set
it gleaming on the drainboard to dry. The same froth clinging to her
mother's arms floated above the rim of the sink, screening the dishes
that filled the bowl. Each time the slim hands disappeared into the
water there was an ominous clatter and rattle, but her mother's fingers
had eyes, sorted out the delicate pieces first, retrieved exactly what
they wanted from the load of dishes. If Lizabeth plunged her own
hands into the soapy water, everything would begin to totter and slide,
broken glass and chipped plates would gnaw her clumsy fingers. Some
larger pieces were handed to her to dry and put away which she did
automatically, never taking her eyes from her mother's swift, efficient
movements at the sink.

"Lizabeth, you go catch the iceman. Tell him five pounds."

Lizabeth shouted, *Five pound, we want five pound.* She knew
better, her mother had told her a hundred times: pounds and miles,
s when you talking bout more than one, but her Daddy said *two pound
a salt pork* and *a thousand mile tween here and home* so when the
wagon was abreast of the last row houses and the echo of the hooves
and the echo of the blues line the iceman made of his call faded down
the narrow funnel of Cassina Way she shouted loud as she could, *Five
pound, five pound, Mister.*

The horse snorted. She thought it would be happy to stop but it
sounded mad. The driver's eyes went from the little girl on the steps
to the empty place in the window where there should be a sign if

anybody in the house wanted ice. When his eyes stared at her again, they said you better not be fooling with me, girl, and with a grunt much like the horse's snort he swung himself down off the wagon seat, jerked up an edge of the canvas from the ice and snapped away a five pound chunk in rusty pincers. The block of ice quivered as the iron hooks pierced its sides. Lizabeth could see splintered crystal planes, the cloudy heart of the ice when the man passed her on the steps. Under the high-bibbed rubber apron, the man's skin was black and glistening. He hollered once *Iceman* and pushed through the door.

If she had a horse, she would keep it in the vacant lot next door. It would never look nappy and sick like this one. The iceman's horse had bare patches in his coat, sore, raw-looking spots like the heads of kids who had ringworm. Their mothers would tie a stocking cap over the shaved heads of the boys so they could come to school and you weren't supposed to touch them because you could get it that way but Lizabeth didn't even like to be in the same room. Thinking about the shadowy nastiness veiled under the stockings was enough to make her start scratching even though her mother washed and oiled and braided her thick hair five times a week.

She waited till the wagon had creaked past the vacant lot before she went back inside. If her pinto pony were there in the lot, nibbling at the green grass her Daddy would plant, it would whinny at the sad ice wagon horse. She wondered how old the gray horse might be, why it always slunk by with its head bowed and its great backside swaying slowly as the dark heads of the saints in Homewood A.M.E. Zion when they hummed the verses of a hymn.

"That man dripping water in here like he don't have good sense. Some people just never had nothing and never will." Her mother was on her hands and knees mopping the faded linoleum with a rag.

"Here girl, take this till I get the pan." She extended her arm backward without turning her head. "Pan overflowed again and him slopping water, too." She was on her knees and the cotton housedress climbed up the backs of her bare thighs. Her mama's backside poked up in the air and its roundness, its splitness made her think of the horse's huge buttocks, then of her own narrow hips. Her mama drew the brimful drain pan from under the icebox, sliding it aside without spilling a drop. "Here," her arm extended again behind her, her fingers making the shape of the balled rag. She had to say *Here girl* again before Lizabeth raised her eyes from the black scarifications in the linoleum and pushed the rag she had wrung into her mother's fingers.

"I don't know why I'm down here punishing these bones of mine and you just standing there looking. Next time . . ."

Her mother stopped abruptly. She had been leaning on one elbow, the other arm stretched under the icebox to sop up the inevitable drips missed by the drain pan. Now she bowed her head even lower, one cheek almost touching the floor so she could see under the icebox. When her hand jerked from the darkness it was full of something blue-black and metal.

"Oh, God. Oh, my God."

She held it the way she held a trap that had snared a rat, and for a moment Lizabeth believed that must be what it was, some new rat-killing steel trap. Her mama set the wooden kind in dark corners all over the house but when one caught something her mother hated to touch it, she would try to sweep the trap and the squeezed rat body out the door together, leave it for John French to open the spring and shake the dead rodent into the garbage can so the trap could be used again. Her mama held a trap delicately if she had to touch it at all, in two fingers, as far from her body as she could reach, looking away from it till she dropped it in a place from which it could be broomed easily out the door. This time the object was heavier than a trap and her mama's eyes were not half-closed and her mouth was not twisted like somebody swallowing cod liver oil. She was staring, wide-eyed, frightened.

"Watch out . . . stand back."

On the drainboard the gun gleamed with a dull, blue-black light which came from inside, a dead glistening Lizabeth knew would be cold and quick to the touch, like the bloody, glass-eyed fish the gun lay next to.

"You've seen nothing. Do you understand, child? You've seen nothing and don't you ever breathe a word of this to a soul. Do you understand me?"

Lizabeth nodded. But she was remembering the man in the alley. Must remember. But that afternoon in the kitchen it was like seeing it all for the first time. Like she had paid her dime to the man at the

Bellmawr Show and sat huddled in the darkness, squirming, waiting for pictures to start flashing across the screen. It had to begin with the caterpillar story.

"I got the most of it then. And if I don't die, she ain't gonna die neither, so stop that sniffling."

Lizabeth has heard the story so many times she can tell it almost as well as her mother. Not with words yet, not out loud yet, but she can set the people—her father, her mother, herself as a baby—on the stage and see them moving and understand when they are saying the right words and she would know if somebody told it wrong. She is nearly six years old and sitting on her mother's lap as she hears the caterpillar story this time. Sitting so they both can look out the downstairs window into Cassina Way.

Both look at the gray covering everything, a late afternoon gray gathered through a fall day that has not once been graced by the sun. Palpable as soot the gray is in the seams between the cobblestones, seals the doors and windows of the row houses across the alley. Lights will yellow the windows soon but at this in-between hour nothing lives behind the gray boards of the shanties across the way. Lizabeth has learned the number *Seventy-Four-Fifteen* Cassina Way and knows to tell it to a policeman if she is lost. But if she is Lizabeth French, she cannot be lost because she will be here, in this house certain beyond a number, absolutely itself among the look-alikes crowding Cassina Way. She will not be lost because there is a lot next door where her Daddy will grow vegetables, and her mother will put them in jars and they will eat all winter the sunshine and growing stored in those jars and there are three wooden steps her Daddy made for sitting and doing nothing till she gets stupid as a fly in that same sun, and sleeping rooms upstairs, her sister snoring and the candle poked in before her Daddy closes the door across the deep well.

The end house coming just before the empty corner lot is Lizabeth and Lizabeth nothing more nor less than the thinnest cobweb stretched in a dusty corner where the sounds, smells and sights of the house come together.

Lizabeth watches her mother's eyes lose their green. She sits as still as she can. She is not the worm now like her mama always calls her because she's so squirmy, she is nothing now because if she sits still enough her mother forgets her and Lizabeth who is nothing at all, who is not a worm and not getting too big to be sitting on people's laps all day, can watch the shadows deepen and her mama's green eyes turn gray like the houses across Cassina Way.

"There was a time Cassina Way nothing but dirt. Crab apple trees and pear trees grew where you see all them shacks. Then the war came and they had a parade on Homewood Avenue and you should have seen them boys strut. They been cross the ocean and they knew they looked good in their uniforms and they sure was gon let everybody know it. People lined up on both sides the street to see those colored troops marching home from the war. The 505 Engineers. Everybody proud of them and them strutting to beat the band. Mize well been dancing down Homewood Avenue. In a manner of speaking they were dancing and you couldn't keep your feet still when they go high stepping past. That big drum get up inside your chest and when Elmer Hollinger hits it your skin feels about to bust. All of Homewood out that day. People I ain't never seen before. All the ones they built these shacks for back here on Cassina Way. Ones ain't never been nowhere but the country and put they children out in the morning, don't call them in till feeding time. Let them run wild. Let them make dirt and talk nasty and hair ain't never seen a comb.

"That's why I'ma hold on to you, girl. That's why your mama got to be mean sometimes and keep you in sometime you want to be running round outdoors."

Lizabeth loves the quiet time of day when she can just sit, when she has her mama all to herself and her mama talks to her and at her and talks to herself but loud enough so Lizabeth can hear it all. Lizabeth needs her mother's voice to make things real. (Years later when she will have grandchildren of her own and her mother and father both long dead Lizabeth will still be trying to understand why sometimes it takes someone's voice to make things real. She will be sitting in a room and the room full of her children and grandchildren and everybody eating and talking and laughing but she will be staring down a dark tunnel and that dark, empty tunnel is her life, a life in which nothing has happened, and she'll feel like screaming at the darkness and emptiness and wringing her hands because nothing will seem real, and she will be alone in a roomful of strangers. She will need to tell someone how it had happened. But anybody who'd care would be long dead. Anybody who'd know what she was talking about would be long gone but she needs to tell someone so she will begin telling herself. Patting her foot on the floor to keep time. Then she will be speaking out loud. The others will listen and pay attention. She'll see down the tunnel and it won't be a tunnel at all, but a door opening on something clear and bright. Something simple which makes so much sense it will flash sudden and bright as the sky in a summer storm. Telling the story right will make it real.)

"Look at that man. You know where he been at. You know what he's been doing. Look at him with his big hat self. You know he been down on his knees at Rosemary's shooting crap with them trifling niggers. Don't you pay me no mind, child. He's your Daddy and a good man so don't pay me no mind if I say I wish I could sneak out there and get behind him and boot his butt all the way home. Should have been home an hour ago. Should have been here so he could keep an eye on you while I start fixing dinner. Look at him just sauntering down Cassina Way like he owns it and got all the time in the world. Your sister be up in a minute and yelling soon as her eyes open and him just taking his own sweet time.

"He won too. Got a little change in his pocket. Tell by the way he walks. Walking like he got a load in his pants, like other people's nickels and dimes weigh him down. If he lost he'd be smiling and busting in here talking fast and playing with youall and keep me up half the night with his foolishness. Never saw a man get happy when he gambles away his family's dinner. Never saw a man get sour-faced and down in the mouth when he wins."

Lizabeth doesn't need to look anymore. Her Daddy will get closer and closer and then he'll come through the door. Their life together will begin again. He is coming home from Rosemary's, down Cassina Way. He is there if you look and there if you don't look. He is like the reflection, the image of mother and daughter floating in the grayness of Cassina Way. There if she looks, there if she doesn't.

She stares at the pane of glass and realizes how far away she has been, how long she has been daydreaming but he is only a few steps closer, taking his own good time, the weight of somebody else's money in his pockets, the crown of his hat taller than the shadowed roofs of Cassina Way.

Her mama's arms are a second skin, a warm snuggling fur that keeps out the grayness, the slight, late-afternoon chill of an October day. She hums to herself, a song about the caterpillar story her mama has just told. Her baby sister is sleeping so Lizabeth has her mother to herself. Whenever they are alone, together, is the best time of the day, even if it comes now when the day is nearly over, sitting at the window in her mama's lap and her mama, after one telling of the caterpillar story, quiet and gray as Cassina Way. Because Lizabeth has a baby sister Geraldine she must love even though the baby makes the house smaller and shrinks the taken-for-granted time Lizabeth was used to spending with her mama. Lizabeth not quite six that early evening, late afternoon she is recalling, that she has not remembered or relived for five years till it flashes back like a movie on a screen that afternoon her mother pulls the revolver from under the icebox.

Her mother screams and smashes her fist through the windowpane. A gunshot pops in the alley. Her Daddy dashes past the jagged space where the windowpane had been, glass falling around his head as he bounds past faster than she has ever seen him move, past the empty, collapsing frame toward the vacant lot. A gun clatters against the cobbles and a man runs off down the corridor of Cassina Way.

My God. Oh, my God.

Her mama's fist looks like someone has tied bright red strings across her knuckles. The chair tumbles backward as her mother snatches her away from the jagged hole. Baby Geraldine is yelping upstairs like a wounded animal. Lizabeth had been daydreaming, and the window had been there between her daydream and her Daddy, there had been separation, a safe space between, but the glass was shattered now and the outside air in her face and her mama's hand bleeding and her mama's arms squeezing her too tightly, crushing her as if her small body could stop the trembling of the big one wrapped around it.

"Lizabeth . . . Lizabeth."

When her mama had screamed her warning, the man's eyes leaped from her Daddy's back to the window. Lizabeth saw the gun but didn't believe the gun until her mama screamed again and flung her fist through the glass. That made it real and made her hear her own screams and made her Daddy a man about to be shot dead in the alley.

If a fist hadn't smashed through the window perhaps she would not have remembered the screaming, the broken glass, the shots when she watched her mama drag a pistol from under the icebox and set it on the bloody drainboard.

But Lizabeth did remember and see and she knew that Albert Wilkes had shot a policeman and run away and knew Albert Wilkes had come to the house in the dead of night and given her father his pistol to hide, and knew that Albert Wilkes would never come back, that if he did return to Homewood he would be a dead man.

"You're a fool, John French, and no better than the rest of those wine-drinking rowdies down at the Bucket of Blood and God knows you must not have a brain in your head to have a gun in a house with children and who in the name of sense would do such a thing whether it's loaded or not and take it out of here, man, I don't care where you take it, but take it out of here." Her mother shouting as loud as she ever shouts like the time he teased her with the bloody rat hanging off the end of the trap, her Daddy waving it at her mama and her mama talking tough first, then shouting and in tears and finally her Daddy knew he had gone too far and carried it out the house . . .

Lizabeth remembered when the gun was dragged from under the icebox so there was nothing to do but lie awake all night and save her Daddy from himself, save him from the trespassing cart and smoking ashes and the blast of a shotgun and dead men and men running away forever. She'd save him like her mama had saved him. At least till he got that garden planted and things started growing and he put up a little fence and then nobody fool enough to dump ashes on something belonged to John French.

YOU OUGHT TO PAINT some yellow stripes and orange stripes on that scar, Mama.

Don't be making fun of my scar. This scar saved your father's life.

I know it did. I'm just jealous, that's all. Because I'll never know if I saved him. I'd sure like to know. Anyway an orange and yellow caterpillar running across the back of your hand would be pretty, Mama. Like a tattoo. I'd wear it like a badge, if I knew.

Don't know what you're talking about now. You're just talking now. But I do know if you hadn't been sitting in my lap, I'da put my whole body through that window and bled to death on those cobblestones in Cassina Way so just by being there you saved me and that's enough saving for one day and enough talk too, cause I can see John French coming down that alley from Rosemary's now and I'm getting sad now and I'm too old to be sitting here crying when ain't nothing wrong with me.

hazel

The day it happened Hazel dreamed of steps. The black steps her
brother Faun had pushed her down. The white steps clinging to the
side of the house she would not leave till she died. Down the steep
black stairwell you always fell faster and faster. In the first few
moments of the dream you could count the steps as parts of your body
cracked on each sharp, wooden edge. But soon you were falling so fast
your body trailed behind you, a broken, rattling noise like tin cans tied
to a wedding car. The white steps were up. You mounted them
patiently at first. The sun made them gleam and printed their shadow
black against the blank, clapboard wall. If you looked up you could
see a pattern repeated endlessly to the sky. A narrow, slanted ladder
of nine steps, a landing, another bank of bare, bone white railings and
steps leaning toward the next landing. Patiently at first, step by step,
but then each landing only leads you to another flight of steps and you
have been climbing forever and the ground is too far away to see but
you are not getting any closer to the top of the building. The sun
dazzles you when you stop to catch your breath. You are dizzy,
exposed. You must hurry on to the next landing. You realize you
cannot stop. You understand suddenly that you are falling *up* and this

318

dream is worse than your brother's hands flinging you down into the black pit.

"Eat your peas now, honey." Her mother was busy halving peas into neat green hemispheres so Hazel wiggled her tongue at the ones prepared for her, the ones her mother had shoved with the edge of her knife into a mound in one compartment of her plate. They're good and juicy her mother said as she speared another pea. Can hardly catch them, she said as she sliced the pea and its two halves disappeared in the gray soup covering the bottom of the plate's largest section. Her mother boiled everything and always splashed water from pan to plate when she portioned Hazel's meals into the thick, trisected platter. If my food had those little wings like fish it could swim to me, Hazel thought. I'd put my lips on my plate and open my mouth wide like the whale swallowing Jonah and my food just swim to me like that.

"Here's the rest now. You eat up now." The knife squeaked through the flood, driving split peas before it, tumbling them over the divider so the section nearest Hazel was as green as she remembered spring.

"Have a nice breast of lamb cooking. By the time you finish these, it'll be ready, darling."

So green she wanted to cry. Hazel wished she knew why her tears came so easily, so suddenly over nothing. She hated peas. Her mother boiled them till the skins were loose and wrinkled. Pure mush when you bit into them. And who ever heard of cutting peas in half. *So you don't choke, darling. Mama doesn't want to lose her baby. Can't be too careful.* She had screwed up her face and stuck out her tongue at the peas just a moment before when her mother wasn't looking but now she felt like crying. Mushy and wrinkled and wet didn't matter at all. She didn't want to disturb the carpet of green. Didn't want to stick her fork in it. It was too beautiful, too green. A corner of spring in the drab room she would never leave.

Her mother never gets any older. She's slim, dainty, perfect as she rises and crosses to the stove, a young girl from the back, her trim hips betraying no sign of the three children they've borne. The long, straight hair they say she inherited from her mother Maggie is twisted and pinned into a bun on top of her head. A picture of Maggie they say when she lets it down and gathers it in her hands and pulls it forward and lets it fall over one shoulder the way Maggie always wore hers. Grandmother Maggie in the oval photograph on the mantelpiece. That's your grandmother, Hazel. Looks like a white lady, don't she? She could sit on her hair. Black and straight as any white woman's. Liked to let it hang like it is in the picture. She'd sit and play with it. Curl the end round her fingers. *That's your grandmother. It's a shame she didn't live long enough for you to see her. But she was too delicate, too beautiful. God didn't make her for living long in this world.*

Not one gray hair in the black mass when her mother swept it over her shoulder, two handfuls thick when her mother Gaybrella pulled and smoothed the dark river of hair down across her breast. Like a river or the wide, proud tail of a horse.

If her mother was not getting older, then she must be getting younger, Hazel thought, because nobody stood still. Hazel knew no one could stand still, not even a person who lives in a chair, a person who is helpless as a little baby, a person who never leaves the house. Even if you become Hazel, a person like that, you can't stand still. Some days took a week to pass. Some nights she'd awaken from her dreams and the darkness would stun her, would strike her across her mouth like a blow from a man's fist and she'd sink down into a stupor, not awake and not asleep for dull years at a time. She knew it hurt to have children, that women sweated and shrieked to wring life out of their bodies. That's why they called that hard, killing work *labor,* called it a woman's bed of pain. She knew it hurt to have a child dragged from your loins but it couldn't be any worse than those nights which were years and years ripped away from the numb cave of nothingness which began at her waist.

You couldn't stand still. You got older and more like a stone each day you sat in that chair, the chair which had been waiting at the foot of the stairs your brother pushed you down. So her mother was growing younger, was a girl again in her grace, in her slim body crossing to the stove and raising the lid to check the boiling breast of lamb.

"It's getting good and tender. It's almost done." Lamb smell filled the room, the shriveled pea halves were already cold to the touch. Hazel mashed one under her finger. As she wiped the mush on the napkin beside her plate she wondered what God used to clean his hands. How He got her off his thumb after he had squashed her in the darkness at the bottom of the steps.

The day it happened she dreamed of steps and thought of swallowing peas and chewing the lamb her mother Gaybrella had boiled to tastelessness. Until the day it roared beside her Hazel had never seen death. Death to her was that special look in her mother's eyes, a sneaky, frightened look which was not really something in the eyes but something missing, the eyes themselves missing from her mother's face. Death was her mother's eyes hiding, hiding for a whole morning, a whole afternoon, avoiding any encounter with Hazel's. Someone had knocked at the door early and Hazel had heard voices in her sleep. Her mother had shushed whoever it was and by the time Hazel was awake enough to listen the whispering on the other side of the door had stopped. Then the outside door was shut and bolted, a woman's footsteps had clattered down the three flights of outside steps and a strange something had emptied her mother's eyes. Hazel hadn't asked who had arrived at dawn, or asked what news the visitor had carried. She hadn't asked because there was no one to ask. Sometimes their three rooms at the top floor of Mr. Gray's house seemed smaller than a dress mother and daughter were struggling to wear at the same time. But the day of the empty eyes her mother found a million places in the tiny rooms to hide. Hazel had hummed all the songs she knew to keep herself company. By two o'clock her nervousness, the constant alert she forced herself to maintain had drained her. She was ready to cry or scream and did both when her mother had appeared from the bedroom in her long black coat. Her mother never left the house alone. Once or twice a year on Ferd's arm she might venture down into the Homewood streets but never alone. With her head tied in a scarf and her body wrapped from ankles to chin in the column of black she had faced Hazel for the first time that day. Her mother Gaybrella had looked like a child bundled up for an outing on a winter day. A child whose wide eyes were full of good-bye.

She's leaving me. She's going away. The words were too terrible to say. They were unthinkable but Hazel couldn't think anything else as she had stared at the pale girl woman who had once been her mother, who was too young now to be her mother, at the child who was going away forever.

"It's John French, sugar." Her mother's eyes had gone again. There was no one to ask why, or how long, no one but her own pitiful, crippled self in the room she would never leave. John French was a big, loud, gentle man who brought her candy and fruit. Her mother smiled at him in a way Hazel had never seen her smile before. Those kisses he planted on Hazel's forehead each time he left smelled of wine and tobacco. Coming and going he'd rattle the three flights of stairs which climbed the outside of Mr. Gray's clapboard house.

"You don't come on down outa here like you got good sense, Gay, I'ma come up and get you one day. Drag you if I have to. Fine woman like you cooped up here don't even see the light of day. I'ma come up here and grab you sure enough."

John French who was an uncle or an in-law or whatever you were to somebody when he married your mother's niece. Cousin Freeda who was Gert's girl. Aunt Gert and Aunt Aida and Aunt Bess your mother's sisters. John French had daughters who would be relatives too. Nice girls he said. *I'ma get those hussies come to see you some time.* How many years had it been since he said that. How many years before Lizabeth knocked on Sunday morning. She said it was Sunday and said she was just stopping by on her way home from church. And said her Daddy said hello. And said he's not doing so well. Heart and all and won't listen to the doctor. My Daddy's hardheaded, stubborn as a mule, she said. How many years ago and Lizabeth still coming, still dropping by on Sundays to say hello. That's how you know it's a Sunday. Lizabeth knocking in her Sunday clothes and, Hi, how you all doing? That's how you know Sunday still comes and comes in winter when she wears a big coat and in summer when she's sweating under her Sunday clothes. She'll take off the little hats she wears and set them on the table. In spring they look like Easter baskets. Girl, it's hot out there. Phew, she'll say and stretch out her legs. Ain't fit for a dog out there. Aunt Gay, she'll say. You should have heard Miss Lewis this morning. She can still sing, Aunt Gay. Old as she is she can still get that whole church shouting. You ought to come the next time she's singing. She always does a solo with the Gospel Chorus and they're on every third Sunday. You ought to come and I'll stay here with Hazel. Or Hazel could come too. We could get somebody to help her down the steps. We could get a wheelchair and somebody would give us a ride. Why don't both you'all come next third Sunday?

John French in Lizabeth's face. His high cheekbones and long jaw. White like her Daddy and his French eyes and the good French hair he used to have and she still does. Lizabeth is like John French always worrying them to come down into the world. A girl then a woman. The years pretty on her. Lizabeth can get up when she's finished with her tea in winter or her lemonade in summer, get up and walk away on two strong legs so the years do not pile up on her. She does not lose them by the fistful in the middle of the night and wake up years older in the morning. Lizabeth is not a thousand years old, she is not a stone heavy with too many years to count.

It's John French, sugar. Her mother had never said more than that. Just stood there in her long black coat, in the body of that child she was becoming again. Stood there a moment to see if her silence, her lost eyes might do what she knew words couldn't. But silence and eyes staring through her, around her, hadn't checked Hazel's sobs so Gaybrella left and tiptoed down the three flights of steps and returned in two hours, tiptoeing again, easing the door open and shut again, saying nothing as she shed the black coat and washed her hands and started water boiling for dinner.

Death was that something missing in her mother Gaybrella's eyes. Death was her mother leaving to go to John French, leaving without a word, without any explanation but Hazel knowing exactly where she was going, and why and knowing if her mother ever leaves that way again it will be death again. It will be Aunt Aida or Aunt Bess if she leaves again, if there is anyone else who can make her tip down the steps, make her lose her eyes the way John French did.

The day it happened (the *it* still unthinkable, unsayable as it was when her mother stood draped in black on the threshold) began with Bess *yoo-hooing* from the yard behind Mr. Gray's house.

"Yoo-hoo. Yoo-hoo, Gay." Little Aunt Bess yodeling up from the yard. That made it Tuesday because that's when Aunt Bess came to do the wash. First the dream of steps, of black steps and white steps, then the day beginning with Aunt Bess hollering *"Yoo-hoo. What you got today? it's Tuesday. What you got for me?"*

Her mother hated to drop the bundle of laundry into the yard but short-legged Bess hated all those steps and since she was the one doing the favor she'd yoo-hoo till she got her sister's attention and got her on the landing and got the bundle sailing down to her feet.

"Oww. Look at that dust. Look at that dust lapping at my things. If they weren't dirty before, they're dirty now."

"You wouldn't be dropping them down here if they wasn't dirty in the first place. I know you're the cleaningest woman in the world, sister Gaybrella, but you still get things dirty."

"Let's not have a conversation about my laundry out here in public."

"Ain't no public to it. Ain't nobody here but us chickens. This all you got for me, Gay?"

"I can do the rest."

"Just throw it all down here. Don't make no sense for you to be doing no rest."

"You know I can't do that. You know I don't let anybody touch the rest."

"You can be downright insultin sometimes. Holding on to them few little things like you don't trust your own sister or something. And me bending over your wash every week."

"If it's too much trouble, I'll do it all myself. Just bring it back up here and I'll do it all myself."

"Shut up, woman. I've been doing it all these years. What makes you think I'ma stop today?"

"Then you know I can't give you everything. You know I have to do our private things myself."

"Suit yourself. Mize well run my head against a brick wall as try to change your ways. If you got sheets in here I'll have to hang them on this line. Won't have room on mine today."

"Go ahead. You know I dry the little business I have right up here."

"Say hello to that sweet angel, Hazel. *Yoo-hoo*, Hazel. You hear me girl?"

"She hears you, Bess. The whole neighborhood hears you."

"What I care about some neighborhood, I'm saying hello to my angel and anybody don't like it can kiss my behind."

"Please, Bess."

"Don't be pleasing me. Just throw the rest of your dirty clothes down here so I can go on my way. Don't you be washing today. Don't do it today."

"I'm going inside now. Thank you."

"And don't you be thanking me. Just listen to me for once and don't be washing youall's underwear and hanging it over that stove."

"Good-bye."

And the door slams over Bess's head. She yells again. *Don't wash today,* but not loud enough to carry up the three flights of steps. She is bending over and pulling the drawstrings of the laundry bundle tighter so there is enough cord to sling the sack over her back. She is a short, sturdy-legged, reddish-yellow woman. Her skin is pocked with freckles. No one would guess she is the sister of the ivory woman who dropped the bundle from the landing. Bess hefts the sack over her shoulder and cuts catty-corner through the backyards toward the intersection of Albion and Tioga and her washing machine.

It happened on a Tuesday because her mother slammed the door and came in muttering about that Bess, that uncouth Bess. Her tongue's going to be the death of that woman. She married below her color but that's where her mouth always wanted to be anyway. Out in the street with those roughnecks and fieldhands and their country nigger ways. Her mother Gaybrella just fussing and scolding and not knowing what to do with her hands till she opened the wicker basket in the bathroom where she stored their soiled private things and ran the sink full of water and started to wash them out. That calmed her. In a few moments Hazel could hear her humming to herself. Hear the gentle lapping of the water and the silk plunged in again and again. Smell the perfumed soap and hear the rasp of her mother's knuckles as she scrubbed their underthings against the washboard.

A warm breeze had entered the room while her mother stood outside on the landing talking to Bess. A spring, summer breeze green as peas. It spread like the sunlight into every corner of the room. Hazel could see it touching the curtains, feel it stirring the hair at the nape of her neck. In the chair she never left except when her mother lifted her into bed each night Hazel tried to remember the wind. If she shut her eyes and held her palms over her ears she could hear it. Pulled close to the window she could watch it bend trees, or scatter leaves or see snowflakes whirl sideways and up in the wind's grasp. But hearing it or watching it play were not enough. She wanted to remember how the wind felt when you ran into it, or it ran into you and pasted your clothes to your skin, and tangled your hair into a mad streaming wake and took your breath away. Once she held her cupped hands very close to her face and blew into them, blew with all her might till her jaws ached and tears came. But it wasn't wind. Couldn't bring back the sensation she wanted to remember.

"Mama." Her mother is stringing a line above the stove. Their underthings have been cleaned and wrung into tight cylinders which are stacked in the basin her mother set on the sideboard.

"Bess never did listen to Mama. She was always the wild one. A hard head. She did her share of digging Mama an early grave. Mama never could do anything with her. Had a mind of her own while she was still in the cradle. I don't know how many times I've explained to her. There are certain things you wear close to your body you just can't let anybody touch. She knows that. And knows better than to be putting people's business in the street."

"Mama."

"What's that, honey?"

"Could you set me on the landing for a while?"

"Honey, I don't trust those stairs. I never did trust them. As long as we've been here I've been begging Mister Gray to shore them up. They sway and creak so bad. Think you're walking on a ship sometimes. I just don't trust them. The last time I went down with Ferdinand I just knew they wouldn't hold us both. I made him go first and held on to his coattail so we both wouldn't have to be on the same step at the same time. Still was scared to death the whole way down. Creaking and groaning like they do. Wouldn't trust my baby out there a minute."

"Is it warm?"

"In the sun, baby."

"I won't fall."

"Don't be worrying your mama now. You see I got these things to hang. And this place to clean. And I want to clean myself up and wash my hair this morning. Don't want to be looking like an old witch when Bess comes back this afternoon with the laundry. We can't slip, darling. We have to keep ourselves neat and clean no matter what. Doesn't matter what people see or don't see. What they never see are the places we have to be most careful of. But you know that. You're my good girl and you know that."

"If the sun's still out when you finish, maybe . . ."

"Don't worry me. I have enough to do without you picking at me. You just keep me company awhile. Or nap if you're tired."

Hazel watched as piece by piece her mother unrolled and pinned their underclothes on the line stretched above the stove. The back burners were lit. Steam rose off the lace-frilled step-ins and combinations.

"I have a feeling Ferdinand will come by today. He said last time he was here he was being fitted for a new suit and if I know my son it won't be long before he has to come up here to his mama and show off what he's bought. He's a good son. Never lost a night's sleep worrying over Ferdinand. If all mothers' sons were sweet as that boy, bearing children wouldn't be the burden it surely is. It's a trial. I can tell you it's a trial. When I look at you sitting in that chair and think of the terrible guilt on your other brother's shoulders, I can't tell you what a trial it is. Then I think sometimes, there's my little girl and she's going to miss a lot but then again she's blessed too because there's a whole lot she'll never have to suffer. The filth and dirt of this world. The lies of men, their nasty hands. What they put in you and what they turn you into. Having their way, having their babies. And worst of all expecting you to like it. Expecting you to say *thank you* and bow down like they're kings of the world. So I cry for you, precious. But you're blessed too. And it makes my heart feel good to know you'll always be neat and clean and pure."

It was always "your other brother" when her mother spoke of Faun. She had named him and then just as carefully unnamed him after he pushed his sister down the stairs. Her mother was the one who blamed him, who couldn't forgive, who hadn't said his name in fifteen years. There was Ferdinand and "your other brother." Hazel had always shortened her brother's names. To her they had been Ferd and Faun from the time she could speak. Her mother said every syllable distinctly and cut her eyes at people who didn't say *Fauntleroy* and *Ferdinand*. I gave my sons names. Real names. All niggers have nicknames. They get them everywhere and anywhere. White folks. Children. Hoodlums and ignorant darkies. All of them will baptize you in a minute. But I chose real names for my boys. Good, strong names. Names from their mother and that's who they'll be in my mouth as long as I live. But she was wrong. Fauntleroy became "your other brother." Faun had forced his mother to break her promise to herself.

Ferd was a timid, little man, a man almost dandified in his dress and mannerisms. He was nearly as picky as their mother. He couldn't stand dust on his shoes. His watch chain and the gold eagle head of his cane always shone as if freshly polished. A neat, slit-eyed man who pursed his lips to smile. When he sat with them he never looked his sister in the eye. He'd cross his leg and gossip with his mother and drink his tea from the special porcelain cups, never set out for anyone but him. Hazel knew he didn't like their mother. Never adored her the way she and Faun always did. To him Gaybrella was never a fairy princess. As a child he made fun of her strange ways. Once he had pursed his lips and asked them: If she's so good, if she's so perfect, why did Daddy leave her? But daddies had nothing to do with fairy princesses and they giggled at the silliness of his question. Then, like their father, Faun had run away or been run away, and ever since in Ferd's voice as he sat sipping tea and bringing news of the world, Hazel could hear the sneer, the taunt, the same mocking question he had asked about their father, asked about the absent brother. Hazel knew her mother also heard the question and that her mother saw the dislike in Ferd's distant eyes but instead of ordering him from the room, instead of punishing him the way she punished Faun for the least offense, she doted on Ferdinand. His was the only arm she'd accept, the only arm she'd allow to lead her down into the streets of Homewood.

Faun was like the wind. There were days when Hazel said his name over and over to herself. Never Fauntleroy but *Faun*. Faun. She'd close her eyes and try to picture him. The sound of his name was warm; it could lull her to sleep, to daydreaming of the times they ran together and talked together and shared a thousand secrets. He was her brother and the only man she had ever loved. Even as a girl she had understood that any other man who came into her life would be measured against

Faun. Six days a week he killed animals. He always changed his clothes at work but Hazel believed she could smell the slaughterhouse blood, could feel the killing strength in his hands when he pinched her cheek and teased her about getting prettier every day. Her big brother who was like the wind. Changeable as the wind. But his mood didn't matter; just staying close to him mattered. That's why they fought. Why they raged at each other and stood inseparable against the world. So when he was twenty and full of himself and full of his power over other women and she was seventeen and learning what parts of him she must let go and learning her own woman powers as he rejected them in her and sought them in others, when they rubbed and chafed daily, growing too close and too far apart at once, the fight in the kitchen was no different than a hundred others, except his slaughter-house hands on her shoulders pushed harder than he meant to, and her stumbling, lurching recoil from a blow she really didn't feel much at all, was carried too far and she lost her balance and tumbled through the kitchen door someone had left unlocked and pitched down the dark steep stairwell to Mr. Gray's second floor where the chair was waiting from which she would never rise.

"I expect him up those stairs anytime." Her mother had let her hair down. It dangled to her waist, flouncing like the broad, proud tail of a horse as she swept the kitchen floor.

Then it happened. So fast Hazel could not say what came first or second or third. Just that it happened. The unspeakable, the unsayable acted out before her eyes.

A smell of something burning. Almost like lamb. Flames crackling above the stove. Curling ash dropping down. Her mother shouting something. Words or a name. A panicked look back over her shoulders at the chair. Hazel forever in the chair. Then flames like wings shooting up her mother's back. Her mother wheeling, twisting slim and graceful as a girl. Her mother Gaybrella grabbing the river of her hair and whipping it forward over her shoulders, and the river on fire, blazing in her fists. Did her mother scream then or had she been screaming all along? Was it really hair in her hands or the burning housecoat she was trying to tear from her back? And as she rushed past Hazel like a roaring, hot wind, what was she saying, who was she begging for help? When her mother burst through the door and crashed through the railing into thin air who was she going to meet, who was making her leave without a word, without an explanation.

FIFTEEN YEARS AFTER the day it happened, fourteen years after Hazel too, had died, Lizabeth rode in the ambulance which was rushing with sirens blaring to Allegheny County Hospital. She was there because Faun was Gaybrella's son and Hazel's brother and she had stopped by all those Sundays and was one of the few who remembered the whole story. She had heard Faun had returned to Homewood but hadn't seen him till one of the church sisters who also possessed a long memory asked her if she knew her cousin was sick. So Lizabeth had visited him in the old people's home. And held his hand. And watched the torment of his slow dying, watched his silent agony because the disease had struck him dumb. She didn't know if he recognized her but she visited him as often as she could. A nurse called the ambulance when his eyes rolled to the top of his head and his mouth began to foam. Lizabeth rode with Faun in the screaming ambulance so she was there when he bolted upright and spoke for the first time in the two months she had been visiting him. "I'm sorry . . . I'm so sorry," was what he said. She heard that plainly and then he began to fail for the last time, tottering, exhausting the last bit of his strength to resist the hands of the attendants who were trying to push him back down on the stretcher. She thought he said, *Forgive me,* she thought those were Faun's last words but they sputtered through the bubbling froth of his lips and were uttered with the last of his fading strength so she couldn't be sure.

the chinaman

The toasts—long, bawdy, rhymed narratives invented by black street bards—contain much new slang but also preserve older words and ways of speaking. In the toasts the Chinaman appears as a symbol of decay and death.
See *Toasts—*
Wm. Labov *et al.*

Outside her window the last snow of the season is white only until it touches the pavement. Freeda's thoughts are her thoughts only until they reach the cloudy pane of glass where they expire silently, damp as tears, like snow against asphalt.

To believe who she is Freeda must go backward, must retreat, her voice slowly unwinding, slowly dismantling itself, her voice going backward with her, alone with her as the inevitable silence envelops. Talking to herself. Telling stories. Telling herself.

Once . . . once . . . her first baby born premature and breathless. The snow falling and her cousin May snatches away the child from the others who have shrieked, keened, moaned and are already beginning to mouth prayers for the dead. The door slams, shaking the wooden row house on Cassina Way, shattering the calm the women's folded hands and bowed heads are seeking. They realize the still, blue baby is gone. And that May is out there in the snow like a crazy woman with the dead child in her arms and ain't took time for coat or nothing she'll catch her death too in the blizzard that has its hand inside the house now and flings the door again and again crashing against its frame.

Once . . . how many years ago . . . Freeda was a baby then, she was forgiving then, burying her head in the wet pillow, hiding her eyes from theirs because she does not want to read the death of her firstborn in the women's faces. She wants to forgive. Forgive John French for the nights he loved her. Forgive the eyes of the women who smiled knowingly when she complained, who showed her their scars and wrinkled flesh, who said *Jesus* and smiled, and winced when she did and said *Everything's gon be all right, child* and *Thank Jesus* and *Ain't she beautiful she carries high like her mama, Gert* and *Her skin's so pretty,* and *Eat, honeychild, eat everything you want you eating for two now.* Who held her hand and rubbed her back and trudged through the snow to boil water and boil rags and stand on tired feet when it was time for her baby to come.

But their eyes are not the eyes of children. She cannot believe they knew everything else and didn't know the baby was twisted wrong side down in her belly. Freeda passes her gaze from one face to the other. They were ready to pray. They had been praying all along so they knew all along and she couldn't forgive. If someone would press her face down into the pillow she would turn blue like her baby was blue. The women's sorrowing, helpless faces would go away. She could forgive them. Her aunts, her neighbors, her cousin May, a girl like she is still a girl. Freeda knows their faces better than she knows her own. She hates what hovers sorrowing in their eyes.

Freeda hears the women rush away. The ragged, noisy lift of a flock of pigeons scared from the sidewalk. They are abandoning her. They were mountains rimming the valley of her pain. They were statues, stiff as the mourning women huddling over the broken body of Jesus in the picture in the Sunday school corner of Homewood A.M.E. Zion Church. Now they are fleeing and she is alone. Not even her baby beside her, if there was a baby borne to her by that sea of pain.

May . . . May . . . They are shouting through the open door.

May is kneeling in the snow across Cassina Way where it has drifted waist deep. She hunches forward shielding the baby from the wind, while she plunges its naked body into the snow. She must turn her face into the wind to see the others. Her hair, her eyebrows and cheeks are caked with white. She is a snow witch and nobody moves a step closer. She hollers something at them which the wind voids.

Then May struggles to her feet, and stomps back through the gaping door with the baby in her arms. She is praising Jesus and Hallelujahing and prancing the floor before anybody can grab the door and get it shut behind her.

"Wouldn't be for that I be telling a different story altogether. Yes indeed. She so tiny could fit in a shoebox. Naw, I ain't lying. If I'm lying, I'm flying. It's the God's truth, sure enough. Didn't weigh but a pound and a half. Weeniest little thing you ever did see. Called her mite. You know like little mighty mite. Course there was something else in that name too. Couldn't help but think that little girl child *might* make it and she *might* not. And everybody scared to call her anything but *mite*. Such a tiny little thing. Feed her with one of them eye droppers. Didn't sleep or nap less it be on somebody's bosom so she stay warm. Little thing curl up just like an eensy-beensy monkey, curl up right on your chest with that thumb in her mouth. The cutest thing. She got that little thumb and gone. Couldn't hardly see the nails on her fingers they so tiny."

The firstborn, Lizabeth, our mother, saved by May in the snow. May's told the story a hundred times but each time it's new and necessary. If she didn't tell the story right, there would be no baby shuddering to life in her arms when she runs through the crashing door. There would be no Lizabeth, none of us would be gathered in my grandmother's house on Finance Street listening to May tell how Geraldine came next. And then the boy, Carl, birthed by my grandmother. Making it all seem so easy. Spring born. Bright and cleansing like the new rain sluicing along the curb. A boybaby in Freeda's arms, plump and crying. Peace. As if his coming was a promise to her of how it would always be. How it should be easy. So when the twins came and died, one at birth, the other named Margaret after Daddy John's sister, holding on a week, whatever peace brought by the first son was shattered, broken and strewn in Freeda's path like bits of glass, like the dry, splintered bones in the Valley of the Shadow she must cross in her bare feet as her body swells again and again life and death share her belly. Finally Martha. Four then. The seasons passing. The children real then. As real as his weight on her body. John French pressing her down into the starched sheets, her body a leaf between the pages of a book. Sometimes, straightening the bed, when she pulls back the homemade quilt she sees her form etched in the whiteness. She touches her edges, her hollows, smooths the wrinkles, pats the indentations, laying her hands where his have been, finding herself as she leans over the sprawled figure his bulk has pressed into the sheets.

Because she knows one day she will roll back the patchwork, velvet-edged, storytelling quilt and there will be nothing. Because her body's outline not deepened by his weight is only a pale shadow, a presence no more substantial than what might be left by a chill wind passing over the sheet.

Freeda watches the snow beat noiselessly against the window. Watches it disappear like the traces of her body when she pounds the white sheet. The faces of the women gather around her again, but they are older now, wrinkle old, gray old, like her own face last time she saw it in the oval mirror of the oak dresser at the foot of their bed. She calls it *their* bed even though she knows the faces, crowded and stomped down as the sooty hills on which Homewood is dying, have come to tell her John French is gone. If you are just a child and marry a man, one day you will grow up and the man will be gone. He can't wait and you can't hurry. Even though trying hard to hurry and to wait are the best part of your love, what makes your love better than what passes for love around you. One day he'll be gone and that will be that. Twice your age when he stole you. Twice your age when he sat with his elbows on his knees and his shoulders hunkered and his eyes downcast, sprawled all arms and legs on the stool in your Aunt Aida's front room while you said to her in the back room where she and Uncle Bill slept, I'm married now and she said, Yes you are now. I can tell just looking at you. John French married you good. Married you real good, didn't he? Saying the words so they hurt so you felt brazen like the ungrateful wench and hussy she didn't say you were. Not calling any names. Not fussing but saying the words so *married* was a door slammed, so *married* was the ashes of all those years Aunt Aida and Uncle Bill had sacrificed to raise her. John French is quiet as she's ever seen him in her life till Aunt Aida leaves her in the dark little bedroom and whispers something to her man Bill and Uncle Bill goes to the closet and gets not the shotgun he had loaded and set inside there but his jug of whiskey and two glasses and pours and hands one to John French.

Yes, she wants to scream. Of course he's dead. What else is he supposed to be with me lying up here an old woman. He was too big to move wedged between the seat of the toilet and the edge of the bathtub. She had heard him fall all the way from the kitchen and flew up the steps two and three at a time getting to him. Ain't no room to put my knees, he'd grumble. Shame when a man can't even squat right in his own house. She crashed open the door with both hands. She had heard him groan once while she rushed up the steps but he lay still now and her heart leaping in her chest was the only sound in the bathroom. But when she clambered on her knees under the sink so she could touch him and raise his face from the pool of vomit spreading on the linoleum she could hear the pipes gurgle and the leaky guts of the toilet hissing. She did as much as she could before she ran to the door and screamed into Cassina Way for help.

It was Fred Clark who came first. Who helped her drag John French from between the toilet and the tub that was always bumping his knees. He must have died while she was at the door because he was dead weight when they lifted him and dead when they laid him across *their* bed.

Someone always comes . . . Homewood people are good about coming. And they're best about coming around when there's nothing they can do. When someone's dead and the faces hovering around you are like flowers cut for a funeral. Fred Clark came and then Vernetta sent that useless pigeontoed man of hers and they got John French laid across *their* bed. And Vernetta Jones down at the bottom of the steps moaning, *Have mercy, Have mercy.* Moaning it like you know she's gon moan it everytime she tells the story she can't wait to tell about John French dying in the bathroom and *I heard Freeda screaming for help and sent Ronald over there and I was so shocked you know how much I done prayed for John French to do right I was so shocked I couldn't even get up the steps I just stood at the bottom praying God have mercy, God have mercy cause I knowed he was dead.*

Freeda counts the faces. There are three. But then there are three more and three more and more threes than she can count above her. Then there is one face hiding behind the others. A face the others cannot see because they stare down at her, stare with their eyes full of tears and their mouths full of prayers so they never see the yellow face grinning behind them, the man who is the only man in the room, the Chinaman with his shriveled yellow walnut of a face. He laughs at her, he is the only one who knows she knows John French is long dead.

The curled edge of the clawfoot tub and the bottom of the sink are cold as she crawls to him. Her feet sneak away and run naked into the snow. Once she had dreamed it would happen this way. A cold, white dream which made her shiver long after she awakened. In the dream the Chinaman sat on a fence. He flashed teeth like gold daggers and laughed and laughed at his ownself trying to make a dollar out of fifteen cents. Chinky, chinky, Chinaman and she was laughing too but then he started to melt, started to run down out of the funny pajama-looking suit he was wearing. Then his face blew up like a watermelon. The skin got fatter and fatter so it swoll up and closed his eyes and closed his mouth and all the rest of him just yellow water running down the fence. And she knew she shouldn't be laughing. Knew that he wasn't laughing at himself but at what was going to happen to her when he finished melting and all the insides of him exploded through that big moon face. She began to shiver when she realized the face was filled with something cold. Like snow only it would be the color of the stuff leaking down out of his pant legs, that pee color and oily like that stuff only cold, colder than anything she had ever touched, cold so the icy pieces of jelly when they flew against her body would turn her to stone.

THREE MONTHS HAD PASSED since my grandmother's death. I had flown to Pittsburgh alone to her funeral. When I returned home I hadn't said much about her. The weather in Pittsburgh had been cold and damp. On the day of the funeral it rained. There wasn't much to say about all of that, about the gray streets and somber gray hills crowded with ramshackle houses and the gray people shrouded in raingear or huddling under umbrellas. I couldn't talk about that because it was too depressing, and I couldn't talk about the storytelling and whiskey all night after we buried my grandmother either. You had to be part of the whole thing to understand why we could laugh and get high while Aunt May, tucked back into an overstuffed chair so her stockinged feet barely touched the rug, told us the stories of Homewood. Our laughter wouldn't seem appropriate unless you had been there through everything and heard how she was saying what she was saying. So I didn't talk much when I got home. I let the trip slowly seep inside me. Sipped it without really tasting it the way I sipped Jim Beam that night May told stories.

Our family had begun its annual migration East. Five hundred miles the first day and another three hundred next day before a flat. There had been a sickening swerve and I hit the brake too hard and lost control but luckily just for an instant and then the Custom Cruiser let me guide it onto the shoulder of the highway. As I began the process of changing the tire, which meant first unpacking a summer's worth of luggage to get at the spare in the back of the station wagon and finding one piece of the jack missing, and cursing the American way of leaving little things out, the sky over my shoulder had divided itself neatly into a layer of dense gray and one of luminous, spooky whiteness. The dark half above squeezing light out of the sky; all the energy in the band of white squirming and heating up as it is compressed into a smaller and smaller space. Then drum rolls of thunder and jagged seams of light splitting the darkness.

We were in Iowa. One of those featureless stretches of Interstate 80 which are a way of getting nowhere fast. Judy yelled at me to get inside the car. She has a morbid fear of lightning so I feel it's my duty to cure her, to treat thunderstorms with disdain and nonchalance and survive. So I take my good time stuffing in the last few boxes and suitcases I had unloaded. The highway would buckle each time a semi passed. I winced every time, stepping backward, swaying in the blast of hot air as the trucks exploded just a few feet away. That sudden caving in of the earth scared me more than the threat of thunderbolts delivered from the sky.

The first rain drops were as big as eggs. Not falling but flung in handfuls so they struck inside the station wagon spattering the bags before I could get the tailgate shut. Behind the wheel again I dried my hands, face and the back of my neck. I felt like I had been running a long time, running fast and strong and the exhilaration of my body had made me slightly breathless, a little giddy.

"Why are you so foolish? Why did you stay out there till the last minute?"

"You wouldn't believe me if I told you."

"It's not funny. Look at the boys. You've managed to terrify them acting like a fool." In the faces of the children strapped in their carseats behind us I could see the echo of their mother's fear, an immense silence welling behind their eyes.

But it was good in a way. The steady drumming on the roof, the windows steamed shut, the windblown sheets of rain suddenly splashing against the metal skin. All hell breaking loose outside, but we were inside, cocooned, safe, together. I liked the isolation, the sudden detour. "Hey, you guys. It's like being in a space ship. Let's pretend we're on our way to Mars. Prepare for blast-off."

And there was the business of assigning roles, the squabbles over rank, the exact determination of a noise level for our rocket motors which would not encourage the migraine Judy felt coming on.

But we were launched successfully from that Iowa plain. Though we were knee deep in water, some of our controls smoking and sputtering, our ark rose, shuddering in the girdle of rain but quickly through it, gathering speed and thrusting pure and swift wherever . . .

So I could relinquish the controls and shut off the intercom and plead the weariness of six days exploring a virgin planet, battling the Dictosaurs, the Todals, the men whose heads grow beneath their shoulders. The ship was safe in other hands so I could shut my eyes and listen to the rockets purr calmly through the Intergalactic night.

That's when I saw her. When my grandmother, Freeda, came to me. She is wearing a thin, gray cardigan, buttonless, perhaps another color once, mauve perhaps as I look more closely or perhaps the purplish blue of the housedress beneath the worn threads gives the wool its suggestion of color. The sleeves of the sweater are pushed back from her wrists. One long hand rests in her lap. The skin on the back of her hand seems dry and loose. If she tried to lift anything heavier than the hand to which it was attached, her fragile wrist protruding from the cuffed and frayed sweater sleeve would snap. She sits in her wooden rocker in front of the fireplace which has been covered over with simulated-brick Contact paper. Just over her head is the mantelpiece crowded with all of our pictures. The television set is muttering a few feet away. Bursts of laughter and applause. Dull flickers of light as the image twitches and rolls. She reaches inside the front of her dress and fumbles with a safety pin which secures the handkerchief cached there against her underclothes. Lilies hidden beneath her dress. Lilies spreading in her lap as she unties the knotted corners of the flowered handkerchief. In the center of the handkerchief a few coins and two or three bills folded into neat squares, one of which she opens as slowly as she had opened the silk. When she learned to talk again after her second stroke, she could only manage a minimal movement of her lips. Her head moves from side to side with the effort of producing the strange, nasal, tonal language of rhythms and grunts. If you listened closely, you could detect the risings and fallings of familiar sentence patterns. The words blurred and elided but you could get the message if you listened.

Take it. Take it. Take it, Spanky. I am leaving home. The first one in the family to go off to college. She thrusts the money in my hand. *Take it. Go on, boy.* A five-dollar bill as wrinkled and criss-crossed as the skin at the corners of her eyes.

Over the wind and rain and rockets and the cars driven by madmen still careening past on the invisible highway I hear her offering the money . . . the strange, haunted whine I would write if I could.

Three months after her death and finally it was time. I needed to talk about her. The storm deserted us. We limped to a gas station and they fixed the flat and promised they'd have a whole jack for us next morning. We decided to stop for the night just down the road a ways in the place the mechanic had recommended, a Holiday Inn overlooking the Mississippi River. After the kids were asleep I began to talk about my grandmother. I wished for May's voice and the voices of my people in a circle amening and laughing and filling in what I didn't know or couldn't remember, but it was just me whispering in the dark motel room, afraid to wake my sons.

For sixteen years they took care of her. My Aunt Geraldine and Uncle Carl, the only son. The other girls, my mother and her sister Martha, had married. Within a week after her husband's death Freeda had a stroke, almost dying, and though her body recovered, her will did not. Wanting only to follow her dead husband everybody said. To be with John French they all said. Yet she was still their mother. And they still lived under her roof, so for sixteen years Geraldine and Carl nursed the shell she had become. The last year of her life she spent mainly in the hospital. She had stopped moving and seldom talked. Her blood thickened so there was always the threat of pneumonia or a clot that needed watching. Endless shots and medicines which might achieve three or four lucid hours a week. During her last month at home before the final confinement in Allegheny Hospital she became deeply agitated. Like a light bulb which glows unnaturally bright just before it pops, she seemed to improve. Her eyes were animated again, she struggled to speak and be listened to. My Aunt Geraldine and Uncle Carl were excited. Talked of miraculous remissions, reprieves, God changing his mind in the eleventh hour. Even though it was terror filling her eyes, even though her gestures and nasal keening described a phantom who had begun to prey on her.

Carl understood the word first, the sound Freeda had begun to repeat constantly. For weeks it had remained a mystery, part of her improved condition, part of her terror. Then, with the certainty of something known all along, Carl matched a word to the sound. A word not discovered but remembered. He couldn't believe the word had escaped him so long once he matched it to the sound she had been shaping. *Chinaman.* When he repeated it back to her the first time aloud, her chin dropped to her chest. A gagging sound came from her throat. As if the word summoned a Chinaman, diabolical and menacing beside the rocker. *Chinaman. Chinky, chinky Chinaman, sitting on a fence. Trying to make a dollar out of fifteen cents.* Hiding in corners. Hovering over her bed at night. Pulling her clothes awry. Raking his nails across her face and hands, inflicting the red wounds she showed them in the morning.

Of course he followed her to the hospital. Every member of the family knew him. The Chinaman's vigil as faithful as the shifts of relatives who tended my grandmother as she lay dying. She slept most of the time. Drugged. Too fatigued to lift her eyelids. I began disbelieving in her. I was glad I was far away and didn't have to trek to the hospital. But the others were faithful. They did the bathing, the touching, the holding on till nothing else remained. It was to them she complained of the Chinaman. But against the background of her slow, painful dying, the Chinaman became for the family a figure of fun. Mama's Chinaman. They talked about him like a dog. Transformed him into an aged suitor courting her with flowers, candy and teenage awkwardness. Made fun of him. Told stories about his appearances and disappearances, his clothes, his hiding places, how he whistled at the nurses and pinched their behinds. The Chinaman became a sort of Kilroy for the family. His signature turning up in unexpected places. His name implicated in any odd or obscene occurrence in the hospital.

One day they moved an Oriental man into a room down from my grandmother's ward. The people in my family became acquainted with his people, sharing cigarettes and gossip in the visitors' lounge. Since both patients slept most of the day, the social gatherings in the lounge offered an opportunity to exchange commiserations, but also a chance to return to the world of health and well-being without totally deserting the realm of the sick . . .

But the story was stiff, incomplete. I said I'd tell the rest when Judy felt better. She fell asleep quickly but I heard paddle-wheeled steamers packed with cotton and slaves ply the river all night long.

Two more days on the road. Then we are in my mother's kitchen. The house is quiet. Relatives and friends in and out all day as always during our summer visits. It's good to see everybody but the days are long and hot and busy so it's also good when the last person leaves. My mother, Lizabeth, and my wife and I are in the kitchen. It's after twelve and the house is quiet. *Five things,* my mother says. *Five things in my life I'll never forget.* One was Faun asking forgiveness in the ambulance. She doesn't tell us what the other three are, but she does tell us about the Chinaman.

"Carl and I were sitting with Mama at the hospital. It must have been around six because I heard them collecting the dinner trays. She had had a bad day. I still don't know how she lasted as long as she did. Her arms weren't any bigger around than this . . . there just wasn't anything left . . . how she held on I'll never know. She had been coughing all day and they were always worried about it getting in her lungs. Anyway we were kinda down and just sitting listening to the awful rattling in her sleep when he walked in leaning on the arm of his daughter. She was a nice girl. We always talked in the lounge. She was steady about coming to see her father. You could tell she was really worried about him and really cared. A pretty girl, too. Well, she only brought him as far as the door. I guess she heard Mama sleeping and how quiet we were so she just waved from there and sort of whispered her father was going home in the morning and good luck. And the old Chinaman peeked around into the room. I guess he was curious about Mama so he poked his head in and looked at her and then they were gone. That's all. Stopped to say good-bye just like we would have said good-bye to them if we could have taken Mama home out of that place.

"Mama never woke up again. She died early the next morning and when I walked down the hall with the nurse I looked in that Chinese man's room and it was empty.

"That's just the way it happened. I was there, I know. He peeked in and Mama never woke up again. I can't tell you how many times I've asked myself how she knew. Because Mama did know. She knew that Chinaman was coming for her. That he'd tip in her door one day and take her away. Things like that happen in people's lives. I know they do. Things you just can't explain. Things that stay with you. Not to the day I die will I understand how Mama knew, but I do know things like that don't just happen. Five times in my life I've been a witness and I don't understand but I'm sure there's a plan, some kind of plan."

I am sleepy but the story gets to me the way it did the first time I heard it. My mother has told it, finished it like I never can. And the shape of the story is the shape of my mother's voice. In the quiet house her voice sounds more and more like May's. My mother doesn't wave her arms like May or rise and preacher-strut like May when May gets the spirit. My mother's hands drum the table edge, or slowly the fingertips of one hand stroke and pull and knead those of the other. For her the story of the Chinaman is a glimpse of her God who has a plan and who moves in mysterious ways. For me the mystery of the Chinaman is silence, the silence of death and the past and lives other than mine.

I watch my mother's pale fingers shuttle in and out of one another. I watch my wife slip into her own quietness, distant and private. The silence is an amen.

the watermelon story

The first time he saw somebody get their arm chopped off was in front of the A&P on Homewood Avenue. They used to pile watermelons outside at the alley corner of the store. A big plate glass window where they stuck Sale signs and Specials This Week signs and propped church posters and advertisements for this and that on the bottom inside ledge was at that end of the store too. A window starting almost on the sidewalk and running up twice as tall as a man so they needed long ladders to wash it when they used to try and keep things clean in Homewood. Watermelons would be there piled three and four high, the green ones shiny, the striped ones cool as if the sunshine couldn't ever melt those pale veins of ice shooting through their rinds. Mostly the winos would stay over in the trees, below the tracks in the Bums' Forest during the heat of the day but sometimes you'd get one straying off, too high or too dry to care, and then he'd wander up where people doing their shopping, wander through there stumbling or singing or trying to get his hands on somebody's change till he got tired of people looking through him and at him and church ladies snorting and kids laughing like the circus was in town or staring like he was some kind of creature from Planet X and then he'd just settle hisself in a piece

343

of shade where the settling looked good and nobody'd mind him no more than they would a cat or dog sleeping under the porch. But the one he saw with his arm hanging by bloody threads, dangling so loose the man in the white apron had to hold the weight of it so it wouldn't just roll on down between the watermelons, that wino had decided for some reason to sit on the stack of melons in front of the A&P.

Must have nudged one of the front ones, the bottom ones holding the stack together and when they all started to rolling like big fat marbles under him he must have leaned back to catch hisself and they pitched him through that plate glass window. Like trying to walk on marbles. Must have been like that. His legs going out from under him all the sudden and him full of Dago Red and dozing in that July sun so he was probably dreaming something and the dream got snoring good to him and Homewood Avenue a thousand miles away. Like having the rug jerked out from under your feet and you know you're falling, know you're going to hit the ground so you throw your arm back to catch yourself and ain't the ground you catch but a whole A&P windowful of glass slicing down on your shoulder.

Must have been easy at first. I mean your fist punches through real quick and busts a clean hole and your arm just passes right on through too. Ain't bleeding, ain't even scratched, it's through that tunnel real easy and quick and nothing hurts, you don't even know you're in trouble, specially with all that sweet wine and sun and you're just waiting for the goddamn watermelons to stop acting a fool so your feet and your behind can find the pavement but then that glass comes down like a freight train, snaps shut like a gator's jaws and you know, you know without looking, without feeling the pain yet either, you know it got you and that screaming behind your ear is not falling, crashing glass anymore, it's you waking up and saying hello and saying good-bye to your arm.

Must have been like that even though he didn't see it happen and he wasn't the man. He dreamed it like that many years later and the dream was his, the throne of watermelons belonged to him, green and striped and holding the heat of the sun. And when it topples and topples him with it into the bath of cool glass, the shattering glass is there ringing like a cymbal in his ear even after he opens his eyes. He dreamed it that way and often without warning when he was walking down the street his shoulder muscle would twitch, would tremble and jerk away from the ax in its dream. Like his arm was living on borrowed time and knew it. The shock of seeing a severed arm in the white aproned lap of the man who had run from inside the store meant that arms didn't have to stay where they were born. Nothing had to stay the way it was. He had wondered if all that blood soaking the apron was wino blood or if the bald white man kneeling beside the hurt wino had brought pig blood and cow blood and blood from lambs and wall-eyed fish from inside the store. Was the man surrounded by the green sea of melons a butcher, a butcher who was used to bloody parts and blood spattered clothes, a butcher cradling the wino's arm so the last few threads won't break. Is he whispering to the wino, trying to help him stay still and calm or is the wino dreaming again, moaning a song to the lost arm in his dream.

The A&P is gone now. They scrubbed the blood from the pavement and stopped stacking watermelons on the sidewalk. One of the grown-ups told him later the wino's life had been saved by a tourniquet. Somebody in the crowd had enough sense to say Forget about that thing. Forget about trying to stick that arm back on and had ripped the apron into strips and made a tourniquet and tied it around the stump to stop the bleeding. That saved him. And he had wanted to ask, Did anybody save the arm, but that sounded like a silly question, even a smart-alecky question, even when he said it to himself so instead he imagined how the only black man who worked in the A&P, Mr. Norris who always sat two rows down toward the front of Homewood A.M.E. Zion Church, pushed his iron bucket that was on wheels through the wide double doors of the A&P. The melons had skittered and rolled everywhere. People trying to get closer to the blood had kicked holes in some, some had plopped over the curb and lay split in the gutter of Homewood Avenue. A few of the biggest melons had walked away when folks crowded around. But it wasn't Mr. Norris's job to count them and it wasn't, he told the produce manager, his job to scrabble around Homewood Avenue picking watermelons, wasn't no part of his job, Mr. Norris told him again as he hummed Farther Along and slopped soapy water on the dark splotches of blood. Mr. Norris had made a neat, rectangular fence of watermelons in front of the broken window to keep fools away. Nobody but a fool would get close to those long teeth of glass, jag-edged teeth hanging by a thread, teeth subject to come chomping down if you breathe on them too hard. Mr. Norris had kept his distance and gingerly swept most of the glass into a corner of his watermelon yard. Then the bucket and mop. When the pavement dried he'd sprinkle some sawdust like they have behind the fish counter. There were smears of blood and smears of watermelon and he'd dust them all. He slooshed the heavy mop up and back, up and back, digging at the worst places with soapy water.

Rather than ask a question nobody would answer and nobody would like, he imagined Mr. Norris taking his own good time cleaning the mess off the sidewalk. Though ninety-nine percent of the shoppers were black, Mr. Norris was the only black man working for the A&P, and that made him special, made him somebody people watched. Mr. Norris had rules. Everybody knew what they were and understood his slowness, his peculiar ways were part of his rules. Watching his hands or his face or the poses he struck, you'd think he was leading an orchestra. The way he carried himself had nothing to do with wiping shelves or scrubbing floors or carting out garbage unless you understood the rules and if you understood the rules, and understood they came from him, then everything he did made sense and watching him you'd learn more than you would from asking dumb questions and getting no answers.

They wouldn't have left the arm for Mr. Norris to broom up. They'd know better so of course they'd take it with them, wherever they took the wino, wherever they took the tourniquet, the stump, the bloody strips of apron.

Don't try to stick it back on. Leave that damn thing be and stop the bleeding.

He hadn't been there when the one man with good sense had shouted out those words. He didn't see how you wrapped a stump, how you put on a handle so you could turn off the blood like you turn off a faucet. Turn and quit. He thought that's what she said at first. Those words made sense at first till she explained a little bit more and told him not "turn and quit," it's *tourniquet,* like you learn in first aid or learn in the army or learn wherever they teach one another such things. Then she said, Uggh. I couldn't do it. I couldn't get down there with my hands in all that mess. They'd have to carry me away if I got too close to it. Me, I wouldn't be no more good. But thank God somebody with good sense was there, somebody with a strong stomach to do what have to be did.

As he listened he heard May saying the words and remembered it was her then. May who told the story of the accident and then told him later, No, he didn't die. He lost that arm but he's still living, he's still back up in the Bum's Forest drinking just as much wine with one arm as he did with two.

And May's story of the lost arm reminded her of another story about watermelons. About once there was a very old man Isaac married to an old woman Rebecca. Was in slavery days. Way, way back. Don't nobody care nothing about those times. Don't nobody remember them but old fools like me cause I was there when Grandpa told it and I ain't never been able to forget much, least much of what I wanted to forget. Well I was there and he told me how it was way back then. There was this Isaac and Rebecca and they was old when it started. Old before those olden days way back, way, way back. It was Africa you see. Or Georgy or someplace back there it don't make no difference no way. Niggers be niggers anyplace they be. If you get my meaning. But this old man and old woman they be living together ninety-nine years and they's tired and they ain't got child the first to hold they old heads, they's childless you see. Old lady dry as a dry well and always was and looks like she's fixin to stay the very same till Judgment Day. So they was some old, sad people. Had some good times together, everybody got good times once in a while, and they was good to each other, better to each other than most people be these days. He'd still pat them nappy knots up under her head rag. She'd rub that shoulder of his been sore for fifty years when he come in from the fields at night. They was good to each other. Better than most. They did what they could. But you ain't never too young nor too old be hurt. And a hurt lived with them all the days of their lives, lived every day from can to caint in that itty bitty cabin in the woods. They loved God and wasn't scared of dying. Naw, they wasn't feared of that like some sinners I know. And they wasn't ungrateful niggers neither. And I could name you some them, but I ain't preaching this morning.

I'm telling youall a story bout two old people didn't never have no babies and that's what hurt them, that's what put that sadness on they hearts.

Youall heard bout Faith? Said I wasn't preaching this morning but youall heard that word, ain't you? Ain't asking if you understand the word. I'ma give you the understanding to go with it. Just tell me if you heard the word. That's Faith! Faith what I'm talking bout. And if you don't know what I'm talking bout just you listen. Just you think on them old, old people in that itty bitty shack in the woods, them people getting too old to grunt. Them people down in Egypt with the Pharaohs and bitter bread and burdens all the days of they lives. Well, they had Faith. Youall heard bout the mustard seed? That's another story, that's another day. But think on it. Old as they was they ain't never stopped praying and hoping one day a child be born unto them. Yes they did, now. This old Isaac and old Rebecca kept the faith. Asked the Lord for a child to crown they days together and kept the Faith in they hearts one day He would.

Well old Isaac had a master grow watermelons on his farm. And old Isaac he have the best knuckle for miles around for thumping them melons and telling you when they just perfect for the table. He thump and Melon, Mr. Melon, he talk back. Tell his whole life story to that crusty knuckle, Uncle Isaac knock at the door. Yoo-hoo, How you do? Melon say, You a day early, man. Ain't ready yet, Isaac. Got twenty-four hours to go. You traipse on down the patch and find somebody else today. Come back tomorrow I be just right, Brother Isaac.

That was in Africa. Way, way back like I said. Where people talk to animals just like I'm sitting here talking to youall. Don't you go smiling neither. Don't you go signifying and sucking your teeth and raisin your eyebrows and talking bout something you don't know. This old lady got sense just good as any you. Like they say. You got to *Go there to Know there.* And ain't I been sitting on Grandpa's knee hearing him tell bout slavery days and niggers talking to trees and stones and niggers flying like birds. And he was there. He knows. So in a manner of speaking I was there too. He took me back. Heard old Isaac. Rap, rap, rapping. Out there all by hisself in that melon patch and Ole Massa say, Fetch me a good, big one. Got company coming, Isaac. My sister and her no good husband, Isaac, so fetch one the biggest, juiciest. Wouldn't give him the satisfaction of saying he ever got less than the best at my table. So old bent Isaac he down there thumpin and listenin and runnin his fingers long the rind. It's low mo hot too. Even for them old time Georgy niggers it's hot. Isaac so old and dry and tough he don't sweat much anymore but that day down in the patch, water runnin off his hide like it's rainin. He hear Rebecca up in the kitchen. Isaac, Isaac, don't you stay away too long. And he singing back. Got sweaty leg, Got sweaty eye, But this here nigger too old to die. And he picks one with his eye. A long, lean one. Kinda like these people going round here you call em loaf-of-bread head. Long like that. He go over and squat down in the vines and thump it once good with that talking knuckle of his.

Now don't you know that melon crack clean open. Split right dead down the middle just like somebody cleave it with a cane knife. And don't you know there's a baby boy inside. A little chubby-legged, dimple-kneed, brown-eyed boy stuck up in there perfect as two peas in a pod. Yes it was now. A living breathing baby boy hid up in there smiling back at Isaac, grabbing that crusty knuckle and holding on like it was a titty.

Well, old Isaac he sing him a new song now. He's cradling that baby boy and running through the field and singing so fine all the critters got out his way. Rattlesnakes and bears and gators. Nothing was going to mess with Old Isaac on that day. They heard his song and seen the spirit in his eyes, and everything moved on out the way.

And here come old Rebecca, skirts flying, apron flapping in the breeze. Took off fifty years in them twenty-five steps tween the back of that itty bitty cabin and her man's arms. Then they both holding the baby. Both holding and neither one got a hand on him. He just floating in the air between them two old, happy people. Thank the lord. Thank Jesus. Praise his name. They got so happy you coulda built a church right over top them. One of them big, fancy white folks' churches like youall go to nowadays and they so happy they'd of rocked it all by theyselves. Rocked that church and filled it with the spirit for days, just them two old happy people and that baby they loved so much didn't even have to hold it. He just floated on a pillow of air while they praised God.

That's just the way it happened. Isaac found that baby boy in a watermelon and him and Rebecca had that child they been praying for every day. It was Faith that bring them that child. Faith and God's will. Now He couldn't do nothing nice like that these days. Youall niggers ain't ready. Youall don't believe in nothing. Old man bring home a baby first thing you do is call the police or start wagging your tongues and looking for some young girl under the bed. Youall don't believe nothing. But the spirit works in mysterious ways his wonders to perform. Yes He does now. In them old slavery Africa times there was more miracles in a day than youall gon see in a lifetime. Youall jumping up and down and ooing and ahhing cause white men is on the moon and you got shirts you don't have to iron. Shucks. Some them things Grandpa saw daily scare the spit out you. And that's just everyday things. Talking to flowers and rocks and having them answer back. Youall don't believe in none that. Youall too smarty panted and grown for that. But old Isaac and Rebecca waited. They kept the faith and that fine son come to light they last days in this Valley of the Shadows.

Now I could say that's all, I could end it right here. Say Bread is bread and wine is wine, If anybody asks, this story's mine. End it happy like that, with a rhyme like the old folks ended their stories. But there's more. There's the rest goes with it so I'ma tell it all.

He heard the rest, and it was how the spirit took back the boy. The rest was the weeping and wailing of old Isaac and Rebecca. The rest was the broken-hearted despair, the yawning emptiness of their lives, a hole in their lives even bigger than the wound they had suffered before the child came. He listened. He'd never heard such a cruel story before. He was scared. He was a boy. For all he knew they had found him in a watermelon. For all he knew he might be snatched back tomorrow. Would the grown-ups cry for him, would they take to their beds like old Isaac and Rebecca and wait for death.

May looked round the room catching nobody's eye but everybody's ear as she finished the rest of her story.

Where was all that praying? Where was all that hallelujah and praise the Lord in that little bitty cabin deep in the woods? I'll tell you where. It was used up. That's where it was. Used up so when trouble came, when night fell wasn't even a match in the house. Nary a pot nor a window. Just two crinkly old people on a shuck mattress shivering under they quilt.

He wanted to forget the rest so he asked if the wino could grow another arm.

May smiled and said God already give him more'n he could use. Arms in his ears, on his toes, arms all over. He just got to figure out how to use what's left.

the songs of
reba love jackson

The First Song Is for Mama

The first song I'm going to sing is for my mama. My first song always been dedicated to Mama and always will be long as I'm drawing breath. Been wearing the white rose in memory of Mama twenty-five years now. Some of you know what I'm talking about. Some of you wore mourning white the first time last Mother's Day Sunday and some been pinning red to they breast gon be pinning white next time round so my first number always been for Mama and always will be long as God give me strength to raise my voice in His praise. Cause that's what Gospel is. Singing praise to God's name. So I'ma sing a praise song and dedicate it to the one loved me best on this earth. The one I loved best and still do. What a Friend. Yes, Lawd. What a Friend We Have.

One for Brother Harris in Cleveland

When the phone rang so much talking and one another thing going on didn't nobody stop to answer it you know how you be busy and everybody think the other person gon get it but it just keep ringing and might be ringing still if there ain't been a napkin close to me that don't look used so I wiped the grease off my fingers and my mouth and picked up the phone.

Hello, hello, I said this the residence of Miss Reba Love Jackson saying the whole name I don't know why but I said it all into the phone and didn't get no answer except for some buzzing at the other end.

Hello, hello again and again I say this Miss Reba Love Jackson's residence.

Then this voice sorta scratchy and faraway sounding like it do when it's long distance. I could tell something wrong. Hear it plain as day in the voice. Poor man talking like he can hardly keep from crying and what I'm supposed to say? Nobody but me still ain't paid no tention to the phone. What with folks eating and talking and somebody at the piano striking off chords, nobody but me still ain't bothered bout no phone, so I'm standing there by myself and poor man must of thought I was Reba Love cause he say his name and commence to telling me his trouble and I felt so bad standing there I didn't want to cut the poor man off and I didn't want to hear what ain't my business to hear but what you going to do?

Finally I had to say wait a minute hold on a minute Sir and I laid down the receiver and got Reba Love to come. I stood beside her while she listened. Seems like I could understand better. Watching how Reba Love listened. How the face of that saint got sad-eyed while she shook her head from side to side. I'm hearing the man and understanding him better than when I was holding the phone my own self. Reba Love nodding like she do when she sings sometimes but she don't say a word.

Then she sighs and talks in the phone, "Yes yes yes. Surely I can do that little thing for you. *I Stood on the Bank of Jordan.* Yes, yes."

And she put her hand over the phone and ask me tell everybody be quiet please. And after some shushing and having to go around and bodily shut some people up, Reba Love's apartment quiet as church on Monday. She still have her hand over the mouthpiece and say, "This is my old friend Brother Harris from Cleveland and he just lost his mama and he needs for me to sing."

And didn't one more chicken wing crack or ice cube bump round in nobody's Coca-Cola. She raised the receiver like it was a microphone and child I ain't never heard no singing like it. Not Mahalia, not Bessie Griffin, not Sallie Martin. None of them, and I done heard them all, not one coulda touched Reba Love Jackson that evening.

She did it alone at first. The first verse all by herself and the chorus too, just her solo. Then the second verse and she stopped and looked around and whispered into the phone, "I got some good folks here with me and they gon help me sing," whispered it and didn't lose a note, made it all seem like part of what she was singing and believe me when it was time for the rest of us to join in we were *there,* Sister, yes we were now, we were *there,* and Hattie Simpson sat her big self down at the piano too and you better believe Cleveland ain't never heard nothing like it.

For Blind Willie Who Taught Me to Sing

The blind man lay drunk and funky, his feet stretched out on the sidewalk so you had to be careful not to trip over them. Precious Pearl Jackson almost shouted, Look child, look and see the kind of man your daddy is, because she knew somewhere in some city her daughter's no good father would be sleeping off a drunk, probably outdoors like this tramp now that it was summer, snoring like him and like him barefaced and past shame. She didn't say a word but clutched her daughter's hand tighter, tugging her over and past the blind man's filthy lap-tongued brogans.

"Mama, you hurting me."

"You ain't been hurt yet, girl. Just come on here and don't be lagging."

Precious Jackson dreams of different streets. Streets lined with gold and glittering jewels. Streets pure as drifted snow where she can promenade clothed in a milk-white garment whose hem touches the pavements but receives no corruption there. If she had the strength, she would run from her door to the door of the church. People could think she was crazy if they wanted to, but if God granted her the power she would run as fast as the wind down Decatour and across

Idlewild and over Frankstown and up the final long block of Homewood, sprinting so her long feet barely touch the ground, clutching her girl to her breast, not breathing till they were safe inside The Sanctified Kingdom of Christ's Holiness Temple. If she could, she would run every step. And it would be like flying. They would not taste of this evil city the Devil had tricked her to, not one swallow of the tainted air. She wondered how it would feel to fly closer to the sun. To have it burn the tacky clothes from her back, and then the skin gone too, all the flesh dropping away like old clothes till the soul rises naked to the Father's side.

Precious Jackson looks down at the gray pavement. She is tall and black and rail thin. Her cropped hair is plastered to her skull by a black net cap. Her round, pop eyes are full and hungry; they burn like the eyes of the saints who never sleep. A sudden breeze drives litter along the high curb and swirls newspapers against the steel gates barricading the shopfronts. Cardboard cartons overflowing with garbage line the curb. Broken glass sparkles in the sunlight. Somebody's crusty, green sock inches down the sidewalk. She knows the blind man. He was a blues singer. Sang the Devil's music in the bars here along the strip. One Saturday night they found him in the Temple. On his knees, they said. Praying in tongues, they said. She remembered him at the mourners' bench. Hunched over on his knees like a man taking a beating. When he arose she expected to see torn and bloody clothing, stripes from the whip. And when he testified it was like reading a book she had sworn to God she would never open. The blind man told it all. She thought the Temple's whitewashed walls would smoke before he finished. So many toils and snares. Listening to the blind man confess his sins, she realized how good her God had been to her. How merciful the straight, hard path He had led her to. Then that mouth of the Devil raised his voice in praise of the Lord. The saints amened his testimony. There was shouting and falling out. The saints offered the hand of Fellowship. The blind man swore by God's grace never to sing blues. Promised to use his voice only to praise God's goodness.

Now he was back in the street again, singing nastiness again. That was him stretched out on the pavement, drunk as sin. She hoped God would snatch his voice as He had snatched his eyes.

The Temple would be visible when they turned the next corner. With its red door as a beacon her eyes would not stray to the fallen city. Precious Pearl envied the people who went to tall churches, churches whose spires could be seen from afar. To be meek and humble, to ask no more than God saw fit to give, to praise affliction because it was a sign of His glorious will, all of this she understood and lived. But she would have liked to worship Him in a cathedral with a mighty organ, and a roof halfway to heaven.

"Come on, gal. Why you lagging this morning?"

Precious Jackson's long feet in flat-heeled shoes slapped the sidewalk. Her daughter was a pitty-pat, pitty-pat keeping up.

"Do you love Jesus?"

"Yes, Mama."

"Do you love Him better than yourself?"

"Yes, Mama."

The words breathless as mother and daughter rushed through the empty, Sunday morning streets. One Sunday in the Temple the blind man sang *Nearer My God to Thee.* Precious Jackson had wept. She had put her arm around her child's stiff, thin shoulders and wept till the song was over.

The sky was a seamless vault of blue. Would it be a sin to paint the ceiling of her church that color. The door, like the door of The Sanctified Kingdom of Christ's Holiness Temple, would be the red of his martyred blood.

A train hooted down by the tracks. Hooted again and Precious Jackson could hear the rattling cars jerked behind it, the sound putting her teeth on edge, then fading, getting soft and white as lamb's wool just before it disappeared. She stopped suddenly and her daughter bumped into her legs. Precious Pearl Jackson felt herself nearly topple. She smacked down where she knew the girl's head would be, her hard head plaited over with cornrows no thicker than scars. Perhaps the world was over. Perhaps everybody was gone. Only the blind blues singer, the girl, and herself, Precious Pearl Jackson, forgotten, left behind. God sweeping the city clean and taking the saints to His bosom in shining silver trains. Perhaps what she had heard was the last load of the blessed taking off for the sun in a beautiful metal bird.

For Old Time Preachin

In those days you could hear real preachin. Not the prancin and fancy robes and sashayin and jump around like wanta be Retha Franklin, James Brown or some other kinda rock and roll superstar with lec- tronics and guitars and pianos and horns and ain't never saying a mumblin word what touch the soul. Real preachin is what I'm talkin about. The man what been there hisself and when he shout for a witness, witness be fallin from they seats and runnin down the aisle. Those old time preachers could tear up a meetin. Tear it up, you hear. And you talk about talkin. Mmmm. They could do that. Yes indeed. *E*pistemology and *Cos*mology and *On*tology and *Deu*teronomy. They was scholars and men and knew the words. Used to be meetins, what you call revivals today, over in Legion Field where the white boys played baseball. Peoples drive they trucks and wagons up here full of chairs just so they can sit in the outfield cause the bleachers packed every day to hear them preachers. Real preachin. What you call testimony. Cause the old timers they knew the world. They knew the world and they knew the Word and that's why it was real.

I could name you some. I can see them now just as plain as day. Now I ain't sayin they didn't use showmanship. Had to do that. Had to draw the people in fore they could whip a message on em, so they had their ways, yes indeed, a sho nuff show sometimes. But that be just to get people's tention. You know what I mean. They had this way of drawin people but there was more to em than that. Once those brothers got hold to you they twist and toss and wrestle you like you seen them little hard-jawed dogs get hold to a rat. And you come out feelin like you sure enough took some beatin, like somebody whipped all the black off you and turned you inside out and ain't nothin ever goin to be the same.

There was one. Prophet Thompson from Talledega. They had this kinda stage set up at one end the ballpark. Well, you could see the preachers and the singers comin and goin. Takin their turns. Now Prophet Thompson he ain't about to walk up to the platform. Noth- ing easy like that for him. When his turn come he rides up on this big, gray, country mule. Yes, he did. And you ought to hear the shoutin. Prophet ain't said a word yet and they carryin people out the stands.

You woulda thought they screamin for the Prophet but all us from the country know those brothers and sisters done got happy behind that lap-eared mule. Mmmp. And the Prophet he knows how to sit a mule. And how to get off one and tie him down so he stays. You woulda believed the place on fire and people burnin up if you heard the tumult and the shoutin from far off. The air be bucklin and them wooden seats rattlin where they stomp they feet and people up off those foldin chairs in the outfield, standin up beatin them funeral parlor chairs like they was tambourines. And the Prophet ain't said nary a word. Just rode in on a mule.

Shoot. That man coulda just rode on out again and left everybody happy. But they was preachers. Real preachers. He knew what to do. That country mule ain't nothin but a trick to get folks' tention. Yes. They knows mules and knows country and the Prophet he just let them have they fun with all that. But when he's on the platform, he knows what to say.

"He brought me up here all the way from the red clay of Talledega, Alabama. So I knows he could get me this little distance to the altar."

And he had to just stand there while the people jump up and down and they clothes fallin like it be raining clothes. Stand there till he ready to say some more, then it's like thunder through the microphone and if he had said *Ground open up and let the spirits of the dead shout too,* nobody been surprised to hear voices comin out that green grass. What he said was, "Some of you all know what I'm talkin about. Some of you know who brought me out of the wilderness and onto this stage in the middle of a darkling plain. Yes, Lord. Some of you know the God I speak of, but some of you still thinkin bout old Martin, my mule, and he's good, he's good and faithful, but he ain't nothin but a mule."

You see how he got em. Got em hooked. They don't know whether to run away or stand still. Whether he's talkin to em or about em. Then he commence to preach.

Real preachin. And Prophet Thompson not the onliest one. I could name a many. Seen women throw down mink coats for a preacher to walk on. Seen the aisles lined with furs. First man I ever saw play piano with his feets, it was right here. Back when they used to meet in Legion Field. Preachin and singin like nobody these days knows how to do. I remember seein Reba Love Jackson and her mama, Precious Pearl Jackson, right here every year till her Mama took her away up North. I remember Reba Love in a little baby gown sittin barebottomed in the grass while all that singin goin on, her and the rest of them barebottomed babies and now I see some of them around here gettin bare on top they heads. They say Reba Love's comin back next spring. Won't that be somethin? Won't it though? I heard her Mama dead now. They say Precious Pearl left the Devil down here and died a fine, Christian woman. I knew her well. Let me tell you what I think. Reba Love Jackson be lookin for her Mama when she come back. And you know somethin, God willin she will find her cause this her home. This where it all began. Yes she will. Find her right here and when she does she's gon sing. Sing it. And by The Grace of the Lord I'll live long enough for to see it. To hear that old time singin one more time before I die.

For Somebody Else

Through the windows of the bus Reba Love tries to imagine what it would feel like to be another person. She had heard one of the singers say just a few minutes before, *New Jersey,* and the name of somebody's hometown in the state, so it is night and they are crossing New Jersey and she knows they will stay in a hotel in Newark because the manager knows somebody there who will let them crowd four or five in a room and pay a special rate. She knows many of the gospel groups stay there. She has heard the hotel's name lots of times on the circuit. But nothing out the window is helping her to be someone else. Everything she thinks of, all of the words or voices coming to her will speak only to Reba Love Jackson, speak to her and who she is or will not speak at all. She tries to picture a person she doesn't know. One of the men she can't help seeing when she sings. A man at a concert or in a church who she has never laid eyes on before and probably will not again. The kind of man she is drawn to in spite of herself. A brown man with soft eyes. A man with meat on his bones. Who could laugh with her and grin at the big meals she loves to cook. But this stranger, this unknown, easy man who is not too beautiful, not too young, who does not seem to belong to some hawk-eyed, jealous body else, this stranger who is not really a stranger because she has seen him every-where and knows she'll see him again, cannot draw her out of herself. This man she has never met, or only met long enough to hear his name before her mother steers him away and returns with some wrinkled, monkey-faced deacon, can not move her from who she is.

She is a Bride of Christ. Sanctified in His service. But there is no mystery here either. What once seemed immense beyond words is as commonplace as cooking and cleaning for a flesh and blood man. Moments of passion surely, surely come, but they are pinpricks of light in the vast darkness which has settled upon her, distant stars which dazzle but do not warm the night sky.

She is not a Bride of Christ. Not since the summer she was thirteen and her mother took her south to visit their People. Seven years away from them and she had just about forgotten her country cousins. Half the people down there seemed to have her last name. Even Tommy Jackson. Little, light-skinned, fast talking T.J. She can't hear him running anymore through the weeds but she can hear T.J.'s holler and the greetings of the others as they bay like bloodhounds over where the picnic cloth is spread under the trees. She is picking up her drawers from the ground. Funny how she was more shamed of her drawers than her bare butt and came out of them so fast she almost scared T.J. away. Once he got his hand up in there she just wanted her underwear gone no matter if she was going to let him do it to her or not. Didn't really seem so important after all. If he did or not. Even after a million warnings and a million threats that this, that or the other thing will happen sure as night follows day or damnation sin, the same old silly stories even after her mother ought to know she knows better. The country girls tell the stories to each other and laugh at them together and mock their mothers telling them. She could never laugh at her mother. Or hurt her any other way. Her mother was a place to stand, a place to lean. Her mama had patched the old underwear so it covered her backside decently. The patches were a secret, a secret between mother and daughter. And though she could open her legs to T.J., she could not share such secrets.

The grass prickly on her skin when she sat down to pull on her drawers. Sitting because she needed to sit. So the pain and the sweet, warm wetness could run out of her body slowly, on her time, according to her mood instead of the way T.J. had rushed it in. Like he was being chased. Sitting with the Sunday dress still like a wreath around her narrow hips. Suddenly she worried about the wrinkles. Would they fall out? Then she thought about the other girls. Sitting on blankets all day. And the careless ones on grass or even dirt and how all the Sunday dresses will need to be scrubbed and scrubbed. She puts her hand there. The springy hair, the wet and sticky. Her hand. Her fingers like his fingers but his didn't learn anything, didn't stay in one place long enough to let her answer them. Like his fingers only hers are dark like the darkness down there. Her skin night skin like the skin over the windows of the bus. Forever, you could be a thing forever. Or once, one time could change it forever.

She couldn't say no. Couldn't say why she had not said no. So she lied once to her mother and perhaps to God and wore the saints' white dress, the Bridal Dress sanctified and holy in His name.

These things she could not speak of. Like she could not speak of the dead man they found that same day stuck in the roots along the riverbank. The dead man who had been lynched, the grown-ups whispered. When they got him up on shore they sent the children away. Away to play. And she couldn't say no. Couldn't speak about some things. She could only sing them. Put her stories in the songs she had heard all her life so the songs became her stories.

Is there ever any other way she asked herself? Am I to be Reba Love Jackson all the days of my life? Her thoughts are lost in the rumble of the bus. Lights wink and blink and climb the night sky. She is racing across New Jersey in a Greyhound. Could her mother follow the swiftness of her flight? Would her mother be watching all night? Did saints need to sleep? Want to sleep?

She would always be Reba Love Jackson. Till He touched her and brought her on home.

For All Her Fans in Radio Land

. . . . . . just for voice level could you please say your full name

Reba Love Jackson

that's fine, just fine. Now lemme do a little lead-in: It is my privilege this morning to be talking to Miss Reba Love Jackson, a great lady who many call the Queen Mother of Gospel. She is here in our studio on behalf of Watson Productions who right now at the Uptown Theatre, Sixtieth and Market, are presenting Miss Reba Love Jackson along with a host of other stars in the spectacular once-a-year Super Gospel Caravan. Yes indeed. The Gospel train is stopping here for three days starting this evening at 7:00 P.M. It's the really big one youall been waiting for so get down to the Uptown and pick up on what these soul-stirring folks is all about . . . that's enough . . . I can fill in later . . . Gotta get some other promo stuff in . . . hmmph . . . but now a Miss a Jackson . . . why don't we start at the beginning . . . Could you tell our audience Miss Reba Love Jackson, Gospel Queen, where you were born

outside Atlanta Georgia in a little place called Bucolia. Wasn't much to it then and ain't much to it now. Little country town where everybody one big family and God the head of the house

I know what you mean. We all know what she means don't we soul brothers and sisters? Yes siree. Down home country. We knows all about it, don't we? Fried chicken and biscuits and grits and the preacher coming over on Sunday wolfing down half the platter . . . Lawd . . . Lawd . . . Lawd . . . but you go on Miss Reba Love Jackson. Tell it like it was.

we didn't have much. But there was only my mama and me and we got along. Mama Precious was a saint. Didn't nobody work harder than my mama worked. Only heard stories about my father. He died when I was a baby. Worked on the railroad my mama said and got killed in an accident. Didn't nobody in Bucolia have much. We children left school about the age of ten, eleven, and worked in the field with the grown-ups. Mighty little childhood then. Folks just didn't have the time they do nowadays to play and get education. What I learned I learned from Sunday school and from my mama. But that's the learning stays with you. Cause it's God's truth. Some educated folks . . .

yes. Yes. Educated fools. We all know some like that. But

let's go on Miss Reba Love Jackson . . . unlike so many entertainers especially your fellow gospel singers, you've been known for a militant stance in the area of civil rights. Could you tell our audience a little about your involvement in the Movement.

I never did understand no movement, nor no politics, nor nothing like that. People just use my name and put me in that stuff. It's the songs I sing. If you listen those songs tell stories. They got words. And I've always believed in those words. That's why I sing them. And won't sing nothing else. God gave me a little strength and I ain't going to squander it on no Devil's work. We's all God's creatures and it ain't in the Bible to sit in the back of no buses or bow down to any man what ain't nothing but breath and britches. White or black ain't meant to rule God's children. He's the only Master.

right on. Right on, Sister.

Trouble is people don't listen to Gospel music. They pat they feet awhile then they go back on out in them mean streets. They Sunday Christians, so somebody can see them say, Look at Miss Jones in her new hat and new coat. Ain't she something. Go to church to be seen, don't go to hear the Word. That's what keeps the world the crying shame it is. There's a song says, This old world can't last much longer, Reeling and rocking so early in the morning. Another one says, They'll be Peace in the Valley someday. Sure enough, it's gonna come. But it's God trumpet say when. Ain't gon be them white folks telling nobody nothing. Not with their Atom bombs and Hydrogen bombs and naked women and selling people dope and liquor and blowing up little girls in church and dogs and hoses they keep just to hurt people with and every one of them from the President on down full of lies. No. We got to stop bleeding for white people and start leading ourselves in the path of righteousness. He gave His only begotten Son to show the way.

well you sure do tell it like it is . . . now could you say a little about how you got into show business . . . I mean how you rose up to become a household word to millions of your fans.

wasn't more'n five or six years ago outside of Memphis and we still going around in a raggedy old station wagon. Seven of us singers and no little people in the group. I remember cause Claretta, bless her soul, was sick and we have to stop every half hour or so and that road was hot and dusty and we had three hundred miles to go before we stop for good and had to sing when we got there and Claretta getting worse cause the car had to keep moving. These two cracker state patrols stop us and everybody out they say. And all us womens standing on that highway in the hot sun and these crackers laughing behind they dark glasses and talking about body searches. And talking nastier and nastier. Only thing save us Claretta she ain't said nothing she too scared like the rest of us to say a thing to these nasty patrol but I see her getting all pale like she did when we have to stop the car. Poor child can't hold it no longer and when she start to going right there standing up beside the road and moaning cause she's so ashamed, well that broke it all up and . . .

yes, mam. I'm sure there are plenty of stories you could tell about the hardships of living in the South

wasn't only South. You find some of your meanest crackers right here walking the streets of Philadelphia and New York. I been coming this way many a year and let me tell you

our audience shares your indignation. We know the crosses you had to bear but I bet folks would like to hear how you rose from your humble beginnings to be a star

God didn't gift me with no fine voice. But he did lay burdens on me and gave me strength to bear them. When I sing people know this. They hear their stories in my songs, that's all

you're too modest. Miss Reba Love Jackson is an inspiring Christian lady. But they don't call her the Queen of Gospel for nothing. You've got to hear her to believe her. Get on down to the Uptown. Better be there bright and early for a good seat

I ain't never had the voice of no Mahalia or Willie Mae Ford or none of them . . . but I listened to the best . . . I was raised on the best holy singing ever was. I remember them all coming to Bucolia . . . Kings of Harmony, Selah Jubilee Singers, the Heavenly Gospel Singers from Spartanburg, South Carolina, the Golden Gates, The Hummingbirds and Nightingales and the Mighty Mighty Clouds of Joy . . . and me sitting with my mama listening and thinking if I ever get to Heaven some day please, please, Jesus, let it be like this. Me at my mama's side and angels shaking the roots of the firmament with their voices. The old time people could sing and preach so good it was like they put their hands inside you and just rooted around till they found where you needed to be touched . . . they . . .

I'm sorry to cut you off but our time is running out and our audience wants to hear a little more about what to expect when they catch you at the Uptown . . . I have a piece in my hand written about one of your performances all the way across the pond in Gay Paree. Listen up, youall: "Reba Love Jackson galvanizes the audience . . . No lady on the stage but a roaring black pantheress, leaping, bounding, dancing her songs . . . she embodies what is primitive and powerful in the African soul."

that must be pretty old. Ain't been to Paris, France but once and that was long ago. They tell me I used to get pretty lively when I sang. Kicking up my heels and what not. To tell the truth I never thought much about it. I just sang the old songs and let them take me where they wanted to go. Now I been out here singing a long, long time. Can't hardly remember a time I ain't been out here singing and I'm getting like the fish when the water gets cold. They stop jitterbugging around and sink down to the bottom and lie real still and they be there on the bottom muck alright but you got to go down deep with something special to get them to move.

we'll go on believing what the French soul brother said about you Miss Reba Love Jackson. Our audience can judge for themselves . . . get a taste of that good old time religion when the Super Gospel Caravan pulls into the Uptown tonight. This is one fan who knows he won't be disappointed. I got a feeling Reba Love Jackson, Queen Mother of Gospel, you'll make these clippings seem tame . . . cut.

One for Her Birthday

It is June 19, her birthday, and she is sixty-five years old and celebrating by going to the ocean beach for the first time in her life. Atlantic City is like nothing she's ever seen. She is almost giddy in her new slacks suit (her mother never wore pants, not even to work in the fields) sitting it seems a mile above the Boardwalk in a cart driven by a black boy. The intermittently overcast day does not dissipate her spirits. Sheets of fine mist blown up from the water refresh when they daintily sprinkle her face. She had worried at first about her voice. The coarse salt air lodging in her throat and the horror of a cold when she faces the crowd in Convention Hall. But she felt fine. Her voice was a brawny animal still secure at the end of its leash. When she tugged it would be there, and she would turn it loose to do its work at the proper time. She tasted the salt on her tongue. The snapping flags, the striped umbrellas, the bright clothes of the passersby, the giant Ferris wheel blazing with light even in the middle of the afternoon, the calliope disembodied within the roar of the surf, everything she could see, smell, hear, and touch celebrated her birthday.

When the cart arrived at a section of beach littered with dark bodies, she commanded the boy to stop. She hadn't noticed colored bathers elsewhere on the white sand. The boy called back ". . . this Chickenbone Beach, mam," and she understood immediately. This was the place she'd been looking for all along even though she hadn't known it until that moment.

"Wait here please, young man." She was paying him by the hour so she knew he would. She was pleased by his obedience, by the extravagance of it all: a suite in the hotel, a taxi to the boardwalk, a new suit just because she wanted it. People knew her name. Strangers would come up to her on the street and say, You Reba Love, ain't you? Pleased to meet you Miss Reba Love. Leaning against the tubular railing which divided the boardwalk from the beach she rubbed her shoes then the nylon Peds from her feet, exposing wrinkled toes and battered, yellowing toenails. Bad feet. Looked like her mother's long toes splayed down there in the hot sand. Her orange bell-bottoms flap in the stiff breeze. As she marches toward the ocean the soles of her feet squeak with each step. The sand whispers, swishing like the sumptuous robes they wear on stage. Black bodies and ivory bodies and every shade between, halfnaked on the sand.

She thinks of her voice again when the first swirl of icy ocean water laps her toes. Backing away quickly she gasps and hikes up the razor creases of her slacks. Behind her the thumping of bongos and conga drums. In front the restless beard of her Father, a million shades of gray and frothy white. The ocean is too large, too restless. All the dead are out there. Rich and poor, black and white, saints and sinners. And plenty room for the living. Room for those bodies stretched like logs drying in the sun. The wind is furrowing the stiff bristles of her Father's beard, tangling them, caking them with dried spittle and foam as He roars His anger, His loneliness. Depths out there the living will never fill. In the thunder of the surf she can hear newborn babies crying.

The motion of the sea becalms the spinning earth. The breakers unraveling from the horizon freeze to a green shimmer. She wishes she could see His eyes. Eyes which never close and never open. His eyes wherever they are. She wants to see what He sees looking down on her bare head.

A gull shrieks. Then cold shackles draw tighter around her ankles. Holes are opening up in the earth, slowly, subtly, drawing her down. She knows if she does not muster her strength and flee, screaming horses will drag her with them under the waves.

One More Time for Blind Willie

Hate to talk about your mommy she's a good ole soul
She got a buck skin belly and a rubber asshole

Oh Shine, Shine, save poor me
I'll give you more white pussy than you ever did see

Blues verses and toasts and nasty rhymes keep the blind man awake with their spinning and signifying. Voices and voices within voices and half the laughter with him and half at him. The bouncer pitched Blind Willie down the steep, narrow stairs of the speakeasy. Old Willie tumbles out of control. "Told you not to come begging around here bothering the customers." Pitching down so many steps Willie can hear the parts of his body cracking as he falls helpless. So many knife-edged steps Blind Willie has time to fear the horrible impact at the bottom, how his body will be curled into the shape of an egg when he reaches the bottom and the last collision will crack him and scatter him.

> *Stagolee begged Billy,*
> *"Oh please don't take my life.*
> *I got three hungry children*
> *And a very sickly wife."*

First he had believed he was in hell when he awoke to all the moaning and groaning around him. A smell of chemicals in the air. Little teasing voices tormenting him. Then he knew he was still alive because he wasn't burning. He was cold, freezing cold. Colder than he'd ever been. He wished for newspapers to stuff under his clothes. He dreamed of the overcoat he lost in a coon-can game down by the railroad tracks. Heard himself singing about cold hearts and cold women. He was too cold to be dead. He was someplace where white people were talking and laughing.

White hands were peeling away his skin. White eyes lay on him like a blanket of snow. White feet stomped on his chest.

Shine, Shine . . .

The bouncer and the fall were black. Black hands had pushed him down the endless steps. But the crash, the dying into a thousand pieces are white.

Lord . . . Help me . . . Help me to hold out

If he could sing now it would be a saint's song. He is on his knees in the Amen Corner of the Temple. He is slamming his fists against the door which even in the darkness throbs red and hot as blood. He smells perfume. Hears a woman's hips, black hips swishing, rubbing against something trying to hold them in. He remembers undressing Carrie May. Pulling down her girdle. The texture of her goosebumpy skin and the rubbery panels. Then how silky she was, how soft with nothing on.

Nearer . . .

The perfume is a cloud over his head. He is swooning, he is trying to catch his breath, and hold his heart in his chest, and will his belly back down where it belongs so his lungs can fill with air. He is trying to remember the words to a song that gal, Reba Love Jackson sings. She is humming it to help him remember. She is smiling and saying *Come on ... Come on in ...* to his sweet tenor. They will sing together. One more time.

This Last Song's for Homewood

Whenever I cross these United States of America it does my heart good to stop here and see youall again. Some of you know I got roots here. Deep roots go way back. Lived here in Pittsburgh for a time. Mama worked for some white folks on Winebiddle Street. We lived in Homewood. Many a day I sat waiting for that trolley to bring my mama home. Stopped at Penn and Douglas Avenue and Mama had to walk five blocks to get home. And some of you knows how long five blocks can be after you been scuffling all day in the white people's kitchen. Yes Lawd. Doing all day for them then you got to ride a trolley and foot slog it five blocks and start to cooking and cleaning all over again for your own. It's a long mile. My mama walked it. Yes she did. We all been walking that long mile many a day. You know what I'm talking about. Yes you do, now. Reba Love Jackson ain't always been standing on stage singing praises to the Lawd. I sang His praises down on my knees, youall. *This is my story. This is my song.* Yes. *Praising my Savior. All the day long.* Sang with a scrub brush in my hand. Sometimes I think I ain't never sung no better than I did all by myself on my knees doing daywork in the white folks' kitchen. But I know something about Homewood. In the summertime I'd walk to meet Mama. I'd take her shopping bag and her hand and walk home beside her. I remember every step. Every tree and crack in the pavement from the trolley stop to our little rooms behind Mr. Macks's Grocery. Wasn't a happier little girl in the world than me when I was walking Mama home. Could tell you plenty about Homewood in those days but youall come to hear singing not talking and that's what I'm going to do now. Sing this last one for Homewood . . .

across the
wide missouri

The images are confused now. By time, by necessity. One is Clark
Gable brushing his teeth with Scotch, smiling in the mirror because
he knows he's doing something cute, grinning because he knows fifty
million fans are watching him and also a beautiful lady in whose
bathroom and bedroom the plot has him awakening is watching over
his shoulder. He is loud and brisk and perfectly at ease cleaning his
teeth before such an audience. Like he's been doing that number all
his life. And when he turns to face the woman, to greet her, the
squeaky clean teeth are part of the smile she devours. This image, the
grinning, self-assured man at the sink, the slightly shocked, absolutely
charmed woman whose few stray hairs betray the passion of her night
with him, a night which was both endless and brief as the time
between one camera shot fading and another bursting on the screen,
may have been in *Gone With the Wind,* but then again just as likely
not. I've forgotten. The image is confused, not clear in itself, nor
clearly related to other images, other Rhett Butlers and Scarlett O'-
Haras and movies flashing on and off with brief flurries of theme song.

It is spring here in the mountains. The spring which never really
arrives at this altitude. Just threatens. Just squats for a day or a few

hours then disappears and makes you suicidal. The teasing, ultimately withheld spring that is a special season here and should have its own name. Like Shit. Or Disaster. Or something of that order. The weather however has nothing to do with the images. Not the wind or the weather or anything I can understand forces this handsome man grinning at a mirror into my consciousness. Nor do geography or climate account for the inevitable succession—the river, the coins, the song, the sadness, the recollection—of other images toppling him and toppling me because it happens no matter where I am, no matter what the season. In the recollection there is a kind of unmasking. The white man at the mirror is my father. Then I know why I am so sad, why the song makes me cry, why the coins sit where they do, where the river leads.

I am meeting my father. I have written the story before. He is a waiter in the dining room on the twelfth floor of Kaufman's Department Store. Not the cafeteria. Be sure you don't get lost in there. He's in the nicer place where you get served at a table. The dining room. A red carpet. Ask for him up there if you get lost. Or ask for Oscar. Mr. Parker. You know Oscar. He's the headwaiter up there. Oscar who later fell on hard times or rather hard times fell on him so hard he can't work anywhere anymore. *Wasn't sickness or nothing else. Just that whiskey. That's whiskey you see in that corner can't even lift his head up off the table.* Ask for your daddy, Mr. Lawson, or ask for Mr. Parker when you get to the twelfth floor. I have written it before because I hear my mother now, like a person in a book or a story instructing me. I wrote it that way but it didn't happen that way because she went with me to Kaufman's. As far as the twelfth floor anyway but she had to pay an overdue gas bill at the gas company office and ride the trolley back to Homewood and she had to see Dr. Barnhart and wanted to be home when I got there. The whole idea of meeting my father for lunch and a movie was hers and part of her idea was just the two of us, Daddy and me, alone. So my mother pointed to the large, red-carpeted room and I remember wanting to kiss her, to wait with her at the elevators after she pushed the button and the green arrow pointed down. If I had written it that way the first time I would be kissing her again and smelling her perfume and hearing the bells and steel pulleys of the elevators and staring again apprehensively through the back of my head at the cavernous room full of white people and the black men in white coats moving silently as ghosts but none of them my father.

The entrance way to the restaurant must have been wide. The way overpriced restaurants are with the cash register off to one side and aisles made by the sides of high-backed booths. Wide but cordoned by a rope, a gold-braided, perhaps tasseled rope, stretched between brass, waist-high poles whose round, fluted bases could slide easily anywhere along the red carpet. A large white woman in a silky, floral patterned dress is standing like she always does beside the pole, and the gold rope swallows its own tail when she loops both ends into a hook at the top of one of the poles.

I must have said then to myself *I am meeting my father.* Said that to myself and to the woman's eyes which seemed both not to see me and to stare so deeply inside me I cringed in shame. In my shyness and nervousness and downright fear I must have talked a lot to myself. Outside the judge's chambers in the marble halls of the courthouse, years later waiting to plead for my brother, I felt the same intimidation, the same need to remind myself that I had a right to be where I was. That the messages coded into the walls and doors and ceilings and floors, into the substances of which they were made, could be confronted, that I could talk and breathe in the storm of words flung at me by the invisible architects who had disciplined the space in which I found myself.

Daddy. Daddy. I am outside his door in the morning. His snores fill the tiny room. More a storage closet than room, separated from the rest of the house so the furnace doesn't heat it. The bed is small but it touches three walls. His *door* is actually a curtain hanging from a string. We live on the second floor so I am out in the hall, on a landing above the icy stairwell calling to him. *Your father worked late last night. Youall better be quiet this morning so he can get some sleep,* but I am there, on the cold linoleum listening to him snore, smelling his sleep, the man smell I wonder now if I've inherited so it trails me, and stamps my things mine when my kids are messing around where they shouldn't be. I am talking to myself when he stirs in that darkness behind the curtain. He groans and the mattress groans under him and the green metal cot squeaks as he shifts to another place in his dreaming.

I say to myself, *Where is he?* I stare at all the black faces. They won't stay still. Bobbing and bowing into the white faces or gliding toward the far swinging doors, the closely cropped heads poised and impenetrable above mandarin collars. Toomer called the white faces petals of dusk and I think now of the waiters insinuating themselves like birds into clusters of petals, dipping silently, silently depositing pollen or whatever makes flowers grow and white people be nice to black people. And tips bloom. I am seeing it in slow motion now, the courtship, the petals, the starched white coats elegant as sails plying the red sea. In my story it is noise and a blur of images. Dark faces never still long enough to be my father.

"Hey, Eddie, look who's here."

There is a white cloth on the table that nearly hangs to the floor. My knees are lost beneath it, it's heavy as a blanket, but Oscar has another white cloth draped over his arm and unfurls it so it pops like a flag or a shoeshine rag and spreads it on top of the other so the table is covered twice. When Oscar sat me down, two cups and saucers were on the table. He went to get my father and told me he'd be right back and fix me up and wasn't I getting big and looked just like my daddy. He had scraped a few crumbs from the edge of the table into his hand and grinned across the miles of white cloth at me and the cups and saucers. While he was gone I had nudged the saucer to see if it was as heavy as it looked. Under the edge closest to me were three dimes. Two shiny ones and one yellow as a bad tooth. I pushed some more and found other coins, two fat quarters neither new nor worn. So there I was at that huge table and all that money in front of me but too scared to touch it so I slid the ten-pound cup and saucer back over the coins and tried to figure out what to do. Knew I better not touch the table cloth. Knew I couldn't help spotting it or smudging it if my hand actually touched the whiteness. So I tried to shove the money with the base of the saucer, work it over to the end of the table so it'd drop in my hand, but I couldn't see what I was doing and the cup rattled and I could just see that little bit of coffee in the bottom come jumping up out the cup and me worried that whoever had forgotten the quarters and dimes would remember and surely come back for them then what would I say would I lie and they'd know a little nigger at a big snow white table like this had to be lying, what else I'm gonna do but lie and everybody in the place know the thief had to be me and I was thinking and worrying and wondering what my father would do if all those people came after me and by that time I just went on and snatched that money and catch me if you can.

"Look who's here, Eddie." And under my breath I said shut up Mr. Oscar Parker, keep quiet man you must want everybody in here listening to those coins rattling in my pocket. Rattling loud as a rattlesnake and about to bite my leg through my new pants. Go on about your business, man. Look who ain't here. Ain't nobody here so why don't you go on away.

Then my father picked up the saucers and balled up the old top cloth in one hand, his long fingers gobbling it and tucking it under his arm. Oscar popped the new one like a shoeshine rag and spread it down over the table. Laid it down quiet and soft as new snow.

"Busboy'll git you a place setting. Eddie, you want one?"

"No. I'll just sit with him."

"Sure looks like his daddy."

"Guess he ought to."

"Guess he better."

I don't remember what I ate. I don't recall anything my father said to me. When I wrote this before there was dialogue. A lot of conversation broken by stage directions and the intrusions of restaurant business and restaurant noise. Father and son an island in the midst of a red-carpeted chaos of white people and black waiters and the city lurking in the wings to swallow them both when they take the elevator to the ground floor and pass through Kaufman's green glass revolving doors. But it didn't happen that way. We did talk. As much as we ever did. Both of us awkward and constrained as we still are when we try to talk. I forget all the words. Words were unimportant because what counted was his presence, talking or silent didn't matter. Point was he was with me and would stay with me the whole afternoon. One thing he must have asked me about was the movies. I believe I knew what was playing at every theater downtown and knew the address of every one and could have reeled off for him the names of the stars and what the ads said about each one. The images are not clear but I still can see the way the movie page was laid out. I had it all memorized but when he asked me I didn't recite what I knew, didn't even state a preference because I didn't care. Going with him was what mattered. Going together, wherever, was enough. So I waited for him at the table. Wondering what I had eaten, running my tongue around in my mouth to see if I could get a clue. Because the food had been served and I had wolfed it down but he was all I tasted. His presence my feast.

He came back without the white coat. He brought a newspaper with him and read to himself a minute then read me bits and pieces of what I knew was there. Him reading changed it all. He knew things I had never even guessed at when I read the movie page the night before. Why one show was jive, why another would be a waste of money, how long it would take to walk to some, how others were too far away. I wanted to tell him it didn't matter, that one was just as good as another, but I didn't open my mouth till I heard in his voice the one he wanted to see.

He is six foot tall. His skin is deep brown with Indian red in it. My mother has a strip of pictures taken in a five and dime, taken probably by the machine that was still in Murphy's 5 & 10 when Murphy's was still on Homewood Avenue when I was little. Or maybe in one of the booths at Kennywood Amusement Park which are still there. They are teenagers in the picture, grinning at the automatic camera they've fed a quarter. Mom looks pale, washed out, all the color stolen from her face by the popping flashbulbs. His face in the black and white snapshots is darker than it really is. Black as Sambo if you want to get him mad you can say that. Black as Little Black Sambo. Four black-as-coal spots on the strip. But if you look closely you see how handsome he was then. Smiling his way through four successive poses. Each time a little closer to my mother's face, tilting her way and probably busy with his hands off camera because by picture three that solemn grandmother look is breaking up and by the final shot she too is grinning. You see his big, heavy-lidded, long-lashed, theatrical eyes. You see the teeth flashing in his wide mouth and the consciousness, lacking all self-consciousness and vanity, of how good he looks. Black, or rather purple now that the photos have faded, but if you get past the lie of the color he is clearly one of those *brown-eyed, handsome men* people like Chuck Berry sing about and other people lynch.

"Here's a good one. Meant to look at the paper before now, but we been real busy. Wanted to be sure there was a good one but it's alright, got a Western at the Stanley and it's just down a couple blocks past Gimbels. Clark Gable's in it. *Across the Wide Missouri.*"

The song goes something like this: *A white man loved an Indian Maiden* and la de da-/-la de da. And: *A-way, you've gone away . . . Across the wide Mis-sour-i.* Or at least those words are in it, I think. I think I don't know the words on purpose. For the same reason I don't have it on a record. Maybe fifteen or twenty times in the thirty years since I saw the movie I've heard the song or pieces of the song again. Each time I want to cry. Or do cry silently to myself. A flood of tears the iron color of the wide Missouri I remember from the movie. *A-way, we're gone a-way . . . Across the wide Missouri.* It's enough to have it in pieces. It's enough to have heard it once and then never again all the way through but just in fragments. Like a spring which never comes. But you see a few flowers burst open. And a black cloud move down a grassy slope. A robin. Long, fine legs in a pair of shorts. The sun hot on your face if you lie down out of the wind. The fits and starts and rhythms and phrases from the spring-not-coming which is the source of all springs that do come.

The last time I heard the song my son called it *Shenandoah.* Maybe that's what it should be called. Again I don't know. It's something a very strong instinct has told me to leave alone. To take what comes but don't try to make anything more out of it than is there. In the fragments. The bits and pieces. The coincidences like hearing my son hum the song and asking him about it and finding out his class learned it in school and will sing it on Song Night when the second grade of Slade School performs for their parents. He knew the words of a few verses and I asked him to sing them. He seemed pleased that I asked and chirped away in a slightly cracked, slightly breathless, sweet, second grade boy's voice.

Now I realize I missed the concert. Had a choice between Song Night and entertaining a visiting poet who had won a Pulitzer Prize. I chose—without even remembering *Across the Wide Missouri*—the night of too many drinks at dinner and too much wine and too much fretting within skins of words and too much, too much until the bar closed and identities had been defrocked and we were all clichés, as cliché as the syrupy Shenandoah, stumbling through the swinging doors out into Laramie's cold and wind.

I will ask my son to sing it again. I hope he remembers the words. Perhaps I'll cheat and learn a verse myself so I can say the lyrics rather than mumble along with the tune when it comes into my head. Perhaps I'll find a way to talk to my father. About things like his presence. Like taking me to the movies once, alone, just the two of us in a downtown theater and seeing him for the whole ninety minutes doing good and being brave and handsome and thundering like a god across the screen. Or brushing his teeth loudly in the morning at the sink. Because I understand a little better now why it happened so seldom. (Once?) It couldn't have been only once in all those years. The once is symbolic. It's an image. It's a blurring of reality the way certain shots in a film blur or distort in order to focus. I understand better now the river, the coins, the song, the sadness, the recollection. I have sons now. I've been with them often to the movies. Because the nature of my work is different from my father's. I am freer. I have more time and money. He must have been doing some things right or I wouldn't have made it. Couldn't have. He laughed when I told him years later about "finding" money on the table. I had been a waiter by then. In Atlantic City during summer vacations from school at the Morton Hotel on the Boardwalk. I knew about tips. About some people's manners and propriety. Why some people treat their money like feces and have a compulsion to conceal it, hide it in all sorts of strange places. Like under the edge of saucers. Like they're ashamed or like they get off playing hide and seek. Or maybe just have picked up a habit from their fathers. Anyway he laughed when I told him and said Oscar probably damned a couple of poor little old white ladies to hell for not leaving him a tip. Laughed and said, *They're probably burning in hell behind you "finding" that money.*

I understand a little more now. Not much. I have sons of my own and my father has grandsons and is still a handsome man. But I don't see him often. And sometimes the grandson who has his name as a middle name, the one who can say *Shenandoah* if he wants to call it that, doesn't even remember who his grandfather is. *Oh yeah,* he'll say. *Edgar in Pittsburgh,* he'll say. *Your father. Yeah. I remember now.*

But he forgets lots of things. He's the kind of kid who forgets lots of things but who remembers everything. He has the gift of feeling. Things don't touch him, they imprint. You can see it sometimes. And it hurts. He already knows he will suffer for whatever he knows. Maybe that's why he forgets so much.

▪ rashad

Rashad's home again. Nigger's clean and lean and driving a mean machine. They say he's dealing now, dealing big in the Big D, Deetroit. Rashad's into something, sure nuff. The cat's pushing a Regal and got silver threads to match. Yea, he's home again. Clean as he wants to be. That suit ain't off nobody's rack. One of a kind. New as a baby's behind. Driving a customized Regal with RASHAD on the plate.

It was time for it to go, all of it. Nail and banner both. Time she said as she eased out the nail on which it hung. Past time she thought as she wiggled the nail and plaster trickled behind the banner, spattering the wall, sprinkling the bare floorboards in back of the chair where the rug didn't reach. Like cheese, she thought. All these old walls like rotten cheese. That's why she kept everybody's pictures on the mantelpiece. Crowded as it was now with photos of children and grandchildren and nephews and nieces and the brown oval-framed portraits of people already old when she was just a child, crowded as it was there was no place else to put the pictures of the people she loved because the rotten plaster wouldn't take a nail.

The banner was dry and crinkly. Like a veil as she rolled it in her hands, the black veils on the little black hats her mother had worn to church. The women of Homewood A.M.E. Zion used to keep their heads covered in church. Some like her Grandmother Gert and Aunt Aida even hid their faces behind crinkly, black veils. She rolled the banner tighter. Its backside was dusty, an arc of mildew like whitish ash stained the dark cylinder she gripped in both hands. How long had the banner been hanging in the corner. How long had she been in this house on Finance street? How long had the Homewood streets been filling with snow in the winter and leaves in fall and the cries of her children playing in the sunshine? How long since she'd driven in the nail and slipped the gold-tasseled cord over it so the banner hung straight? No way to make the banner stand up on the mantelpiece with the photos so she'd pounded a nail into the wall behind the overstuffed chair cursing as she had heard the insides of the rotten wall crumbling, praying with each blow of the hammer the nail would catch something solid and hold. Because embroidered in the black silk banner was the likeness of her granddaughter Keesha, her daughter's first baby, and the snapshot from which the likeness on the banner had been made, the only photo anybody had of the baby, was six thousand miles away in her daddy's wallet.

Rashad had taken the picture with him to Vietnam. She had given it up grudgingly. Just before he left, Rashad had come to her wanting to make peace. He looked better than he had in months. I'm clean, Mom. I'm OK now, he'd said. He called her mom and sometimes she liked it and sometimes it made her blood boil. Just because he'd married her daughter, just because there'd been nobody when he was growing up he could call mom, just because he thought he was cute and thought she was such a melon head he could get on her good side by sweet talking and batting his droopy eyelashes and calling her mom, just because of all that, and six thousand miles and a jungle where black boys were dying like flies, just because of all that, if he thought she was going to put the only picture of her granddaughter in his hot, grabby, long-fingered hand, he better think again. But he had knocked at her door wanting to talk peace. Peace was in him the way he'd sat and crossed one leg over his knee, the way he'd cut down that wild bush growing out the top of his head, and trimmed his moustache and shaved the scraggly goat beard, peace was in his hands clasped atop his knees and in the way he leaned toward her and talked soft. I know I been wrong, Mom. Nobody knows better than me how wrong I been. That stuff makes you sick. It's like you ain't yourself. That monkey gets you and you don't care nothing about nobody. But I'm OK now. I ain't sick now. I'm clean. I love my wife and love my baby and I'ma do right now, Mom.

So when he asked she had made peace too. Like a fool she almost

cried when she went to the mantelpiece and pulled out the snapshot
from the corner of the cardboard frame of Shirley's prom picture. She
had had plans for the photo of her granddaughter. A silver frame from
the window of the jewelry shop she passed every morning on her way
to work. But she freed it from the top corner of the cardboard border
where she had tucked it, where it didn't cover anything but the fronds
of the fake palm tree behind Shirley and her tuxedoed beau, where it
could stay and be seen till she got the money together for the silver
frame, freed the snapshot and handed it to her granddaughter's daddy,
Rashad, to seal the peace.

Then one day the package came in the mail. The postman rang and
she was late as usual for work and missed her bus standing there
signing for it and he was mad too because she had kept him waiting
while she pulled a housecoat over her slip and buttoned it and tied a
scarf around her head.

Sign right there. Right there where it says received by. Right there,
lady. And she cut her eyes at him as if to say I don't care how much
mail you got in that sack don't be rushing me you already made me
miss my bus and I ain't hardly answering my door half naked.

I can read, thank you. And signs her name letter by letter as if
maybe she can read but maybe she had forgotten how to write. Taking
her own good time because his pounding on the door again after she
hollered out, Just a minute, didn't hurry her but slowed her down like
maybe she didn't quite know how to button a housecoat or wrap her
uncombed hair in a scarf and she took her time remembering.

Thank you when she snatched the package and shut the door louder
than she needed to. Not slamming it in the mailman's face but loud
enough to let him know he wasn't the only one with business in the
morning.

Inside, wrapped in pounds of tissue paper, was the banner. At first
she didn't know what it was. She stared again at the rows of brightly
colored stamps on the outside of the brown paper. Rashad's name and
number were in one corner, "Shirley and Mom" printed with the same
little-boy purple crayon letters across the middle of the wrapping
paper. Handfuls of white tissue inside a grayish box. Then the black
silk banner with colored threads weaving a design into the material.
She didn't know what it was at first. She held it in her fingertips at

arm's length, righting it, letting it unfurl. It couldn't be a little fancy China doll dress Rashad had sent from overseas for Keesha, she knew that, but that's what she thought of first, letting it dangle there in her outstretched arms, turning it, thinking of how she'll have to iron out the wrinkles and be careful not to let her evil iron get too hot.

Then she recognized a child's face. Puffy-cheeked, smiling, with curly black hair and slightly slanting black eyes, the face of a baby like they have over there in the jungle where Rashad's fighting. A pretty picture with a tiny snowcapped mountain and blue lake worked into the background with the same luminous threads which raise the child's face above the sea of black silk. Though the baby's mouth is curled into a smile and the little mountain scene floating in the background is prettier than anyplace she has ever been, the banner is sad. It's not the deep creases she will have to iron out or the wrinkles it picked up lying in its bed of tissue paper. It's the face, something sad and familiar in the face. She saw her daughter's eyes, Shirley's eyes dripping sadness the way they were in the middle of the night that first time she ran home from Rashad. Pounding at the door. Shirley standing there shaking on the dark porch. Like she might run away again into the night or collapse there in the doorway where she stood trembling in her tracks. He hit me. He hit me, Mama. Shirley in her arms, little girl shudders. You can't fight him. He's a man, baby. You can't fight him like you're another man.

Shirley's eyes in the baby's face. They used to tease her, call Shirley *Chink* because she had that pale yellowish skin and big eyes that seemed turned up at the corners. Then she remembered the picture she had sent away with Rashad. She read the word in the bottom corner of the banner which had been staring at her all this time, the strip of green letters she had taken for part of the design till she saw her daughter's eyes in the baby face and looked closer and read *Keesha*.

How many years now had they been teasing Keesha about that picture hanging in the corner of the living room?

Take it down, Grammy. Please take that ugly thing down.

Can't do that, baby. It's you, baby. It's something special your daddy had made for you.

It's ugly. Don't look nothing like me.

Your daddy paid lots of money for that picture. Someday you'll appreciate it.

Won't never like nothing that ugly. I ain't no chinky-chinky China-man. That's what they always be teasing me about. I ain't no chinky baby.

How many years had the banner been there behind the big spaghetti gut chair in the dark corner of her living room? The war was over now. Rashad and the rest of the boys back home again. How long ago had a little yellow man in those black pajamas like they all wear over there held her granddaughter's picture in his little monkey hand and grinned at it and grinned at Rashad and taken the money and started weaving the face in the cloth. He's probably dead now. Probably long gone like so many of them over there they bombed and shot and burned with that gasoline they shot from airplanes. A sad, little old man. Maybe they killed his granddaughter. Maybe he took Rashad's money and put his own little girl's face on the silk. Maybe it's the dead girl he was seeing even with Keesha's picture right there beside him while he's sewing. Maybe that's the sadness she saw when she opened the package and saw again and again till she learned never to look in that corner above the mush springed chair.

Keesha had to be eleven now, with her long colty legs and high, round, muscley butt. Boys calling her on the phone already. Already getting blood in her cheeks if you say the right little boy's name. Keesha getting grown now and her sister Tammy right behind her. Growing up even faster cause she's afraid her big sister got a head start and she ain't never gonna catch up. That's right. That's how it's always gon be. You'll have to watch that child like a hawk. You think Keesha was fast? Lemme tell you something. You'll be wishing it was still Keesha you chasing when that Tammy goes flying by.

They get to that certain age and you can't tell them nothing. No indeed. You can talk till you're blue in the face and they ain't heard a word. That's the way you were, Miss Ann. Don't be cutting your big China eyes at me because that's just the way you were. Talked myself blue in the face but it was Rashad this and Rashad that and I mize well be talking to myself because you were gonna have him if it killed you.

She unrolls the banner to make sure she didn't pull it too tight. It's still there, the bright threads still intact, the sad, dead child smiling up at her. The dead child across the ocean, her dead granddaughter Kaleesha, her own stillborn son. When you looked at it closely you could see how thicker, colored threads were fastened to the silk with hundreds of barely visible black stitches. Thinner than spider's web the strands of black looped around the cords of gold and bronze and silver which gave the baby's face its mottled, luminous sheen. From a distance the colors and textures of the portrait blended but up close the child's face was a patchwork of glowing scars, as ugly as Keesha said it was. Rashad had paid good money for it sure enough but if the old man had wept when he made it, there must have been times when he laughed too. A slick old yellow man, a sly old dog taking all that good money and laughing cause it didn't matter whose face he stuck on that rag.

She had heard Rashad talk about the war. One of those nights when Shirley had run back home to Mama he had followed her and climbed through a basement window and fallen asleep downstairs in the living room. She heard him before she saw him stretched out on her couch, his stingy brim tipped down over his eyes, his long, knobby-toed shoes propped up on the arm of the couch. His snores filled the room. She had paused on the steps, frightened by the strange rumbling noise till she figured out what it had to be. Standing above him in the darkness she'd wanted to smack his long shoes, knock the hat off his nose. He's the one. This is the nigger messing over my little girl. This the so-called man whipping on my baby. She thought of her sons, how she had to beg, how she just about had to get down on her knees and plead with them not to go to their sister's house and break this scrawny nigger's neck.

He's sick, Mama. He can't help it. He loves me and loves the baby. He came back sick from that filthy war. They made him sick again over there.

She looked down at Rashad sleeping on her couch. Even with the trench coat draped over his body she could see how thin he was. Skin and bones. Junkie thin because they just eat sugar, don't want nothing but sugar, it's all they crave when that poison gets hold to them. Her sons wanted to kill him and would have if she hadn't begged them on her knees.

She has to fight her own battles. Your sister's a grown woman. Stay away from there, please.

She had felt the darkness that night, heavy as wind swirling around her. She had come downstairs for a glass of wine, the sweet Mogen David in the refrigerator which once or twice a month would put her to sleep when nothing else would. She had a headache and her heart had been pounding ever since she opened the door and saw Shirley with Keesha in her arms standing on the porch. There had been calls earlier in the evening, and Keesha howling in the background and Shirley sobbing the second time and then it was midnight and what was she going to do, what could she say this time when the baby was finally asleep and the coffee cups were empty and there were just the two of them, two women alone in the middle of the night in that bright kitchen. Finally Shirley asleep too but then her stomach and her pounding heart turned her out of bed and she checked Shirley and the baby again and tipped down the steps needing that glass of wine to do the trick and there he was, the sound of his snoring before she saw him and then the night swirling like a wind so she was driven a thousand miles away from him, from his frail, dope-smelling bones under that raggedy trench coat, a thousand miles from him and anyone, anything alive.

It was his screaming which broke her sleep again, the last time that night or morning because one had bled into the other and she heard him yell like a man on fire and heard Shirley flying down the stairs and by the time she got herself together and into her robe and downstairs into the living room, Shirley was with him under the trench coat and both were quiet as if no scream had clawed sleep from her eyes and no terror had nearly ripped his skinny body apart.

Sunday morning then, too late and too tired to go to church then so it was the three of them at the table drinking coffee and nodding with that burden of no sleep from the night before, Shirley, Rashad, her own weary self at the table when he talked about the war.

I was a cook. Had me a good job. You know. Something keeps your butt away from the killing. A good job cause you could do a little business. Like, you know. A little hustle on the side. Like be dealing something besides beans to them crazy niggers. Little weed, little smack. You get it from the same gooks sold you the salt and pepper.

Had me a nice little hustle going. Been alright too cept some brothers always got to be greedy. Always got to have it all. Motherfucker gon gorilla me and take my little piece of action. Say he's the man and I'm cutting in on his business. Well one thing led to another. Went down on the dude. Showed him he wasn't messing with no punk. Eyes like to pop out his head when I put my iron in his belly. You know like I thought that was that and the nigger was gon leave me alone but he set me up. Him and some of them jive MPs he's paying off they set me up good and I got busted and sent home. Still be in jail if I hadn't copped a plea on possession and took my dishonorable.

Yeah, they be killing and burning and fragging and all that mess but I only heard stories about it, I had me a good job, I was feeding niggers and getting niggers high. Getting them fat for the jungle. And getting my ownself as messed up as you see me now, sitting here at this table not worth a good goddamn to nobody.

She knew there was more to tell. She knew he had been in bad fighting once because her daughter was always reading the newspapers and calling her on the phone and crying and saying, He's dead, Mama. I know he's dead and my poor little girl won't never know her daddy. That was before his good job, before the dope he said was as easy to get as turning on a faucet. But he wouldn't talk about the fighting. He'd dream about the fighting and wake up screaming in the night but he wouldn't talk.

Now she had it down, rolled in her hands, and had to put the banner someplace. It was time to take it down, she knew that but didn't know where to put it now it was off her wall. Where the nail had been, a dug-out, crumbly looking hole gaped in the plaster. If she touched it, the rotten wall might crack from floor to ceiling, the whole house come tumbling down around her heels. A knuckle-sized chunk of wall gone but she could fix it with patching plaster and in the dark corner nobody would hardly notice. The paint had sweated badly over the chair and a stain spread across the ceiling over the corner so one more little spot a different color than the rest wouldn't matter because the rest wasn't one color, the rest was leaks and patches and coming apart and faded and as tired of standing as she was tired of holding it up.

One day she'd like to tear the walls down. Go round with a hammer and knock them all down. She knew how the hammer would feel in her fist, she knew how good each blow would feel and she could hear herself shouting hallelujah getting it done.

But she needed someplace to put the banner. She was late as usual and Shirley and the girls would be by soon to go to church. Shirley might be driving Rashad's new car. On Sunday morning he sure wouldn't be needing it. Be dinnertime before he was up and around so he might give Shirley the keys so she could drive the girls to church in style. The girls loved their daddy and he loved them. When he came to town it was always a holiday for the girls. Presents and rides and money and a pretty daddy to brag on for months till he appeared again. She wondered how long it would be this time. How long he'd be flying high before somebody shot him or the police caught up with him and then he'd be dead or in jail again and he'd fall in love again with "Shirley and Mom."

Here she was with the banner still in her hand and the kitchen clock saying late, you're late woman and she's still in her robe, hasn't even filled the tub yet but she just had to stop what she was supposed to be doing and take it down. Well, when the girls come knocking at the door, calling and giggling and signifying and Shirley sits behind the wheel honking to rush her, she'll fling open the door and stuff it in their hands. It will be gone then. Someplace else then, because she never really wanted that sad thing in the first place. She didn't understand why she'd left it hanging this long, why she let it move in and take over that dark corner behind the chair. Because it was a sad thing. A picture of somebody wasn't ever in the family. More of Rashad's foolishness. Spending money when he has it like money's going out of style. Rashad living like a king and throwing a handful of money at the old yellow man when the banner is finished. Rashad living fast because he knows he's gonna die fast and the old chink grinning up at the black fool, raking in the dollars Rashad just threw on the floor like he got barrels of money, stacks of money and don't know how to give it away fast enough.

She loves him too. That handful of money he throws over his shoulder would feel like the hammer in her hand. She'll pray for Rashad today. And Tommy. So much alike. A long hard prayer and it will be like hoisting the red bricks of Homewood A.M.E. Zion on her shoulders and trying to lift the whole building or trying to lift all of Homewood. The trees and houses and sidewalks and all the shiny cars parked at the curb. It will be that hard to pray them home, to make them safe.

She starts up the stairs with the rolled banner still in her hand. She'll soak a little in the tub even if it makes her later. They can wait awhile. Won't hurt them to wait a little while. She's been waiting for them all the days of her life and they can just sit tight awhile because she needs to pray for them too. Pray for all of them and needs all her strength so she'll soak in the tub awhile.

At the top of the steps, at the place they turn and her sons have to stoop to get by without bumping their heads on the low ceiling, at that turning where she always stoops too, not because her head would hit if she didn't but because the slight bend forward of her body brings them back, returns her sons to this house where they all grew tall, taller than the ceiling so they had to stoop to get past the turning, at that place near the top of the stairs when she stoops and they are inside her again, babies again, she thinks of the old man sewing in his hut no bigger than a doghouse.

Rashad would lean in and hand him the photo. The peace offering she sent with him all those miles across the ocean. The old man would take the snapshot and look at it and nod when Rashad pointed to the banners and faces hanging in the hut. A little wrinkled old man. A bent old man whose fingers pained him like hers did in the morning. Swollen fingers and crooked joints. Hands like somebody been beating them with a hammer. She had kept it hanging this long because he had sewn it with those crippled fingers. She took it down because the old man was tired, because it was time to rest, because Keesha was almost grown now and her face was with the others decorating the mantel.

She saw him clearly at that turning of the stairs and understood the sadness in the eyes. The lost child she would pray for too.

■ tommy

He checks out the Velvet Slipper. Can't see shit for a minute in the darkness. Just the jukebox and beer smell and the stink from the men's room door always hanging open. Carl ain't there yet. Must be his methadone day. Carl with his bad feet like he's in slow motion wants to lay them dogs down easy as he can on the hot sidewalk. Little sissy walking on eggs steps pussy-footing up Frankstown to the clinic. Uncle Carl ain't treating to no beer to start the day so he backs out into the brightness of the Avenue, to the early afternoon street quiet after the blast of nigger music and nigger talk.

Ain't nothing to it. Nothing. If he goes left under the trestle and up the stone steps or ducks up the bare path worn through the weeds on the hillside he can walk along the tracks to the park. Early for the park. The sun everywhere now giving the grass a yellow sheen. If he goes right it's down the Avenue to where the supermarkets and the 5&10 used to be. Man, they sure did fuck with this place. What he thinks each time he stares at what was once the heart of Homewood. Nothing. A parking lot and empty parking stalls with busted meters. Only a fool leave his car next to one of the bent meter poles. Places to park so you can shop in stores that ain't there no more. Remembers

389

his little Saturday morning wagon hustle when him and all the other kids would lay outside the A&P to haul groceries. Still some white ladies in those days come down from Thomas Boulevard to shop and if you're lucky get one of them and get tipped a quarter. Some of them fat black bitches be in church every Sunday have you pulling ten tons of rice and beans all the way to West Hell and be smiling and yakking all the way and saying what a nice boy you are and I knowed your mama when she was little and please sonny just set them inside on the table and still be smiling at you with some warm glass of water and a dime after you done hauled their shit halfway round the world.

Hot in the street but nobody didn't like you just coming in and sitting in their air conditioning unless you gonna buy a drink and set it in front of you. The poolroom hot. And too early to be messing with those fools on the corner. Always somebody trying to hustle. Man, when you gonna give me my money, Man, I been waiting too long for my money, Man, lemme hold this quarter till tonight, Man. I'm getting over tonight, Man. And the buses climbing the hill and turning the corner by the state store and fools parked in the middle of the street and niggers getting hot honking to get by and niggers paying them no mind like they got important business and just gonna sit there blocking traffic as long as they please and the buses growling and farting those fumes when they struggle around the corner.

Look to the right and to the left but ain't nothing to it, nothing saying move one way or the other. Homewood Avenue a darker gray stripe between the gray sidewalks. Tar patches in the asphalt. Looks like somebody's bad head with the ringworm. Along the curb ground glass sparkles below the broken neck of a Tokay bottle. Just the long neck and shoulders of the bottle intact and a piece of label hanging. Somebody should make a deep ditch out of Homewood Avenue and just go on and push the row houses and boarded storefronts into the hole. Bury it all, like in a movie he had seen a dam burst and the flood waters ripping through the dry bed of a river till the roaring water overflowed the banks and swept away trees and houses, uprooting everything in its path like a cleansing wind.

He sees Homewood Avenue dipping and twisting at Hamilton. Where Homewood crests at Frankstown the heat is a shimmering curtain above the trolley tracks. No trolleys anymore. But the slippery

tracks still embedded in the asphalt streets. Somebody forgot to tear
out the tracks and pull down the cables. So when it rains or snows
some fool always gets caught and the slick tracks flip a car into a
telephone pole or upside a hydrant and the cars just lay there with
crumpled fenders and windshields shattered, laying there for no reason just like the tracks and wires are there for no reason now that
buses run where the 88 and the 82 Lincoln trolleys used to go.

He remembers running down Lemington Hill because trolleys
come only once an hour after midnight and he had heard the clatter
of the 82 starting its long glide down Lincoln Avenue. The Dells still
working out on *Why Do You Have to Go* and the tip of his dick wet
and his balls aching and his finger sticky but he had forgotten all that
and forgot the half hour in Sylvia's hallway because he was flying, all
long strides and pumping arms and his fists opening and closing on
the night air as he grappled for balance in a headlong rush down the
steep hill. He had heard the trolley coming and wished he was a bird
soaring through the black night, a bird with shiny chrome fenders and
fishtails and a Continental kit. He tried to watch his feet, avoid the
cracks and gulleys in the sidewalk. He heard the trolley's bell and
crash of its steel wheels against the tracks. He had been all in Sylvia's
drawers and she was wet as a dishrag and moaning her hot breath into
his ear and the record player inside the door hiccuping for the thousandth time caught in the groove of gray noise at the end of the disc.

He remembers that night and curses again the empty trolley
screaming past him as he had pulled up short half a block from the
corner. Honky driver half sleep in his yellow bubble. As the trolley
careened away red sparks had popped above its gimpy antenna. Chick
had his nose open and his dick hard but he should have cooled it and
split, been out her drawers and down the hill on time. He had fooled
around too long. He had missed the trolley and mize well walk. He
had to walk and in the darkness over his head the cables had swayed
and sung long after the trolley disappeared.

He had to walk cause that's all there was to it. And still no ride of
his own so he's still walking. Nothing to it. Either right or left, either
up Homewood or down Homewood, walking his hip walk, making
something out of the way he is walking since there is nothing else to
do, no place to go so he makes something of the going, lets them see

him moving in his own down way, his stylized walk which nobody could walk better even if they had some place to go.

Thinking of a chump shot on the nine ball which he blew and cost him a quarter for the game and his last dollar on a side bet. Of pulling on his checkered bells that morning and the black tank top. How the creases were dead and cherry pop or something on the front and a million wrinkles behind the knees and where his thighs came together. Junkie, wino-looking pants he would have rather died than wear just a few years before when he was one of the cleanest cats in Westinghouse High School. Sharp and leading the Commodores. Doo Wah Diddy, Wah Diddy Bop. Thirty-five-dollar pants when most the cats in the House couldn't spend that much for a suit. It was a bitch in the world. Stone bitch. Feeling like Mister Tooth Decay crawling all sweaty out of the gray sheets. Mom could wash them every day, they still be gray. Like his underclothes. Like every motherfucking thing they had and would ever have. Doo Wah Diddy. The rake jerked three or four times through his bush. Left there as decoration and weapon. You could fuck up a cat with those steel teeth. You could get the points sharp as needles. And draw it swift as Billy the Kid.

Thinking it be a bitch out here. Niggers write all over everything don't even know how to spell. Drawing power fists that look like a loaf of bread.

Thinking this whole Avenue is like somebody's mouth they let some jive dentist fuck with. All these old houses nothing but rotten teeth and these raggedy pits is where some been dug out or knocked out and ain't nothing left but stumps and snaggleteeth just waiting to go. Thinking, that's right. That's just what it is. Why it stinks around here and why ain't nothing but filth and germs and rot. And what that make me? What it make all these niggers? Thinking yes, yes, that's all it is.

Mr. Strayhorn where he always is down from the corner of Hamilton and Homewood sitting on a folding chair beside his iceball cart. A sweating canvas draped over the front of the cart to keep off the sun. Somebody said the old man a hundred years old, somebody said he was a bad dude in his day. A gambler like his own Granddaddy John French had been. They say Strayhorn whipped three cats half to death try to cheat him in the alley behind Dumferline. Took a knife off one and whipped all three with his bare hands. Just sits there all summer selling iceballs. Old and can hardly see. But nobody don't bother him even though he got his pockets full of change every evening.

Shit. One of the young boys will off him one night. Those kids was stone crazy. Kill you for a dime and think nothing of it. Shit. Rep don't mean a thing. They come at you in packs, like wild dogs. Couldn't tell those young boys nothing. He thought he had come up mean. Thought his running buddies be some terrible dudes. Shit. These kids coming up been into more stuff before they twelve than most grown men do they whole lives.

Hard out here. He stares into the dead storefronts. Sometimes they get in one of them. Take it over till they get run out or set it on fire or it gets so filled with shit and nigger piss don't nobody want to use it no more except for winos and junkies come in at night and could be sleeping on a bed of nails wouldn't make no nevermind to those cats. He peeks without stopping between the wooden slats where the glass used to be. Like he is reading the posters, like there might be something he needed to know on these rain-soaked, sun-faded pieces of cardboard talking about stuff that happened a long time ago.

Self-defense demonstration . . . Ahmed Jamal. Rummage Sale. Omega Boat Ride. The Dells. Madame Walker's Beauty Products.

A dead bird crushed dry and paper-thin in the alley between Albion and Tioga. Like somebody had smeared it with tar and mashed it between the pages of a giant book. If you hadn't seen it in the first place, still plump and bird colored, you'd never recognize it now. Looked now like the lost sole of somebody's shoe. He had watched it happen. Four or five days was all it took. On the third day he thought a cat had dragged it off. But when he passed the corner next afternoon he found the dark shape in the grass at the edge of the cobblestones. The head was gone and the yellow smear of beak but he recognized the rest. By then already looking like the raggedy sole somebody had walked off their shoe.

He was afraid of anything dead. He could look at something dead but no way was he going to touch it. Didn't matter, big or small, he wasn't about to put his hands near nothing dead. His daddy had whipped him when his mother said he sassed her and wouldn't take the dead rat out of the trap. He could whip him again but no way he was gon touch that thing. The dudes come back from Nam talking about puddles of guts and scraping parts of people into plastic bags. They talk about carrying their own bags so they could get stuffed in if they got wasted. Have to court-martial his ass. No way he be carrying no body bag. Felt funny now carrying out the big green bags you put your garbage in. Any kind of plastic sack and he's thinking of machine guns and dudes screaming and grabbing their bellies and rolling around like they do when they're hit on Iwo Jima and Tarawa or the Dirty Dozen or the Magnificent Seven or the High Plains Drifter, but the screaming is not in the darkness on a screen it is bright, green afternoon and Willie Thompson and them are on patrol. It is a street like Homewood. Quiet like Homewood this time of day and bombed out like Homewood is. Just pieces of buildings standing here and there and fire scars and places ripped and kicked down and cars stripped and dead at the curb. They are moving along in single file and their uniforms are hip and their walks are hip and they are kind of smiling and rubbing their weapons and cats passing a joint fat as a cigar down the line. You can almost hear music from where Porgy's Record Shop used to be, like the music so fine it's still there clinging to the boards, the broken glass on the floor, the shelves covered with roach shit and rat shit, a ghost of the music rifting sweet and mellow like the smell of home cooking as the patrol slips on past where Porgy's used to be. Then . . .

Rat Tat Tat . . . Rat Tat Tat . . . Ra Ta Ta Ta Ta Ta Ta . . .

Sudden but almost on the beat. Close enough to the beat so it seems the point man can't take it any longer, can't play this soldier game no longer and he gets happy and the smoke is gone clear to his head so he jumps out almost on the beat, wiggling his hips and throwing up his arms so he can get it all, go on and get down. Like he is exploding to the music. To the beat which pushes him out there all alone, doing it, and it is Rat Tat Tat and we all want to fingerpop behind his twitching hips and his arms flung out but he is screaming and down in the dirty street and the street is exploding all round him in little volcanoes of dust. And some of the others in the front of the patrol go down with him. No semblance of rhythm now, just stumbling, or airborne like their feet jerked out from under them. The whole hip procession buckling, shattered as lines of deadly force stitch up and down the Avenue.

Hey man, what's to it? Ain't nothing to it man you got it baby hey now where's it at you got it you got it ain't nothing to it something to it I wouldn't be out here in all this sun you looking good you into something go on man you got it all you know you the Man hey now that was a stone fox you know what I'm talking about you don't be creeping past me yeah nice going you got it all save some for me Mister Clean you seen Ruchell and them yeah you know how that shit is the cat walked right on by like he ain't seen nobody but you know how he is get a little something don't know nobody shit like I tried to tell the cat get straight nigger be yourself before you be by yourself you got a hard head man hard as stone but he ain't gon listen to me shit no can't nobody do nothing for the cat less he's ready to do for hisself Ruchell yeah man Ruchell and them come by here little while ago yeah baby you got it yeah lemme hold this little something I know you got it you the Man you got to have it lemme hold a little something till this evening I'll put you straight tonight man you know your man do you right I unnerstand yeah that's all that's to it nothing to it I'ma see you straight man yeah you fall on by the crib yeah we be into something tonight you fall on by.

Back to the left now. Up Hamilton, past the old man who seems to sleep beside his cart until you get close and then his yellow eyes under the straw hat brim follow you. Cut through the alley past the old grade school. Halfway up the hill the game has already started. You have been hearing the basketball patted against the concrete, the hollow thump of the ball glancing off the metal backboards. The ball players half naked out there under that hot sun, working harder than niggers ever did picking cotton. They shine. They glide and leap and fly at each other like their dark bodies are at the ends of invisible strings. This time of day the court is hot as fire. Burn through your shoes. Maybe that's why the niggers play like they do, running and jumping so much cause the ground's too hot to stand on. His brother used to play here all day. Up and down all day in the hot sun with the rest of the crazy ball players. Old dudes and young dudes and when people on the side waiting for winners they'd get to arguing and you could hear them bad-mouthing all the way up the hill and cross the tracks in the park. Wolfing like they ready to kill each other.

His oldest brother John came back here to play when he brought his family through in the summer. Here and Mellon and the courts beside the Projects in East Liberty. His brother one of the old dudes now. Still crazy about the game. He sees a dude lose his man and fire a jumper from the side. A double pump, a lean, and the ball arched so it kisses the board and drops through the iron. He could have played the game. Tall and loose. Hands bigger than his brother's. Could palm a ball when he was eleven. Looks at his long fingers. His long feet in raggedy ass sneakers that show the crusty knuckle of his little toe. The sidewalk sloped and split. Little plots of gravel and weeds where whole paving blocks torn away. Past the dry swimming pool. Just a big concrete hole now where people piss and throw bottles like you got two points for shooting them in. Dropping like a rusty spiderweb from tall metal poles, what's left of a backstop, and beyond the flaking mesh of the screen the dusty field and beyond that a jungle of sooty trees below the railroad tracks. They called it the Bums' Forest when they were kids and bombed the winos sleeping down there in the shade of the trees. If they walked alongside the track all the way to the park they'd have to cross the bridge over Homewood Avenue. Hardly room for trains on the bridge so they always ran and some fool always yelling, *Train's coming* and everybody else yelling and then it's your chest all full and your heart pumping to keep up with the rest. Because the train couldn't kill everybody. It might get the last one, the slow one but it wouldn't run down all the crazy niggers screaming and hauling ass over Homewood Avenue. From the tracks you could look down on the winos curled up under a tree or sitting in a circle sipping from bottles wrapped in brown paper bags. At night they would have fires, hot as it was some summer nights you'd still see their fires from the bleachers while you watched the Legion baseball team kick butt.

From high up on the tracks you could bomb the forest. Stones hissed through the thick leaves. Once in a while a lucky shot shattered a bottle. Some gray, sorry-assed wino motherfucker waking up and shaking his fist and cussing at you and some fool shouts *He's coming, he's coming.* And not taking the low path for a week because you think he was looking dead in your eyes, spitting blood and pointing at you and you will never go alone the low way along the path because he is behind every bush, gray and bloody-mouthed. The raggedy, gray clothes flapping like a bird and a bird's feathery, smothering funk covering you as he drags you into the bushes.

He had heard stories about the old days when the men used to hang out in the woods below the tracks. Gambling and drinking wine and telling lies and singing those old time, down home songs. Hang out there in the summer and when it got cold they'd loaf in the Bucket of Blood on the corner of Frankstown and Tioga. His granddaddy was in the stories. Old John French one of the baddest dudes ever walked these Homewood streets. Old, big-hat John French. They said his granddaddy could sing up a storm and now his jitterbug father up in the choir of Homewood A.M.E. Zion next to Mrs. Washington who hits those high notes. He was his father's son, people said. Singing all the time and running the streets like his daddy did till his daddy got too old and got saved. Tenor lead of the Commodores. Everybody saying the Commodores was the baddest group. If that cat hadn't fucked us over with the record we might have made the big time. Achmet backing us on the conga. Tito on the bongos. Tear up the park. Stone tear it up. Little kids and old folks all gone home and ain't nobody in the park but who supposed to be and you got your old lady on the side listening or maybe you singing pretty to pull some new fly bitch catch your eye in the crowd. It all comes down, comes together mellow and fine sometimes. The drums, the smoke, the sun going down and you out there flying and the Commodores steady taking care of business behind your lead.

"YOU GOT TO go to church. I'm not asking I'm telling. Now you get those shoes shined and I don't want to hear another word out of you, young man." She is ironing his Sunday shirt hot and stiff. She hums along with the gospel songs on the radio. "Don't make me send you to your father." Who is in the bathroom for the half hour he takes doing whatever to get hisself together. Making everybody else late. Singing in there while he shaves. You don't want to be the next one after him. "You got five minutes, boy. Five minutes and your teeth better be clean and your hands and face shining." Gagging in the funky bathroom, not wanting to take a breath. How you supposed to brush your teeth, the cat just shit in there? "You're going to church this week and every week. This is my time and don't you try to spoil it, boy. Don't you get no attitude and try to spoil church for me." He is in the park now, sweating in the heat, a man now, but he can hear his mother's voice plain as day, filling up all the empty space around him just as it did in the house on Finance Street. She'd talk them all to church every Sunday. Use her voice like a club to beat everybody out the house.

His last time in church was a Thursday. They had up the scaffolding to clean the ceiling and Deacon Barclay's truck was parked outside. Barclay's Hauling, Cleaning and General Repairing. Young People's Gospel Chorus had practice on Thursday and he knew Adelaide would be there. That chick looked good even in them baggy choir robes. He had seen her on Sunday because his Mom cried and asked him to go to church. Because she knew he stole the money out her purse but he had lied and said he didn't and she knew he was lying and feeling guilty and knew he'd go to church to make up to her. Adelaide up there with the Young People's Gospel Chorus rocking church. Rocking church and he'd go right on up there, the lead of the Commodores, and sing gospel with them if he could get next to that fine Adelaide. So Thursday he left the poolroom, *Where you tipping off to, Man? None of your motherfucking business, motherfucker,* about seven when she had choir practice and look here, Adelaide, I been digging you for a long time. Longer and deeper than you'll ever know. Let me tell you something. I know what you're thinking, but don't say it, don't break my heart by saying you heard I was a jive cat and nothing to me and stay away from him he ain't no good and stuff like that I know I got a rep that way but you grown enough now to know how people talk and how you got to find things out for yourself. Don't be putting me down till you let me have a little chance to speak for myself. I ain't gon lie now. I been out here in the world and into some jive tips. Yeah, I did my time diddy bopping and trying my wheels out here in the street. I was a devil. Got into everything I was big and bad enough to try. Look here. I could write the book. Pimptime and partytime and jive to stay alive, but I been through all that and that ain't what I want. I want something special, something solid. A woman, not no fingerpopping young girl got her nose open and her behind wagging all the time. That's right. That's right, I ain't talking nasty, I'm talking what I know. I'm talking truth tonight and listen here I been digging you all these years and waiting for you because all that Doo Wah Diddy ain't nothing, you hear, nothing to it. You grown now and I need just what you got . . .

Thursday rapping in the vestibule with Adelaide was the last time in Homewood A.M.E. Zion Church. Had to be swift and clean. Swoop down like a hawk and get to her mind. Tuesday she still crying and gripping the elastic of her drawers and saying *No.* Next Thursday the only singing she doing is behind some bushes in the park. *Oh, Baby. Oh, Baby, it's so good.* Tore that pussy up.

Don't make no difference. No big thing. She's giving it to somebody else now. All that good stuff still shaking under her robe every second Sunday when the Young People's Gospel Chorus in the loft beside the pulpit. Old man Barclay like he guarding the church door asking me did I come around to help clean. "Mr. Barclay, I wish I could help but I'm working nights. Matter of fact I'm a little late now. I'm gon be here on my night off, though."

He knew I was lying. Old bald head dude standing there in his coveralls and holding a bucket of Lysol and a scrub brush. Worked all his life and got a piece of truck and a piece of house and still running around yes sirring and no mamming the white folks and cleaning their toilets. And he's doing better than most of these chumps. Knew I was lying but smiled his little smile cause he knows my mama and knows she's a good woman and knows Adelaide's grandmother and knows if I ain't here to clean he better guard the door with his soap and rags till I go on about my business.

Ruchell and them over on a bench. Niggers high already. They ain't hardly out there in the sun barbecuing their brains less they been into something already. Niggers be hugging the shade till evening less they been into something.

"Hey now."

"What's to it, Tom?"

"You cats been into something."

"You ain't just talking."

"Ruchell, man, we got that business to take care of."

"Stone business, Bruh. I'm ready to T.C.B., my man."

"You ain't ready for nothing, nigger."

"Hey man, we're gon get it together. I'm ready, man. Ain't never been so ready. We gon score big, Brother Man . . ."

THEY HAVE BEEN walking an hour. The night is cooling. A strong wind has risen and a few pale stars are visible above the yellow pall of the city's lights. Ruchell is talking:

"The reason it's gon work is the white boy is greedy. He's so greedy he can't stand for the nigger to have something. Did you see Indovina's eyes when we told him we had copped a truckload of color tee vees. Shit man. I could hear his mind working. Calculating like. These niggers is dumb. I can rob these niggers. Click. Click. Clickedy. Rob the shit out of these dumb spooks. They been robbing us so long they think that's the way things supposed to be. They so greedy their hands get sweaty they see a nigger with something worth stealing."

"So he said he'd meet us at the car lot?"

"That's the deal. I told him we had two vans full."

"And Ricky said he'd let you use his van?"

"I already got the keys, man. I told you we were straight with Ricky. He ain't even in town till the weekend."

"I drive up then and you hide in the back?"

"Yeah dude. Just like we done said a hundred times. You go in the office to make the deal and you know how Indovina is. He gon send out his nigger Chubby to check the goods."

"And you jump Chubby?"

"Be on him like white on rice. Freeze that nigger till you get the money from Indovina."

"You sure Indovina ain't gon try and follow us?"

"Shit, man. He be happy to see us split . . ."

"With his money?"

"Indovina do whatever you say. Just wave your piece in his face a couple times. That fat ofay motherfucker ain't got no heart. Chubby his heart and Ruchell stone take care of Chubby."

"I still think Indovina might go to the cops."

"And say what? Say he trying to buy some hot tee vees and got ripped off? He ain't hardly saying that. He might just say he got robbed and try to collect insurance. He's slick like that. But if he goes to the cops you can believe he won't be describing us. Naw. The pigs know that greasy dago is a crook. Everybody knows it and won't be no problems. Just score and blow. Leave this motherfucking sorry-ass town. Score and blow."

"WHEN YOU AIN'T got nothing you get desperate. You don't care. I mean what you got to be worried about? Your life ain't shit. All you got is a high. Getting high and spending all your time hustling some money so you can get high again. You do anything. Nothing don't matter. You just take, take, take whatever you can get your hands on. Pretty soon nothing don't matter, John. You just got to get that high. And everybody around you the same way. Don't make no difference. You steal a little something. If you get away with it, you try it again. Then something bigger. You get holt to a piece. Other dudes carry a piece. Lots of dudes out there holding something. So you get it and start to carrying it. What's it matter? You ain't nowhere anyway. Ain't got nothing. Nothing to look forward to but a high. A man needs something. A little money in his pocket. I mean you see people around you and on TV and shit. Man, they got everything. Cars and clothes. They can do something for a woman. They got something. And you look at yourself in the mirror you're going nowhere. Not a penny in your pocket. Your own people disgusted with you. Begging around your family like a little kid or something. And jail and stealing money from your own mama. You get desperate. You do what you have to do."

THE WIND is up again that night. At the stoplight Tommy stares at the big sign on the Boulevard. A smiling Duquesne Pilsner Duke with his glass of beer. The time and temperature flash beneath the nobleman's uniformed chest. Ricky had installed a tape deck into the dash. A tangle of wires drooped from its guts, but the sound was good. One speaker for the cab, another for the back where Ruchell was sitting on the rolls of carpet Ricky had stacked there. Al Green singing *Call Me.*

Ricky could do things. Made his own tapes; customizing the delivery van. Next summer Ricky driving to California. Fixing up the van so he could live in it. The dude was good with his hands. A mechanic in the war. Government paid for the wasted knee. Ricky said, Got me a new knee now. Got a four-wheeled knee that's gonna ride me away from all this mess. The disability money paid for the van and the customizing and the stereo tape deck. Ricky always have that limp but the cat getting hisself together.

Flags were strung across the entrance to the used car lot. The wind made them pop and dance. Rows and rows of cars looking clean and new under the lights. Tommy parked on the street, in the deep shadow at the far end of Indovina's glowing corner. He sees them through the office window. Indovina and his nigger.

"Hey, Chubby."

"What's happening now?" Chubby's shoulders wide as the door. Indovina's nigger all the way. Had his head laid back so far on his neck it's like he's looking at you through his noseholes instead of his eyes.

"You got the merchandise?" Indovina's fingers drum the desk.

"You got the money?"

"Ain't your money yet. I thought you said two vans full."

"Can't drive but one at a time. My partner's at a phone booth right now. Got the number here. You show me the bread and he'll bring the rest."

"I want to see them all before I give you a penny."

"Look, Mr. Indovina. This ain't no bullshit tip. We got the stuff, alright. Good stuff like I said. Sony portables. All the same . . . still in the boxes."

"Let's go look."

"I want to see some bread first."

"Give Chubby your keys. Chubby, check it out. Count em. Make sure the cartons ain't broke open."

"I want to see some bread."

"Bread. Bread. My cousin DeLuca runs a bakery. I don't deal with *bread.* I got money. See. That's money in my hand. Got plenty money buy your television sets buy your van buy you."

"Just trying to do square business, Mr. Indovina."

"Don't forget to check the cartons. Make sure they're sealed."

. . .

SOMEBODY MUST be down. Ruchell or Chubby down. Tommy had heard two shots. He sees himself in the plate glass window. In a fishbowl and patches of light gliding past. Except where the floodlights are trained, the darkness outside is impenetrable. He cannot see past his image in the glass, past the rushes of light slicing through his body.

"Turn out the goddamn light."

"You kill me you be sorry . . . kill me you be real sorry . . . if one of them dead out there it's just one nigger kill another nigger . . . you kill me you be sorry . . . you killing a white man . . ."

Tommy's knee skids on the desk and he slams the gun across the man's fat, sweating face with all the force of his lunge. He is scrambling over the desk, scattering paper and junk, looking down on Indovina's white shirt, his hairy arms folded over his head. He is thinking of the shots. Thinking that everything is wrong. The shots, the white man cringing on the floor behind the steel desk. Him atop the desk, his back exposed to anybody coming through the glass door.

Then he is running. Flying into the darkness. He is crouching so low he loses his balance and trips onto all fours. The gun leaps from his hand and skitters toward a wall of tires. He hears the pennants crackling. Hears a motor starting and Ruchell calling his name.

"WHAT YOU MEAN you didn't get the money? I done wasted Chubby and you ain't got the money? Aw shit. Shit. Shit."

He had nearly tripped again over the man's body. Without knowing how he knew, he knew Chubby was dead. Dead as the sole of his shoe. He should stop; he should try to help. But the body was lifeless. He couldn't touch . . .

Ruchell is shuddering and crying. Tears glazing his eyes and he wonders if Ruchell can see where he's going, if Ruchell knows he is driving like a wild man on both sides of the street and weaving in and out the lines of traffic. Horns blare after them. Then it's Al Green up again. He didn't know how, when or who pushed the button but it was Al Green blasting in the cab. *Help me Help me Help me . . .*

Jesus is waiting . . . He snatches at the tape deck with both hands to turn it down or off or rip the goddamn cassette from the machine.

"Slow down, man. Slow down. You gonna get us stopped." Rolling down his window. The night air sharp in this face. The whir of tape dying then a hum of silence. The traffic sounds and city sounds pressing again into the cab.

"Nothing. Not a goddamn penny. Wasted the dude and we still ain't got nothing."

"THEY TRACED the car to Ricky. Ricky said he was out of town. Told them his van stolen when he was out of town. Claimed he didn't even know it gone till they came to his house. Ricky's cool. I know the cat's mad, but he's cool. Indovina trying to hang us. He saying it was a stickup. Saying Chubby tried to run for help and Ruchell shot him down. His story don't make no sense when you get down to it, but ain't nobody gon to listen to us."

"Then you're going to keep running?"

"Ain't no other way. Try to get to the coast. Ruchell knows a guy there can get us IDs. We was going there anyway. With our stake. We was gon get jobs and try to get it together. Make a real try. We just needed a little bread to get us started. I don't know why it had to happen the way it did. Ruchell said Chubby tried to go for bad. Said Chubby had a piece down in his pants and Ruchell told him to cool it told the cat don't be no hero and had his gun on him and everything but Chubby had to be a hard head, had to be John Wayne or some goddamned body. Just called Ruchell a punk and said no punk had the heart to pull the trigger on him. And Ruchell, Ruchell don't play, brother John. Ruchell blew him away when Chubby reached for his piece."

"You don't think you can prove your story?"

"I don't know, man. What Indovina is saying don't make no sense, but I heard the cops ain't found Chubby's gun. If they could just find that gun. But Indovina, he a slick old honky. That gun's at the bottom of the Allegheny River if he found it. They found mine. With my prints all over it. Naw. Can't take the chance. It's Murder One even though I didn't shoot nobody. That's long, hard time if they believe Indovina. I can't take the chance . . ."

"Be careful, Tommy. You're a fugitive. Cops out here think they're Wyatt Earp and Marshall Dillon. They shoot first and maybe ask questions later. They still play wild, wild West out here."

"I hear you. But I'd rather take my chance that way. Rather they carry me back in a box than go back to prison. It's hard out there, Brother. Real hard. I'm happy you got out. One of us got out anyway."

"Think about it. Take your time. You can stay here as long as you need to. There's plenty of room."

"We gotta go. See Ruchell's cousin in Denver. Get us a little stake then make our run."

"I'll give you what I can if that's what you have to do. But sleep on it. Let's talk again in the morning."

"It's good to see you, man. And the kids and your old lady. At least we had this one evening. Being on the run can drive you crazy."

"Everybody was happy to see you. I knew you'd come. You've been heavy on my mind since yesterday. I wrote a kind of letter to you then. I knew you'd come. But get some sleep now . . . we'll talk in the morning."

"Listen, man. I'm sorry, man. I'm really sorry I had to come here like this. You sure Judy ain't mad?"

"I'm telling you it's OK. She's as glad to see you as I am . . . And you can stay . . . both of us want you to stay."

"Running can drive you crazy. From the time I wake in the morning till I go to bed at night, all I can think about is getting away. My head ain't been right since it happened."

"When's the last time you talked to anybody at home?"

"It's been a couple weeks. They probably watching people back there. Might even be watching you. That's why I can't stay. Got to keep moving till we get to the coast. I'm sorry, man. I mean nobody was supposed to die. It was easy. We thought we had a perfect plan. Thieves robbing thieves. Just score and blow like Ruchell said. It was our chance and we had to take it. But nobody was supposed to get hurt. I'd be dead now if it was me Chubby pulled on. I couldna just looked in his face and blown him away. But Ruchell don't play. And everybody at home. I know how they must feel. It was all over TV and the papers. Had our names and where we lived and everything. Goddamn mug shots in the Post Gazette. Looking like two gorillas. I know it's hurting people. In a way I wish it had been me. Maybe it would have been better. I don't really care what happens to me now. Just wish there be some way to get the burden off Mama and everybody. Be easier if I was dead."

"Nobody wants you dead . . . That's what Mom's most afraid of. Afraid of you coming home in a box."

"I ain't going back to prison. They have to kill me before I go back in prison. Hey, man. Ain't nothing to my crazy talk. You don't want to hear this jive. I'm tired, man. I ain't never been so tired. . . . I'ma sleep . . . talk in the morning, Big Brother."

He feels his brother squeeze then relax the grip on his shoulder. He has seen his brother cry once before. Doesn't want to see it again. Too many faces in his brother's face. Starting with their mother and going back and going sideways and all of Homewood there if he looked long enough. Not just faces but streets and stories and rooms and songs.

Tommy listens to the steps. He can hear faintly the squeak of a bed upstairs. Then nothing. Ruchell asleep in another part of the house. Ruchell spent the evening with the kids, playing with their toys. The cat won't ever grow up. Still into the Durango Kid, and Whip Wilson and Audie Murphy wasting Japs and shit. Still Saturday afternoon at the Bellmawr Show and he is lining up the plastic cowboys against the plastic Indians and boom-booming them down with the kids on the playroom floor. And dressing up the Lone Ranger doll with the mask and guns and cinching the saddle on Silver. Toys like they didn't make when we were coming up. And Christmas morning and so much stuff piled up they'd be crying with exhaustion and bad nerves before half the stuff unwrapped. Christmas morning and they never really went to sleep. Looking out the black windows all night for reindeer and shit. Cheating. Worried that all the gifts will turn to ashes if they get caught cheating, but needing to know, to see if reindeer really can fly.

◼ solitary

To reach the other world you changed buses twice. The first bus took you downtown and there you caught another to the Northside. Through the Golden Triangle, across the Sixth Street Bridge, the second bus shuttled you to Reed Street on the Northside where you waited for one of the infrequent expresses running out Allegheny River Boulevard to the prison. With perfect connections the trip might take an hour and three quarters each way but usually a whole day was consumed getting there and getting back with the visit to her son sandwiched between eternities of waiting. Because the prison was in another world. She hadn't understood that at first. She had carried with her into the prison her everyday expectations of people, her sense of right and wrong and fairness. But none of that fit. The prison mocked her beliefs. Her trips to see her son were not so much a matter of covering a certain distance as they were of learning the hostile nature of the space separating her from him, learning how close and how far away he would always be. In the time it took to blink, the time it took for a steel gate to slam shut behind her, he would be gone again, a million miles away again and the other world, gray and concrete, would spring up around her, locking him away as abruptly as the prison walls.

One Sunday, walking the mile from the prison gate to the unsheltered concrete island which served as a bus stop and shivering there for over an hour in freezing November rain she had realized the hardships connected with the visits to her son were not accidental. The trips were supposed to speak to her plainly. Somebody had arranged it that way. An evil somebody who didn't miss a trick. They said to reach him you must suffer, you must fight the heat and cold, you must sit alone and be beaten by your thoughts, you must forget who you are and be prepared to surrender your dignity just as you surrender your purse to the guard caged outside the waiting room entrance. In the prison world, the world you must die a little to enter, the man you've traveled so far to see is not your son but a number. He is P3694 and you must sit on a hard, wooden bench in a filthy waiting room until that number is called. Then it's through steel doors and iron bars and buzzing machines which peek under your clothes. Up stairs and down stairs and across a cobbled corridor dark and chill even in summer and you are inside then and nothing you have brought from the outside counts. Not your name, your pain, your love. To enter you must be prepared to leave everything behind and be prepared when you begin the journey home to lose everything again.

That is the trip she must take to see him. Not hours and buses but a brutal unraveling of herself. On the way back she must put herself together again, compose herself, pretend the place she has been doesn't exist, that what surrounds her as the bus lumbers along the Boulevard is familiar and real, that the shopping center and factories and warehouses crowding the flanks of Allegheny River Boulevard served some useful, sane purpose and weren't just set out to taunt her, to mock her helplessness. Slowly she'd talk herself into believing again. This bus will take me to Reed. Another will cross the bridge into town. I'll catch the 88 and it will shudder over the Parkway and drop me five blocks from home. And when I am home again I will be able to sit down in the brown chair and drink a cup of coffee and nod at some foolishness on TV, and nothing I do, none of these little lies which help me home again will hurt him or deny him. Because he is in another world, a world behind stone walls higher than God's mercy.

Sometimes she says that to herself, says the prison is a place her God has forsaken. But if He is not there, if His Grace does not touch her son then she too is dwelling in the shadow of unlove. If she can make the journey to the Valley of the Shadow, surely He could penetrate the stone walls and make His presence known. She needs weeks sometimes to marshall her strength for the trip. She knows what it costs her: the sleepless nights, the rage and helplessness, the utter trembling exhaustion bracketing the journey. How she must fight back tears when she sees his face, hears his voice. How guilt and anger alternate as she avoids people's faces and shrinks into a corner of a bus. She prays the strangers won't see her secrets, won't laugh at her shame, won't shatter in the icy waves of hatred pouring from her frozen heart. She knows her blood pressure will soar sky high and the spasms of dizziness, of nausea will nearly knock her off her feet. She needed weeks to prepare for all of that and weeks of recovering before she gathered strength enough to begin planning another trip, but she rode the buses and walked the miles and waited the eternities. Surely the walls weren't too tall, too thick for Him. He could come as a cloud, as a cleansing wind.

The prison was built close to the river. She wondered if the men could see it from their cells. She had meant to ask Tommy. And if her son could see it, would the river flowing past make him feel better or feel worse. In spring the sloping bank beyond the iron fence of the visitors' parking lot turned green. The green wasn't fair, didn't make sense when she noticed it for the first time as she stopped in the asphalt and gravel margin between the prison's outer wall and the ten-foot-tall iron fence along the river. A border of green edging the brown river which didn't make sense either as she stopped to blow her nose. For a moment as she paused and stared across the water everything was absolutely still. A wad of tissue was balled in her fist, the river glided brownly, silently past but nothing else was real. Everything so still and quiet she believed that she had fallen out of time, that she had slipped into an empty place between worlds, a place unknown, undreamed of till that moment, a tiny crack between two worlds that was somehow in its emptiness and stillness vaster than both.

The green was sectioned by the iron spears of the fence. Between the sharp points of the spears clusters of spikes riveted to the top railing of the fence glittered in the sun. The sky was blue, the river brown, the grass green. The breeze off the water whispered spring and promised summer but God let his sunshine play in the crowns of needle-pointed spikes. Near the top of the wall she could make out a row of windows deeply recessed, darker than the soot-grimed stones. If Tommy was standing at one of the screened windows could he see the river, the green, the gray pit into which she had slipped?

A coal barge hooted. She stuffed her tissue back in her purse. She thought she could hear the men's voices echoing from behind the walls, voices far away in a cave, or deep inside a tunnel, a jumbled, indistinct murmur out of which one voice would eerily rise and seem to mutter inches from her ear. If she could, she would have run from the yard. The voices hated her. They screamed obscenities and made fun of everything about her. She didn't have the strength to run but wouldn't have run if she could because that would only give them more to laugh at, would bring them howling and nipping at her heels as she fled to the bus stop.

From the visitors' entrance to the bus stop was a walk of nearly a mile. A nameless street paralleled one black prison wall, then crossed a flat, barren stretch of nothing before it intersected Allegheny River Boulevard. From the bus stop she looked back at the emptiness surrounding the prison. The dark walls loomed abrupt and stark. Like the green river bank the walls had no reason to be there, nothing connected them to the dusty plain of concrete. The walls were just there, like the lid of a roasting pan some giant hand had clamped down. It made no sense but it was there and no one could move it, no one was trying to disturb the squat black shape even though her son was dying beneath it.

This is the church and this is the steeple. Open the doors and out come the people. She let her hands form what she was thinking. Her wiggling fingers were ants scrambling for a wedge of daylight.

Her God had razed the proud walls of Jericho with nothing more than screaming horns. She let her hands fall to her sides and closed her eyes, but the walls were still there when she looked again.

On the first of the buses back to Homewood she tried to think of what she'd say to the others. What she would tell them when they asked, How is he? Should she say he's a million miles away? That his name is different in the other world? That he is heavier, thicker in the shoulders, but the baggy prison clothes hang loosely on his body so he seems like a little boy? Should she say his bitterness toward her is mellowing? Or does his anger hurt her less now only because she has listened so many times to his accusations? He says he has relived every single moment of his life. He turns the days over and over, asking questions, reconstructing incidents, deciding what he should have done, analyzing what he did do and what others did to him. In the story of his life which he dreams over and over again, she comes up a villain. Her love, her fears are to blame. She held the reins too tightly or she let him run loose; she drowned him in guilt with her constant questions, her tears at his slightest trespass or she didn't ever really pay enough attention to him. His hurting words would tear her down. She'd stop trying to defend herself, grow numb. His voice would fade from her consciousness and her mind would wander to a quieter, safer place. She'd daydream and free herself from the choking web of his bitterness. She'd want to ask him why he thought she made these wearying journeys. Did he think she came to be whipped? Did he think he had a right to take out his frustrations on her just because she was the only one who'd listen, who'd travel the million miles to where he was caged? But she wouldn't ask those questions. She'd listen till she drifted to that leaden, numb place where nothing could touch her. If someone to scream at was what he needed, she'd be that someone.

She wouldn't tell them anything like that when they asked, How is he? At the bus stop on Reed street she rehearsed what she would say, what she always said, *Better. He's doing better. It's a hateful place but he's doing better.* Corrugated tin sheeting and transparent plastic panels formed a back and slanting half-roof partially enclosing the platform. Like standing in a seashell when the roar of traffic buffeted her. This morning only an occasional car rumbled by. All over town they were ripping up the old trolley tracks and asphalting their cobblestone beds but at this end of Reed street anything that moved rattled against the cobbles like it was coming apart. She was alone till a boy crossing from the far side of the street joined her on the platform. His transistor radio was big as a suitcase and his music vibrated the shelter's tin roof. He was skinny like Tommy had been.

A string bean, bean pole like her son Tommy and like him this one pranced when he walked and danced to the music while he was standing still.

Tommy was *Salim* now. She had told them his new name but she had no words for what had happened to his eyes, his cheekbones, the deepening shadows in his face. To herself she'd say his eyes burned, that his flesh was on fire, that the bones of his face were not hard and white, but something kindling beneath his skin, that the fire burned with sharp knife edges and his skin hung on the points of flame and the dark hollows of his face were where the fire shone blackly through his brown skin. His eyes screamed at her. It hurt him to be what he was, where he was, but he had no words for it either. Only the constant smoldering of his flesh, the screaming of his eyes.

"He's stronger, much stronger. The Muslim business and the new name scare me but it's something for him to hold on to. They have their own little group. It gives him a chance to be somebody. He has his bad days of course. Especially now that the weather's getting nice. He has his bad days but he's made up his mind that he's going to stay on top of it. He's going to survive."

She'd say that. She'd answer with those words each time one of them asked about him. She'd say the words again and again till she was certain she believed them, till she was certain the words were real.

He'd been in the Behavior Modification Unit six weeks now. Six weeks out of the six months of solitary confinement they'd slapped on him. They called it the B.M.U., the Hole. To her it was a prison within a prison. Something worse happening after she thought she'd faced the worst. Twenty-three hours a day locked in his cell. Forty-five minutes of exercise in the yard if a guard was free to supervise him. If not, tough. Twenty-four hours alone in a ten by eight box. One meal at eleven, the other at two. *If you could call them meals, Mom.* Nothing till the next eleven o'clock meal except coffee and a hunk of bread when he was awakened. Two meals in three hours and no food for the next twenty-one. A prison within a prison. A way of telling him and telling her never to relax, never to complain because things could always get worse.

Instead of staying on the last bus till it reached her stop she got off at Frankstown and Homewood. They had both stood when the visiting room guard called his number. Tommy had wrapped his arms around her and hugged her, drawn her as close as he could to the fires alive inside him. Then he had turned from her quickly, striding across the scarred floor toward the steel gate from which he had entered. He hadn't turned back to look at her. The smell of him, the warmth, the strength of his arms circling her so suddenly had taken her breath away. She had wanted to see his face again, had almost cried out at those shoulders which were a man's now, which sloped to his arms and long, dangling hands and tight round butt and gangly legs with his bare ankles hanging down out of the high water prison pants. She had believed nothing could hurt more than the bottled-up anger he spewed at her but she had been wrong. The hug hurt more. His arms loving her hurt more. And when he turned like a soldier on his heel and marched away from her, eyes front, punishing the floor in stiff, arm rigid strides she was more alone than she had ever been while he raged.

So she stepped off the bus at Frankstown and Homewood because she didn't want to be alone, didn't want to close her front door behind her and hear the bolts and chains clicking home in the stillness, and didn't want to greet the emptiness which would rush at her face, pelt it like the dusty, littered wind when it raced across the barren plain outside the prison walls.

This was his street, Tommy's stomping ground. One hot summer night they'd burned it. Looted and burned Homewood Avenue so the block between Hamilton and Kelley was a wasteland of vacant lots and blackened stone foundations and ramshackle wooden barricades guarding the craters where stores and shops had once done business. This was the same Homewood Avenue her Daddy had walked. Taller than the buildings in his high-crowned, limp-brimmed hat. Big-hat John French strutting like he owned Homewood and on his good nights he probably did, yes, if all the stories she had heard about him were true, he probably did own it. Her father, her sons, the man she married, all of them had walked up and down Homewood Avenue so she got off before her stop because she didn't want to be alone. They'd walk beside her. She could window-shop in Murphy's 5&10, listen to the music pouring from the open door of the Brass Rail and Porgy's Record Shop, look at the technicolored pictures advertising coming attractions at the Bellmawr Show. She could hear it and see it all, and walk in the company of her men even though the storefronts were boarded or demolished altogether or transformed to unfamiliar, dirty-looking shops and her men were gone, gone, gone.

On the far corner of Homewood and Kelley the brick and stone Homewood A.M.E. Zion church stood sturdy and solid as a rock. She almost crossed over to it. Almost climbed the cement steps and pushed through the red door. She knew she'd find silence there and knew at the foot of the purple-carpeted aisle she could drop to her knees in a familiar place and her God would listen. That if she left her pride in the ravaged street and abandoned her hate and put off her questions He would take her to His bosom. He would bathe her in the fount of His Grace and understand and say well done. She almost stepped off the broken curb and ran to His embrace but the stolid church they had purchased when white people started running away from Homewood didn't belong on the Avenue this afternoon. She stared at it like she'd stared at the prison and the green river bank. He had to have a plan. For her life or anybody's life to make sense He had to have a plan. She believed that and believed the plan would reveal His goodness but this long day she could only see gaps and holes, the way things didn't connect or make sense.

Now she knows she is walking to the park. Homewood Avenue with its ghosts and memories was not what had drawn her off the bus early. Homewood Avenue was just a way to get somewhere and clearly now she understood she was walking toward the park.

She turned left at Hamilton, the street where the trolleys used to run. Then past the library where the name of her great uncle Elmer Hollinger was stamped on the blackened bronze plaque with the rest of the Homewood veterans of World War I. The family went back that far. And farther when you listened to May and Gert tell about the days when bears and wildcats lived in Homewood and Great-great-grandfather Charley Bell was the one first chopped down a tree here. Past the library then across Hamilton and up the hill alongside old Homewood school. The building in which she had started first grade was still standing. Tinny looking outcroppings and temporary sheds hid most of the old walls but her grade school was still standing. Somewhere she had a picture of her third grade class posed on the front steps, between the thick columns which supported the porch of old Homewood school. More white faces than black in those days, and long aproned dresses, and stiff collars and she is a pale spot at the end of one row, couldn't tell she was colored unless you looked real close and maybe not even then. No one was smiling but she remembered those days as happy, as easy, days she quickly forgot so each morning was like starting life all over again, new and fresh. Past the school yard where they're always playing basketball, past the pool the city stopped filling years ago so now it's just a huge garbage can you can smell from blocks away in the summer. At the top of the hill a footbridge to the park crosses the railroad tracks. They say the little house below the bridge on a platform built out from the park side of the tracks was where the trains stopped for George Westinghouse. His private station, and any train his people signaled knew it better stop for him. He was like a king they said. Owned half of Pittsburgh. The park belonged to him. The two white buildings where the maintenance men keep their tools and tractor were once a stable and a cottage for his servants. It was Westinghouse Park because the great man had donated it to the city. Kids had broken all the windows in the little house. For as long as she could remember it had been an empty shell, blind and gutted, a dead thing beside the tracks.

From the footbridge she could look down on the shape of the park, the gravel paths dividing it into sections, the deep hollow running along Albion Street, the swings and slides in a patch of brown over near the tracks, the stone benches, the whitewashed buildings at the far end. In spite of huge trees blocking her view she saw the park in detail. She had been coming to Westinghouse Park since she was a baby so she could see it with her eyes closed.

From the bridge the grass seemed a uniform green, a soft unbroken carpet the way it is in her dreams when she comes with her mother and her sisters and brother to sit on the steep sides of the hollow. On summer Sundays they'd wear white and spread blankets on the grass and watch the kids whooping like wild Indians up and down the slope, across the brown floor of the hollow their feet had rubbed bare. She had wondered why her mother dressed them in white then dared them to come home with one spot of dirt on their clothes. She had envied the other children romping and rolling down the sides of the hollow. Sunday is the day of rest her mother would say, God's peace day so she'd dress them in white and they'd trudge up Tioga Street to the park with rolled blankets tucked under their arms. Her mother would read the magazines from the Sunday paper, watch the grown-ups promenade along the paths, and keep track of every breath her children drew. *Mama got eyes like a hawk,* her brother would whisper. *Eyes in the back of her head.* Sooner or later he'd escape just long enough to get grass stains on his knee or backside, just long enough for his sisters to see a white streak flashing in the whirl of dark bodies down in the hollow. Then she'd get mad at her brother Carl and join her voice with her mother's summoning him back. *Running with that pack of heathens like he ain't got good sense.* Sometimes her bones ached to tumble and somersault down the green slope, but there were moments, moments afloat with her sisters on the calm, white clouds of their dresses, when she knew nothing could be better than the quiet they shared far away from anyone, each in her own private corner of the bluest sky.

SHE CALLS her brother from the open door of the Brass Rail. *Carl, Carl.* Her voice is lost in the swirl of music and talk animating the darkness. The stale odor of beer and pee and disinfectant blocks the entrance. Her brother Carl is at the far end of the bar talking to the barmaid. He is hunched forward, elbows on the chrome rail, his long legs rooted in the darkness at the base of his stool. He doesn't hear her when she calls again. The stink rolling in waves from the open door of the men's room works on her stomach, she remembers she's eaten nothing since coffee in the morning. She starts when a voice just inside the door shouts her brother's name.

"Carl. Hey Carl. Look here, man."

Her brother turns toward the door and frowns and recognizes her and smiles and begins to dismount his stool all at once.

"Hey Babe. I'm coming." He looks more like their daddy every day. Tall like him, and bald on top like John French, even moving like their father. A big man's gentle, rolling shuffle. A man who walked softly because most things had sense enough to get out of his way. A large man gliding surely but slowly, like John French once did through the streets of Homewood because he wanted to give the benefit of the doubt to those things that couldn't move quite so quickly as others out of his path.

"Could you walk with me a minute? Walk with me up to the park?"

"Sure, Babe. Sure I'll walk with you."

Did he sound like John French? Was his voice getting closer to their father's? She remembers words John French had said. She could hear him laugh or hear his terrible coughing from the living room that year he sat dying in his favorite chair. Those noises were part of her, always would be, but somehow she'd lost the sound of her father's speaking voice. If Carl was getting more like him every day maybe she'd learn her father's voice again.

"I've just been to see Tommy."

"No need to tell me that. All I had to do was look at your eyes and I knew where you'd been."

"It's too much. Sometime I just can't take it. I feel like I'd rather die than make that trip."

"You try and relax now. We'll just walk a little bit now. Tommy knows how to take care of hisself in there and you got to learn how to take care of yourself out here. Did you take your medicine today?"

"Yes. I swallowed those hateful pills with my coffee this morning for all the good they do."

"You know how sick you get when you don't take em. Those pills are keeping you alive."

"What kind of life is it? What's it worth? I was almost to the park. I got as far as the bridge and had to turn around and come back. I wanted to walk over there and sit down and get my nerves together but I stopped halfway across the bridge and couldn't take another step. What's happening to me, Carl? I just stood there trembling and couldn't take another step."

"It's hard. It's hard out here in the world. I know that and you know that, it's hard and cold out here."

"I'm no child. I'm not supposed to break down and go to pieces like I did. I'm a grown woman with grown children. I walked all the way from Frankstown just to go to the park and get myself together but I couldn't get across that silly bridge. I need to know what's happening to me. I need to know why."

"Let's just walk. It's nice in the park this time of day. We can find us a bench and sit down. You know it'll be better in the park. Mama'll keep her hawk eyes on us once we get to the park."

"I think I'm losing Him."

"Something happen in there today? What'd they do to Tommy?"

"Not Tommy. Not Tommy this time. It's God I'm losing. It's Him in me that's slipping away. It happened in the middle of the bridge. I was looking down and looking over into the park. I was thinking about all those times I'd been to Westinghouse Park before. So much on my mind it wasn't really like thinking. More like being on fire all over your body and rushing around trying to beat down the flames in a hundred places at once and doing nothing but making it worse. Then I couldn't take another step. I saw Mama the way she got after her stroke, the way she was when she stopped talking and walking after Daddy died. You remember the evil look she turned on anybody when they mentioned church or praying. I saw her crippled the way she was in that chair and I couldn't take another step. I knew why she cursed Him and put God out of her life when she started talking again. I knew if I took another step I'd be like her."

She feels Carl's arm go around her shoulder. He is patting her. His big hips get in the way and bump her and she wants to cry out. She could feel the crack begin at the top of her forehead, hear it splitting and zigzagging down the middle of her body. Not his hard hip bone that hurt. She was a sheet of ice splintering at the first touch.

"I'd lose Him if I took another step. I understood Mama for the first time. Knew why she stopped walking and talking."

"Well, I'm here now. And we're gon cross now to the park. You and me gon sit down under those big pretty trees. The oldest trees in Homewood they say. You musta heard May tell the story about the tree and the bear and Great-great-granddaddy Bell killing him with a pocket knife. That woman can lie. You get her riding a bottle of Wild Turkey and she can lie all night. Keep you rolling till your insides hurt."

"Mama was right. She was right, Carl."

"Course she was. Mama was always right."

"But I don't want to be alone like she was at the end."

"Mama wasn't never alone. Me and Gerry were there under the same roof every morning she woke up. And you and Sissy visited all the time. Mama always had somebody to do for her and somebody she could fuss at."

She hears her brother's words but can't make sense of them. She wonders if words ever make sense. She wonders how she learned to use them, trust them. Far down the tracks, just beyond the point where the steel rails disintegrated into a bright, shimmering cloud on the horizon line she sees the dark shape of a train. Just a speck at this distance. A speck and a faint roar rising above the constant murmur of the city. She had never liked standing on the skimpy bridge with a train thundering under her feet. Caught like that on the bridge she wouldn't know whether to run across or leap under the churning wheels.

Her God rode thunder and lightning. He could be in that speck the size of a bullet hurtling down the tracks. If you laid your ear on the track the way Carl had taught her you could hear trains long before you'd ever see them. In a funny way the trains were always there, always coming or going in the trembling rails so it was really a matter of waiting, of testing then waiting for what would always come. The black bullet would slam into her. Would tear her apart. He could strike you dead in the twinkling of an eye. He killed with thunder and lightning.

She stopped again. Made Carl stop with her in the middle of the bridge, at the place she had halted before. She'd wait this time, hold her ground this time. She'd watch it grow larger and larger and not look away, not shut her ears or stop her heart. She'd wait there on the shuddering bridge and see.

the beginning
of homewood

I have just finished reading a story which began as a letter to you. A letter I began writing on a Greek island two years ago, but never finished, never sent, a letter which became part of the story I haven't finished either. Rereading makes it very clear that something is wrong with the story. I understand now that part of what's wrong is the fact that I never finished the letter to you. The letter remains inside the story, buried, bleeding through when I read. What's wrong is the fact that I never finished the letter, never sent it and it is buried now in a place only I can see. Because the letter was meant for you. I began by trying to say some things to you, but they never got sent, never reached you so there is something wrong about the story nothing can fix.

In a way the story came before the letter. The story concerned the beginning of Homewood and a woman, a black woman who in 1859 was approximately eighteen years old. She was the property of a prosperous farmer who employed slave labor to cultivate the land he owned near Cumberland, Maryland. I wanted to tell the story of the woman's escape, her five-hundred-mile flight through hostile, danger-ous territory and her final resettlement in Homewood, a happy ending

420

or beginning from our point of view since this woman turns out to be Great-great-great-grandmother Sybela Owens. The idea of the story had been on my mind for years, ever since I'd heard Aunt May tell it the night of Grandpa's funeral. For some reason being in Europe again sharpened the need to get it down on paper. Maybe the trip to the concentration camp at Dachau, maybe the legend I'd heard about Delos, an island sacred to Apollo where no one was allowed to be born or to die, maybe the meals alone in restaurants where no one else was speaking English, maybe the Greek word *helidone* which means swallows and sounds like a perfect poem about birds, maybe all of that had something to do with sharpening the need. Anyway I was sitting in a cafe scribbling messages on postcards. Halfway through the stack I got tired of trying to be cute and funny and realized the only person I needed to write was you. So I started a letter in my notebook. And that's when the first words of Sybela Owens's story said themselves. Five or six sentences addressed to you and then the story took over.

Aunt May's voice got me started on the story. Sitting in a cafe, staring out at the gray sky and gray sea, and mad because it was my last morning on the island and I'd been hoping for blue skies and sunshine, sitting there trying to figure out why I was on a Greek island and why you were six thousand miles away in prison and what all that meant and what I could say to you about it, I heard Aunt May's voice. She was singing Lord reach down and touch me. I heard the old church rocking through the cries of sea birds. *Lord, reach down and touch me,* the Gospel Chorus of Homewood African Methodist Episcopal Zion Church singing, *Touch me with Thy holy grace* because *Lord if you would touch me, Thy touch would save me from sin.* And Aunt May was right there singing with them. You know how she is. Trying to outsing everybody when the congregation harmonizes with the Gospel Chorus. She had on one of those funny square little hats like she wears with all the flowers and a veil. I could hear her singing and I could feel her getting ready to shout. In a minute she'd be up and out in the aisle shaking everything on her old bones she could shake, carrying on till the ushers came and steadied her and helped her back to her seat. I could see the little hat she keeps centered just right on top of her head no matter how hard the spirit shakes her. And see her eyes rolling to the ceiling, that yellow ceiling sanctified by the sweat of Deacon Barclay and the Men's Auxiliary when they put up the scaffolds and climb with buckets of Lysol and water and hearts pumping each year a little less strongly up there in the thin air to scrub the grit from the plaster so it shines like a window to let God's light in and let the prayers of the Saints out.

That's when the story, or meditation I had wanted to decorate with the trappings of a story began. At least the simple part of it. The part concerning the runaway and her dash for freedom, the story I had been trying to tell for years. Its theme was to be the urge for freedom, the resolve of the runaway to live free or die. An old, simple story, but because the heroine was Great-great-great-grandmother Sybela Owens, I felt the need to tell it again.

What was not simple was the crime of this female runaway set against your crime. What was not simple was my need to tell Sybela's story so it connected with yours. One was root and the other branch but I was too close to you and she was too far away and there was the matter of guilt, of responsibility. I couldn't tell either story without implicating myself.

This woman, this Sybela Owens our ancestor, bore the surname of her first owner and the Christian name, Sybela, which was probably a corruption of Sybil, a priestess pledged to Apollo. The Sybil of Greek myth could see the future but her power was also a curse because like the black woman tagged with her name centuries later, Sybil was a prisoner. A jealous magician had transformed the Greek Sybil into a bird, caged her and robbed her of speech. She possessed only a song and became a bauble, a plaything in a gilded cage set out to entertain dinner guests in the wizard's palace. This was to be her role for eternity, except that once, addressed by a seer who heard a hauntingly human expressiveness in her song, she managed to reply, "My name is Sybil and I wish to die."

On the plantation Sybela Owens was called Belle. Called that by some because it was customary for slaves to disregard the cumbersome, ironic names bestowed by whites, and rechristen one another in a secret, second language, a language whose forms and words gave substance to the captives' need to see themselves as human beings. Called Belle by others because it was convenient and the woman answered to it. Called Belle by a few because these older slaves

remembered another black woman, an African who had lived with a
cage on her shoulders for twenty years and the cage had a little
tinkling bell attached to it so you knew when she was coming and
naturally they had started calling her Bell, in derision at first, mocking
her pride, her futile stubbornness on a point most of the women had
conceded long before, a point which peopled the plantation with
babies as various in hue as the many colors of Joseph's coat, then Belle
because she had not broken, Mother Belle finally because she was
martyr and saint, walking among them with the horrible contraption
on her shoulders but unwavering, straight and tall as the day the iron
cage had been fitted to her body; her pride their pride, her resistance
a reminder not of the other women's fall, but of the shame of those
who had undone them. Called Belle because they saw in this beautiful
Sybela a striking resemblance, a reincarnation almost of the queenly,
untouchable one who had been sent to suffer with them.

Every morning the slaves were awakened by the blast of a conch
shell. Blowing the conch horn would have been a black man's job. To
be up before everybody else while the sky was still dark and the grass
chilly with dew. A black man would have to do it. And do it to the
others who hated to hear him as much as he hated the cold walk in
his bare feet to the little rise where he was expected to be every
morning and every morning like he was some kind of goddamn
rooster stand there and blast away on the conch till other feet started
shuffling in the rows of dark huts.

Sybela would have heard the conch shell a thousand mornings.
Strangely, the first morning of her freedom when she heard nothing
but bird cries and the rasp of crickets, she missed the horn. The three
or four dresses in which she had cocooned herself unfurl as she rolls
away from Charlie Bell's hard back. She shivers as a draft runs up
between her clothes and her skin, breaking the seal of heat. She stares
at the horizon while the sky drifts grayly across the mirror of her eyes.
In the rifts between the dark hills, mist smolders dense and white as
drifted snow; the absolute stillness is still and more absolute because
of the ground noise of birds and insects. She rises to a sitting position
and lifts her arm from the rags beneath which her children sleep and
hugs the mantle of her entire wardrobe closer to her body. In the quiet
moments of that first morning of freedom she misses the moaning

horn and hates the white man, her lover, her liberator, her children's father sleeping beside her.

Charlie Bell had stolen her, her and the two children, stolen them from his own father when he learned the old man intended to include them in a lot of slaves sold to a speculator. She had no warning. Just his knock, impatient, preemptive as it always was when he decided to take her from her sleep. Using no more words than he did when he demanded her body, he made it clear what he wanted. In a few minutes all that was useful and portable was gleaned from the hut, the children roused, every piece of clothing layered on their backs and then all of them rushing into the night, into the woods bordering the northern end of the plantation. He pushed them without words, a rage in his grunts, in his hands, rage she felt aimed at her and the frightened children though it was the forest he tore at and cursed. The dark woods responded to his attack with one of their own: branches whipped at the runaways' faces, roots snarled their feet, dry wood snapped loud enough to wake the dead.

It began, like most things between them, in silence, at night. After an hour or so they had to carry the children. Charlie Bell lifted Maggie who was older and heavier than her brother, and Sybela draped Thomas in the sling across her chest not because she conceded anything to the man's strength but because when she bowed into the darkness she reached for the sobs of fear and exhaustion she knew the man could not quiet. Maggie would cling to Charlie Bell, the plunge through the forest would become a game as she burrowed her head into his shoulder. She would be riding a horse and the jostling gallop, the fury of the man's heartbeat would lull her to sleep. But the boy was frightened more by the white man than the crashing forest. Thomas was not much more than a baby but he would scramble along on his thin, bowlegs till he dropped. Never complaining, Thomas would pick himself up a hundred times and not even notice the shrieks of invisible animals, but he could not abide the man's presence, the man's anger, and he whined until Sybela pressed him to sleep against her body.

The first morning of her freedom she looked quickly away from the white man, forgetting the knife-thrust of hatred as she listened to the complaints of her body and surveyed the place where exhaustion had forced them to drop. Charlie Bell must know where they are going. She had heard stories of runaways traveling for weeks in a great circle that brought them back to the very spot where they had begun their escape. The man must know. All white men seemed to know the magic that connected the plantation to the rest of the world, a world which for her was no more than a handful of words she had heard others use. The words *New Orleans, Canada, Philadelphia, Cumberland* were impossible for her to say. Except silently to herself, sifting them through her mind the way old heathen Orion was always fingering the filthy string of beads he wore around his neck. She did not hear the conch shell and realized for the first time in her life she was alone. In spite of the children still tied to her with strings that twisted deep inside her belly, in spite of the man, she knew she could just walk away from all of them, walk away even if the price was heavy drops of her blood dripping at every step because she was nowhere and no one was watching and the earth could swallow her or the gray sky press down like a gigantic pillow and snuff out her life, her breath, the way Charlie Bell had tried once, and it would be nobody but her dead, nobody knowing her death just like nobody heard in the silence of this morning her thoughts; and that was the thing she would not walk away from, the drone of her voice speaking to itself, monotonous and everlasting as cricket hum. She could not leave it, or bury it and cry over it; she was nothing but that sound, and the sound was alone.

I wanted to dwell on Sybela's first free morning but the chant of the Gospel Chorus wouldn't let me sit still. *Lord, reach down and touch me.* The chorus wailing and then Reba Love Jackson soloing. I heard May singing and heard Mother Bess telling what she remembers and what she had heard about Sybela Owens. I was thinking the way Aunt May talks. I heard her laughter, her amens, and *can I get a witness,* her digressions within digressions, the webs she spins and brushes away with her hands. Her stories exist because of their parts and each part is a story worth telling, worth examining to find the stories it contains. What seems to ramble begins to cohere when the listener understands the process, understands that the voice seeks to recover everything, that the voice proclaims *nothing is lost,* that the listener is not passive but lives like everything else within the story. Somebody shouts *Tell the truth.* You shout too. May is preaching and dances out between the shiny, butt-rubbed, wooden pews doing what she's been doing since the first morning somebody said *Freedom.* Freedom.

One of the last times I saw you, you were in chains. Not like Isaac Hayes when he mounts the stage for a concert or poses for an album cover, not those flaunted, ironic, who's-shucking-who gold chains draped over his ten-thousand-dollar-a-night brown body but the real thing, old-time leg irons and wrist shackles and twenty pounds of iron dragged through the marbled corridors of the county courthouse in Fort Collins, the Colorado town where they'd finally caught up with you and your cut buddy Ruchell. I waited outside the courtroom for a glimpse of you, for a chance to catch your eye and raise my clenched fist high enough for you and everybody else to see. I heard a detective say: "These are a couple of mean ones. Spades from back East. Bad dudes. Wanted in Pennsylvania for Murder One."

You and Ruchell were shackled together. In your striped prison issue coveralls you were the stars everyone had been awaiting. People murmured and pointed and stared and the sea of faces parted for your passage. In the eyes of the other green-coveralled prisoners waiting to be arraigned there was a particular attentiveness and awe, a humility almost as they came face to face with you—the Big Time. Your hair was nappy and shot straight out of the tops of your heads. Made you look a foot taller. Leg irons forced you to shuffle; your upper bodies swayed to make up for the drag of the iron. Neither of you had shaved. Neither looked down at the gaggle of deputies shooing back the crowd. The two of you could have been a million miles away discussing Coltrane or pussy. Everything about your faces disclaimed the accident that was happening to your bodies. The slept-in, too small coveralls, the steel bracelets, the rattling pimp-strut shuffle through the marbled hallway some other black prisoner had freshly mopped. You were intent on one another, smiling, nodding, whispering inside a glass cage. I thought of your ambition to be an entertainer. Admired the performance you were giving them.

Bad dudes. Mean nigger men. Killers.

If they had captured Great-great-great-grandmother Sybela Owens, they would have made a spectacle of her return to the plantation, just as they paraded you, costumed, fettered through the halls. Because they had not allowed you soap or combs or mirrors or razors, you looked as if you had been hiding for days in the bush, bringing some of its wildness with you into the clean halls of justice. She too, if they had caught her, would have returned part wild thing. Her long hair matted, her nails ragged and caked with mud, her skirts in tatters, the raw smell of the woods soaked into her clothes and skin. She would have struggled to walk unbowed behind the horses, at the end of the rope depending from her wrists to saddle horn. Her eyes would have been fixed in the middle distance, beyond the slumped backs of the sleepy riders, above the broken line of slave row cabins the hunting party finally reached. Her shoes would be gone, her wrists bloody. There would be dark splotches across her back where the coarse homespun cloth has fused with her flesh. The shame she will never speak of, more bearable now than it will ever be because now it is a fiery pain in her groin blotting out the humiliation she will remember and have to deal with once the pain has subsided. A funky, dirty black woman, caught and humbled, marched through the slave quarters like the prize of war she is, like the pawn she is in the grand scheme of the knights on horseback. But her eyes are on the moon. Like yours. I ask myself again *why not me,* why is it the two of you skewered and displayed like she would have been if she hadn't kept running. Ask myself if I would have committed the crime of running away or if I would have stayed and tried to make the best of a hopeless situation. Ask if you really had any choice, if anything had changed in the years between her crime and yours. Could you have run away without committing a crime? Were there names other than "outlaw" to call you, were there words other than "crime" to define your choice?

Mother Bess is down off Bruston Hill now. She talks about you and asks about you and says God give her strength she's crossing that river and coming over to see you. She talks about Sybela Owens. May saw Sybela Owens too. May was staring at the tall, straight trees behind the house when she felt eyes on her, eyes which had burrowed right down into the place where she was daydreaming. May let her own eyes slowly find the ones watching her. Cautiously she lowered her gaze down past the tall trees, the slant of the roof, the rhythmed silhouette of gray shingles and boards, down past the scarred post supporting the porch roof, the knobby uprights of the rocking chair's back, stopping finally at the old woman who sat dark and closed as a fist. Sybela Owens's ancient eyes blinked in the bright sunlight but did not waver; they had waited patiently as if they had all the time in the world for May to reach them. Then it was May's turn to wait. She quieted everything inside herself as the old eyes shushed her and patted her and said her name in a way she had never heard it said before. *May.* The eyes never left her, but after an instant which seemed forever, May was released. Sybela Owens's eyes never left her but they had fallen asleep again. Among the million brown wrinkles and folds in the old woman's face were two invisible shutters which slid down over her eyes. They were in place again and though May could not see through them, she understood that Grandmother Owens could still look out.

"And let me tell you all something. That's right. You all listen up because I'm gon tell you what you ain't never heard. That's right. And you heard it from May and May be long gone but you all remember where you heard it. Yes indeed. About Grandmother Owens now. She had power. A freeing kind of power. I heard them say it and you might hear somebody say it and think that's just old people talking or them old time down home tales don't nobody believe no more but you listen to me and hear me tell it like it was because I was there, me, May, and I wasn't nothing but a child in knickers but I had sense enough to know it when I felt it, sense enough to let the power touch me, yes Lawd, reach down and touch me, and I felt it from my nappy head down to my dirty toes, felt it even though I was a child, felt it raising me up from scratching at my backside and playing in dirt. Grandmother Owens touched me and I felt it. Felt all the life running out me and something new filling me up at the same time. Just as clear as a bell I heard her say my name. And say so many other things there ain't no words for but they all rushing in so fast felt my whole self moving out the way to make room. Thought her power gon bust me wide open. Bust me clean open and I be running down off that hill like melting snow."

And Mother Bess said, Tell the truth. Said. Yes. Yes. And May kept on telling.

"That's all. Ain't no more. Old as she was and young as I was, she let me feel the power. And I'm a witness. That's what I am now. Your Aunt May's a witness. I'm telling you it happened and I don't know much else about Grandmother Owens except what I been told cause that's the only time I seen her. Just before they brought her down off Bruston Hill. Didn't last a month they say. Took her down off that hill and she was dead in a month, a month after they carried her down. Strong enough to fight when they came for her. But she let them take her. Know she let them cause if she set her mind on not moving, nobody on God's green earth could budge that woman a inch. Because she had the power. I'm a witness. Had it still as sure as she sitting in that rocking chair in petticoats and a black cape and a long black dress. Sun hot as fire and she never sweat one bit. Had it and touched me with it. And changed my life. Yes she did. Told me to live free all this time and be a witness all this time. And told me come a day her generations fill this city and need to know the truth.

"Yes, Lawd. Everybody talking about heaven ain't going there. Hmmph. And everybody talking about freedom ain't been free and never gon be. If the Lord set a burden on you so heavy you can't move nothing but one thumb, you better believe what I'm telling you, the wiggling of that one thumb make you the freest thing in the world. Grandmother Owens now. She suffered in Egypt. She suffered under them cruel pharaohs. Told her when to jump and when to spit and beat her unmerciful she didn't jump or spit fast enough to suit em. That's what it was all about. Evil pharaohs and Hebrews who was God's chosen people, chosen to suffer and get hard like iron in a fire. Now youall see people just like I do, see them every day strutting round here in them fancy clothes or riding them big cars and they don't know they's still jumping and spitting when they told. They don't know it. Too ignorant to know it. Hmmph. And tell you *gwan out my face, nigger,* you try and tell them something. But it be the same. Pharaohs and Hebrew children. Cept some few like Grandmother Owens get up one morning and gone. Run a hundred miles a day with little children on her back, her and that white man Charlie Bell and them babies run by night and sleep by day, crisscrossing rivers and forests full of alligators and wolves. Now that's something, ain't it? Grandmother Owens wasn't hardly no more than a child. Hardly old as Shirley sitting there but she got up one bright morning and heard the freedom trumpet and lit out not knowing a thing but she was gon keep running till she free. . . ."

On the first night of her first day of freedom after the children had finally fallen asleep under her arm and Charlie Bell's restless tossing had quieted to the grunting and twitching of a hound dog dreaming of a hunt, and the stars and insects reigned absolute in the darkness, Sybela thought she saw a star fall and remembered the old story about a night when all of heaven had seemed to come unstuck and hundreds of stars plummeted from the sky and you couldn't hear the rooster or the conch horn next morning for the prayers rising from the cabins. Niggers took the fiery night for a sign of Judgment Day coming. And the story said didn't nobody go to work that morning and didn't none the white folks come round and say a mumbling word neither. She believed she saw the star go, let go like a leaf does a tree, then tumble not like a leaf but with a stone's dead heaviness through water. But the dark waters of the sky closed up without a ripple so she couldn't be sure whether she saw a star fall or not. The swift turning of her eye loosed one of the tears brimming there and it slanted coolly and hotly down her cheek and she didn't know its source any more than she understood why one star tumbled and the other didn't and after she dug the back of her hand into both eyepits and her eyes were bone dry again she couldn't be sure if there had been a tear any more than she could be sure the flicker of motion crossing a corner of her eye had been an actual star's dying.

"They some the first settle here in Homewood. On Hamilton Avenue where Albion comes in. Trolley cars used to be on Hamilton but Charlie and Sybela Owens come here long before that. Most the city still be what you call Northside now. Old Allegheny then. Wasn't but a few families this side the river and hardly none at all out this way when Grandmother Owens come. Brought two children from slavery and had eighteen more that lived after they got here. Most born up on Bruston Hill after the other white men let Charlie know they didn't want one of their kind living with no black woman so Charlie he up and moved. Way up on Bruston Hill where nobody round trying to mind his business. Stead of killing them busybodies he took Grandmother Owens up there and that's the start of Homewood. Children and grandchildren coming down off that hill and settling. Then other Negroes and every other kind of people moving here because the life was good and everybody welcome. They say the land

Charlie owned on Hamilton was fixed. After he left, nothing grow or prosper there. They say Grandmother Owens cursed it and Charlie warned all them white folks not to touch his land. He said he would go to keep peace but nobody better not set a foot on the land he left behind. That spiteful piece of property been the downfall of so many I done forgot half the troubles come to people try to live there. You all remember where that crazy woman lived what strangled her babies and slit her own throat and where they built that fancy Jehovah Witness church over on Hamilton that burnt to the ground. That's the land. Lot's still empty cept for ashes and black stones and that's where Grandmother Owens first lived. What goes round comes round, yes it does, now."

And Mother Bess said Preach. Said Tell the truth.

Sybela's story could end here but it doesn't. I still hear May's voice: "It hurts me. Hurts me to my heart. I remembers the babies. How beautiful they were. Then somebody tells me this one's dead, or that one's dying or Rashad going to court today or they gave Tommy Life. And I remembers the babies. Holding them. Seeing them once or twice a year at somebody's wedding, somebody's funeral or maybe at the Westinghouse picnic. Sitting on a bench at Kennywood Park watching the merry-go-round and listening to the music and a brown-skinned boy walk by with his arm around a little gal's shoulder and he grin at me all sheepish or turn his head real quick like he don't know the funny looking old lady on the bench, and I know he's one of the babies and remember the last time I saw him and how I patted his nappy head and said *My, my, you sure are getting big* or *My, my, you're grown now, a big man now,* and remember him peeking at me with the same sheepish grin and don't you know that's what I remembers when I hear he's robbed a store or been sent to prison or run off from some girl he's left with a baby, or comes around on Westinghouse picnic day at Kennywood Park to ask me for some ride money or to show me his family, his babies and let me hold them a minute."

My story could end here, now. Sybela Owens is long dead, rocking on the porch in her black cape like the sea taxis on their anchors when the water is too mean for the journey to Delos. Great-great-great-grandmother Owens is meeting May's eyes, gazing through the child to the shadowy generations, to storms which will tilt the earth on its axis. The old woman watches her children fall like stars from the night sky, each one perfect, each one a billion years in the making, each one dug from her womb so the black heavens are crisscrossed infinitely by the filaments of her bright pain which no matter how thinly stretched are unbreakable and connect her with her progeny and each point of light to every other. The vision blinds her. She sighs and crosses her wrists under the ruins of her bosom.

It could end here or there but I have one more thing to tell you. The Supreme Court has decided to hear a case in which a group of inmates are arguing that they had a right to attempt an escape from prison because conditions in the prison constituted cruel and unusual punishment and thereby violated the prisoners' human rights. It's a bitch, ain't it? The Court has a chance to say yes, a chance to author its version of the Emancipation Proclamation. The Court could set your crime against Sybela's, the price of our freedom against yours. The Court could ask why you are where you are, and why the rest of us are here.

So the struggle doesn't ever end. Her story, your story, the connections. But now the story, or pieces of story are inside this letter and it's addressed to you and I'll send it and that seems better than the way it was before. For now. Hold on.

John Edgar Wideman is the author of *A Glance Away,*
Hurry Home, The Lynchers, Damballah, Hiding Place, Sent
for You Yesterday, Brothers and Keepers, Reuben, Fever,
and *Philadelphia Fire.* He lives in Amherst, Massachusetts.